THE LEGEND OF JOKTAN

AND THE DAUGHTER OF THE

BLOOD GODDESS

PART ONE

THE CHARGE OF THE GODDESS

By

AZRIEL ST. MICHAEL

the charge of the goddess

The Legend of Joktan and The Daughter Of The Blood Goddess

Part One
THE CHARGE OF THE GODDESS

Azriel St. Michael

An original publication by Shemyaza Press

FIRST REVISED EDITION
CANADA
ISBN 978-0-9876921-2-2

This book is a work of fiction. The characters, situations, dialogue, and events are drawn and conjured from the author's imagination and are not to be construed as real. Any resemblance to actual events or persons, living, dead, undead, or otherwise, is entirely coincidental. He isn't talking about you; don't flatter yourself. The contents of this book belong solely to the author and are his intellectual property.

For further information address the publisher at Shemyaza Press, RR5 Site 17 Comp 49 Prince Albert, Sk, Canada. S6v-5r3.

www.azrielstmichael.com

www.audiopornmusic.com

SHEMYAZA PRESS

A DIVISION OF THE SHEMYAZA SYNDICATE GROUP

THE CHARGE OF THE GODDESS

17 years ago i opened a door within my mind to a dark and strange new world....

INTRODUCTION

For untold centuries, the name of Joktan and his legendary life lay shrouded in the mists of ancient legends and shadowed myths, only vaguely remembered by a few, and believed by even less to be true.

Like glorious Atlantis with her gleaming spires of gold, ivory and precious stones, the name of Joktan was considered to be nothing more than the time-twisted memories of mumbling old men and fables told by old women dreaming of other lives in times more suited to the fairy tales of the enchanted centuries and millennia past. And finally, after thousands of years, the legendary life of Joktan was all but forgotten.

That is, until Sir William Ferdinald Milton Sagelt stumbled upon some broken shards of decaying pottery tablets while exploring high up in the Himalayan Mountains in 1879.

According to his journal, Sagelt had embarked upon an extensive journey deep into the snow-covered peeks of Nepal on what would later prove to be an unsuccessful attempt at capturing the mysterious and elusive Yeti.

On the twenty-third day of his ascent into the treacherous crags, a severe blizzard caught Sagelt and his men unawares, rendering further progress impossible.

While seeking shelter from the bitter storm, he sank through the snow and fell some distance before coming to rest upon solid ground. The sudden impact rendered Sagelt temporarily unconscious, and upon coming to, he became painfully aware of just how dreadful the fall had been. He had broken his right leg and no less than five ribs.

Knowing that it would be some time before help arrived, Sagelt tried his best to remain calm in spite of the seriousness of his injuries.

He'd been deposited into a small mountain cave through a jagged chasm of ice, and never a man prone to wasting precious time, the adventurer immediately began to explore his surroundings as best he could. Soon his eyes grew accustomed to the dim light, and he noticed a number of small earthen vessels strewn about the rough stone floor.

Snow filtered down into the tiny cavern through the crevice above, and clay jars were frozen into the ice around them. Many of the jars were cracked and broken, and those that weren't readily crumbled during his attempts to free them. As luck would have it, however, one vessel survived intact. Imagine his amazement when he removed the lid and discovered within the two clay tablets that are now commonly known as the Nepali Plates. Despite the fact that they were in a very poor state of preservation, Sagelt was elated.

After returning safely to his modest estate in England some two months later, he could hardly wait to examine his rare find more closely. With the aid of several colleagues, Sagelt immediately began the painstaking process of piecing together what was left of the mysterious writing engraved upon the ancient tablets. His efforts were carefully conducted within the confines of the Royal British Historical Museum in London.

Upon preliminary study the writing appeared to be an unknown dialect of Phoenician cuneiform. After seventeen months of laborious research, Sir William was finally able to translate what was still visible of the nearly faded inscriptions.

Translated on August 21, 1880, the text on the Nepali Plates was discovered to be a partial account of the life of an ancient hero by the name of Joktan.

In the years following Sagelt's translation, the Nepali Plates became the center of much-heated debate. Secular historians were understandably stumped, having never heard of Joktan. Biblical scholars, however, insisted that the tablets were proof of the descendants of Noah's favorite son, Shem. Religious leaders the world over were elated, as this was the first archaeological evidence of a written account detailing the life of Noah's closer descendants.

However, when carbon dating was introduced, the Nepali Plates were dated to approximately 8550 BCE. This put the biblical Joktan out of the picture completely, as he would not even be born until some time after 4000 BCE.

Clearly, the two accounts were not of the same man.

Once more darkness crept in upon the legends of Joktan, and his memory slowly faded from the minds of men. Then in 1928, Professor Isaac Walsh unearthed the Hittite Padden Stone while conducting a dig near the ancient Hittite city of Hatusha.

The Padden Stone is a pyramid-shaped block of solid crystalline rose quartz. It is indeed a most beautiful artifact, and an immensely heavy one as well. It measures 71 inches in height and 71 inches across its base. The surface is perfectly smooth on each of its three sides and base, save for the inscriptions etched upon them from top to bottom.

What is most remarkable about this rare artifact is that each surface is inscribed in a different language! Stranger still is the fact that starting with the most recent of the texts written upon the Padden Stone, each following side is inscribed in a language pre-dating the one before it. The writing upon this stone was performed over a period of some 3000 years!

Fortunately, Professor Isaac Walsh unearthed the Padden Stone perfectly intact, as it remains to this very day. However, when work crews lifted the stone from it's resting place, Walsh also discovered a small container buried beneath it....a human skull, fitted together precisely and plated in solid gold.

Inside this macabre relic the Professor found the very tools used to etch the Padden Stone---- four cylindrical forged iron rods with faceted diamond tips. These iron tools were carbon dated to approximately 18,725 BCE!

The Padden Stone does not offer a single clue as to who inscribed it or who made the etching tools themselves, currently in the care of the Smithsonian Institute in London.

In 1936 Dr. Thomas Soll translated the Padden Stone, and at long last the name of Joktan was heard once more!

This artifact tells us of a young man named Joktan, born in the Sabertooth Tribesland, a wild and mountainous region. He was sold into slavery as a child, but through some miraculous intervention of fate----and perhaps even the gods themselves----he eventually frees himself and becomes an adventurer of great renown.

We are told of battles and victories with only the briefest of details. Joktan is about sixteen or seventeen years of age at first mention, and approximately twenty-five years old at the point where the text ends.

Unfortunately, the exact dates of these events are unknown. However, with the discoveries of the Sanskrit Steedman Scrolls in Iraq in 1951 by Dr. John Dee Steedman, the Egyptian Papyrus Temple Records unearthed in 1957 at the Valley of the Kings by Fred

Mancusey, as well as the Petro glyphs in a series of isolated mountain caves in Northern France (discovered by Raphael Zintowski in 1973), a rough sketch of Joktan's life begins to emerge.

We have a collection of scattered events which transpired in the life of Joktan that seem to be of great significance, as well as other accounts given by various individuals he came into contact with throughout his rather extensive travels.

To date, the Steedman Scrolls have been only partially translated. They were housed for a number of years in a museum near Baghdad, Iraq, but the ruling government at that time refused to allow outsiders a chance to view them.

Several attempts were made during the Gulf War in the early 1990's to bribe various individuals in key positions close to these priceless artifacts, endeavoring to obtain them at whatever means possible. Many heroic men and women lost their lives during those tumultuous years. Tragically, most of our attempts to capture the Steedman Scrolls during this time proved unsuccessful.

However, there were a few exceptions.

During the subsequent Dessert Storm Campaign, the museum was overrun and looted. Every artifact of value disappeared literally overnight, many of which were soon auctioned off to the highest bidder on the black market. Of the thousands of ancient texts that went missing, it is estimated by scholars that over three hundred of them related almost solely to the Legends of Joktan.

Through the diligent and concerted efforts of some very close and expensive friends, I have managed to obtain a large number of these rare artifacts within the last few years.

Although certain of the manuscripts are not in my personal possession at the moment, I have been afforded some excellent photographs of the complete collection. Through the wonders of digital enhancement, I have at last succeeded in translating over thirty of the Steedman Scrolls in their entirety. These portions include not only the Royal records of Straltonia and the Temple Records of Redon, but also several important religious texts from other influential kingdoms such as Dendera, Ahmhutonia, and Escalon.

The Egyptian Papyrus Temple Records are currently on display at the Cairo National Antiquities Museum in Egypt, and the Bronze Amorite Tablets are now the property of the Society for Historical Research in Miami, Florida.

While there have been several other notable discoveries in recent years, the manuscripts and artifacts mentioned above have proven to be of the most significance. Almost without exception, they contain the same accounts as other partial texts. In every instance, however, these records have provided me with vastly more detail.

As a result, we can safely place the era in which Joktan lived somewhere in the neighborhood of 160,000 years BCE.

Of course, the accuracy in pinpointing an exact time and date to such an important pre-historical figure as Joktan is very difficult, to say the least!

Indeed, it is an almost insurmountable feat to merely identify and affix a date to something occurring in such recent history as the sinking of Atlantis and the disappearance of the land of Mu.

At the risk of sounding vain, I must make it perfectly clear that for such precision in the instance of Joktan, I am indebted to myself immensely. Certainly I do not suppose to know everything about this ancient legend, for what foolish man would attempt to claim such nonsense?

Yet I can with great assurance inform you that although we do not yet know the details regarding Joktan's death, we are quite certain that he lived to be extremely old by our present standards. It was not uncommon for people to live well over one thousand years in ages long ago, and such remarkable traits were no less unusual in Joktan's time as well.

Legend tells us nothing of his death. There is rumored evidence of an ancient oral tradition, which once claimed that Joktan journeyed to the shores of the Eastern Sea, supposedly choosing to spend the final years of his life in solitude. It is more likely, however, that our hero retreated to the Nephilim Isles, and there is a fair amount of circumstantial evidence to support this view.

As new discoveries are made, I will continue to publish them as often as I can. Perhaps one of the manuscripts I have yet to translate will one day clarify this particular aspect of these ancient legends.

I must say that in recounting what I know of Joktan's life, I've made every effort to stay as close to the facts as presented to us today by modern archeological evidence. However, I do not deny that at times I have taken the liberty of embellishing a bit here and a little there; but of course, what decent, self-respecting historian could possibly restrain himself from such things?

Besides, such liberties are, almost without exception, absolutely necessary. They serve wonderfully to enhance the narrative for the reader, while at the same time enabling the writer to accurately impart a more vivid mental picture of the era in which such a man as Joktan might once have lived.

Thus, to truly grasp and envision that era, you must first understand that the world in which Joktan lived was relatively new.

It was a time when the Earth was yet in Her infancy, and creation was still vibrant and pristine. Her magnificent beauty had once been marred by a violent war between the Star People and the Gods; but that was long before even the most ancient history of Joktan's era. Very few people remembered the War of the Gods, and the ones who did knew of it only from ancient manuscripts.

Since that time the Earth had been healed of Her ancient wounds, and although some scars yet remained, she was virtually unspoiled by the carelessness of men.

The air was pure once more, the water clean, the sky an even darker, deeper, shade of sapphire blue. And the land was different too, for given time, the Earth can heal herself of almost any devastation. Only a few places remained where the ancient mistakes of men and other races could be detected, and such lands held mysteries that were uniquely their own.

There were vast, luscious plains where grasses grew taller than a full-grown man and all manner of wild beasts roamed----not in the mere hundreds or thousands----but in millions, teaming with life and vitality.

The jungles were dense and humid, filled with mystic wonder and enchantment, and there too unusual creatures lived that are now long since extinct.

Up from the plains and jungles the mighty mountains began to rise, at first just humble, thickly wooded hills rolling gently into the distance; then suddenly soaring into jagged, snow-crested peaks, thrust high into the heavens above.

From these lofty spires, icy-cool glaciers slowly inched their way down to emerald-green valleys far below. Snow-fed waterfalls and cataracts plummeted from head-spinning heights into wild, rugged gorges and bottomless chasms. White-water torrents rushed in wild abandon over impossible cliffs, then raced along through narrow canyons at breathtaking speeds on an unstoppable journey towards shimmering oceans and endless seas that beckoned from far, far away.

There were deserts too, where pure white sands and windswept dunes stretched as far as the eye could see, and in the searing temperatures strange and wonderful creatures dwelt, such as have never been seen since by the race of men.

Perhaps most curious of all, however, was the Moon. For when one looked up and gazed into the evening heavens above, they did not see just one Moon, but rather a Moon with two smaller Moons of Her own, one of a reddish hue, the other a yellowish blue.

And because these two smaller Moons orbited opposite each

other, they were always visible at the same time, one on each side of the Mother Moon, and so it was that they were commonly known as "the Heavenly Twins", though some preferred to call them the "Sisters of Mercy".

Although few now know it, the ancient symbol of the full Moon set between two crescent moons, a modern symbol of witchcraft, originated during this era, for once a month when the Mother Moon was full, one of the Sister Moons would be waning, while the other would be waxing.

It was during the lifetime of Joktan that these two sister moons would vanish from the heavens forever.

This was a time when Magick was mighty, and by some, mightily feared! It was said to be better for one to cut off his own private parts than to suffer grief at the hands of an angry mage, but it was not only wizards who possessed the knowledge of The Craft in those ancient eons long since forgotten. For there have always been those who are born with such gifts, those chosen few blessed with otherworldly powers and sinister charm.

It was an age when both beauty and repugnance were absolute. There were mermen and mermaids, centaurs, dragons and innumerable herds of unicorns in the deep, misty forests. There were Elves, Dwarves, Fairies and Nymphs; and there were also some things that are better left unmentioned.

For naming a thing can give it immense power, and there are some things which are far too terrible for one to imagine, and much too dark for the human mind to comprehend.

At times their presence is fleetingly glimpsed in the flickering light of tallow tapers, when shadows dance around the bedroom like angry ghosts about an undertaker's trampled tomb. Restless souls lurk in those grey, haunted shadows, creeping ever closer in the dead, black watches of the night. They wait, ever anxious for weary lids to fall, to feast on mortal flesh.

But I digress....

The Earth held her breath and waited, much as does a virgin, for a brave man to explore her with nothing more than a strong body, a relentless will and of course, a long, sharp sword.

This was a time when a man was judged by his actions, and his actions were limited only by the courage of his own heart. When gods and goddesses spoke to men and walked beside them across enchanted lands.

It was an age where the strong survived, and woe to the weak! A time when a peasant could become rich beyond his wildest dreams, and a kingdom could be won or lost upon nothing more than the

keen edge of a sword.

In this ancient era of magic and wonder, heroes and heroines were born.

Many became myths.

A few became legend.

These are the Legends of Joktan.

Azriel St. Michael

October 31, 2000

prologue

"Who dares risk his worthless life to defile my sacred privacy?" Skeltar's words were hissed, rather than spoken. They cut the dank, musty air like sharpened blades.

The intruder had thrown himself prostrate to the cold stone floor the instant he'd burst through the cumbersome wooden doors. His long, brown, stringy hair was dirty and unkempt. It hung limply about his sickly face in thin, matted strands. His garments were tattered and frayed, and the frail, diminutive form they concealed trembled visibly as he made his reply with a fearful voice.

"It is only I, your humble and loyal servant Cral. Please forgive my foolish error, master, but I thought….."

"Forgiveness has never been one of my strong points, you quivering fool!"

Skeltar's evil hiss cut off Cral's timid voice in mid-sentence, his tone sinister and venomous as he continued, "and thinking has never been one of yours, or else you would have done so before breaking down my door so rudely and unannounced".

He glared at Cral through eyes as black as tar. "Now what was it that seemed so important to you?"

"M-m-m-my lord," Cral stammered, risking a glance at his master. "A rider awaits your presence at the gates."

"At this early hour?" Clearly the mage wasn't impressed. "Well, show him in, you skulking rat".

"But your Excellence," the servant pleaded, "he will not so much as even stand under the gate. The man refuses to enter. He claims that this place is evil and accursed."

Skeltar peered at Cral, his eyes narrowing to tiny blackened slits.

"Of course it is you fool! I made it that way." His tone lowered. "Whence came this haughty messenger?"

"He says only that he is here by King Xalton's command, and that he is expressly forbidden to speak with anyone except for you, my Lord."

Skeltar, still seated at his scrying table, motioned to his cowering servant with a wave of his bonny, skeletal hand. "Wait for me outside."

So, his plan was proceeding smoothly! He smiled inwardly and settled back into his black, cushioned chair.

Skeltar was a thin wisp of a man, so thin in fact, that he more closely resembled a skeleton encased in tightly stretched, urine-colored parchment instead of a living, breathing human. Every tiny bone in his frail frame stood out in garish relief, and his eyes were sunken in their sockets like hardened pools of brackish sludge. His gnarled grayish-green fingernails were sharpened into hideous looking claws, and his lips, which never seemed to move when he spoke, were twisted into an ever-present sneer.

His most distinguishing feature, however, was his thick, long hair, for it was silver with black speckles scattered unnaturally throughout.

Few knew that Skeltar's disturbing appearance was a direct result of his life-long immersion in the arcane arts. An invading army had killed his parents when he was barely six years of age, and being an only child, Skeltar, then known as Malachi, had been left an orphan.

He had loved his parents deeply, but after their deaths the only person who would take him in was the village mage. Malachi had lived with the decrepit wizard until the age of twelve, learning all he could from his elderly mentor. When he felt he could discover no more, the boy concealed himself within the bedchamber of his mentor and waited patiently until the wizard was fast asleep. Then, ever so quietly, he crept out of his hiding place. Unsheathing his dagger, Malachi slowly pressed the blade into his teacher's wrinkled throat, watching with cruel interest as an expression of horror filled his dying eyes.

Under cover of darkness, he stole away from town that very night and took up residence far away. So it was that he had began his life as a usurper of the black arts. Malachi moved constantly from one city to the next, becoming the acolyte of whatever sorcerers would take him in, learning all he could from each one, then killing them and moving on to his next arcane victim.

Now, after decades of deceit, treachery, and cold-blooded murder, Malachi had become the most feared and powerful mage in all of the western kingdoms.

Treachery, however, has its own price, and his physical features were now living proof of this fact. For not all wizards were as easily fooled as his first mentor had been, and in their dying moments many of his victims had cursed him. Those curses were to leave a lasting mark on Malachi's flesh and bones. They were an ever-present reminder that his teachers had taken secrets to their graves, secrets never revealed to their murderous apprentice.

During his youth, Malachi had been considered quite attractive by all accounts. Women had been drawn to him like moths to a flame, but as his features slowly changed, their affection for him subsided. They had begun to call him cruel names behind his back, foolishly imagining that he could not hear. That was how he had come to be known as Skeltar. It was a slur of the word "skeleton" in the common tongue of the Westermarch.

Skeltar had, nevertheless, learned the hard way to be thorough, and his dark fibrous robe attested to this grim fact. Woven from the hair of every sorcerer he had ever known, it covered his head in a thick, concealing hood and flowed down to the floor. The sleeves were wide and completely hid his skeletal hands. A broad leathery belt, braided from the skin of each butchered mage, wrapped around his narrow waist and tied in front in a tight, square knot. The loose ends hung limp down past his knees.

With a menacing laugh, Skeltar rose to his feet and walked across the darkened room to the doorway. The items he would need were already packed away and waiting. These he gathered up as he exited the room, closing the doors securely with an uttered incantation before turning down the musty hall.

Cral, still cowering outside the doorway, sprang to his feet and silently fell into step behind his master, who moved unusually fast for such an ancient looking man.

That he hated Skeltar was a fact Cral kept secretly inside, never allowing his festering contempt to be seen. The slightest sign of anything but abject loyalty on his part could illicit Skeltar's demonic rage in an instant.

There was a room in the belly of this forbidding keep, a tiny stone cubicle that once had been a dungeon. Often Cral had been shut up within it all alone, on occasions when the wizard's temper had gotten the best of him.

He shuddered at the mere thought of that hellish pit. It was infested with rats and other vermin, scurrying incessantly over the floor and along the walls. Spiders and scorpions dwelt there too, of unbelievable size, but such creatures were not the reason for the lowly servant's deep-seated terror of that place.

Lurking within the darkness, other entities waited, forms whose shapes he had never truly determined, but whose touch was frighteningly real nonetheless. Cral hated them even more than his master. They tormented him relentlessly every time he was locked inside, forcing him to endure the most unspeakable assaults.

It was one thing to be raped by a man----his father had taught him that much as an adolescent child----but a demon's lust was far crueler and never fully sated. It could last for hours on end, and continue for days at a time....

Notwithstanding such nightmares, being *Skeltar's* slave did have some definite advantages from time to time.

For starters, Cral was never treated like a slave by anyone other than his master. The commoners of Zebulon paid him the utmost respect. They even went out of their way to lend him assistance when needed, and on occasion he was given gifts, too. Many times people braved their fears in seeking out Skeltar's assistance, and Cral always offered to present their case to his master for an appropriate price.

Almost without exception, they were flatly rejected.

Skeltar suddenly halted his steps and Cral, lost in thought, nearly ran right into him.

"You foolish rat!"

His master's eyes had that look again. They seemed to burn holes into Cral's very flesh.

"Well! Don't just stand there. Open the gate!" Skeltar hissed at him from beneath his hooded robe.

Cral hurried to draw back the rusty iron bars that held the aging bronze gate closed, struggling as he pressed his full weight against the massive metal frame. The hinges squeaked in belligerent defiance, then the gate grated against the granite cobblestones, swinging outward with a scraping groan.

Skeltar shoved his way past Cral, stepping through the opening to squint at the dismounted rider who waited anxiously outside. His bitumen eyes were accustomed to the gloom within the sanctum of his forbidding keep, and the brilliant sunlight outside caused them to burn and water involuntarily.

The rider was one of King Xalton's Palace Guards, as the wizard could plainly see by the gleaming golden eagle insignia on his silver-plated Imperial armor. It glared brightly in the blazing sunshine and caused Skeltar's eyes to burn even more intensely.

That the King took great pride in the appearance of his Palace Guardsmen was immediately apparent. From the crimson horse-hair plume on the hammered silver helm, the long scarlet silken cloak, clasped at the shoulders and about the neck; to the intricate designs graven into the silver-plated armor that covered chest, midriff and torso, the chain mail leggings and arm sleeves, even the thick leather sandals, this man was a living symbol of King Xalton's immense power and immeasurable wealth.

His silver-sheathed short-sword was strapped tightly at his hip by a wide, red leather belt, the scarlet tassels on it's pommel dangling almost to the mans knees. Each individual tassel was woven with bright yellow strands of the purest gold.

Cral stared enviously at the guardsmen's attire. He wore more wealth than many small towns had locked away in their treasuries. The man's fear of Skeltar was apparent, but to his credit he made a noble effort of keeping it concealed. He stood erect, wide shoulders set square, his massive legs slightly apart.

"I am Brutus, second officer of the King's Palace Guard, sent to summon the great wizard Skeltar to the palace of the King of Straltonia at the urgency of his Highness," the rider announced boldly. "Make haste, for the King would see you immediately!"

The wizard's smoldering obsidian eyes were narrow slits beneath his obtrusive hood, and sudden anger danced within his molten stare as he met the messenger's gaze. His words were slow and deliberate, uttered from unmoving lips. "I take orders from no one, least of all you and your impotent little King."

The soldier looked as if he had been smitten across the face, but before he could speak the mage continued. "You say you are the king's second officer?"

Brutus puffed out his chest in obvious pride, his arrogance plainly visible. "Yes" he replied, "I am second officer of his Majesties Royal Palace Guards. I have been in his service for nearly twenty-two years, and I take my orders directly from the king himself."

"Nevertheless," Skeltar sneered mockingly, "you are second. You have been second, all your pathetic, subservient life, and second you shall always be."

Brutus' face turned crimson instantly, a mask of seething rage, but before he could respond he heard the mage's voice inside his head. *"Where is Marcus?"*

The soldier blanched visibly. *How could he possibly know?*

"Yes!" the wizard's voice sneered telepathically, *"even now his*

blood cries out to me from the ground!"

Brutus started to respond, but Skeltar prevented him, directing his acidic demeanor towards the humble servant Cral. "Fetch our mounts, rat! Quickly now, for we shall leave at once!"

The poor wretch disappeared in an instant, and Brutus waited without a word, until presently Cral returned, leading their mounts by weathered leather reins.

Skeltar stepped up to his horse, swinging himself into the saddle with the ease of a man half his age. After settling himself comfortably, he addressed Brutus in a calculated tone.

"You can tell your men to come out of the trees behind you. Only an imbecile would attempt to hide his soldiers within a forest of green while clad in polished silver armor."

1

The heavens were shrouded in swirling, angry clouds. They blotted out the moonlight with a forbidding, hateful gloom, and the sky was as black as the darkest pits in the demon-haunted bowels of Hell. An impenetrable fog spread heavily across the sopping, soggy ground, obscuring even the nearest details from view.

It seemed as if the gods were venting their frustrations in unison upon the world of men. Rain pelted the earth in a torrential downpour, turning the recently bone-dry and dusty soil into a slough of mud and washed-out debris. The wind blew with all the violent fury of a hurricane's wrath. Once shallow streams were now raging rivers, spilling over their banks and mercilessly washing away anything unfortunate enough to be caught within their paths.

The unusual storm had begun twelve days earlier, yet it showed no signs of relenting. Thunder roared deafeningly overhead as bolts of brilliant blue-white lightning tore through the chaos above, crisscrossing the boiling sky with intense, electrifying rage.

In the small trade town of Luxantia the streets were all but deserted, and even the rats sought shelter from the malevolence of the storm.

The gatekeeper pulled his cloak tight around his shoulders in a futile attempt at gaining some warmth as he peered out into the heavenly onslaught from his lonely post near the heavy wooden gates.

No one had ventured out from the town since this storm had begun, and there had been no sign of anyone outside the wall as well. Not that he was surprised. During storms only half this bad no one ventured forth, preferring the comfort of a roach infested room in one of Luxantia's many shabby inns. Even a leaky roof above their heads was better than no roof at all, and a moldering, flea-infested cot of straw was still better than the sticky mud outside. A goatskin of wine or a flagon of watered-down ale could adequately warm up any man's stomach and ease the chill of the bitter damp in their aching bones.

The gatekeeper was a large, portly fellow with broad and sagging shoulders. His once muscular frame had grown soft and flabby over the course of many years of relatively easy living and his love for ale and mead.

Luxantia was a trade route town, where merchants and adventurers from all around stopped over night to buy supplies, relax in the shadows of a dimly lit tavern, or seek out other, more personal pleasures and services, before continuing on their journeys towards the coastal kingdoms of the Western Sea.

Built around a small, shallow lake, Luxantia had literally sprouted over night. What was once a small cluster of tents and shacks had grown quickly into a hastily thrown-up mass of shoddy brick and wooden buildings. A maze of muddy streets and dirty alleys spider-webbed the bustling little town. The wooden palisade surrounding it was built more to protect the residents from the elements than from pillaging invaders, for windstorms were common in this region.

Situated along the northwestern fringe of Straltonia, Luxantia had certainly seen its share of violence in years gone by. Two hundred years ago, King Severus had sought to enlarge the borders of the kingdom, and the town had been filled with thousands of soldiers. The merchants here had grown rich quickly in those days, for men of arms had an insatiable lust for women, gambling and ale.

Luxantia had been the size of a small city then, but soon the armies had been sent to the south, and shortly thereafter hordes of savages swept down across the plains, pillaging, burning, and looting.

Sabertooth warriors, half-naked men who rode Sabertooth war tigers and fought as though they were possessed, had led them.

The once dusty plains had run red with slaughter, soaked in a veritable sea of Straltonian blood.

Although most of the small towns and villages along the borders had been burned to the ground, Luxantia had somehow managed to survive. The war had been extremely violent but short-lived, and as peace began to return, so too did the traders, prospectors, and adventurers. Soon the streets were bustling with travelers seeking to replenish their supplies and merchants vying for their gold.

These days, all signs of war were long gone. Luxantia still had its rowdy moments, as did any trade-route town, but generally life here was peaceful and nothing extraordinary took place. Even the savages that visited the town from time to time sought only to trade with the local merchants, who for their part came and went, living here just long enough to become wealthy. Then they would move on to bigger cities where life was more civilized and refined, places such as Zebulon or Ostila, where there were theaters and magnificent temples dedicated to every deity in the civilized kingdoms of the world.

This being the case, the gatekeeper's job was one of little physical exertion. He was quite content to sit quietly in his lookout, passing the long hours over mugs of ale and games of chance. Certain months of the year saw far less travelers than others, and frequently during these occasions his nights were spent in solitude. However, that is not to say that he was truly alone at such times, for Luxantia was also home to a multitude of women who would provide their pleasures to any man----or woman----for a moderate fee.

Tonight he was busy enough just trying to stay warm and dry. The constant din of thunder overhead was deafening, and in all his years as gatekeeper this was the worst storm he had ever seen.

If the rain doesn't let up soon the whole town will wash away, he thought to himself, reaching for another steaming mug of spiced wine. Already the lake had reached a frightening level, swelling far past its shallow banks on account of the terrible storm. He was about to tilt the hot mug to his lips, when suddenly a bolt of lightning flashed nearby. The resounding clap of thunder was so close it made him jump half out of his seat, spilling the scalding liquid down the front of his woolen tunic and burning his chest as well.

"Dagon's slimy scales!" he cursed, leaping angrily to his feet. He tried in vain to relieve the blistering pain, tugging the soiled tunic away from his burning chest. "When will this accursed storm ever..."

He stopped in mid-sentence, peering down through the fog and rain at the muddy ground below. At first he thought his eyes were playing tricks on him, and he rubbed them with his hairy paws while trying to recount how many mugs of spiced wine he'd drank tonight.

He leaned forward and peered once more at the wooden gates, and slowly it dawned on him that what his drink-blurred eyes beheld was not some illusion in the swirling mist.

For standing there below him in the full malevolence of the storm appeared the fog-veiled form of a man, and a very wet man he was indeed! As the gatekeeper gaped in disbelief, the man began to pound mightily on the gong outside the wall, although the sound of it could not be heard above the clamor of the wind and rain.

Regaining his senses, the gatekeeper hurriedly snatched up his rain cloak. He did his best to carefully descend the thirty or so slippery stairs leading down to the narrow, muddy street. As he sloshed his way through the slimy ooze, he abruptly lost his footing and fell face down into the muck.

Instantly a stream of profanity and curses issued from his lips. He pushed himself back up onto his feet and started towards the gates, but as soon as he took his first step the gatekeeper slipped and fell once more, this time landing heavily on his back. It was a hard fall, nearly robbing him of his breath, and as he struggled to rise once again another lengthy burst of expletives ensued. There was mud caked into his eyes and splattered across his face----most embarrassing, to say the least!

He covered the remaining distance gingerly, taking care not to fall again. When he finally reached the gates he peered out at the newcomer apprehensively.

The traveler was a youth of average height, no more than eighteen years of age by the looks of it, wrapped in a heavy fur robe. His long hair was drenched and matted. It stuck to his back and face as if glued there by the greasy mud, which seemed to encase him completely from head to toe.

On his back was slung a long sword, a quiver of arrows and an unstrung bow. A thick leather belt strapped around his waist secured a fur breechcloth and several daggers and blades of various sizes. Leather knee-high moccasins, adorned with elaborate beadwork, completed the only clothing this stranger wore.

He could not have weighed much more than a couple sacks of horse fodder, even soaking wet as he was, but his body was lean, compactly muscular and well proportioned.

Right now he was stooped over at the waist as if in pain, one hand on his knee, the other arm wrapped around his ribcage. The stranger's body shook as if in convulsions.

The gatekeeper was about to hail the man and inquire as to what ailed him until he realized that the man was not in pain at all. Quite the contrary, this newcomer was, in fact, laughing hysterically!

Bewilderment swept the gatekeeper's features. Here stood a man who was half naked, covered in mud and grime and soaked to the bone, in the midst of the worst storm this land had ever seen....and he was laughing like a mad man!

"Ho there!" shouted the stranger in a fit of roaring mirth," that was the most entertaining act I've seen in nearly two damned weeks!"

He was trying hard to stifle his peels of laughter, but to no avail. Suddenly the gatekeeper understood that he himself was the source of the stranger's mirth, and his eyes began to narrow as embarrassment gave way to indignation.

"Have you gone mad?" he shouted at the man, half believing such to be the case.

The stranger straightened himself to his full height before leaning heavily against the gates. Amid chuckles he shouted back through the clamor of the storm, "I am not mad, friend," he replied, "just exceedingly humored by your clumsiness. I pray you forgive my mirth, but save for this moment, I have not laid eyes upon another human for quite some time!"

He took a step toward the gatekeeper. "I am Joktan, of the Sabertooth Tribesland. I am bound for Endrakana. If it were not for this foul weather, I might have already been there days ago. Now I find myself in dire need of lodging and rest, not to mention a good hot meal or two."

The gatekeeper considered his words for a moment. Endrakana was in Bezakzia, Straltonia's western neighbor. This man was either lying, or else must be truly lost....but the chances of a savage getting himself lost around these parts was slim indeed.

The tribesman paused for a moment to wipe the grime off his face with the back of a dirty hand, then leaned forward. "Are you going to let me in, or am I to drown in this cursed rain?"

"Of course", the gatekeeper muttered, signaling the guards to let him in. "Welcome to Luxantia."

He stood back and watched as the guards moved swiftly to raise the heavy bar, bracing themselves against the weight of the wooden frame and the onslaught of the harsh, driving winds. This done, it took the strength of three men to open the gates just enough to allow Joktan to squeeze between them, and he had to step through quickly to avoid getting struck hard as the gates slammed shut behind him. They closed with a solid thud, and the savage turned to eye them skeptically.

The gatekeeper motioned him over to the registry booth, a small wooden enclave at the side of the street. It was protected from the elements by a canvas tarp stretched tightly over a framework of bent poles and saplings. "That'll be one silver piece for entrance," said the gatekeeper, holding out a wet, muddy hand to Joktan matter-of-factly.

Joktan eyed him suspiciously. "What is the rate of copper and silver here?" he inquired, knowing it was different in every town and city, even if they were in the same province or country.

"Twelve coppers for one silver piece and three pieces of silver for one gold."

"One silver is quite high for such a town as this," Joktan replied thoughtfully. "I shall give you seven coppers and no more."

"Seven coppers is robbery!" the gatekeeper howled, "and for all my trouble! I should have left you outside in the storm." He folded his arms across his chest. "One silver it is and not one copper less."

Joktan smiled widely at the gatekeeper, and a sudden look of apprehension swept across the man's face. He noted the savage's extended upper canine teeth, a distinguishing trademark of Sabertooth Tribesmen. They were two and a half times the size of his other teeth, and even though people from his homeland frequently visited many of the small towns along the border, the sight of a man with fangs still seemed unsettling to most civilized men. Two hundred years might have erased the visible signs of war, but bitter memories yet lingered.

The gatekeeper hesitated, and Joktan took a step forward. "Maybe you *should* have left me out in the storm," he growled, "but nevertheless, I am here now, and the gates are closed. You can try to throw me out if you like, but I'm betting you are smarter than you look. I will give you eight coppers, and not one copper more. As you can see, I am not a rich man."

Joktan's azure eyes twinkled with amusement as the keeper, who had hoped to make a bit of a profit, ruefully agreed at last. It was unwise to anger any civilized man who was well armed, especially on a night as foul as this. It was absolute folly to anger a savage. He nodded his head. "Eight coppers it is then," the man begrudgingly conceded.

He muttered under his breath as Joktan produced the agreed-upon amount. Snatching at the coins in his outstretched hand, the keeper thumbed them into a bulging pouch hanging from his sagging belt.

"Is there an inn here with a bath?" Joktan asked when he had finished stowing away the coins.

The portly man grunted and motioned with his bronze helmed head. "You might try the Open Arms Tavern over yonder. It's the second building on the right, just past this first street here. Most of the better inns are filled up, but many of the taverns still have some room." He gave Joktan an appraising look, then added, "That is, of course, if you don't mind the bugs!"

Joktan was of no mind to sleep with vermin tonight. "What of this tavern you speak of then? Is it full of bugs too?"

The man shook his head. "Of course not! I would never send a man to a den of flees, no matter how queer he might seem!" The gatekeeper laughed heartily, then grew more serious. "You might want to get yourself a decent change of clothes as well, tribesman.

There are shops here aplenty in Luxantia that can give you a fair exchange for those mangy hides you wear."

"Thanks," Joktan replied dryly, "but I'm actually quite fond of them." He grinned and turned to step outside the registry booth, then stopped and turned once again to the gatekeeper. "I didn't catch your name."

"I am Nolan," the gatekeeper answered with a broad, toothsome smile, "gatekeeper, diplomat and merchant. I can find anything you desire," then with a sheepish look he lowered his voice and added, "for a modest fee, of course." Joktan didn't miss his meaning. The gatekeeper was always the first person to greet anyone who came into a town. He knew everyone's business, where they were traveling to, when they planned to leave, and what they brought into town with them. If anyone were going to know where to get contraband goods or services, it would almost certainly be him.

Joktan nodded an understanding gesture. "Of course," he replied knowingly. "I shall keep that in mind."

With that he stepped back out into the rain and set off down the slippery street in search of the Open Arms Tavern, while the gatekeeper worked his way back up the greasy steps to his lookout on the palisade above, where a most welcome flagon of hot, spiced wine awaited him.

2

The Open Arms Tavern was a weathered wood and brick building, thrown together quickly with little attention to outward appearances. A gray battered sign hung haphazardly above the low, narrow doorway. It announced the tavern's name in old red painted letters that had started cracking and peeling away years ago.

Located on the main street of Luxantia, it looked as though it had survived at least one fire since being built, which must have been around the time that the town had first began her transformation from a jumble of tents into a small town.

When he pushed open the door and stepped inside, he was immediately greeted by the stench of sweat and the thick smell of burning grease. A dense haze of wood smoke hung heavily in the dimly lit room. This was not uncommon, but tonight it was thicker than usual due to the prevailing winds, which forced the smoke back down the chimney of the old stone fireplace built into the wall on the far side of the dingy room.

The floor was simple enough; just hard packed dirt. This alleviated the need for frequent sweeping, although it also created a lot of extra dust. The haze of grease, smoke and dust mixed together in the air and slowly settled, leaving a brownish oily sludge, which lightly coated nearly everything inside the tavern.

Small, rough wooden tables were scattered at random about the room, and soot-blackened tallow lamps hung from the rafters and pillars, economically spaced apart.

Tonight the tavern was empty, save for a disheveled looking drunk who appeared to be unconscious, passed out with his head face down at a table in the corner nearest the entrance door. His clothes were ragged and dirty with clumps of dried mud smeared here and there.

The only other patrons were two trulls, seemingly bored from a lack of recent work. They sat at a table on the far side of the room by the roaring hearth-fire, lazily sharing a clay jug of cheap wine. They glanced over at the doorway upon Joktan's entrance, a sudden tinge of interest in their heavily painted eyes.

He approached the bar and rang the small brass bell for service. After a moments wait, the barkeep emerged from behind a dirty curtained doorway at the opposite end of the counter.

The man was a short, stocky fellow with flabby arms and a round potbelly that sagged down over his belt well past the crotch of his over-sized breeches. His face looked bloated and misshapen, and a web of tiny purple veins covered his stubby, bulbous nose and bright red cheeks. A black mustache, streaked with gray, hung below the pudgy folds of skin, which sagged underneath his double chin. His big, round eyes were lined in dark circles, and beads of perspiration stood out upon his furrowed brow. The short-cropped hair on his balding head mirrored the mixture of black and gray in his mustache. He wore a grimy, white linen vest and apron, which did little to conceal the thick mat of hair that carpeted his back and chest. The only jewelry he wore were dull copper bands clasped about his wrists, each one nearly a hands breadth wide.

He looked at Joktan in startled surprise, obviously not expecting new-comers during such a violent storm and at this late hour, but the barkeep's face instantly lit up in an overjoyed smile as he waddled towards him. The man's fat belly jiggled with each hasty step.

"Well! What have we here?" he bellowed happily as he made his approach. His brown eyes were bright with curiosity and humor at once. "You look like a drown rat washed up from the lake!"

"Indeed," replied Joktan, still dripping with rain. "I have but just arrived from this foul storm, and I am sorely in need of a room and a hot meal."

"And a hot bath, by the looks of ye!" the barkeep interjected. Even in towns as far flung as this, Straltonians were still fond of their baths. To them it was not just a matter of personal hygiene; it was a mark of civilization.

"Aye," Joktan nodded, then continued. "The gatekeeper spoke highly of you and this fine tavern."

"Ha!" exclaimed the jolly man, a cheerful grin spreading widely across his fat face, "and what did Nolan tell you? That I make my living off of his evening losses at the tables?"

"No," Joktan chuckled, feeling much at ease in the presence of such an affable fellow, "but he *did* say that your prices are reasonably low," he lied, "and your rooms are some of the best in Luxantia."

"Now *I know* you jest!" the barkeep laughed, "but come, sit down and warm yourself with a tankard of the finest ale this town has to offer." He motioned towards a table near the hearth. "Haven't had a Tribesman through these parts for quite some time now, I'd say," the man informed him. "How long did you say you plan to stay?" he was greedily eyeing the leather pouch of coins tied securely at Joktan's belt while trying not to seem too conspicuous about it.

"I didn't," said Joktan, knowing full well what was on the round man's mind.

"Well, then," the man said slowly, a sly, concerned tone edging his voice, "this storm may last another week or more, you know. You could end up being stuck here in Luxantia for a while longer than you intend."

"I don't care how long it lasts," Joktan muttered wearily.

"Nonetheless," the fat man hastily replied, "no one travels in such weather, if they can help it. Sort of like tempting the gods, you might say. I would imagine that you will want to remain here until it clears up a bit." He poured ale from a flagon into an earthen mug and placed both upon a table as Joktan took a seat.

"I have traveled in this damned storm since it began, and I will leave whenever I please. I don't care if it clears or not." He lifted the flagon to his lips and drank deeply. It wasn't bad, he thought, although if it was truly Luxantia's best the town was in dire need of a new ale merchant. However, he had journeyed in these miserable conditions for what seemed to be weeks on end, with only muddy water and rain to quench his thirst, and even watered-down camel's milk would have been a refreshing change just now.

"What did I tell you?" the fat man asked exuberantly, "is our ale not the finest in town?" He gestured as he spoke, waving his chubby hands in the air.

"It's not bad," Joktan granted, "but as you know I've only just arrived, and have not had the opportunity to drink ale in other taverns yet." He grinned at the barkeep, "How should I know if it's the best in town?"

"You will see soon enough," the man promised, "although most people in these parts drink from the cup, not the flagon…."

Joktan merely shrugged, then lifted the flagon once more and downed nearly half its contents in one draught before motioning to the barkeep to take a seat across from him at the small table. "I suppose there is the matter of payment," he said as the fellow settled onto the bench.

"Ah! Yes," replied the man with an anxious nod, his eyes once again lighting up brightly.

Joktan produced his coin pouch. Opening it up, he searched through its contents thoughtfully before withdrawing a gleaming golden object and placing it on the table before the tavern owner. It was round, about the size of a man's palm, and inscribed with curious designs. Strange writing and symbols were etched upon it, and a number of precious jewels were set at equal distances about the objects circumference. A larger stone was set in the center of the disc, and it shone brightly even in the dim interior of the tavern. The barkeeper's eyes grew very large as Joktan examined the piece briefly before handing it to him.

"This should cover my stay here for the next ten days, as well as my meals and drinks, should it not?"

The man hefted the golden jewel in his hand and held it up for inspection appraisingly.

"It has blood on it," he noted, as if that would make some difference in the costly bauble's worth.

"Aye," Joktan replied dryly, taking another mouthful of ale and swishing it around in his mouth before swallowing. "There is more on my blade where that came from."

The barkeep looked startled, then shrugged his broad shoulders noncommittally and turned it over for further examination. It truly was a costly object, and Joktan noted the greed in the fat man's eyes. "Rather fascinating, it is," he mumbled more to himself than anyone else. "How did you come by it?" he asked curiously, as he ran his chubby fingers over it's engraved and jeweled surface. There was a golden loop mounted along the upper edge, obviously to allow the piece to be hung from a chain or cord.

"You needn't trouble yourself with such trivial concerns," Joktan replied, "but I assure you it was not stolen, if that's your worry. The previous owner was a very unsavory sort, if you know what I mean. He lost his head, and after that the trinket was of little use to him."

The man smiled knowingly, then thought for a moment. "Eight days," he said at last, "including your room, baths, meals, and ale." He paused for a moment, then added, "But wine will be extra."

"So be it," Joktan consented, "and I will throw in an additional silver piece per day to be kept well informed, but tonight my wine is free."

The small man frowned, then grunted his approval, thrusting out his hand. "My name is Paltro," he declared with an air of importance, "though I'm sure the gatekeeper told you that as well?"

Joktan smiled and clasped his hand. "I will look after your needs personally," said the man. "You must be starving!"

"Aye," he replied, "I thought you'd never ask!"

"Very well. I'll have the cook prepare you a meal at once." With that Paltro turned and waddled back towards the bar, disappearing behind the soiled curtain.

Joktan sat back and warmed himself by the blazing hearth. After spending the last twelve days in wet clothing in continuous freezing rain, the heat from the fire felt only too good. A flagon of ale pressed to his lips felt even better, and presently he began to relax.

For the last three months he'd been roaming the Harwood Mountains, about eighteen or nineteen days travel from Luxantia if one were to make the journey in descent weather. He'd spent his time in the wilds completely alone, save for the beasts that dwelt in the highlands and desolate peaks.

Originally he had meant to cross over that area, on his way south through Bezakzia, but while traversing the mountains he'd discovered some gold nuggets in a cold, glacial stream. Further investigation higher up had yielded even more gold in the black creek-bed sands, and Joktan had decided to stay and collect as much as could be found.

Many days of prospecting had paid off, resulting in a large, heavy bag full of the gleaming nuggets, which he had strapped securely to his horse before beginning his descent from the mountains, but his luck ended abruptly. He had traveled only a short distance before being set upon by a horde of hairy apes. It was very rare to encounter such creatures this far west, but Joktan felt little fondness about the affair.

In the ensuing battle, his beleaguered mount was slain, and Joktan himself might have been too, had he not been knocked off his feet during the fray by a particularly massive ape, wielding a tree-stump as a weapon. He'd wrestled viciously with the beast, before being tossed over the cliffs near the summit. He could still feel the sudden rush of panic, which had surged through him as he plummeted from dizzying heights into a pool of icy water far below.

Stunned from the fall, he was swept away by a small river fed by the mountain streams and cataracts. How long he'd been unconscious was anyone's guess. The fall alone should have killed him, not to mention the terrific blows he had received during his struggle with the apes. That he had not been drown by the river was a further miracle, too.

Eventually he had awakened to find himself resting upon the bank of the river. Disoriented and hopelessly lost, he was battered and bruised. There were cuts and scrapes all over his body, and his gold was forever gone.

The river had carried him far from the mountains and into an area unfamiliar to him, with no recognizable signs of civilization to be found, but being born in the Savage Tribesland, he was no stranger to wild places. Joktan had subsequently chosen to stay until his wounds had healed and he could provision himself to travel once more. In the end, however, he had spent more time there than he'd first planned, due largely to a continuing streak of inescapable misfortune.

His hunting efforts had been for the most part futile; game fled from him before he could get a chance at bring it down. Roots, berries and various other wild plants became the bulk of his diet, something he had not found pleasing at all, and the lack of more substantial fare caused his strength to return much more slowly than he'd expected.

After that his luck had went from bad to worse. He was set upon by bandits, and narrowly escaping death at their hands----and incidentally bringing about theirs----he was then caught in a severe storm. It was the very same one which even now raged in full-blown fury outside the tavern's protective walls.

The golden trinket with which he'd paid for his lodgings and food had fallen into his possession shortly before Joktan had begun his ill-fated journey through the Harwood Mountains.

It had been the property of a slimy cutpurse in Striebe, who'd had the not-so-bright idea of relieving him of his money and life. The lout had stabbed him in the back with a poison-tipped dirk. Taking Joktan's coin-purse, he had then fled into the dark of the night, leaving him for dead on the filthy street.

Joktan had been found lying bleeding and unconscious by a local trull, who was returning to her quarters from an unsuccessful night of business. She'd taken care of him for a couple of weeks, during which time his strength began to return once more.

As his health had improved, so too his desire for vengeance, and Joktan began to hunt the loathsome thief. He'd eventually found the man behind a local tavern and promptly cut off his head. It was then, while searching his lifeless corpse for anything of value, that Joktan had acquired the golden disk. At the time he was hoping to sell the bauble for its weight in gold coins.

After thanking the trull who had saved his life, and giving her a few gold pieces for her trouble, he took his booty to a local merchant and tried to sell it. But the man had refused to even touch it, saying it was a cursed object, and that whoever possessed it would suffer great sorrow and misfortune. The merchant had went on to inform him that he would surely die unless he got rid of the golden disk.

At the time Joktan had laughed at the superstitious old man before going on his way, and after discovering gold high up in the Harwood Mountains some days later, he'd remembered the merchant's words and laughed at him all the more.

Now, as he sat beside the crackling fire in the Open Arms Tavern, Joktan began to mull over the recent course of events which had transpired in his life. He wondered if maybe the old merchant in Striebe wasn't so crazy after all. Truly, it did seem like his luck had went sour ever since he'd taken possession of the golden trinket.

Oh, well, he thought silently as he took another swig of ale. *I no longer own that accursed jewel, and all the better. Let's see if my luck changes now, for it certainly cannot get any worse than it has been!*

His thoughts were suddenly interrupted by Paltro, who, true to his word, had returned from the kitchen with a steaming tray of food big enough for ten men. He placed the hot tray on the table before Joktan with great care, eyeing the feast as if starving himself.

"I think you will find our fare here immensely palatable," Paltro beamed with obvious pride. He raised his bushy eyebrows and gestured invitingly, "Eat up, my man. I prepared it myself!"

And he had indeed cooked the meal himself, because his kitchen help had went home for the night shortly before Joktan's late arrival.

He eyed his meal appraisingly; a thick slab of sizzling beef loin, charred almost black on the outside, but red and bloody within. The very sight of it made his mouth water! A mess of greens, a fresh baked trencher of thick, meaty stew and a flagon of wine completed the more than ample meal.

"Paltro!" he exclaimed hungrily around a mouthful of the delicious beef, "you certainly know how to make a decent meal. Perhaps I'll stay here a little longer than eight days after all!"

Paltro nodded, looking exceedingly pleased. "If you need anything else, just let me know."

"Aye, I'll be sure to do so," Joktan replied as he set about devouring the feast before him. *Maybe,* he thought to himself, *just maybe, my luck is starting to change after all!*

Paltro retreated to the front of the tavern behind the bar, towel in hand, and busied himself by cleaning the counter and stowing away clean mugs for the morning patrons. After a short while he disappeared behind the curtain into the kitchen, and Joktan was left in peace to finish his meal.

This he did with a veracious fervor, and in little time all that remained before him was a few bones, an empty tray and his flagon of wine. Then, just when he had finished eating, the silence was broken by a husky, female voice.

"Care for some company, stranger?"

He looked up to see the two trulls approach, each one carrying a flagon of wine in their hands. So intent had he been on the meal before him that Joktan had completely forgotten about the women, who for their part had been kind enough to at least let him finish eating before making their presence known.

The whores wobbled and swayed, doing their best to saunter across the tavern towards him, obviously drunk from the large amount of wine they'd imbibed throughout the course of the evening. Both were of pale complexion, thin, and by all accounts attractive. They made every effort to accentuate their sensuous curves and abundant endowments as they sidled up beside him.

The one who had spoken had long, wavy, brunette hair that spilled down over her round breasts and ended just above her ruby-studded navel. Her long legs were bare up to her hips and thighs, which were covered in silken wraps, leaving little to the imagination of what they vaguely concealed. A full bosom was clad in a thin silk strip of cloth that strained to hold her ivory breasts in place. Silver bracelets and armbands completed her scant, exposing outfit.

The other whore had straight, thick, auburn hair that stopped just above her generous, firm breasts. She was dressed almost identically to her companion.

Their full lips were colored bright red, their cheeks and eyes painted even more heavily than he had at first noticed upon entering the tavern.

Joktan returned their inviting gaze with a look of mild interest. He had not yet had sex with a trull, but the savage had no intention of changing things tonight. No matter how beautiful and sensuous they might appear, he knew all too well that the few silver pieces he could spend for a brief night of pleasure would be multiplied many times over by the apothecary to rid him of the putrid puss or discomfiting sores which they could give him in return. Not to mention the loathsome vermin that could infest a man's private parts....

The pair were a sight for sore eyes nonetheless, and he inhaled sharply as they stepped into the light of the glowing fire. He was not inclined to be rude to women, no matter who they were. Joktan viewed women as creatures of exquisite beauty, and often preferred their company to that of other men.

"No thanks," he replied to the brunette who had addressed him, "you are both very beautiful, and tempting, to say the least, but right now I need a good nights rest."

Neither one made any move to leave. "Perhaps we could persuade you differently."

It was the trull with the auburn hair which spoke. She now touched her full, round breasts with the tips of her long, crimson nails. Her thick lashes fluttered as she gazed side-eyed, a seductive pout playing upon her face. The brunette licked her luscious lips with the tip of her wet, pink tongue insinuatingly. Joktan watched silently as her empty hand slid slowly downward between her naked thighs. Her hips moved erotically as she closed her eyes and touched herself there....

Despite his distaste for harlots, Joktan felt his manhood instantly stiffen. His hard erection throbbed within the confines of his fur-lined loincloth, and he suddenly realized just how long it had been since he had last enjoyed such pleasures.

He cleared his throat and did his best to appear unaffected by their unabashed behavior, becoming painfully aware of the rushing blood that pounded in his head.

"Like I said," he replied, trying hard to maintain a steady tone, "I really need to get a good nights sleep. Besides, I wouldn't be very good company tonight."

The two women ceased their posturing, looking dejected and sullen. Even so, they sat down at his table, one across from him, the other by his side. *They must be in sore need of some coin*, he thought to himself while trying hard to calm his hormones.

"You can't have my silver, but I'm on my way to my room, and this flagon is nearly full. It would be a shame to waste it." He pushed the wine towards them and smiled, "You might as well enjoy it," he said, getting to his feet.

Instantly their faces lit up in genuine joy. The auburn trull picked up the wine and tipped it to her lips, taking a long draught before passing it to her companion, who followed suit. They winked at him and cooed almost in unison, "Thanks, stranger." The surprise in their voices was unmistakable.

Joktan left the table and headed to the tavern counter. "Paltro!" he bellowed, "I'm ready to see my room!"

The barkeep appeared immediately from behind the kitchen curtain and led the savage up a rickety narrow staircase to the second floor above the tavern. "Quite a pair, those two, are they not?" the fat fellow said as he puffed his way up the steps.

"Aye," Joktan agreed.

Paltro led him into a long, dimly lit hallway with creaky wooden floorboards worn with many years of frequent use. He stopped in front of a door about halfway down. "I'm afraid that this is all I've got left," he informed him, giving it a heave with his left shoulder. "Haven't had time to clean the rest yet, but it's not a bad room at all, as you can plainly see for yourself."

Joktan stepped inside and looked around. He was somewhat surprised. Three oil lamps that hung from sconces on the walls lighted the room. A bucket and a wooden tub of steaming water sat in the center of the floor upon a small square mat of woven reeds. A linen towel and washcloth were placed nearby on a small stool with a bar of soap.

Instead of the small cot he'd expected, a large bed sat in the corner of the room, and against the wall at the foot of it was piled a fresh mat of straw.

A table sat along the opposite wall to the right, and upon it was placed an earthen wash basin. A clay tankard and flagon of ale had been put there as well, which Joktan noted with an approving smile.

"This will do," he told Paltro with a nod.

"*This will do?"* Paltro retorted, as if insulted, "what more would you like, your majesty! Perhaps a dozen roses and a few naked women to bathe your stinking carcass?" The barkeep laughed uproariously. "Maybe some imported food to glut yourself on too, I suppose?" He threw his hands up in the air in mock frustration, his fat belly jiggling from sudden motion. "For a Tribesman of the north lands, you really have quite a sense of humor, Joktan!"

He marched to the door and called out over his shoulder, "If you need anything else, your Highness, just yell for little old Paltro." He turned and gave an ungraceful bow before waddling off down the hallway, laughing as he went.

*Well, at least the entertainment is good here!*_ Joktan thought to himself as he closed and bolted the door.

Upon further inspection of his quarters he was pleased to find the place absent of bugs, something quite common in most other places such as this.

Removing his weapons, he placed them on the floor beside the tub where they would be in easy reach, then stowed his few possessions beneath the bed. This done, he quickly disrobed and settled into the steaming water, it's warmth instantly soothing to his travel-weary muscles.

"Ah!," he moaned contentedly, sinking down into the bath, "truly my luck *is* better already!"

Joktan stretched his aching frame out in the tub as much as it would allow, resting his head on the wooden rim. Outside the storm continued, and the room shook from its rage. Rain poured down in torrents on the roof above his head, and somewhere nearby a frightened occupant prayed desperately to deaf and silent gods.

Joktan breathed a long, deep, sigh and closed his blood-shot eyes. Sleep beckoned like a long-lost lover, and he sank groaning into her waiting arms.

Where have my long years hastened?
Whence comes this gray, grim dawn?
Where hope once dared to linger,
Now gaping darkness yawns;
Dusk falls cold and frigid,
Pale frost on brittle bones;
Grinning specters gather,
To lead the way back home.

----Memoirs of King Xalton

The ride to the Imperial Palace in Zebulon was a quiet one. Skeltar's venomous personality saw to that well enough indeed, and his obvious disdain for anyone but himself compelled Brutus and his men to keep a considerable distance between themselves and the dour mage. Brutus couldn't help imagining what immense pleasure his would be in cleaving Skeltar's hooded skull in two.

While entertaining such thoughts, the soldier kept a watchful eye about himself and his men as they made their way into the city, for it was rumored that Skeltar never traveled anywhere without the protection of an evil spirit. According to many well-informed sources, this demon appeared in the form of a large black dog, and it could only be killed by magick, something he knew nothing about. Though it didn't seem to be present at the moment, one could never be too careful, and a sudden shiver ran down his spine.

Just what type of defense could be mounted against such a foe

Brutus hardly knew, but if confronted by something which could not be dispatched with sharpened steel, flight did not seem to be a dishonorable option.

Skeltar, on the other hand, was lost deeply in his own dark thoughts and appeared to pay no attention to the men around him. His paramount concern of late was focused upon an ancient arcane amulet. The wizard had been attempting to locate its whereabouts, an obsession that had kept him occupied for over ten months now. He'd spent countless hours locked away in his chambers, gazing into his scrying glass in search of the sacred relic.

Just once, Skeltar had thought he'd discovered its location, in the small northwestern city of Striebe. It had been in the possession of a common thief, if he had judged correctly, which was a difficult thing to do sometimes when scrying.

Often one had to trust their own intuition when interpreting the images revealed within the glass, allowing plenty of room for error. Scrying had definite risks as well, for if done over extended periods of time one's physical vision could be permanently damaged. Skeltar knew of many methods to remedy this, but all were extremely time-consuming. He did not wish to become sidetracked with other matters of less importance.

After concluding that the amulet was in Striebe, the wizard had traveled there immediately, only to discover that it had once more vanished, this time in the hands of a tribesman from the north lands.

Skeltar had returned to his keep outside of Zebulon empty-handed, and once again locked himself in his private chambers. Failure had never bode well with him. It was a feeling he'd experienced only rarely during his lifetime, and it caused the wizard to redouble his efforts. Further gazing into his crystalline ball of visions, however, had been confusing at best. The smooth, achromatic surface became an adumbration of a man within a sea of swirling chaos, surrounded by bolts of lightening and the tumultuous roar of thunder.

The vision had remained unchanged with each passing day for nearly two full weeks now, and the mage was slowly becoming exasperated. Still, he would not relent, for the foundation of his scheme was starting to take shape.

Once the amulet was in his hands, he would be able to break the curses which had kept him disfigured for so many years. Through the secret of the amulet he could wield unimaginable power. Unlimited wealth would be his for the taking. He would be a god! The mage adjusted the hood of his robe to better shield his eyes from the blazing glare of the sun. How he abhorred such foul weather!

_Ah!_ he thought silently, a grim look of determination settling across the twisted features of his skeletal face*; I will change that as well……!*

4

Joktan woke late the next day to find himself still stretched out in the tub of water, which had now been cold for quite some time. His legs were cramped and numb, and his skin was white and wrinkled from being submerged in water for so many hours.

Apparently it was still raining outside, and he sat for a moment listening to the downpour as it battered against the clay tiles outside on the roof above his room. Since he was still in the tub, he decided to finish getting himself cleaned up before venturing out from his quarters.

He washed out his loincloth, and while it dried he busied himself by cleaning and sharpening his weapons, which had suffered a great deal of abuse during his time out in the storm. After rubbing his sword, dagger and throwing darts with a piece of tallow from an old candle stub, he carefully returned them to their appropriate places before getting dressed and heading downstairs.

Breakfast consisted of generous helpings of eggs, sausage, back bacon, fresh baked ash cakes with butter and hot jasmine tea, served enthusiastically by Paltro, who was in as good a mood as ever there could be.

"Are you always this cheerful?" Joktan inquired of the barkeep as the fat little fellow scurried about the tavern.

"Why shouldn't I be?" He beamed, "this storm is doing wonders for business!" Paltro waddled over to his table and plopped himself down on the rough wooden seat across from him, while Joktan concerned himself with shoveling down the hearty breakfast. He noticed the barkeep eyeing his food hungrily and wondered how the obese man could ever manage to satisfy his own appetite and still have food to spare for his customers.

Paltro sat back, staring at Joktan curiously. "You are the talk of the town," he said at last. "Nobody travels in weather like this. Even the men here in Luxantia only leave their house if it's absolutely necessary."

Joktan, busy stuffing a greasy link of sausage into his mouth, merely shrugged his shoulders silently and continued chewing a mouthful of food. After washing it down with several gulps of lukewarm tea, he looked over at the barkeep. "I've traveled in worse conditions on many occasions, but it wasn't like I had a choice in the matter this time. The storm caught me by surprise, out in the open."

He guzzled back the last of the tea and handed the empty pot to the barkeep. "Got any Muscat wine?"

"Aye," Paltro muttered, shaking his head as rose to his feet. He paused a moment, then said, "you are a lucky man, Joktan. You should be as sick as a dog right about now. But instead here you sit, healthy as an ox and swilling wine without a care. Do you make a habit of tempting the gods?"

"Only when they piss me off," he replied with an devilish grin, "besides, walking in the rain never hurt anybody." He then grew suddenly curious.

"Why the questions?"

Paltro lowered his head slightly, and seemed to become more than a little uneasy. "Well," he began slowly, "not that I believe this myself, mind you, but some of the people here in Luxantia think maybe your presence here is a bad omen."

"How so?" Joktan demanded to know.

"It's just that, well…"

"Come on, man! Out with it!" Joktan's tone was a commanding one, and Paltro's chubby face at once grew fearful.

"You came in from the storm," he said in a pleading voice, "and your teeth make people….nervous…"

"My teeth are nothing more than a feature I was born with!" Joktan retorted. "Living so close to the border, you would think people here would know that by now. They are a distinction of my people, and any child born without them in my homeland would be deemed cursed, and therefore killed immediately," he informed Paltro factually. "As for this miserable rain and wind, you might recall that it started up long before my arrival."

He scowled at Paltro and cursed under his breath in his native tongue. "Nolan has a loose tongue. Perhaps I should gut him first."

The barkeep put his hand on Joktan's shoulder and looked him in the eyes. "Come, my friend. I did not mean to offend you in any way. If I have done so, please accept my most sincere apologies." He was very serious, and Joktan could plainly see that the man spoke the truth.

"I don't believe in mumbo-jumbo," he confessed, "nor do I believe in curses, or any deity either. You have paid me well, and I intend to honor my word to you. But do take care if you decide to venture out into the town, for there are many other people who are not of the same mind as I. Luxantia has seen many Sabertooth Tribesmen in the past, but now they come here only rarely. There are many foreigners in town, merchants from distant places, that have taken up residence here in the hopes of becoming wealthy."

The barkeep shook his head in dismay. "They know nothing of your people, nor of the other tribes that live along the borders. Even less of the past wars in these parts."

"Well," Joktan growled, "all that I need is a good mount and some provisions. If the city folk are as superstitious and distrusting as you say, it might be a good idea to hire someone to purchase the supplies I need."

Suddenly Paltro's face lit up with a good-natured grin, and his eyes once again sparkled with their usual cheerfulness. "I'll go get you that wine," he declared, "and then we shall both have a drink, for whatever it is that you need, I can find it, and at a cheaper price than anyone else."

"That I don't doubt," Joktan replied dryly. He gave the man an appraising look and laughed. "You don't seem like the type to pass up an opportunity to make a profit!"

Paltro almost looked genuinely insulted, and there was a haughty edge to his words as he retorted, "well! I *am* a business man, but then of course, what would a savage such as yourself know of that?"

"Fetch the wine, fat man," he chuckled, "and we shall see what I know of doing business!"

Paltro hurried away and returned shortly with a flagon of the Muscat wine Joktan had asked for, as well as two earthen mugs. He positioned himself once more across from him, and poured them both a drink. "As long as I'm drinking with you, tribesman, we will drink from a cup instead of the bottle," he said, handing one of the cups to Joktan.

"Very well," he replied, "I can act civilized too when I desire."

"I would wager that's not very often," the barkeep intoned.

"You may be right."

"Now then, lets talk business, shall we?" Paltro said with a sly look on his face, "for as I recall, I'm a greedy, money hungry man, waiting to make some easy coin."

"Fair enough," Joktan agreed with a smile. "First, I need two swords, and not long swords either."

“Why not long swords? Too cumbersome, perhaps?”

“Aye, and I already have one,” Joktan answered. “I don’t much care for it.”

“Then why don’t you trade it, towards a new sword of your liking?” the barkeep suggested.

“What, and be unarmed? I think not!” Joktan exclaimed indignantly.

“But you just told me that you don’t like it, so why *not* sell it?” Paltro reasoned, “after you have purchased new swords that are more to your liking.”

Joktan’s brow furrowed as he thought for a moment before consenting. “Very well.”

“Now we’ve established that you don’t like long swords,” Paltro surmised, “so what manner of sword are you looking for?”

“I want one to have a single edge, and another a double edge, and both are to be not much longer than my arm.”

“I’ll see what I can do, of course, but you must understand that Luxantia is not an armory,” the barkeep replied. “I don’t understand why one sword is not sufficient.”

Joktan smiled broadly, his ivory canines fully visible in the dimly lit tavern. “Two blades are always better than one, my friend.”

“Anything else?”

“I need two short daggers, one long knife, a few throwing dirks, and two hundred arrow staves,” Joktan paused for a moment, then continued. “I fletch my own shafts. I'll also need two coils of strong rope, a grappling hook, a couple bundles of cordage, two wool blankets, a good strong belt, and general provisions for two weeks.” He downed his wine, then added, “and a good, stout horse that can carry it all, and me as well.”

He leaned forward with a smirk. “You got all that? Maybe you should write it down.”

Paltro raised his bushy eyebrows and snorted through his bulbous nose. “I got it,” he said, tapping his temple with a pudgy finger, “my memory is excellent.” He sipped some wine and shook his balding head. “You sure don’t ask for much, do you tribesman?”

“I’m traveling bare bones here,” he returned, ”it’s not really all *that* much.”

“No,” the barkeep scoffed, “not for a small army. I don’t even want to know where you are going with all this stuff.”

“That is how I intend to keep it, too,” Joktan informed him.

He scratched his head and thought for a moment. “This will be expensive.”

“How much?” Joktan growled, his face darkening.

Paltro squinted his eyes and began going through the list of supplies under his breath, his round pate moving back and forth as he quickly made some mental calculations. His sweat-beaded brow furrowed in silent contemplation, then finally he looked up. "Thirty pieces of gold. For everything."

"That sounds reasonable," Joktan agreed, surprised. "I'll give you fifteen now, and the other fifteen when all is ready," then in a lower voice, "take as much time as is necessary to be discreet. I don't want to cause suspicions. If this town is truly as superstitious of my kind as you say it is, it wouldn't take too much to do it."

"Of course."

"In the mean time, I'm going to wander around a bit. It would not seem right if I were to just stay inside for days on end without venturing out even a little."

"Then we have a bargain?" Paltro inquired.

"Yes, that we do," he replied.

Then, in the customary sign of agreement, the two grasped forearms, slapping the back of each other's hand with their free hand. Paltro for his part looked very pleased, and he smiled enthusiastically. "What you ask will take some time, but consider it done," he assured him. "And *please* try not to kill anyone if you do go out and about," Paltro advised.

"I'll do my best," he smirked.

A look of apprehension swept across the barkeep's face, and he shook his finger at him. "I'm very serious!"

"I'm sure you are," Joktan confirmed with a mischievous grin. He reached into his coin pouch and thumbed out the agreed upon amount of gold, which the barkeep snatched up hastily and secreted away. Paltro turned and waddled back to the kitchen, muttering under his breath and wagging his head as he went.

Joktan left the table and climbed the stairs leading back up to his room, contemplating what to do next. He needed the provisions and weapons to continue his journey south. The truth of the matter was he had lied to the gatekeeper when he'd first arrived. He had no intention of traveling to Endrakana at all. But then he had not intended to travel through Straltonia either, a kingdom where there was still a hefty price on his head. If he had not lost his bearings in the storm, he would have been in Bezakzia right now.

Luxantia was situated along the fringes of Straltonia, the nation over which King Xalton now ruled. The chances of being caught by his soldiers were very slim at the moment, considering the distance that stood between the palace in Zebulon and this small trade town.

Nonetheless, Joktan was being careful. There were numerous

armed patrols that roamed about the country in Xalton's service. He knew that if he were to be captured a second time, the king's men would handle him much more carefully.

No, his real destination lay much further south. He was bound for the Nephilim Isles; a place that most people thought only existed in myths and legends.

A few months earlier he had traveled to his homeland, a place he had not been since early childhood. He'd went there to visit his mother. She was much older now then she had been when he had last seen her, and he knew instinctively that the time of her passing would soon draw near.

The once beautiful features of her face now bore deep scars, etched by the ravages of time and untold grief, but there was still a fire that burned brightly in her emerald gaze, which the years had been unable to quench.

She was a powerful woman, although not in terms of physical strength. Her name was a secret few would ever know, for she was a *Scathach,* a witch of the Sabertooth Tribes, greatly renowned as a seer and wise in the ways of magick. The very name "Scathach" meant "woman who strikes fear". Her true name was *Uathach,* which in the language of Joktan's people meant "The Very Terrible One". She was the last summoner, one who could call the tigers.

A witch never revealed her name to anyone, for names have a power all their own, and tradition held that if one were to discover a witch's name, he would have power over her. Never before had there been a witch in the Savage Tribesland as powerful as Uathach.

Joktan had spent nearly two months with his mother, and during that time she'd told him many things he'd never known, not only about her own life, but his as well. The sound of his steps reverberated down the stairs as he went up to his room. Deep in thought, he reflected back on the last night he had seen her alive.

"When I was younger I traveled to many lands," she had said that night as they sat by the fire in her hut. Her eyes had seemed so distant, as if looking past the flickering flames, into another place and time. Her voice trembled with age as she spoke.

"Very few know what I am about to tell you, Joktan. I am older than any of our kind who now live. My mother was a powerful Scathach, as was her mother, and her mother before her. All of the women in our family have been strong in the ways of magick, ever since the coming of our people to this land."

She looked at him, studying his face. "Throughout the history of our family, the women have given birth to only one child during their lives, and always that child was female."

A look of pride settled over her features as she spoke. "You are the first male child born by the women of our bloodline. However, my father was not of our kind. He was from a land far to the south called Ellyllon. It is the land where the Elves live."

"Do you mean to say that Elves actually exist?" Joktan asked in surprise. Perhaps his mother had grown fanciful in her old age.

"Aye," she assured him, "they most surely do. And not only do they exist, but they have their own kingdoms, not only in the western lands of the world, but the east as well. I have told you that my father was of their race, but the truth is that all of the women in our bloodline have had fathers who were Elves. The men of our own kind have never impregnated us. That is why we have always been so strong in the ways of magick."

Uathach searched her robes with a trembling hand, then found her pipe. They sat in silence as she packed it with tobacco, lighted it, and passed it to Joktan. He took several puffs before handing it back to her as the old woman went on with her strange tale.

"I journeyed to the kingdom of Ellyllon when I was still quite young, not much older than what you are now. It is a beautiful land, and I lived with the Elves for many summers before returning home. But during my stay there, I also journeyed to a place that lies at the end of the world."

She paused for a moment, allowing him time to consider what she was saying. "Perhaps you have heard of it. It is called the Nephilim Isles."

"Aye," he replied. "I have heard of it, but like the land of Ellyllon, I have never believed it to exist."

"Well, I can assure you that it does," his mother said in a low tone. "That is the place where the Watchers live."

"I don't understand," he replied. "Why are you telling me this?"

Her voice became a whisper, but her words were clear and distinct. She gazed at him intently. *"That is the homeland of your father!"*

"My father…?" Joktan was stunned.

His mother shook her head solemnly. "Yes, my son. Your father was a Watcher."

"I thought the Watchers were a myth," he exclaimed. "According to every legend I've ever been told, it was forbidden for them to have sex with humans."

"They are no myth," she responded seriously, "and we are not completely human. For generations upon generations our bloodline has been so mingled with that of the Elves that there is little human left in us at all."

"I find that very hard to believe," he replied obstinately. "I have the teeth to prove it."

"As do I," Uathach confirmed. "But what I am telling you is the truth. That is why I chose someone of a different race to be my consort. That is why I gave birth to a boy and not a girl. You are not like other men. In time you will see."

"And what then of my father?" Joktan had wanted to know.

Uathach sighed heavily. "Do you remember when you were taken away?"

"Aye," Joktan growled bitterly. Even though he had been but a child, the memory of that day was still as clear as if it had just happened. "I remember it well."

"You were too young then to know why you were taken." His mother's face looked pained as she searched her thoughts. She looked at him evenly.

"The men who captured you were the servants of a necromancer. You were taken only as bait, for the one he truly sought was your father. You must understand that the Watchers never leave their land. It is forbidden for them to do so, for they are pure in every respect. They protect the Earth, but in the times of old, many of them became.....tainted. Since those days, only a select few of them are permitted to travel abroad, and then only for short periods of time, and with the utmost care. Your father was one of those few, and somehow the necromancer discovered this. He wanted to capture a Watcher, undoubtedly for some evil purpose, for their blood is very valuable to those who delve into the black arts. But the necromancer could not figure out a way in which to capture him."

"So he sent his servants to steal you, knowing that if he did this, your father would hunt him down. In this way, he did not have to search for a Watcher, one would come to him. His plan worked well. Your father sought to rescue you and was taken in a trap. He was captured and imprisoned, and you were no longer of any use to the mage, so he sold you as a slave."

Joktan's eyes narrowed. He remembered the face of that man, even after all these years. Because of him, he had come to know the cruelty of slavery and the red-hot sting of the whip. Even if he could somehow forget it, the scars where still etched indelibly upon his back.

Tears welled up within his mother's eyes, and she stared into the flames. "I used to speak to your father every day. I heard his voice in my head, and he could hear mine as well....that is how we talked to each other when we were apart. But in time his voice fell silent..... "

"So he is dead then," Joktan surmised.

"For years I thought it so," Uathach replied. "But of late I have begun to hear his voice once more."

"And what does he say?"

She looked at him thoughtfully. *"He is calling me home."*

Joktan didn't know what to say. His mother's words triggered memories within his mind that had been long suppressed. He fought to make sense of it all, but his head felt like it was about to explode.

"I thought this place was your home," he muttered sullenly.

"It has been for many years," she answered, "but home is where the heart is, and for me, that is with your father."

Joktan was silent. He had just recently gotten to know Uathach. Now it seemed that he might never see her again.

"What of this wizard?" he inquired. "What has become of him?"

"I am glad you ask, for the necromancer yet lives!" she whispered, a sinister smile tugging at her lips. "I have never asked anything of you. Will you promise me something now?"

"You know I will," he blurted.

Her eyes grew cold and narrow, and her voice became unearthly. "Carve that wretched mage to pieces and feed his flesh to the jackals!"

His mother's sudden outburst of rage was so unexpected and frightful that it caused a chill to run down his spine. In that instant, he realized why his people called her "the terrible one".

"How will I find him?" Joktan was almost afraid to ask.

"His name is Skeltar," his mother practically spat the words. "Head for the south. You will not have to search for him. He will soon find you."

Joktan hardly felt reassured. If the mage had been crafty enough to capture a Watcher, he would be a formidable foe indeed. Uathach seemed to sense his apprehension.

"Do not fear. When I have gone, our people will take me to the mountain, to the sacred stone. They will leave my body there for three days, according to our tradition. You must go with them."

"I will," he promised.

She pointed at him with a gnarled finger. "On the third day they will return, to burn my flesh to ashes."

Joktan started to speak, but she cut him off sharply. "Do not be sad about this, for my body is old and withered now. It feels more like a prison with every passing day. You must go with them to light the fire."

"I understand," Joktan said hollowly.

"Swear to me that you will slay the necromancer when I am gone!" she said.

"I will."

"Swear it!" she demanded.

Joktan looked her in the eyes. "I swear it."

"Very well," she sighed with relief. "Head toward the Nephilim Isles when you have left this land. That is how you will meet your destiny."

She then lit her pipe once more. After a few puffs, she offered it to him with a smile. "Now let us speak of more cheerful things."

"Aye," Joktan replied, returning her smile as he accepted the pipe. He closed his eyes and inhaled deeply, making an effort to clear his mind as best he could, but he found it difficult to rid himself of the heaviness filling his heart.

Sometime during the night Uathach died. Her lifeless body was carried to a plateau that rose high above the northern plains and placed upon a massive stone altar which had been built there in some ancient age that had long passed out of memory.

The stone was etched with strange designs and symbols which no living soul could now interpret, but they had been considered by Joktan's people to be very sacred for countless generations.

Her body was left there for three days and nights, after which time Joktan and the rest of their Tribe returned, intending to burn her corpse and scatter the ashes upon the ground, according to the custom of the Sabertooth Tribes. But when they returned to the altar her body was missing! A thorough search of the area failed to yield any clues as to where her body might have gone.

Such a thing had occurred often in the past, when the body of a powerful Scathach was brought to this sacred place, but it was very rare now, for very few of the Wise Ones were as strong in the art of magick as the witches of old had been.

It troubled him deeply, though his people regarded her vanishing to be a blessing from the Gods, a reminder that they still remained in the world of men and that their people had not been forgotten.

However, Joktan also wondered secretly if this unusual event might have something to do with the Watchers, and he pondered his mother's last words to him. She had said that he was different than other men, yet as far as he could tell, there wasn't any sign of it. *"In time, you will see,"* she had promised. Perhaps time itself would reveal what that difference truly was.

For now he needed to fulfill his oath to his mother, to kill the necromancer, but he wasn't anxious to get started just yet. Besides, she had said that the mage would come looking for him. If that was correct, then it did not matter where he chose to go. They would meet soon enough. Hopefully he would be able to keep his promise when the time came and succeed where his father had failed.

Joktan shoved open the door to his room and stood off to one side, surveying it carefully before entering. Satisfied that there had been no intruders during his breakfast in the tavern below, he strode across the floor to the bed and reached beneath it for his utility pouch, a soft leather bag that strapped around his waist.

After a brief inspection of its contents he slung the pouch over his shoulder and exited his room, scooping up his muddy robe as he went and heading back down to the tavern. During his brief absence the two trulls had returned. They casually draped themselves by the hearth with a flagon of wine.

As he glanced about the room he noticed that the drunk who'd been in the tavern upon his arrival the night before had returned. He sat sipping a pint of ale in the far corner, quietly passing his time playing a game of some sort with a deck of parchment cards.

He looked up from his game when Joktan entered the room, but quickly averted his eyes, returning to his ale and cards.

The interior of the tavern was not as dim now as it had been the night before, and even though he'd merely swept his eyes across the room, Joktan had noticed every detail.

The man was middle-aged, disheveled looking, and hadn't seen a razor in at least a month. His dark hair was greasy and matted, but it was his hands that particularly caught his attention, for they were perfectly clean, unlike the usual drunkards that one would see in such places.

Come to think of it, those sandals he wore looked fairly new and much too well made for a common drunkard to afford. And the face; narrow mouth, drooping eyes set into bony chiseled features, the long hawk-like nose and high forehead spider-webbed with bright red veins. They were very familiar looking.

He continued across the tavern and stepped outside into the street. *"I know I've seen that man before,"* he mussed aloud as he went, *"but where?"*

For the moment the answer eluded him, much to his annoyance, but it seemed obvious that the man was a spy. There were too many discrepancies in his appearance for him to be a poor, luckless drunk. But why would someone be spying in a town such as this? Luxantia was just a common trade town, and surely nothing very exciting ever happened here, at least not enough to warrant sending out a spy to investigate it.

Oh well, no use troubling myself over it at the moment, Joktan surmised as he set off down the slippery street. Time would reveal who and what the drunkard really was, though he made a mental note to question Paltro upon his return.

He wandered the small town in search of a taxidermist, and presently located one just a short distance from the Open Arms Tavern. Due to the present weather conditions, business had been very slow of late. Even so, the man greeted Joktan with a look of apprehension upon his aging face. He showed him his soiled robe and asked how much it would cost to have it cleaned.

The taxidermist, a tall man with heavily callused hands, examined the garment and offered to clean it for a modest fee.

"Don't see musk-ox skin much in these parts," he remarked rather curiously as he unrolled the robe and went to work cleaning it with an assortment of bristle-brushes and metal combs.

Joktan made no comment, and began browsing through the selection of hides and leathers in the small shop, many of which were from animals that he'd never before seen or heard tell of, and there was a great variety of goods fashioned from these which were displayed for sale. At length he selected a rabbit-skin loincloth, a gray and black wolf-skin cloak, a pair of dark brown buckskin leggings and a soft, tan leather tunic. He piled them all upon the counter while the hide merchant continued working on the robe, then selected a pair of knee-high boots with thick soles and soft, durable tops.

The merchant was overjoyed as he paid for the goods. Joktan informed him that he would be back in a sort while to collect his things, then headed back out into the muddy streets to familiarize himself with the town. There were very few people wandering about, and most of those that were seemed to pay little attention to him as they scurried along, going about whatever business they had in mind.

The ones who did notice gave him queer, furtive glances while keeping a safe distance away. Before too long he headed back to the taxidermist to collect his things. The man bundled up the various items for him, making them easier to carry on his way back to the tavern.

Back in his room, Joktan stripped off his old clothing, throwing it into a heap in the far corner of the room before getting redressed and going back downstairs to the tavern. He was getting hungry, and had a hankering for a draught of ale.

The cook prepared him a meal of roast mutton, corn, fried mushrooms and a loaf of bread, with a bowl of drippings in which to dip it. Paltro set it down before him with a pitcher of foaming ale. Joktan cut off a bite-sized hunk of the meat, skewered it with his dagger and thrust in into his watering mouth. It was still bloody on the inside, just the way he liked it, and the barkeep smiled, noting the look of satisfaction on the tribesman's face.

"You've got an excellent cook!" he managed around a mouthful of the juicy meat, "I might have to take him hostage when I leave."

"Ha!" the fat man exclaimed, "you've been eating mud and rain for so long that anything would taste good!"

He had that usual mischievous twinkle in his eyes as he spoke, and Joktan nodded his agreement as he continued to stuff his mouth. "Aye, and that mud was hard on my teeth!"

He set to devouring his meal with all the grace of a ravenous tiger, belching his approval loudly when he'd finally cleaned off his plate, which was the custom in these lands. He wiped the grease off his face with the back of his hand before draining his ale and motioning for more. When Paltro returned with another pitcher, Joktan handed him his plate.

"What of my provisions?" he asked.

"I'm working on it," he assured him, "but you have to give me some time, you know. I have a tavern to look after, and what you ask is very unusual, especially for a savage such as yourself. I don't know what plans you have or where you intend to go, nor do I want to know for that matter."

"True," Joktan intoned, "but you have no need to trouble yourself with such details."

"Do you know how much trouble you will cause me?" Paltro was incredulous. "Do you have any idea in that thick skull of yours how much effort I am having to go through just to be discreet about things? And had I known I would be feeding a horse instead of a man I would have doubled the price!"

"You've been paid well, my friend," Joktan answered dryly, "and for your troubles you will be paid fairly, though I care not what pains you must endure to provide me with the things I need." An amused smile played upon his lips.

"Humph!" Paltro snorted, "you are an ungrateful savage too!"

"That is true, of course," Joktan allowed, "but what I lack in gratitude I can make up for in gold, which makes you grateful enough for the both of us."

The barkeep scowled at him, then bust into a boisterous roar of laughter, "Only because you have a fine sense of humor, my friend!" he declared, "and speaking of which, Nolan still thinks you are touched with madness."

"Why?" Joktan asked defensively.

"Why? Because you laughed at him so when he fell on his face in the mud, that's why! I believe you're the only person who's ever laughed at him and lived. He despises being made fun of, even in jest. The man has a dreadful temper."

The barkeep leaned down, bracing his weight on the table and nearly overturning it. "How I would have enjoyed seeing his face when he realized that he was the source of your merriment. I would have paid in gold to witness that!"

As Paltro made his way back over to the counter Joktan muttered to himself, "Yes, the look on the gatekeepers face had been priceless indeed!"

He sat silently for a while then, lost in his own thoughts, when presently the barkeep returned with another pitcher of frothing ale. As he placed it on the table, Joktan leaned forward and spoke in a low voice. "That drunk in the corner," he inquired discreetly, "has he been here long?"

"Aye," he confided, raising his bushy eyebrows, "he came in just before the storm began. He says nothing, and no one knows where he's from. Even Nolan does not know. Seems he slipped into town unnoticed, though how I have no idea."

He shot a quick glance in the strangers direction, then went on. "Before your arrival he came into my tavern now and then, but since he has only left a few times, and only for a short while."

A concerned look fixed itself upon the barkeeps face as he moved his head in the direction of the two trulls, still seated beside the glowing hearth. "Even Luena and Glona trust him not."

He now leaned over closer, his words a barely audible whisper. "I've seen the cards he lays upon the table. They're not the usual sort for gambling, if you know what I mean. There are strange symbols on them."

Joktan's brow furrowed with interest. "What sort of symbols?"

"Evil ones, that's what sort they are!" the barkeep hissed.

"And you say he spooks even the whores?" Joktan asked with a hint of surprise.

"Aye," Paltro's countenance vividly portrayed his uneasiness.

"Where does he lodge?" Joktan questioned, draining his drink tankard, then refilling it with the last of the remaining ale and handing the pitcher to the barkeep.

Paltro shrugged, "I don't know. He comes in early and leaves late, but the man is no vagrant, mind you. He pays with coppers that bear King Xalton's face, and he drinks very slowly. He feigns drunkenness, which is suspicious, and if you ask me, he looks like the sort that deals in black magick."

Joktan thought for a moment. He had no reason to doubt the barkeeps word, and the more he learned, the more he began to think that the stranger was indeed a spy of some sort. He turned to Paltro. "I'm going to step out for a moment and wait," he informed him quietly. "If he leaves, I will follow him and see where he goes."

The man's face showed sudden concern, "Be careful, my friend," he admonished him softly. "I think that lout may be a priest of Dhampir. I would not want my best customer to get hurt." An impish grin formed on his lips, which only Joktan could see in the dim light of the tavern. Then speaking in a loud voice for all to hear he asked, "Would you like some more ale?"

"No thanks," Joktan answered in like manner, "I'll be on my way."

He pushed back his seat and strode to the door, shooting Paltro a secret wink as he went. "Thanks for directions," he called out over his shoulder, "and if that jewelry merchant is what you say, I shall extend my stay a while longer and enjoy much more of your ale!" He stepped out the door, hoping that the stranger would buy his ruse and soon follow.

Walking down the street, he ducked quickly into an alleyway, pressed his back to the wall and peered back in the direction from which he'd just come. Evening was setting in now, and the streets were growing dark as he waited, silent as a ghost. He did not have to wait long.

Within a few moments the door of the tavern swung open, and the drunkard stepped out into the mud. He glanced furtively to each side before starting in Joktan's direction, moving along at a brisk pace.

The savage held his breath as the splatter of hurried footsteps grew steadily closer, and he melted into the brick wall at his back, blending into the shadows like an unseen phantom. As the stranger drew near, Joktan crouched behind a pile of wood to avoid detection, and his quarry scurried past the alleyway, continuing off down the deserted street. Joktan emerged from the shadows and trailed behind at a safe distance.

The man sped along with his head down, winding through a maze of muddy streets and dark alleys, until he stopped at a small wooden door set into a brick building on the far side of the small lake which Luxantia was built around.

Opening the door, he disappeared quickly inside. Joktan paused, scowling. The building did not appear to be a tavern or inn of any sort. It looked more like an old warehouse.

The tribesman put his ear to the door and listened carefully for any sounds coming from within before slowly opening it and treading softly inside. He moved quickly into the nearest corner, waiting for his eyes to adjust to the darkness. After several moments he began to notice the details of his surroundings. He was standing in a corridor, the floor of which slanted downwards. The walls and ceiling were made of brick and wood. The floor was hewn stone.

The shape of the interior was square near the doorway, but as he began to advance stealthily along the passage it began to take on a hexagonal shape, a fact which struck him as rather odd. Small torches set in copper sconces lit the gloom with a flickering glow, and he took one from its place on the wall and held it out in front of him to better illuminate the darkness of the corridor.

The wavering flames cast ghastly shadows along the walls. They danced unnaturally, like demons escorting a dead soul down into the black maw of the abyss. In certain places the passage was flooded with muddy water, probably due to the recent rains, and eventually he could make out another doorway looming in the blackness up ahead.

As he drew nearer, the torchlight revealed a brass rung fastened securely to the door. It functioned as a handle, and Joktan tugged at it cautiously. Peering beyond, he nearly let out a gasp of sudden surprise at the sight he beheld.

The room was very large. He judged it to be about sixty paces across, each way. The walls, floor and ceiling were of chiseled stone, for the entire vault had been hewn into solid bedrock. It was brightly lit by strange lamps that hung from bronze chains, fastened to the ceiling some forty feet above.

At the far corner of the chamber the man from the tavern sat at a large, semi-circular stone table, the hood of his robe thrown back to reveal a completely shaven head. Joktan frowned. A dirty wig lay nearby, tossed carelessly upon the floor. His back was turned towards the savage, and an assortment of curious objects were placed purposefully upon the top of the table.

The man seemed to be in a trance, staring deeply into a crystalline obsidian stone in front of him, a stone which had been craftily shaped into the perfect likeness of a human skull. He appeared to be speaking to someone, as if receiving commands, but Joktan could not recognize the language that the strange man uttered. It had an unearthly tone to it that sent shivers down his spine. The tribesman knew instinctively that it was a long forgotten tongue, malignant and arcane.

So immersed was magician in the gleaming black object before him that he seemed oblivious to his immediate surroundings. A small leather bag sat precariously on the edge of the table, and from the lumps and bulges inside it Joktan surmised that it must be full of gold.

All this his well-trained eyes took in at a glance, but what made him gape in surprise was the only other object in the center of the cavernous room.

For before him was one of the most beautiful women he'd ever seen. She was inside a huge brazen cage, and she was completely nude.

Her long, wavy hair was the color of living flame, cascading down to the cheeks of her pale, rounded buttocks. She had lean, muscular thighs, arms and legs, as if well accustomed to physical exertion. The woman's generous breasts were the size melons, tipped by dark-pink nipples that stood erect in the frigid chill of the damp, musty air.

Joktan blinked hard to tear his eyes away from her breasts, only to find himself transfixed by the sight of the dark patch of her pubic mound between milky thighs.

Her green eyes were the color of emeralds, and the features of her face were finely sculpted in perfect proportion, flowing down with artistic symmetry to the graceful curve of her slender neck. Her parted crimson lips were full--the kind of lips that begged to be kissed--Joktan thought, feeling his manhood stiffen the moment the idea shot through his head.

She was suspended by her wrists at the center of the cage by an iron chain and manacles, and although her luscious breasts heaved with each painful gasp of breath, not a single sound escaped her. The woman's clothing had been tossed into a heap outside the door of the giant cage.

Joktan's instant rage was immeasurable.

How anyone could be so cruel to a woman, let alone a beauty such as this, was beyond his comprehension. Anger welled up inside him so suddenly that he completely forgot about stealth. He curled up his lips in a fearsome, throaty growl, ivory fangs glistening in the brilliantly lit interior. His deep blue eyes burned with molten fire as he leapt towards the robed figure seated at the table, bounding with the ease and speed of a rabid panther.

The man wheeled in his chair, his face a picture of terror and surprise, as Joktan's sword hissed from it's leather sheath and sang through the air in a deadly arc. It narrowly missed it's mark, for the man had wisely jerked his bald head backwards just in time to avoid loosing it.

Joktan closed in on him, and stepping ahead lightly with his left leg, his right knee came up. His foot was a blur as it snapped suddenly forward. Twisting at the hips, he released the devastating power of a well-trained front kick. It struck his foe in the solar plexus with violent force.

The man flew off of his seat, sailing backwards in the air, his back smashing into the stone wall behind him with a muffled thud. He fell to the floor in a crumpled heap, gasping desperately for breath. His breastbone had been shattered by the shear force of Joktan's blow, and dark bloody foam began to froth from his mouth and drip onto the cold, granite floor.

Joktan swept towards him and placed his foot on the man's sunken chest. Lowering his sword, he held the razor tip of the blade to his enemies' unprotected throat.

"Who are you!" he growled angrily at his victim, as the man sputtered and coughed for breath. There was no reply.

Joktan pressed his sword harder against the soft flesh of his neck, and a stream of crimson blood began to flow instantly from the wound. "What is your name?" he demanded ferociously.

His enemy stifled a terrified howl of pain, wincing grotesquely. "Don't kill me!" he pleaded weakly, "I am but a lowly priest of Dhampir…"

"That much is obvious," the tribesman grated. "Whose spy are you, and what of this woman?" Joktan demanded, motioning with his free hand in the direction of the brazen cage.

"You have an amulet," the priest choked as more blood sprouted from his lips. "I was sent to locate it and return it to the rightful owner."

"And the wench?" Joktan snarled, his azure gaze cold as a winter's chill.

"She is a gift to our god, Dhampir," the priest gurgled thickly.

"A *gift?"* Joktan's eyes narrowed to thin, deadly slits. "A sacrifice more likely! I know well what you and your ilk do with *gifts."* He glared at the frail man as he spat out the final word.

"As you should, Joktan of the Sabertooth lands," the priest's voice took on an ugly, sinister tone. "You," he said accusingly, "are the thief who tried to rob our holy temple! You are the vagabond that defiled our god's sacred dwelling place! Maybe you escaped the king's dungeon, tribesman, but you cannot hide from the wrath of Dhampir."

He coughed up another mouthful of bloody ooze, then continued, "You are but one man. We are many. We know where you are, and I am not here alone."

Suddenly Joktan knew where he'd seen the man's face.

7

A year before, he'd been in the city of Zebulon. He had traveled there for one purpose; to rob the Temple of Dhampir of treasures hidden away in a subterranean vault, which Joktan had discovered lay beneath the central Temple altar.

After locating the vault and gathering up all the gold and jewels he could possibly carry away, he had tried to escape undetected, but was caught by several of the priests. They immediately called the guards, and Joktan had been hauled off to the King's dungeons.

There he was suspended spread eagle from the granite ceiling of a cell by iron chains, then left to slowly rot and die. Water and filth from the latrines on the dungeon's upper levels had dripped down upon him as he'd hung there, high above the stone prison floor, which was littered with human bones, blood, feces and urine.

Every manner of foul insect crawled upon the prison floor, procreating and feeding on the maggots amid the putrid filth. And the stench!

It burned the nostrils like acid and his eyes had swelled nearly shut on account of it. He'd hung there for almost a week when the priests had come for him. They had devised their own way to torment him apparently, and had persuaded the king to release him into their custody.

They'd drug him from the cell and over to an iron block to remove his bonds, after which they intended to tie him up securely and carry him away.

Somehow, Joktan had managed to grasp onto a small

sledgehammer, a tool which the guards used to pound rivets into the prisoner shackles with.

He'd brained several of the priests before they knew what was happening, then took two of their swords and fought his way through the dungeon, killing all who crossed his path.

After what had seemed to be an eternity he had finally escaped, but ever since that day there was a price upon his head, not just by the priests, but by the king of Straltonia as well.

Now Joktan glared at the wretch with contempt as he lay there upon the stone floor, trying in vain to wipe the dark foam from his lips. The priest looked up at him with a sinister grin.

"If you kill me, you will still die."

The savage smiled grimly at his bleeding foe, baring his mighty teeth. "I know who you are!" he snarled thinly, "you are the treacherous fiend who sold me to King Xalton's Imperial Guards. You were the reason I spent so many days and nights in that loathsome cell, breathing foul air that burned my eyes and reeked of rotting flesh. I couldn't place you until just now." He tightened his grip on the handle of his long sword as he spoke.

The helpless priest let out a sudden peel of wicked laughter, his voice echoing eerily within the subterranean vault. "We will kill you," he hissed, "and death at Dhampir's hand is more fearsome and terrible than you can possibly imagine in that dimwitted skull of yours. Spare my life, and I can make your death a quick one, but know this; no one has ever defiled the temple and lived. You in your arrogance thought to steal from our god, and for that alone you should surely die, but we can make a bargain right now, you and I, and by doing so you can spare your own life and Dhampir may grant you mercy."

"I don't deal with your kind," Joktan retorted angrily. "And you are hardly in a position to be advising me."

"But you have the amulet!" the priest rasped, "the golden disk."

"I have never seen such a thing," the savage spat.

"You lie! You acquired it in Striebe," the priest insisted.

So, his bad fortune *had* begun with that accursed bauble, Joktan thought silently. Suddenly he laughed out loud. "Perhaps, but I don't have it anymore, nor do I want the foul thing you seek."

The priest sputtered and coughed through the gore that foamed in profusion from his lips, holding his hand to his fractured chest and wincing in pain. His gaze was almost pitiful, but the words he uttered were edged in sarcasm. "Then we cannot make a deal, I fear, and you shall still die, for the priesthood will follow you to the ends of the Earth."

Joktan's eyes brimmed with fury, and a hatred that seethed like a volcano's molten wrath welled up inside his chest as he glared vengefully at the evil scoundrel.

"Promise?" he growled, and thrust his blade through the man's pale throat.

Blood shot through the air like a crimson fount, and the priest's eyes went wide in terror, bulging from their sockets. He clawed desperately at his throat, but to no avail. As he choked on his own blood, his legs thrashed about and his body convulsed violently, then went slack and limp as his eyes glazed over in a lifeless stare.

Joktan turned and strode across the room towards the bronze cage, the dead man's blood dripping from his blade and staining the stone floor with every step.

Reaching the square door, he bent down and grasped the lowest bar, sliding it up as he rose. Holding the door open with one hand, he stretched out the other and secured the latch, then stepped inside.

"Are you all right?" he asked the woman while inspecting her wrists and iron bonds from below.

She had to breath hard for air to speak, and her large breasts heaved with the effort. "Do I look all right?" she replied sarcastically, gasping for air. "Just hurry up and get me down."

Joktan was stunned. He'd expected gratitude, or at the very least a thank-you. His gaze followed the chains at her wrists up to the top of the cage. They were slung over a large iron hook, fastened to the center of the cage roof where all the vertical bars met in a peeked dome. He would have to climb up there and lift the chains, as well as the woman's full weight, over the end of the hook to let her down.

His eyes met hers. "I'll have to climb up to the top to get you down," he informed her, then added with a smirk, "just hang on."

"I suppose I don't have much choice, do I?" she muttered as he took hold of the bars and began pulling himself up the side of the cage, ignoring her remark.

At the top, he swung his legs upwards, thrusting them between the bars of the roof and hooking both his knees over one of them, anchoring the rest of his body. He let go with his hands to hang upside down, and grabbed hold of the chains on each side of the iron hook, pulling with all his strength. Every muscle in his arms, shoulders and legs strained to lift the chains over the tip of the hook, and then he had to do his best to let her down slowly to prevent her from crashing to the stone floor. He groaned painfully with the effort, looking down from his perch above her. The veins in his forehead swelled with a sudden rush of blood, his face turning pink, then red.

The woman looked up from below, her head back, green eyes staring at Joktan in agonizing desperation. *"Pull!"* she screamed tersely.

"I am pulling, you ungrateful wench!" he growled back at her through clenched teeth.

"Well pull harder!" she retorted.

He heaved with all his might, and his legs felt as if they were going to give. Then the chain slipped over the hook and he struggled to lower her to the floor as best he could. The woman collapsed as her weight settled on her legs.

"Watch your head!" he shouted, letting go of the chains and then dropping to the ground. He landed gingerly on his feet, his knees absorbing the shock, as the woman rolled to one side. The heavy chains struck the floor beside her, rattling with a metal hiss and narrowly missing her head.

"Fool!" she sputtered in rage, "you almost brained me with these blasted chains!" She made a great effort to stand up, but her legs were too weak to support her body and she fell back onto the floor.

"Get up," Joktan ordered as he squatted panting, trying to catch his breath. He felt very annoyed with the woman's caustic personality.

She looked up at him in humiliated exasperation, "Don't you think I would if I could?"

"All right," He muttered with a sigh. "I'll have to carry you then."

Joktan stooped over, and putting her hands over his shoulders, grabbed her by the waist and hefted her up. Much to his delight, her bare thighs pressed against his face as he carried her out of the cage and over to the stone table a short distance away. She was about the same height and weight as he, but he managed to set her down with as much grace as could be expected under the circumstances.

"Now," he said as he unloaded the woman gently, "where did

this priest put the keys to your shackles?"

He fought to keep his gaze from feasting upon her more than ample naked beauty.

He'd never felt more uncomfortable in all his life.

She seemed to read Joktan's thoughts, and shot him a look that was as cold as ice.

"I don't know," she replied cynically, "I never saw any keys. But maybe after you've finished staring at my tits you could try to hack the cuffs off with your sword."

"I don't want to damage my blade," he returned dryly, "besides, I might miss and lop off one of your pretty little hands."

He stepped over to the dead priest and began searching the lifeless man's clothing.

"Can you dawdle any longer?" came the woman's voice from behind him as he rummaged through a pouch containing various personal belongings.

"Why? You going anywhere?" he quipped, laughing. He found a brass ring with several keys attached to it in the man's leather pouch, and turned back to the wench. "What's your name?" he questioned her curiously.

"What's it to you? Don't think I owe you anything just because of what you've done here," she retorted. "Besides, I think you've gotten a good eyeful already."

"I don't think you owe me anything," Joktan stated with a smile, "I only came here to kill this worthless piece of carrion," he motioned towards the lifeless priest. "Had I been looking for an unthankful trull, I would have stayed at the tavern."

Fire leapt instantly into her eyes and her cheeks flushed, bright red with anger. "I am no trull!" she shouted at him in rage, "I am Sheba of Lothair, a warrior far greater than you shall ever dream of becoming." The woman glared at him defiantly.

Joktan threw back his head and laughed, which did nothing to ease her indignation. "I should have left you to rot in that cage, wench Sheba!" he proclaimed mockingly, trying the different keys in the manacle locks.

"Then why didn't you?" she asked haughtily.

Finally finding the right key, he removed the first iron bond as she waited for a reply.

"Because," he said, running a hand along the outside of her thigh, "when I saw you chained up in that cage....your body dripping wet with sweat," he paused and openly looked her over from head to toe with lustful, hungry eyes, "I began to think of much better uses for that cage....and you!" He smiled wickedly at her.

"Swine!" she screamed and swung her right hand at his face, intending to slap him viciously, but at the same instant she let out a yelp of surprise and pain. She grabbed her shoulder with the other hand and bent forward.

"Oww!" she growled through clenched teeth.

"Easy now," Joktan commanded sternly, "your shoulders are dislocated. That happens when you get hung like that. Trust me, I know. Now sit still so I can finish getting these cuffs off. We can fix your shoulders later."

Sheba sat up, murmuring a stream of angry curses under her breath while he removed the other manacle. He shoved the chains off of the table and they hit the floor, making a dull, rattling noise.

"Are those your clothes?" he pointed to a crumpled pile.

"Yes," Sheba hissed, her temper cooling down only slightly.

"Very well. Lets get you dressed then."

"I can dress myself."

"O.K.," Joktan shrugged, "suit yourself, wench."

"My name is *Sheba*!" the woman retorted angrily.

"Whatever," he replied unconcerned, "you do that while I take a look around."

He picked up the leather bag that still sat upon the table and hefted it. It felt heavy. He opened the bag and looked inside. It was full of gold coins. He dumped them out on the table for inspection. They were mostly Straltonian, bearing the image of King Xalton upon them in bold relief.

He scooped the coins back into the bag and stowed it away, then began to take a closer look at the table itself.

It was made of perfectly smooth stone. About the length of a man, it curved in a broad semi-circle. There was a wooden drawer on the side closest to him which he opened. It was full of miscellaneous items and a strange looking dagger, probably for use in rituals or sacrificial ceremonies, he thought, thrusting it into his belt.

The various other items that had been laid out upon the tabletop he piled together, then went over to the corpse on the floor.
Stripping the dead priest of his robe, Joktan heaped the items from the table onto it, placing the crystal skull in the center, then he wrapped them up into a small bundle.

Meanwhile, Sheba had been making a valiant effort to clothe herself, but with very little progress. She was now muttering profane curses and vulgarities the likes of which Joktan had heard very few men equal. He stood and watched her humorous attempts to garb herself, making no effort to conceal his mirth.

Finally, when she was near total exasperation, he spoke up,

"Would you like some help?" he asked innocently.

"I can't get my arms through the sleeves of my tunic," she glowered begrudgingly.

He went to her side and gingerly helped her into the shirt, a brown silk affair set off with elaborately stitched silver designs. Beneath this a tight wrap of silk held her generous breasts firmly in place. The remainder of the woman's garb consisted of close-fitting, thigh-high boots and a silken loincloth, which hung down to her, knees in front and behind. It matched her tunic in color and design, and was secured with a thin leather belt, decorated with flat silver wire that had been threaded along the length of each edge.

Merely dressing her made his manhood ache with desire. Her naked flesh was soft to his gentle touch, and her feminine aroma made him painfully stiff with an irrepressible, burning lust.

"Now," he said once the beauty was fully dressed, "I will take you with me to the Open Arms Tavern. Once we reach my quarters I'll fix your shoulders and divide what wealth I've gathered here, but you will need to take it easy for a while so your body can heal."

"*To your quarters?"* she asked indignantly," what makes you think I want to go to *your* quarters? You will not have your way with me, if that is what you have in mind."

"Look, if I wanted to rape you, I'd have already done it," Joktan informed her. "I'm from the Sabertooth Tribesland in the north. We honor our women and treat them as equals, we do not ravish them against their will." He gave her a long look, then said, "You have my word that I will not force myself upon you. If you choose to remain in my company until your strength returns, no harm will come to you."

Sheba looked at him thoughtfully, as if trying to make up her mind.

"Alright," she said at last, "but I will need to get some new clothes, as well as a sword. All my weapons and jewelry were taken from me when I was captured."

"Like I said," he replied, holding up the bundle of goods, "once we divide this up, you shall have more than enough coin to purchase the things you need, and plenty extra too."

The woman gave him an appraising stare, and for the first time she actually smiled. "What are we waiting for then? Let's get out of here."

"Very well," he said, placing his right arm around her narrow waist. "I'll help you along, but we must be wary. There may be more of these vile priests about."

King Xalton sat sprawled out on his bed in the Royal Palace at Zebulon, making a great effort to appear casual and relaxed for his meeting with the wizard Skeltar.

His bed, which had been crafted from exotic woods found deep in the jungles of Ramaya, was blanketed in fine silks and hides, all of which had been imported from distant lands so far away that few had ever heard of them. Every visible inch of wood had been overlaid with gold and silver, inlayed with ivory and encrusted with precious stones.

The bed floated in a crescent-shaped pool of deep, blue-green water. A score of naked, lithesome beauties from as many different nations perched themselves on the edges of the bed in sultry fashion or frolicked playfully about in the cool, glistening water.

Rare turquoise flamingos, swans, brightly feathered ducks and exotic fish of countless variety also inhabited this magnificent pool.

He sipped his favorite Balsin Berry wine, a sapphire colored beverage distilled from a rare type of blue raspberry, which only grew high up in the mountains of the far eastern lands. His goblet was crafted of gold and fine amethyst crystal. It was held to his lips by a nubile, naked girl, usually his most recently acquired maiden, all of whom were there to serve his every whim and desire.

All of these beautiful women serviced the King by their own choice, not through obligation or enslavement. They were his pride and joy, and he loved them and his immeasurable wealth more than any other thing or person in all of Straltonia.

Everyone in his kingdom and in many of the nations abroad had heard rumors about the King's bevy of beauties. Indeed, they were said to be the most exquisite women in the entire world.

However, what few people would ever know is was that these luscious, naked goddesses were the King's most elite, personal guards.

They were unparalleled by the vast majority of his most brutal soldiers, and far more ruthless and bloodthirsty in combat than any man could ever be. These women possessed cunning, guile and strength enough to defeat any adversary, disguised beneath flawless beauty unsurpassed in all the world.

Even the King's personal guards had no idea of their hidden talents, and if they ever found out, the unfortunate men mysteriously disappeared. Usually they were called upon for a personal audience with the King, after which they were never seen or heard of again.

The King despised affairs of state, and it was very seldom that he left his royal chambers. Everything he desired overflowed in abundance within its marble walls.

Recently, however, his health had begun to fail him, and his once seemingly endless supply of strength and stamina were rapidly fading away. Each day left him more tired and gaunt.

No matter how much he slept and rested, he never felt truly refreshed, and all his physicians were now at a loss when it came to finding a cure. They couldn't even diagnose the cause of his mysterious illness, which troubled the king even more.

He'd brought in a renowned herbalist from the southern lands, but even he had been unable to provide him with anything more than temporary relief. There was a constant, dull aching in his bones, and although the herbalist had given the king a tonic which eased the suffering considerably, it didn't last for very long. The discomfort seemed to be even worse afterwards. King Xalton had spent a lot of money getting the old geezer to Zebulon, and for what?

He still continued to die a little more with each passing day.

The only wisdom anyone could offer was to seek out a powerful sorcerer, for it was a strange and mysterious illness, one which to the royal apothecary reeked of the black arts. Their logic was, if the illness was created by some fell magick, then it must take stronger magick to make it disappear.

Of course, no one had been too comfortable telling the king so, for it was well known throughout the kingdom that King Xalton despised wizards. At one time he'd even contemplated having them all put to death upon the gallows.

The idea had seemed wise to him at the time, but his counselors advised him in no uncertain terms that to attempt to exterminate all those who dealt in the dark arts was to risk their arcane retaliation. No kingdom could ever hope to withstand the wrath of a legion of vengeful wizards.

And so the King had permitted them to continue practicing their magicks, albeit begrudgingly, but now the irony of him seeking out the feared and dreadful wizard Skeltar for help was most humiliating! He was keeping it a closely guarded secret, to be sure. If word was to escape that the king was seeking out the aid and services of such a one as Skeltar, suspicion and rumors would run rampant throughout the kingdom.

Lost deep in his thoughts, King Xalton jumped with a start as a dark-skinned beauty with small, perky breasts suddenly burst up from beneath the water right beside him. He was showered in a spray of droplets as she emerged, her nipples hard and erect from the cool depths of the pool.

Her slender body glistened with wetness from her brief swim under the surface. Rivulets ran down over her buttocks and dripped from her neatly shorn mound as the woman pulled herself up onto the bed. Her dark, wavy hair was soaked and flowed down to her tailbone. There was an anxious look within her almond eyes as she sat down beside the King.

Neither she nor any of his other lovely women needed to be addressed by Xalton before speaking to him, and she immediately drew near to him and pressed her lips to his ear. She spoke in a low, breathy tone that bore a heavy southern accent.

"Your Highness, Skeltar waits outside the chamber door."

He could feel the flutter of her long thick lashes against his cheek. "Thank-you, Elliasha," the King replied. "Tell the guards to show him in." He paused a moment and then added, "but only him. No one else."

Elliasha moved close again and kissed him softly on the lips, then disappeared beneath the surface, swimming under the water towards the far edge of the pool. King Xalton smiled as he watched her lithe, graceful form glide effortlessly below the water. She was truly an exotic beauty indeed! Elliasha re-emerged moments later, slipping up onto the floor and padding softly to the door.

She's a naughty little vixen, that one! Xalton thought inwardly. *I should give her a proper spanking…*

The King motioned to be moved closer to the waters edge, and twelve of his maidens surfaced beside the floating bed. They held onto it with their hands and guided it forward, their feet churning up the water as they swam.

No sooner had he reached the side of the pool when Skeltar appeared, escorted by four attractive maidens, one in front, one on each side, and one bringing up the rear.

Skeltar, for his part, seemed totally unaffected by his surroundings, and his brooding pitch-black eyes betrayed not the slightest hint of human warmth as he came in silence toward the King. He halted abruptly, standing within a few feet from the King. Something in his movements made the Xalton feel suddenly uneasy, for the wizard seemed to glide rather than walk, as he moved across the marble floor.

He did not bow, nor did he kneel, but stood erect, his pale form shrouded by the dark robe wrapped tightly about him like a fibrous cocoon. The mage's ever-present sneer played upon his garish lips, and his lack of respect was immediately apparent.

Not waiting for an introduction, Skeltar addressed the King in a hollow, hissing tone that seemed more demanding than inquisitive, his mouth unmoving as he spoke. "I am Skeltar. Why have you summoned me?"

The King noticed the wizard's motionless lips, and an eerie chill sent shivers up his spine. The hair on the back of his neck began to stand on end.

"I have a problem," King Xalton began. "I grow weaker with each passing day. My bones ache endlessly, and my dreams are filled with foul demons and terrors, which I cannot even begin to describe. No one has been able to make me well, and it is only out of frustration that I call on you."

"I can cure your illness, oh King," the sorcerer responded, "but the price for your health and peace of mind may be more than you are prepared to pay."

The King burst into a violent peel of laughter that shook his withering frame from stern to stem and ended in a spasm of choking coughs.

"I am prepared to pay you whatever it is you desire, sorcerer," he replied with a flourish of his hand. "As you can plainly see, I am the wealthiest and most powerful man in all the Westermarch."

Skeltar's eyes took on a life of their own, as if some fell evil waited just within to be unleashed. He glared at the King in open contempt.

"Wealthiest?" The mage shrugged. "Perhaps. Powerful?" His eyebrows arched. "Doubtful. Power comes in many guises. I wield more power than your fragile mind can comprehend."

The king looked smitten. "Do not test me, wizard," he sneered. "You claim to have a cure for an illness I suffer. Name your price so I can be rid of it, but toy with me, and I will have you drawn, quartered, and flayed in the market square."

The wizard eyed him stolidly. "I require three things."

"Say on," the King replied, obviously annoyed.

"First, I need a goblet filled with your own blood. Second, a hundred of your best soldiers, all expendable and obedient to my command, to secure a talisman I will need to cure you. And thirdly, a certain woman for which my plans are not of your concern."

"That's it?" Xalton responded.

"That is all," the mage intoned.

The King's forehead furrowed. It seemed at present that this magician had no interest in women at all. He hadn't so much as even glanced at the ones surrounding him right now, and they were without doubt the finest women in the world. Not to mention naked!

"What woman do you seek?" he inquired curiously. "Surely you do not mean one of my own."

"A warrior. Her hair is red like fire, her eyes the color of emeralds. She is from the southern lands, but even now she resides in the north of your kingdom." The wizard drew closer to the King, and Elliasha stiffened instantly.

"The woman I seek keeps company with a fearsome savage from the Sabertooth Tribes, and he protects her," the wizard hissed. "She is presently injured, however only temporarily. She cannot be captured easily when she is well, as soon she shall be." He moved slightly closer.

"Timing is critical."

Xalton was immediately interested, but strove his best to seem unconcerned. "What is so special about her?' he yawned. "She does not sound so interesting to me."

Skeltar was growing impatient, and his voice grew louder now as he replied. "She is the daughter of the Blood Goddess, known in the south as *Cihuacoatl*. As such, she possesses certain powers and abilities which I desire the benefit of, and without which you shall not be cured," the mage informed him. "The priests of Dhampir captured her, hence her current injuries, but they were foolish as always, and she escaped them. She must be captured, as she will not come willingly, but under no conditions whatsoever must she be molested or harmed."

The wizard's molten gaze seemed to burn holes into the King's very soul, and his words were now edged with an urgent, sinister hiss. "Your life, King Xalton, depends on this precariously!"

The King raised his eyebrows in silent contemplation. "Very well," he sighed resignedly, "what is the woman's name?"

"Sheba," the sorcerer's unmoving lips intoned.

"And what about this savage of whom you speak?" the King queried. "Sabertooth warriors are not to be trifled with. My forefathers discovered that the hard way!"

"Which is why I have requested the use of your soldiers," the mage answered thinly. "He has the talisman which I spoke of. It may be that he has allies, with which I will be forced to contend."

The King frowned. "And that is all?"

"That is much more than you could possibly comprehend. But yes, that is all."

"Then lets be on with it!" Xalton snapped. He'd about had it with this wizard's blatant disrespect. His patience was nearly spent.

"Very well. Is that goblet from which you drink valuable to you?" Skeltar asked.

"It is my favorite," the King proclaimed. "It is the only one from which I drink. Amethyst is said to remove poisons from wine and other drink, but I'm sure I need not tell you that. A wizard such as yourself would know those things."

"It will do," the mage replied thinly. "Give it to me."

"Are you crazy?" the King exclaimed incredulously, "I just told you it is my favorite. What manner of game do you think to play with me?"

"This is no game!" Skeltar's words resounded like thunder inside the royal chamber, its preternatural volume and intensity nearly deafening. "This is your life we are talking about, or have you forgotten already? I must use that cup, for there can be no room for error." He stretched out a skeletal hand toward the King. "Now give it to me!"

Xalton sat stunned. No one ever used such a tone of voice with him, and his harem of women began to stealthily arm themselves, bristling in his defense.

"Now!" the wizard cried, though his lips still did not move.

King Xalton held out the goblet.

"I will not mislead you, oh King," the mage hissed, "this is going to be very painful. But the *cup must* be the one from which you drink, and it must be filled with your blood. It may be that the sickness in your body was administered to you as a poison, in this very chalice."

Xalton shook his head mutely in understanding, baring his left arm. The wizard's voice seemed to compel him to obey his commands.

"Come," the wizard commanded a nearby maiden, "hold this cup under his wrist."

The woman looked at the king, then at the wizard, before obeying without comment. She moved rigidly towards the king, as if controlled by some alien force outside of herself.

Skeltar took hold of the Xalton's hand, and with a gnarled, sharpened fingernail pierced the vein on the inside of his wrist.

"Oww!" the King howled in pain and pulled back his hand involuntarily, as a sudden burning sensation traveled up his arm and across his chest. It felt like coals of searing fire.

When the goblet was nearly full, Skeltar let go of the King's wrist and took up the cup of blood in his sinewy hands. He looked the King in the eyes, his evil gaze almost hypnotizing the sickly man.

"You will feel pain no longer. This is all the blood I require." He reached into his robe and withdrew a tiny orange object. "Swallow this now."

King Xalton shook his head as if to clear it. He accepted the pill and examined it skeptically before tossing it into his mouth. After a moment he addressed the mage. "My wrist still bleeds."

"Don't worry, it will cease in a moment," the wizard replied, and to the King's amazement, even as the wizard spoke the blood stopped flowing and the wound closed up completely. The King blinked, for there was now not even a trace of the cut, which had bled profusely only seconds before.

Skeltar pointed a bony finger at him.

"One payment you have made. Two still yet remain. You will send the troops to my castle tonight, when it is dark."

The King consented and the mage added, "They must obey me explicitly, to their deaths, if need be, for this is no game that I embark upon to cure your disease. They should be men who will not be missed if perchance they lose their lives, for the suspicion that could cause would be troublesome to both of us."

King Xalton was still staring at his wrist in disbelief.

"Do you understand, King Xalton?" the wizard's booming voice shocked him back to his senses.

"Yes, yes, of course," he said quickly, "and I will send agents to capture the girl, this Sheba of whom you speak. If anyone can find a woman, it is I." He was inspecting his wrist, spreading his fingers wide, then clenching them tightly into a fist and flexing his arm in front of him.

"I think I feel better already!" he exclaimed, sucking a deep breath of air into his lungs and expelling it sharply. "Come to think of it, I haven't felt this good in weeks!"

"Enjoy it while it lasts," Skeltar advised, "this replenishment you feel is only temporary. Without my further services you will once again become weak, and within a short while your body will wither and die."

"So to what do I owe this surge of vitality?" the King demanded.

"Consider it a token of our agreement. A brief taste of what is to come."

King Xalton sighed heavily, but then his eyes grew bright once more. "If this is just a taste, then I shall surely enjoy it to the fullest!" he boasted vigorously. "Now leave me. All will be done as you have requested."

"Very well," the wizard hissed his reply as he moved towards the chamber doors, gliding backwards across the marble floor. "I will be counting on it. But be warned! No harm is to befall the daughter of Cihuacoatl! She is not to be molested in any way. If she is even slightly injured, you will surely die."

He paused at the doors and lowered his voice. "Mark my words, O King, for your eternal soul hangs in the balance!" With that he disappeared through the doors, and they closed behind him as he went, as if slammed shut by some unseen force.

King Xalton stood and watched as the wizard left. *Why must sorcerers always be so serious?* He wondered inwardly. The King turned to his pride of maidens with undisguised enthusiasm. It had been at least three full weeks since he'd last truly enjoyed their charms. If this sudden surge of vitality was to last only briefly, he would make the most of it while he still could.

"Come!" he proclaimed with a joyous leap upon his bed, "let us play while I yet live!"

10

"Ahhh!" Sheba snarled through clenched teeth, her lips twisting in pain as Joktan gave her shoulder one last sudden snap. The bone popped into place with a sinewy, crunching sound.

"Are you sure that you've done this before?" she growled fiercely.

"Yes. Several times, in fact, but only to myself," he replied, releasing his grip and chuckling quietly.

"I'll bet you tell all your women that," she muttered bitterly.

"Oh, so now you think your my woman? I hardly know you!" he returned with a grin.

"Like *that's* ever made a difference to you before!" she exclaimed.

He ignored her jibe. "Hurts a bit though, doesn't it?" he commented while massaging the bruised upper muscles of her back and neck.

"Aye," she managed with a wince, "but it does feel much better now." She slowly moved her shoulders in circles as she spoke.

"Well, don't be moving like that for a while. Your muscles are weakened around your shoulder joints and they could easily slip back out of place right now."

"Thanks," she groaned softly, "I owe you one."

"One what?" he asked coyly.

"Not what your thinking!"

Joktan stared at her for a moment. He was smiling too. She certainly seemed to be in much better spirits now. "Right now, I think we could both use a drink," he said. "Killing always makes me thirsty. Why don't we go downstairs? You must be starving."

"That is the best thing you've said yet," Sheba agreed.

They left the room and made their way down the rickety stairs to the tavern below, choosing a table close to the hearth. The storm outside had begun to subside, but both of them were sill soaking wet from their jaunt in the rain, and the heat from the crackling fire felt wonderful.

Paltro greeted them with his usual exuberant grin, but when he saw Sheba his eyes grew bright with sudden interest and curiosity.

"Joktan, you have not introduced me to this beautiful friend of yours!"

She smiled demurely at the barkeep and shot Joktan an impish look. "That is because he is a savage, without the manners of civilized men," she scolded with an air of aloofness. "My name is Sheba. And you are....?"

"I am Paltro the owner of this tavern, and I am at your service," he bowed as gracefully as his portly belly would allow. "A friend of Joktan's is a friend of mine," he added boisterously, "especially one so lovely!"

"Well, Paltro," she replied, tossing her long hair over her shoulder and looking up at the barkeep charmingly, "Joktan and I are utterly famished, and *very* thirsty too."

"Ah!," he beamed, "Joktan is always hungry and thirsty! But I will fix up a mess for you both. Would you prefer a flagon of wine, or a pitcher ale?"

"Ale," she purred, "and you'd best bring two."

"Very well." He shuffled away, returning a few moments later carrying pitchers of frothy brew. "Your dinner will be ready shortly," he informed the pair as he placed their drink on the table. Joktan motioned to him to lean close.

"What of my provisions?" he questioned in a low voice.

"I still have a few items to locate, but you must be patient, my friend," he confided quietly. "I *do* have a tavern to look after, remember?"

Joktan nodded and the barkeep scurried away. He looked up to see Sheba eyeing him appraisingly, a quizzical expression upon her perfectly sculpted features. "Paltro is securing some provisions for me," he explained with a hushed tone. "I plan to leave town as soon as they are ready."

"You can't buy your own things?" she asked.

"My teeth frighten the locals," he said, "and they are superstitious of me because I came into town at night, during the worst of the storm. Also, my people fought a bloody campaign against the border towns once. They have not yet forgotten it."

"Will you be walking or riding when you leave?" the woman

asked.

"Riding."

"And where are you bound?" she prodded.

"Far to the south." He really felt no desire to elaborate further.

"There are many lands in the south," she snorted, "could you be a little bit more forthcoming, perhaps?"

Joktan studied her face for a moment, then spoke. "I am going to the Nephilim Isles," he stated flatly, "but no one, except for you now, knows it. They believe me to be headed for Endrakana."

A look of recognition passed over her face. "The place you seek is south of my homeland," she informed him, "it is truly at the bottom of the world. However, I fear it may be folly for any mortal man to go there. The Watchers do not allow it. They keep to themselves."

"That remains to be seen," he replied wryly.

She sipped her drink and sat silent for an instant, as if in thought. "Before I was captured, I was on my way to the southern lands as well," she confided. "I was bound for Lothair, my home."

"I have heard of it," he replied with interest. "I don't believe I've ever met anyone who hailed from there, until now, of course."

"And what have you heard of it?" she queried.

"That it is a land of dark jungles, inhabited by all manner of strange beasts and birds. They say that Fairies live there, and that there are Dwarves in the mountains. And gold."

"Aye," she replied softly, "it is that and much more. Lothair is the most beautiful place in all the Earth," she paused to take another sip of ale. "It is a land of magick."

"I hope not the type of magick that our friendly priest practiced," he commented dryly, reaching for his tankard.

"No, silly!" she laughed, "the Fairy folk wouldn't stay if people like him were living there."

"Am I to believe in Fairies then?" he scoffed lightheartedly.

She merely smiled. "There are many wonders in the south. Believe whatever you please, but men are not the only race to inhabit this world."

"Oh," he muttered, feeling somewhat embarrassed. He guzzled the rest of his ale, re-filled his tankard, then changed the topic.

"Why are you so far from home?" For the moment he had no wish to discuss things such as Fairies. They reminded him of Elves. And Watchers.

"Why are you so far away from yours?" Sheba smiled, returning the question.

"I was taken from my homeland when I was just a child," he

replied, noting her efforts to evade his question. "I lived as a slave for a time."

"Well, I see that you are no slave now, so I presume you either escaped or were set free," she said, "but you have not answered my question." She studied him thoughtfully, waiting for a response.

"I escaped, obviously" he replied, "but I am still wanted in that land, and a few others as well, but you have not answered my question either."

"There you have it then," she told him, her husky voice almost a purr. "We have much in common." She lifted her tankard to her lips and swallowed the last of the contents in one large gulp. Wiping the foam from her mouth, she gingerly sat the mug back down on the table, holding it between two slender fingers and looking at him tauntingly. "I'll bet I can drink you under this table, Joktan," she said with a mischievous smile.

"Remind me of that when I have finished my meal," he laughed, "and I may take you up on your challenge." He tossed back the rest of his drink and slammed his tankard down, then added with a smirk, "though I think you will lose!"

"Ha!" she exclaimed, "I never lose!"

Just then Paltro arrived. He was bearing a steaming feast in his arms on a large wooden tray which he placed on the table before hurrying off again. The meal consisted of two trenchers of beef stew, a roasted rabbit, which had been cooked with the head and feet still attached and then halved down the middle, two loaves of bread, some boiled vegetables and two flagons of wine.

The conversation ended abruptly as the pair set to, devouring the food with gluttonous vigor. Sheba, who'd not eaten for more than a week, couldn't put away nearly as much as Joktan, and before long she gave him the rest of her meal. In a short time all that remained was a pile of clean-picked bones and the rabbit's tiny skull, which he cracked open to scoop out the brains. These he devoured with obvious relish while Sheba turned up her nose. Soon the two of them were relaxing beside the fire, enjoying the warmth as it dried out their damp clothing.

"So," Joktan spoke up presently, "you never did tell me why you want to go back to your homeland."

Sheba sat back and put her feet up on the edge of the hearth, stretching her legs. "Well," she began with a sigh, "its quite a long story, really. Suffice it to say that I've been away from home for a very long time. I would like to see my family and friends once again." She took a long draught of wine. "It *would* be nice to live in comfort for a while."

She looked over at him thoughtfully. "What about you? Do you ever visit your homeland?"

"Aye," he replied pensively, "I went there not very long ago. It was the first time I'd been home since I was a child."

"But you did not stay too long, did you?"

He took another long drink of wine, a contemplative look upon his face. "No," he said at last, "I went there to see my mother before she died."

"I'm sorry," Sheba said softly. "Parting with a loved one is never easy. Particularly when it is your mother."

Joktan sighed. "After she died I left. I doubt that I will ever return. There is nothing for me there now."

"How can you say such a thing?" she asked in surprise. "After all, they are your people."

He studied her in quiet contemplation. "I can never seem to stay anywhere for very long," he said thoughtfully. "In my homeland the people are very proud of their heritage and traditions, although now there are not many of them left. To them, it is foolish to wander the Earth like a nomad. They believe that men should stay at home and raise families, so that our people's numbers will grow once more, and be strong. But that is not the life for me. I don't fit in there."

"I understand what you are saying, Joktan," she mused. "How can they expect you to *want* to stay there? You've spent the better part of your life thus far in other places."

"Aye," he agreed, "after seeing the world outside the borders of my homeland, I could never go back. Besides, it would be so *boring!"* He lifted his flagon and took another swig. "I'm sure you know what I mean though."

"Yes, that I do," she sighed wearily. "In my country I am the future Queen." Her eyes met his briefly. "Does that surprise you?"

"Yes, and no," he answered truthfully. "You seem to be a woman who is used to getting her way, giving commands and having them carried out quickly, so I guess it *could* be possible that you are a princess." He gazed at her for a moment. "I mean, judging from the little time I've spent with you so far, you can be very.... demanding....at times."

He expected her to become defensive, but instead she let out a quiet laugh. "So what you're saying is that I'm a bitch!"

"Precisely," he smiled.

"I know," she agreed quietly, "I can't help myself at times. There are moments when I just don't care." She leaned closer, and in her eyes there was a calm defiance. "But nobody, and I mean *nobody,* jerks me around. If I don't like someone, I'll tell them so, and if that is a problem then I will gladly kill them."

She adjusted herself in her seat and continued speaking softly. "If someone hurts me, I will hurt them back worse. If they treat me well, then usually I treat them equally, and this brings me to something I wanted to tell you earlier."

"And what would that be?"

"I wanted to kill that priest."

"Aye, I'm sure that you did," he nodded, "but I couldn't help myself."

"Oaf!" she retorted, "in killing him you robbed me of vengeance." Her green eyes narrowed as she glared at him intently.

"Relax," he chuckled gently, "I laid my claim to vengeance on him long before you did."

Sheba bristled, "I don't care!" she burst out, "I wanted to gut that bastard myself!"

"And how?" he suddenly demanded, "you couldn't even raise your arms until I fixed them. How did you plan to kill him, with your personality?"

"Oh!" she howled angrily, "that wasn't very nice at all!" She sat for a few minutes glaring at him before leaning back once more. She downed the last of her drink. "You owe me another one then," she proclaimed.

"Fine," he conceded with amusement, "the next priest we meet is yours."

"Really?" she replied, "how sweet. But I meant that you owe me another flagon of wine! After all, I have no money." She smiled, then added, "but I'll take the next priest too!"

Joktan frowned. "Your going to need a blade then." For a brief moment his eyes wandered over her supple body. "And you'll definitely need some more clothes."

He tugged at a leather thong on his belt. "Here," he said, handing her a fist-sized pouch. "That's all the coins I took from the priest. I have plenty of gold for now, and the way I see it, your entitled to it more than I."

She accepted the bag gratefully and weighed it in her palm, then opened it and looked inside. Her eyes grew wide. "There's a lot of gold here," she observed, "are you sure you don't want any of it?"

"I don't need it," he assured her. "I have enough to last me a while. Besides, I took a couple jewels and the crystal skull that was on the table. They should fetch me a fair profit somewhere." He pointed at the pouch. "If you empty it out, you'll find a few jewels in there as well."

"Strange that a priest would carry so much wealth," she mused.

"Aye," he agreed, "but that lout was not just a common priest. I reckon he was one of the high priests. He was obviously in charge of guarding you, which implies that he was highly trusted by his order, and that cage is no ordinary cell either."

"How so?" she asked curiously.

"You obviously haven't spent as much time as I have behind bars," he laughed bitterly. "There were symbols on each of the bars. It was not just designed to keep someone a prisoner," he confided. "I've been thinking about it, and it seems to me that it must have been made to contain some type of evil as well," he gave her a knowing look, "such as Dhampir himself, perhaps."

A sudden shudder passed over Sheba, and for an instant the fire in the hearth didn't seem to cast as much warmth as it had just a moment before. They both fell silent for a while, each of them lost deeply in their own thoughts, until presently the heaviness in the air about them was dispelled as Paltro's cheerful voice broke the silence. "More wine?"

A look of relief swept over Joktan's sullen features and a broad smile lit up his eyes. "Yes, my friend, bring us two more flagons," he responded merrily.

The barkeep hurried off, returning shortly to hand them their drinks before once more scuttling away to look after other things. Joktan turned to her once Paltro had gone. "You're going to need a place to stay now," he said.

"Aye," she agreed, "and it is growing late."

"You can room with me if you like," he offered.

She smiled and gave him a discerning glance. "Don't you mean that *you* would like that?"

"Look," Joktan explained, "even though you're a bitch, I like you, and what's more, I like your company."

Her gaze hardened. "If you intend to bed me…."

"I would love to bed you!" he interrupted her with a devilish grin, "but right now there are more important matters which must be taken care of."

"Yes," she replied, looking at her outfit ruefully. "I need my boots repaired, and I also need a good horse, as well as a few other things."

Joktan took a pull from his flagon, then nestled it in his lap. "You can room with me if you like. I can have Paltro send up another cot and blankets, and a bath if you care for it. My meals and room are paid for already, so for a few silvers more your meals will be covered too."

Sheba appeared thoughtful, and he looked at her earnestly. "I won't harass you, if that's your worry. Once the priests of Dhampir find their dead companion there's sure to be trouble, and for the moment you are in no condition to be fighting. You will be safest with me."

She studied him silently. "I'll stay with you," she decided, "but you have to knock before you come into the room from now on."

He growled begrudgingly, then finally nodded his consent, and she settled back in her seat. "A bath does sound wonderful," Sheba reflected with a weary sigh.

Joktan spotted the barkeep and motioned him to their place by the hearth. "Sheba will be rooming with me," he informed the man. "Can you have another bed made up for her in my quarters?"

"Of course," he smiled sheepishly.

"This should cover the extra bed and her meals for the duration of my stay," he said to the barkeep, handing him several silver pieces. Paltro inspected the coins, then shoved them into a pocket.

"Can you have a bath drawn for her as well?" Joktan asked.
The round man nodded. "Consider it done," he replied, "and will you be needing more wine?"

"Certainly," Joktan answered, "send a couple flagons up to my room, and bring us another as well."

Sheba laughed as he waddled away. "You didn't give him very much silver," she observed.

"I've given him plenty already," he assured her.

"You did not need to pay for me, though," she objected.

"I paid for you because you will need most of your gold to purchase the things you require," he replied.

"Your concern is appreciated," she said softly, "but you needn't worry about me so."

"I'm not worried," he returned. "I'm being fair."

"Are you so fair with everyone?" she queried.

Joktan shrugged. "Maybe. Maybe not. It depends on the person and the situation."

She grew silent, then turned to him. "I am going to return to my homeland. Since we are both headed in the same direction, why don't we travel together, Joktan?" she suggested suddenly. "From there you can carry on to the Nephilim Isles, if you so desire."

His brow furrowed in thought as he pondered the idea. "That is not a bad idea," he said at last. "It is a long and dangerous journey, and two swords would be better than one. Provided you how to use it, of course."

"I am quite familiar with the southern lands," she told him. "The nations that border my country I know very well, and I speak many of the languages used by the people there." She leaned closer and gazed at him fiercely. "And I am no stranger to steel."

"You must understand that I have a price on my head in Straltonia," he confessed. "I must therefore travel through some very treacherous areas."

"All the better!" she enthused, "I've traveled the main roads and trade routes in the past, but now I feel it would be wise to be as careful as possible. I have many other foes than just those priests. It would be to my advantage, having you with me."

Joktan considered what she'd said. It would be much wiser for both of them to travel together, and it made sense too. They *were* going in the same direction. And he would be hard pressed to find a better looking companion with which to make such a journey. Even so, women seemed to always bring trouble, and that was a very big drawback.

Sheba was growing impatient for a response. "I can also give you an armed escort to the land of the Watchers, once we reach my country."

"How so?"

"I've already told you," she replied, "I'm the next Queen."

"So you say," he muttered.

"So I am!" she bristled.

"I'm curious about something," he informed her. "You say you are from Lothair, but your skin is pale as ivory."

Sheba merely smiled. "Like I said, I *will* be Queen."

"And what, pray tell, does that have to do with the color of your skin? I have never met anyone from the southern lands that didn't have a dark complexion. At the very least you should have a good tan. But you don't, and that seems a bit odd to me."

"You are quite correct, of course," she replied. "Nearly everyone in the southern lands are dark skinned. In Lothair *all* the people are." She took a swig of wine, then went on. "All the people of my homeland are dark skinned *except* for Royalty, and we are all very pale, as you have obviously noticed. It is a most unique distinction between those who lead the nation and what you might call the common people."

Joktan shook his head. "The sun darkens everyone's skin."

"Not mine," Sheba smiled coyly, "I have been pale since the day of my birth, and I shall always be so, just as my mother before me and her mother before her."

Suddenly she leaned toward him, her emerald eyes narrowing. "You don't like my skin color then?" she inquired sharply.

"I don't care if your skin is blue," he ejected. "I just think it is odd that you do not tan, that's all."

She smiled and relaxed once more, a gleam of satisfaction in her stare. "You see, Joktan," she said, "that is precisely why we should travel together. Once you reach the mountains on the northern borders of Lothair it will be impossible for you to travel any further south, unless you are in the company of someone who is a native of those kingdoms. There are sights so spectacular, you simply cannot imagine. The jungle holds mysteries all her own, and many undreamed of things await within to be discovered and experienced. I could show you more than any other person, even among those that live in my land, for I have traveled and explored it more than anyone else, and as a future Queen, I could show you things that no other man will ever see."

"The truth is, I don't have any idea of how to get there," Joktan confessed. "I don't even have a map. My plan is just to head south and keep going."

"Why, that is the silliest thing I've ever heard of!" the woman exclaimed.

He shrugged his shoulders. "Like you said, the Nephilim Isles are at the bottom of the world. If I travel south long enough, I'm sure to get there sooner or later."

Sheba shook her head in wonder. "So what of it then?" she asked. "Shall we travel together? At least I know where I'm going."

"Well," he nodded with a laugh, "it would appear to be in the best interest of us both." His eyes traveled over her magnificent figure lustily. She caught his gaze and moved a little in her seat.

"You really must stop looking at me so if we are to be companions," she scolded.

"Don't be so prudish!" he laughed, "I was merely appreciating your beauty."

"I can read your thoughts like an open book," she replied somewhat haughtily.

"Read on then!" he exclaimed, laughing once more.

"I also saw how you looked at me when I was hanging in that cage," she informed him lowly. "You are a savage."

"That is hardly a secret!" he shot back. "Your a spoiled wench!"

"Maybe so," she accepted, "but this wench has wealth beyond your wildest dreams."

"And a lot of good it does you now," Joktan remarked. He moved closer to her, and all traces of warmth disappeared from his azure eyes. He lowered his voice.

"Let's get one thing straight right now. I take orders from no one. If we run into trouble, and surely we will, you do as I say, understand? It could mean the difference between life and death."

Sheba's gaze met his with in an equally icy stare. "I can handle myself just as well as you," she growled. "You may find that hard to believe right now, but you will find out soon enough." They eyed each other for a moment appraisingly, not saying a word. The air between them grew tense as they silently appraised each other.

Presently she spoke up. "I know that you do not trust people easily," she said, "you probably never have, and I'm sure that you have some very good reasons." She took another drink of her wine. "I give you my solemn oath that I will not betray your trust, Joktan. A Queen cannot break an oath."

She studied his face for a few seconds. "If I ask you to do something, I expect you to trust my reasons, just as much as you expect it of me. If I must trust my life to you, then you must also trust yours to me."

Joktan considered what she'd said silently. He had learned long ago that it was not wise to put any great amount of trust in others. It also seemed that whenever he'd gotten into real trouble, a woman was usually to blame. This woman was different though. He could see it in her eyes. It was in the way she spoke too, and she had a way with words that made what she said sound very believable.

"Agreed," he said at last.

Sheba smiled. "Give me your dagger."

"Why?"

"We've made an agreement, have we not?"

"Aye, we have," he said.

"Then we must seal it," she replied.

"Of course," he said, feeling a bit foolish. It was the custom in many lands to seal an oath in blood. He drew his dagger and passed it to over, hilt first. She accepted it and pressed the blade into her palm, making a small but deep cut. There was not the slightest sign of pain in her expression as blood welled up from the wound.

Joktan took up the blade and did likewise, then the pair clasped hands firmly. Sheba closed her eyes as she gripped his hand tighter and grew silent for a long moment, as if in quiet contemplation. When her eyes opened again there was a genuine warmth deep within them, and when she spoke her voice was a satin purr. "My life for yours," she promised softly.

"Aye," he returned the oath, "and mine for yours."

He sat as if entranced by her beauty. Sheba's gaze seemed to beckon him, pulling him closer and closer like a moth to a flame.

"You have the beauty of a goddess," he whispered softly, feeling a knot beginning to form in the pit of his stomach.

She merely smiled and drew closer. "You have no idea," she replied slowly, "but I believe we will make perfect companions."

Joktan shook his head, as if to clear it. He almost felt as if he'd just awakened, like somehow he had briefly passed into a dream.

"Well," he said quickly, "I need some more wine." He waved to Paltro and the barkeep started over immediately.

Sheba rose from her seat with feline grace. "I'm going to head upstairs and have that bath now," she told him. "I won't be long." She picked up his dagger and twirled it lightly between her finger. "Mind if I keep this for the night?"

"I would actually feel much better if you did," he responded. "It is not wise to be without a weapon."

"Especially with your raging hormones so close to me," she teased.

Sheba turned to the barkeep. "Goodnight, Paltro!" she said, and then glancing at Joktan, "don't let him get too drunk!"

"I'll do my best," he assured her with a grin.

After she'd gone Joktan ordered up another flagon of wine and a plate of meat. Paltro shook his head as he placed the food before him. "I envy you, Joktan," he said with a sigh. "You drink and eat like a bear and still you are not fat. What's your secret?"

Joktan grinned. "Lots of exercise."

"In that case, I should be losing some weight quite soon," he joked. "I've made all the arrangements, and your provisions should be ready tomorrow night. I did not want to say much around your lady friend."

"That is good news indeed," he said, "but it seems I will be needing another mount as well."

Paltro looked surprised. "Then I take it that you will not be traveling alone?"

"No," he answered.

A quizzical look swept over the mans face. "Tell me," he asked, "is your new companion a certain red-haired woman?"

"You are very observant," Joktan replied dryly. "I trust this won't be a problem for you then?"

"No, not at all," the barkeep was quick to assure him.

"Good," he said, "when we are ready to leave, I'll let you know."

"And what of our friend the drunkard?" Paltro inquired curiously. "I see he has not yet returned."

Joktan gave him a sly smile. "Your questions seem to have no end. But if you must know, it turns out he *was* a priest, not a drunk," he replied. "And I doubt he'll be around much anymore."

11

Skeltar gloated as he sat once again before the table of visions, recounting the recent events silently in his mind.

"What a fool this King Xalton is!" he thought, a contemptuous smirk settling upon his thin lips. Beside him on the table was a box containing the King's goblet and blood. As long as it stayed safely within the confines of this container, it would not be polluted in any way. The spell would keep King Xalton's blood just as fresh as it had been the moment it had spilt from his veins.

Peering intently once more at the scrying glass before him, he noted with satisfaction that the chaos in the vision was beginning to dissipate. The bolts of lightening and clashes of thunder were now gone. Only dark clouds remained, and it was evident that the downpour of rain was steadily lessening.

If he judged correctly, it seemed that the sacred amulet he coveted had changed hands, for the vague outline of the person in the glass was much different than had been before.

However, the fact that the apparition was still enveloped in swirling chaos gave him hope. It meant that the amulet was still in the same location.

"The savage must have sold it," he muttered in disgust to himself. He wondered how much he had gotten for it, knowing that there were others like himself who would pay almost any price. He also knew that very few people would ever guess the power the amulet possessed, and without that knowledge, it was just another strangely crafted piece of gold.

Skeltar sat considering his next course of action. It was clear that he would have to travel to the amulet. He'd known all along that it would certainly not come to him of its own volition. His recent travel to the palace had been tiring, and he knew that the troops he was receiving from the King would be arriving very soon.

Getting up from the table, he strode across the darkened chamber to his favorite chair. It had a thickly cushioned seat raised an arms-length off of the floor, and it was fashioned so as to allow the occupant to stretch out fully upon it.

The chair sat facing a mirror, and a cord attached to the side of the seat was strung to a brazen bell outside of the room, serving to summon his lowly servant Cral.

Skeltar now tugged on the cord, and Cral appeared almost instantly, opening the door to the chamber and standing silently before his master, his eyes averted to the floor.

"Bring me something to eat," the wizard commanded, "I wish to have my dinner now. And bring me a kettle of hot water as well."

"Yes, Master," the servant replied, immediately withdrawing from the room and closing the door.

For Skeltar, "something to eat" was always the same; a bowl of fatty beef broth and simmered marrow, seasoned heavily with hot spices and peppers. He never ate anything else, and Cral kept a pot of it simmering constantly, for his master never ate at regular intervals. Indeed, he could go for several days without eating at all, sometimes even weeks at a time. But other days he consumed such vast quantities that Cral was hard pressed to keep up with the wizard's sudden, insatiable appetite. In truth, the simple fact that Skeltar ate at all was the only visible characteristic of mortality in his existence.

The servant returned momentarily carrying an unadorned copper tray. Upon it rested the soup, a kettle of hot water, a bowl and a spoon fashioned from bone. He sat the tray down carefully beside his master's seated form.

"Cral," Skeltar intoned as his servant made to exit the room.

"Yes, Master?" his voice trembled as he answered.

"We are going on a journey. Prepare victuals for several days travel. Also prepare my carriage, and see that you do it with care," the Mage demanded. "Be quick about it, for all must be ready soon."

"Yes, Master," the servant responded quietly.

"Get to it!" Skeltar snapped, "and advise me when you are done."

Cral fled from the room, leaving the mage in solitude to eat his spicy soup. Once finished, Skeltar leaned forward in his seat, thrusting an emaciated hand into the folds of his dark robe. He withdrew a small black pouch containing an assortment of tiny glass vials. These were filled with various arcane powders, liquids and oils.

He sat it on the tray next to him, and reaching over to a ledge positioned just below the mirror, he snatched up a small grayish cup. He held it fondly for a few brief moments before filling it with steaming water from the kettle.

To this he added the dried powder of Datura Stramonium, then a drop of his own virulent blood, which he also kept in one of the many small vials laid out before him.

The mixture began to bubble, and a greenish black foam formed upon the surface of the liquid in the cup. Picking up the spoon, he scooped off this putrid looking substance, then held the cup to his lips and swallowed the contents in a single gulp. He tilted his head back and closed his brackish eyes.

"Ahh!" moaned Skeltar through sealed lips as the malignant drink coursed through his veins. He could feel it inside of him, under his urine colored skin, which began to take on a translucent, eerie glow.

He lazed back on his chair and fully relaxed, holding the small cup in his hand. If Skeltar's face was truly capable of displaying the slightest hint of affection, it did so now as a reminiscent stare crept across his twisted features, and he slipped slowly into a trance-like sleep.

For this wretched mage had once been a father, and the cup that he now nestled in his hand had been fashioned from the skull of his only child.

Long ago he had discovered the secret of the Datura Stramonium plant. Commonly known as the Death Weed, if used incorrectly the effects were fatal, causing blurred vision, delirium, uncontrollable fits and coma, finally resulting in death. Only after years of trial and error had he eventually learned the proper method for the ancient plant's arcane use.

He'd then taken captive a high priestess from the Temple of Ashtoreth and carried her away to a distant land. In the sixth month, when the Mother Moon had passed through her waning and became void of course, he had raped her upon an ancient altar which had been crafted in ages long past and dedicated to a now forgotten goddess. The priestess became pregnant with his child, a baby girl. It was not only the virgin priestess who had been defiled by this despicable act, but the ancient goddess also. It was not enough to violate the human vessel. The divinity must be defiled as well.

From that moment, until the time of her delivery, Skeltar had taken very special care of the priestess, for the child had to be perfect in every way. No expense was spared to make her comfortable and keep her health intact.

Then, just as the expecting mother went into labor, he'd taken a sacred, consecrated dagger and slit her pale belly open. Removing the unborn child amid the mother's horrified screams, he'd held the child close to his chest and waited for the midnight hour. He had listened with cold indifference to the innocent child's cries for her mother's nourishing milk. Even now he could still recall the terror in the mother's eyes as she'd bled to death upon the altar, and the very memory of it brought a look of satisfaction to his unearthly features.

At the appointed hour, Skeltar had taken up the dagger once more. Holding the baby by its feet, high above the flames of a fire fed by evil powers and caustic substances, he'd cut her throat. The infants blood had drained into the fire, sizzling upon the glowing embers while foul spirits from the black realms of Hel gathered round to witness the abominable rite and feast upon the innocent baby's blood.

Once the child's life was gone, he'd left portions of her flesh behind to further appease the demons. Packing her corpse into a crate filled with maggots, he buried her in the Black Earth of Bileth. He waited for another six months, during which time the maggots stripped her tiny body of all its flesh, leaving only her whitened skeletal frame. It was from this that Skeltar had fashioned the chalice which he now held in his hand.

The sleep of the Datura plant was a long-forgotten secret, rumored to have been first discovered by Kethros in the distant past. Even amidst the most knowledgeable wizards, only a few had ever learned to use it, and it was fewer still that tried. But for Skeltar it had become a matter of life and death.

For it rejuvenated the body, while allowing the spirit to soar free and travel wherever one desired, and right now he was interested in a certain little trade town in the north-western region of Straltonia.

As he lay back in his chair, the mage opened his bitumen eyes and gazed into the mirror that hung upon the wall. It was tilted at an angle, so as not to reflect his own image back upon him. The only thing reflected in the dark glass was a small light veiled by the gloom which brooded heavily in the room. The light was cast by a small oil lamp hung on the far side of the chamber.

Now as he gazed into the mirror, the glass suddenly began to ripple, like the surface of a pond when a stone has been cast into it. It took on an eerie depth, and billowing clouds of rolling gray smoke appeared within. The mage closed his eyes once more.

His sealed lips parted ever so slightly and a fine mist began to emerge. It was like a translucent vapor that emerged from his thin mouth. It seemed to have a life of its own, and it hovered above his slumbering form, slowly becoming a dense haze. In his minds eye Skeltar imagined himself stepping into the mirror as if it were an open door into another plane of existence, and the mist began to move. It rose above his body and poured into the mirage, then disappeared in the swirling smoke beyond.

12

Joktan and Sheba awoke late the next day, each on their respective cots. Neither one had slept well. Their dreams had been filled with dreadful images and a strange dark figure clothed in black, billowing robes.

After a hearty brunch in the tavern, Sheba set out to secure some new clothes and various other items she would need for the coming journey.

Paltro had managed to gather the provisions ahead of schedule, a fact that he made certain Joktan was aware of. He led the savage down a side street to a small stable tucked away out of sight.

Joktan frowned as he rummaged through the items spread out before him. "Paltro!" he shouted, "where are my swords?" *Surely the barkeep hadn't forgotten them….*

"Ah!" Paltro exclaimed as he scurried over to Joktan's side. "I was saving those for last, my friend!"

"I don't want them last," he growled impatiently, "I want them now!"

"Very well, then," the man muttered indignantly. "You savages are worse than children! Come over here." He motioned to a table on the opposite side of the room. It was covered by a thick cloth, which the barkeep now threw back. A smile instantly lighted Joktan's gaze.

There were over a dozen swords and twice as many daggers placed carefully upon the table. "I was not sure which ones you would like best, so I had them all brought over," the man said proudly. "This way, you can take your pick, and then I'll just return the rest to the merchant."

Joktan raised his eyebrows in surprise. "They must trust you immensely."

The barkeep shrugged and laughed. "I've had the tavern for over twenty years now. They know I'm not going anywhere, and everyone knows where they can find me."

He hefted various weapons and swung them about, getting a feel for the weight and balance of each one, then moving on to the next. Some he passed over completely, while others he scrutinized endlessly, inspecting the wrapping on the handles, the etchings, comparing types of wood, and so forth until he narrowed down his selection.

"I'll take these three," he told Paltro presently, setting them to the side. One was a long scimitar, crafted in Dendera by the looks of it, for the blade was made of layered steel. The long curved edge had been finely honed and was razor sharp.

The other two were broadswords, double-edged affairs. They were light and well balanced, yet strong enough to withstand serious abuse without being broken.

He selected two short swords as well, which he could carry across his back beneath his quiver. Each had a single edge, the back of which was flat and nearly as thick as a man's finger. They were graceful looking, but built stoutly.

Eventually he also decided upon an assortment of small daggers and dirks, as well as two large knives, nearly long enough to be considered short-swords.

"You've done well, my friend," he commented to Paltro as the fellow bundled up the weapons. "I did not expect you to obtain such an excellent collection."

"I have many friends," he replied proudly, "and the wares of many kingdoms pass through Luxantia."

He carefully checked through the various bundles and packages, making sure that everything he'd asked for had been delivered.
Satisfied at last, he turned to the barkeep. "Here is the rest of the gold I owe you," he said, handing him a small pouch of coins. He accepted them and counted out the money.

Joktan stowed away the rest of the provisions, then looked at Paltro. "I will be leaving tomorrow at dawn," he informed him.

"So soon?" the barkeep was surprised. He'd hoped that Joktan would stay for several more days. "You paid for eight days lodging, and there are still a few days left."

"I know," he reassured him with a smile, "but I need to get on my way. Just throw in a few extra wineskins and some food and call it even."

"Very well," Paltro replied, "although I don't need to tell you that the skies have not yet cleared. You could be headed right back into that same storm all over again."

"Possibly," he returned, "but I believe it will be fine by tomorrow."

After a bit of discussion, they soon arrived at an agreeable price for the extra weapons and supplies which Joktan had chosen, and having no other pressing matters to attend to, he wandered back to the tavern for some more ale.

He quickly downed the first tankard and ordered another, as well as a flagon of wine. "I won't be seeing another tavern for a while," he told Paltro, "so I might as well enjoy my last day in this one."

No sooner did it arrive than the tavern door was flung open and Sheba strode in. Peering about the room, she spotted him in the corner by the fire and made her way over. She stopped and stood directly in front of him, hands on her hips, as if waiting for a response.

Joktan whistled softly, and his eyes grew wide. He lowered his tankard with a lusty grin.

She wore a one-piece outfit made of black silk, the edges of which had been hemmed with silver embroidery. It was split below the navel into two strips, each side tapering upwards in a wide, revealing "V" which fastened behind her neck. The back and sides were completely open, except for a few thin strands of braided silk, which were attached below her breast and along the sides. These wrapped around and secured behind, holding both the top of the outfit and her bosoms firmly in place. From the waist down it was open along each thigh and leg, forming a long, narrow loincloth of sorts that tied together at the hips. It ended just below her knees in the front and back.

She'd had her boots refurbished; they were laced up the sides and rose halfway up her thighs, where a sheathed dagger was strapped securely on each leg. Below her knees, a sheathed dirk had been fastened to each of her boots.

A broad leather belt around her waist held two more daggers, a large knife and two short, single bladed battle-axes. Over her back was slung a scimitar that looked remarkably similar to the one which Joktan had just purchased.

"I'm impressed," he blurted honestly, "you look magnificent!"

"You like it?"

He gave her an enthusiastic grin. "I love it," he confirmed.

She smiled. "You have no idea how much it costs to look this good!"

He nodded in agreement. "Nice choice of weapons too."

She reached behind her back and produced the dagger he'd given her earlier. "You can have this back," she said, throwing the blade at the table. It stuck into the wood with a solid thud. "I don't need it anymore."

Sheba sat down across from him as he pulled the point of the dagger out of the table with a concerned frown.

"It has blood on it," he noted dryly as he inspected the blade.

"Oh?" she smiled coyly and reached across the table for his ale. "I hadn't noticed."

She took a deep draught, nearly draining his tankard. "All that shopping makes a girl thirsty," she said, "and very hungry too."

"I see," he observed, quickly thrusting the dagger beneath his belt. "And who's blood is on my blade?"

"Oh, I don't know," she remarked innocently, "I must've forgotten to catch their names."

"So you were attacked, I presume?" he asked.

"Not exactly," she replied casually.

"I trust it wasn't a merchant," he pressed.

"Oh, no," she replied, "just a couple of priests. You said that I could have the next one, remember?"

Joktan snorted. "I thought I told you to take it easy too! Fighting won't help you heal. And it could get us into a lot of trouble before we leave."

"But I didn't fight anybody," she defended, picking up his flagon of wine.

"Then what did you do?" he demanded.

Sheba's eyes sparkled with glee. "I merely pricked them."

Joktan drew the dagger from his belt and laid it on the table. "Do you see this?" he reprimanded her. "There is blood all the way to the hilt!" He stowed the blade away and glared at her once more. *"That is not a prick!"*

Sheba stared at him blankly for a moment, but then her expression changed completely and her face lit up with excitement. "I got some other things today too," she enthused. "I got some more clothes for wet and cold weather, a cloak, a pair of leather gloves that go up to my elbows...."

She stopped talking for an instant and looked about the room. "Paltro!" she yelled with a wave, "can we get some more wine over here?"

The barkeep hurried over right away with two flagons of wine. "I'm famished, Paltro dear," Sheba coed, "can you fix me up something?"

"Of course," he replied, "what did you have in mind?"

"Oh, I don't know," she hesitated, "how about something red....and bloody?"

"A beef steak, perhaps?" he suggested.

"Oooh! That sounds delicious!"

Paltro looked at Joktan. "And the same for you?"

"Sure, why not," he sighed. He knew pressing her any further was pointless.

When the barkeep had gone Sheba looked at him. "Don't chide me about drawing blood. I can handle myself, in case you hadn't noticed. Get used to it."

"I just don't want the city guard to find a pile of dead priests somewhere. This town is too small. They would suspect us immediately....at least me anyway....and I don't want them trying to arrest me the night before we leave." His tone was icy thin.

"I'll try to restrain myself," she spat sarcastically.

Where have I heard that before? he thought silently. They were very much alike in many ways, though he justified his killing of the priest in the cavern because it had been necessary in order to free her. She seemed to have done it for the mere pleasure. Then again, he knew all too well just how sweet revenge could feel at times....

The air between them was tense for a while as they both sat there, glaring at each other like a pair of angry wolves. Presently the silence was interrupted as Paltro placed their food before them. As they ate their food, he decided to let the matter rest. If trouble arose from it, they would just have to deal with it as best they could.

He ordered another flagon of wine when the barkeep came back to clear away their plates. Sheba had made short work of his.

"I believe you said that you could drink me under the table," he reminded her mischievously.

"Anytime," she smiled coolly, eyes sparkling.

"Then how about right now?" he suggested. "It's going to be a while before we're in another town."

"O.K." she accepted, "but you pay for the wine."

He shook his head obstinately. "No. The loser pays."

"I know," she replied, "and you're going to lose, so you might as well be prepared."

Joktan laughed. "Your on, wench!" he said, knowing how much she hated being addressed so. It had the desired effect.

She glared at him from her side of the table. "I've already bloodied my blade once today. Pray I don't do it again, savage."

"You bloodied *my* blade," he corrected her, "and the next time you'll clean it off afterwards."

She gave him a taunting stare. "I know where you sleep, and in a little while you'll be passing out, so don't piss me off!"

He chuckled softly, but inwardly he made a mental note. She did have a point, although he doubted that she would kill him in his sleep. After all, he'd saved her from what would have been a grim and painful death.

However there were certain things about the woman that disturbed him. Like the way she moved her shoulders, seemingly without pain. And they now bore not a single trace of bruising or injury, which was quite odd indeed.

And the cut on her palm.

His was still visible, a narrow scab having formed over the wounded flesh, as would anyone else's for that matter. Except for Sheba, apparently.

And if she truly was going to be a Queen, what was she doing so far from her kingdom? Shouldn't she be taking care of her people instead of adventuring in some distant land? He wondered if her future subjects would even want her back when she returned, for it seemed that she cared very little about them. He'd never heard of a princess that acted in such a manner.

He decided that, while she wasn't outright lying to him, she was obviously omitting a few important details, and that troubled him. It was like a puzzle with missing pieces.

Oh well, what difference did it make to him? He was traveling with her as a means of added protection. Most of the lands they would be traveling through he'd never seen before. If she was familiar with them then they would make much faster progress.

In spite of it all, part of him really *did* like her. She was beautiful, spirited, and had a sharp sense of humor. And she obviously liked adventuring, not some pampered, fluffy wench who would cry over a broken nail or scraped elbow. Plus he desperately wanted to bed her!

Sheba interrupted his thoughts. "What shall we drink to?" she asked, raising her flagon.

Joktan was caught off guard. "I don't know," he shrugged, "I usually drink to my hearts content."

She rolled her eyes. "How about we drink to having a fruitful partnership and to not being hung over tomorrow?"

"Sounds good to me!" he grinned.

They touched their flagons together with a dull ring, and Sheba tipped her head back and emptied hers in one big, long draught. Not to be outdone, Joktan did the same, then they tossed their empty flagons into the hearth. The jugs smashed into small shards against the stones and scattered amid the burning embers of the fire. This was standard custom in most lands, and there was no backing out now. The gauntlet had been thrown down, as it were, and they would drink until one of them was unconscious.

Joktan smiled inwardly. He couldn't wait to see her face in the morning, for he had no intention of losing. He'd drank men three times his size into oblivion, and indeed he'd never yet lost a drinking contest to anyone. He knew without a doubt that she would lose. There wasn't any question about it.

She may as well pass out right now, he told himself as he reached for another flagon and gave Sheba a gracious nod....

King Xalton lay exhausted upon his luxurious bed, his recent burst of vitality completely spent. His bones felt as if they were on fire, and his skin was cold and clammy. His body quivered and his limbs shook incessantly, and he was unable to rest due to the violent, racking cough that had once again returned.

The strange illness that plagued him was far worse now than it had been before the wizard's recent visit. As he lapsed into another painful series of raged, hacking coughs, he inwardly cursed himself for ever inviting Skeltar to the Palace in the first place.

Although he now regretted his pact with the mage, he was also wise enough to know that if he broke it his death would be almost guaranteed. He realized suddenly that he now had two afflictions to deal with instead of only one; the illness on one hand, and the fell wizard on the other. It was anyone's guess which one would destroy his life first, but one thing was certain; from now on, he could not afford to take any chances.

He'd been smitten by the illness only three weeks before the arrival of the wizard. Skeltar had to be gotten rid of, but such a thing would not be an easy task, to be sure. Killing a wizard was serious business, especially one so powerful. Nonetheless, it must be done, for he now suspected that he was being played for a fool, and the thought of it angered him all the more.

The red-haired woman of whom the mage had spoke was another consideration to be accounted for. She was obviously important, and even if the wizard had no intention of curing him, it was clear that he desperately desired to find the her. From the wizard's description of Sheba, she seemed to be a very interesting woman indeed. Could it be that it was she who could cure him, and not the wizard?

He knew that if he sent out his usual agents in search of this mysterious woman they would be successful in capturing her.

However, Skeltar had been crystal clear on one thing; she was not to be harmed or molested in any way, which ruled out the usual agents. If she was only half as beautiful as what the mage had described, his men would be sure to rape her many times over before bringing her to him, for such men had little reverence for anything. They would not restrain themselves in such a situation.

Besides, supposing that she was capable of curing his disease, she would be sure to refuse if treated poorly. Abusing women was not in the King's nature, and the thought of it stirred his temper. His agents were only effective because they were unscrupulous and degenerate, capable of the most vile and despicable acts. Their priority was in satisfying their lust for gold, and King Xalton always paid well.

While such methods served more than adequately in other instances, they clearly would not suffice in this particular situation. She would not help him if she were brought by force, he decided.

The solution, he concluded smugly, was to send members of his secret guard to find her. She would be more easily coerced by women than by men, and his women would never fail in carrying out his wishes.

He called Elliasha to him now. She was his favorite maiden, and he was confident in her abilities above all the rest. She slid onto the bed beside him.

"I do not trust the wizard," he confided.

"Nor do I," she replied, "and watching him leave with a portion of your blood concerns me greatly. I fear he will work some foul magick upon it that will not bode well for you."

He nodded his agreement. "I thought that he might be able to cure me, and I brought him here only out of desperation. Now I deeply regret it." He could see the worry in her dark eyes.

"I would love nothing more than to cut out his wicked heart," she said bitterly, "but I fear that killing him would only hasten your death."

"I have been thinking about the matter," he replied, "and I too have decided that he must be killed, but there is another thing which troubles me as well."

"You are thinking of the woman," she blurted. It was almost as if she were jealous….

“Yes, and I’m not sure if even she can cure me, but it is clear that Skeltar seeks her out, so she must be of some worth. I have thought of sending you and a few of the others to find her.”

Elliasha’s face grew fearful. “You must be very careful, my Lord, in regards to her, for she is known to us,” she informed him earnestly.

The King had not expected this. “Then you must tell me what you know,” he replied, “for I fear that one false move now could bring about my death more swiftly than before.”

She was silent and lowered her head for a moment, and when she finally spoke her voice was low and solemn.

“Many of us have heard of this woman. She is truly the daughter of Cihuacoatl, the Goddess of Blood. In that the wizard spoke the truth. In the southern lands, Cihuacoatl protects many people, and it is because of her that they dwell in safety amid the many dangers of the jungles. She is greatly loved for this, and she blesses all those who seek her in peace. But to those who displease her, her wrath and vengeance are utterly dreadful.”

She paused, and when she continued her voice was nearly a whisper and filled with fear.

“If this woman is the daughter of the Blood Goddess, then she may have great power too. If she is harmed, you will have both her *and* her mother to worry about, and that would be a dreadful thing. It would be better to anger a thousand wizards than to invoke the malice of Cihuacoatl.”

“I have heard of many Gods and Goddesses, but I know of no one who has actually seen one, nor been killed by them for that matter!” he replied.

“You do not understand!” she insisted, “the one of whom we speak is real. She is flesh and blood, and ancient as the mountains. She does not die, and the night is her refuge. I fear it would be folly to treat her daughter unwisely.”

“If she is flesh and blood, then she can be killed, and is no more of a worry to me than any other living soul,” he retorted, felling somewhat perturbed.

Elliasha shook her head. “You hear me, but you do not listen,” she said sorrowfully. “This Goddess cannot be killed. Not by swords, or spears, nor any other weapon you possess. Against her, the might of your armies is useless. She will come as a mist upon the wings of darkness, and there will be no way to turn her back when she seeks revenge.”

“How do you know this?” he demanded.

“It is no secret in my homeland. In my youth, when I was just a little girl, Trolls invaded our village. There were thousands of them, and she killed them all in one night. When I was older we were attacked by a horde of Goblins, and she destroyed them in less time than the Trolls…."

He stared at her in disbelief. "Do you mean to say that such creatures exist?" he asked incredulously.

"Aye," she replied, "and they are not the worst of the dreadful things which yet linger in the dark places. I have seen them with my own eyes."

He fell silent for a moment, then looked at her once more. "You have never lied to me, and although I am not given to believing in Gods and Goddesses, I have never seen the world outside of my kingdom, so in such matters I must trust your judgment."

"Then do not aid Skeltar in capturing her!" she pleaded. "You must not allow harm to befall her, neither by your hand nor by any other power at your command, for you will surely die!"

The King pondered her words. He'd never before seen such fear in Elliasha's eyes, and that was troubling, but now he realized that his situation had grown far worse than he'd suspected. Still he had come to trust her judgment more than that of any other.

"So let me get this straight," he replied presently. "It can be surmised that by trusting in Skeltar I may lose my life by some evil of his own design. By aiding him in capturing this woman my death is assured as well, and if I capture her, or cause her any sort of trouble, I will also be killed. Have I missed anything so far?"

"No," she replied, "it is so."

"I'm so screwed my ass hurts!" he lamented. "What other options do I have?"

She thought for a moment. "We must first tell the rest of the women. Then send some of us to find this Sheba of whom Skeltar spoke. We will inform her that the mage seeks your death and hers as well, and we shall tell her of your illness. It may be that if she really does have the power to heal you she will return with us."

"And if she can't?" he inquired.

"If not then we will trouble her no more, but it may also be that she will help us destroy the wizard, for he is a danger now to us all," she replied.

"Aye," the King sighed regretfully, "and now he is armed and protected by a hundred of my own soldiers." He smiled grimly. "I tricked him though! I did not send my best men with him. What King in his right mind would? Only one was of worth."

"I know him," she confessed, "and he is a good soldier. What others did you send?"

He smiled slyly. "Just common riffraff. Men recruited as foot soldiers for the front lines. They are the ones who would be the first to die in battle."

Her almond eyes brightened. "Wise decision, my Lord!" She kissed him, and he ran his hands along the contours of her supple body. "We should call the others," she suggested.

"Yes," he sighed in agreement, "there is much work to be done."

"One last thing, My Lord," Elliasha said.

"What is it, my little raven?"

"Do not send me on this excursion. I will be better able to serve you here." Her fingers lightly caressed his manhood, and the King smiled instantly. Elliasha could do things with her tongue and lips that few other women could equal....

"Very well," he decided quickly. "Perhaps, afterwards, you can refresh my memory..."

"Of course, My Lord!"

They summoned the other women, and explained the plight of the King and the conclusion he and Elliasha had finally reached. After further careful consideration and discussion, it was eventually agreed by all that their proposal would be the best course of action.

After deciding upon which women would go, the chosen warriors hastily gathered their weapons and the few necessities that they would need. The King selected his most proficient warrioress to lead them. No food or water were packed, for the idea was to travel light and move swiftly. Such provisions could be secured along the way as required.

Soon they exchanged farewells and exited the Palace through a secret door. Chia, a young beauty from the eastern kingdom of Zhenya, led them downwards from the King's chambers into a maze of tunnels beneath the city. Further on underground they went, toward the hills several miles outside the walls of Zebulon.

There were only two exits from these tunnels. One was in the King's chambers, which was the one they used now. The other was located in the hills far away from the city. The floor and walls of the tunnels were mostly earth and clay, although brick and stone had also been used in many places to support the higher portions of the ceiling where various tunnels intersected. In these spots the ceiling consisted chiefly of heavy wooden planks. In numerous places water dripped from above, and several of the lower passages were half flooded with water.

The air at times was foul and dank, but as they climbed gradually upwards toward the plains surrounding Zebulon, the air became clean and wholesome.

The women knew their way about these tunnels intricately, for they never entered or exited the palace by any other means. Each one knew every twist and turn by heart. This maze had been built long ago----by whom no one could now recall----but ever since Xalton had taken the throne, the tunnels had been designated as an emergency exit for the King in times of peril.

Now they moved with great speed, silent as phantoms upon the evening breeze, winding through the spider-web of subterranean passages expertly, guided only by their own familiarity and the light of a single torch.

These women were no ordinary palace concubines, nor were they soft and tender from a life of ease and comfort. They were warriors, tried and true, having distinguished themselves through the course of many battles in the lands of their nativity. Hunters, trackers, and assassins all, equally familiar with the arts of diplomacy and intrigue as with those of war and death.

They emerged in single file from the mouth of the entrance, concealed within the forest of the distant hills. Their faces were painted grimly with determination. They were loyal to the King alone, and each of them knew that if this quest proved unsuccessful, their ruler would die. If they failed, their dignity would be forever tarnished, not just in the eyes of the King, but in their own as well.

They had no fear of death, but to die in dishonor, now that was something truly unspeakable.

The setting sun cast long, bloody shadows across the land as the small band of women moved steadily towards the horizon, their minds and wills centered upon one all-important objective; *find the daughter of Cihuacoatl. Find Sheba!*

14

Paltro slept the sleep of one who has been physically drained. In truth he had been, only a few hours before, though most pleasantly indeed, for he'd been exhausted though sexual satisfaction. Luena and Glona, the two whores from the tavern, both slept deeply beside him, having first gratified the portly barkeep, then each other. Paltro, being a short, fat man in every respect, had little stamina in the bedroom.

His lack of endowment was not aided by his sagging belly, and both of these combined made intercourse difficult at best. Luena and Glona often took turns bringing him to orgasm on successive nights. They were accustomed to awkward situations, so to speak, and over the years had become adept at giving the barkeep the results he so desired, and doing so rather quickly.

Tonight had been no different than any other. He had fallen fast asleep with a contented smile on his pudgy face while watching the two women pleasure each other, their lithe bodies soaked in sweat while they orally indulged their carnal passions.

Luena lay on her back, while Glona straddled her facing the opposite direction, and judging by the moans they elicited from each other with their pink, lapping tongues and probing fingers, this position proved most beneficial for both of them.

Soft sighs gradually mounted in volume, surging into screams of erotic desperation. Their bodies arched, one against the other, and Glona's painted nails clawed desperately at Luena's glistening flesh. Her muscles contracted within her, and she thrust her hips involuntarily, pressing her quivering mound against the other's open mouth.

Luena responded in like fashion. Gasping for air in violent release, they rocked in the throws of explosive climax. At length they collapsed in a passionate embrace, their hands exploring familiar contours as their bodies lay intertwined, like two serpents coiled together.

Paltro had not been witness to the results of their frenzied lovemaking tonight, feeling rather spent from the effects of Glona's unrelenting mouth, and now all three slept soundly on the bed.

In truth, no one knew of the relationship the barkeep carried on with the two trulls, which was the result of some shrewd bargaining on his part. It had continued in secret for quite some time now.

Years before, the two women had arrived in Luxantia with a caravan of nomadic Gypsies. They had grown weary of travel and thought to take up residence in the small town, making a living by plying their trade. Luxantia offered all the comforts they desired. It was a resting place for sojourning merchants and adventurers, and a surprisingly vast amount of wealth poured into the coffers of the small, unassuming town. All manner of desires and pleasures were easily acquired in abundance, for a price, of course, and so too were Luena and Glona.

Their needs were few; a place to live, a tavern to work in, food and drink. The Open Arms Tavern was the first such establishment one saw when entering town, and the pair had quickly chosen it as the perfect place to conduct business.

Paltro, on the other hand, had only one desire that was difficult for him to satisfy, due to his lack of stature and wanton obesity, and that just happened to be the one thing which Luena and Glona specialized in providing.

So it was not by chance that the three had worked out a bargain, one night long ago. They wanted lodging, food, drink, and a place that allowed them to conduct business without having to compete with other women employed in the same trade.

Paltro agreed to supply such needs, so long as the pair satisfied his own cravings, whenever they quite literally arose. In addition, he also received a portion of their earnings once a month. It was a small price to pay when compared to the wealth the two trulls could rake in during that time, and he never really knew just how much they chose to charge their customers.

They set their price as they saw fit, and as the years passed they began to amass an immense amount of wealth. So much, in fact, that if the truth were told and their gold counted, it would have far surpassed that of the richest merchant in town.

Many times they had discussed in private what they should do with their growing fortune, till at last they agreed upon a plan. They decided to purchase an old storage house on the far side of Luxantia. It had several old stables attached to it, which were now deserted and collapsed. The buildings were of little value, but that did not matter.

In fact, it made the spot all the more perfect. They would tear down the old structure and build a new one. They would hire a score of women and open a brothel that would also comprise a tavern and an inn. They could charge their hirelings a modest fee, and soon they would become truly rich indeed!

After years of prostituting themselves out to innumerable scores of men, and on occasion, even women, Luena and Glona were anxious to put their plans into action.

So far no one had discovered their deal with Paltro. It would not be beneficial to any of them if word of their illicit bargain got out to the rest of the town folk. His reputation was impeccable, at least in as much as any merchant's could possibly be.

As for the whores, the fact that they serviced Paltro would not bode well with many of their regular clients. So all three kept their little secret to themselves, and there had never been a problem between them ever since it had been agreed upon.

Now they lay upon the bed, each one slumbering peacefully, but unbeknown to them, a thick cloud of misty vapor had begun to seep into the room. It crept under the door in the darkness of the night and slowly spread across the floor like a restless phantom risen from the grave.

The women's clothing lay strewn about the room, having been hastily stripped away only a few short hours before, and now smoky tendrils fingered a stealthy path amongst their scant, discarded garments. The vapor moved with intention, and as more of the wisps slipped silently into the room, they began to coalesce at the foot of the bed.

Slowly it took shape, as if being sucked upwards from below, swirling into a pillar of living smoke. The eerie visage began to emit a translucent, greenish colored glow, and quickly gathered itself into the shape of a dark, robed figure. It towered to the ceiling in the cluttered little room while the threesome lay sleeping unawares.

Two tendrils of smoke crept forth from the apparition now standing beside the bed, reaching out like decrepit hands into the blackness of the night. Paltro rolled over on his back, still fast asleep. His mouth gaped and his lower jaw hung slack. He snored noisily.

The tendrils drifted across his sleeping form to hover silent above his head. Then they seemed to sprout fingers and join together, almost as if folded in prayer. Suddenly, a wisp of purple vapor emerged from between the smoky hands. It took on the form of a death adder, and settled downwards in the direction of the sleeping barkeepers mouth. After a moments pause, it slithered between his open lips and disappeared inside Paltro's throat.

The barkeep snorted and coughed a few times, then rolled onto his side and drifted once more into sleep. The hovering hands of smoke withdrew hastily into the mysterious form, which began to swirl faster and faster at the edge of the bed. Slowly it dissolved, and an instant later, completely vanished from the room.

Far away Skeltar's mirror of visions rippled once again. The glass surface took on the appearance of water, and as clouds of dark smoke broiled within its depths, a misty vapor moved out from the image and entered the room.

It hovered above him before spreading out over his body, then slowly seeped into his sleeping form as if being absorbed into his very flesh.

The mirror suddenly shook, and then the scene was gone. It once more reflected only the interior of the room and the faint shimmer of the lamplight glowing dimly on the far wall.

Skeltar opened his eyes and rose up from his chair, frail hands clenched triumphantly into tiny fists. The talisman was already his!

15

Joktan's head felt as though it had been smashed in by a blacksmith's hammer. He couldn't remember the last time he had suffered such a splitting headache.

The savage never imagined that the first person to best him in a drinking contest would be a woman. Last night was a blur, and he couldn't even guess how much wine and ale he'd consumed. Only the gods and Sheba knew for sure, and the gods weren't telling. As for Sheba, the numbers kept getting smaller all the time as she recounted for the umpteenth time this morning the groggy details of the previous nights events.

He moaned out loud as she launched into another endless tirade of how men were chauvinistic dogs. They never gave women the credit they justly deserved. Men were oppressive and placed little value on women's lives.

She blamed men for the existence of so many predominantly male deities within the more civilized lands. Men, she proclaimed, had introduced gods of fire and war. In many lands where the worship of such gods was dominant, women were thought of as being unclean during their menstrual cycles, a time when a woman's powers of regeneration and fertility should instead be honored and venerated. Yet in numerous places men viewed it as "the woman's curse." How despicable!

Sheba pointed out that the majority of whores were women. Few queens ever kept a harem of male concubines, even though they could if they so desired. And few men truly satisfied the women they slept with. If a woman had numerous lovers, she was labeled a whore, but a man could lie with as many women as he chose and it was perfectly acceptable.

In certain kingdoms men could actually kill their wives without it being considered a crime. She emphasized the fact that if a woman were to kill her husband she would surely die, most likely by stoning or being burnt at the stake. She said that it was also common practice in many kingdoms for female children to be killed at birth, for they could never carry on the father's name and so were of little value. Male children were never killed. In fact, the birth of a baby boy was usually celebrated.

Finally, Sheba stated, the ultimate proof that men were a vile species was the fact that so many women were raped each day. She herself had never heard of a man being raped by a woman. Even if such a thing *were* to happen, she surmised, the man would be sure to find great pleasure in it.

Joktan covered his ears tightly with both hands as a peel of thunder roared off in the distance.

"Enough already!" he shouted at his companion, to which she simply smiled, her emerald eyes taunting him as she rode sidesaddle on her mount.

He tugged at the stopper on his wineskin. Maybe a few draughts would ease the throbbing in his skull, he thought. He lifted it to his lips and took another lengthy swig.

"Oh," Sheba sneered playfully, "Still trying to catch up to me I see!"

"You were lucky," he spat, obviously not in a very good mood.

"Really!" she laughed mockingly, "and how would you know? You couldn't even stand up."

"O.K!" he exclaimed, "you beat me. Are you happy now?"

"And I defeated you fairly too," she goaded him.

He sighed heavily. "Yes, you beat me fairly. Is there anything else you need to hear before you cease your endless babble?"

"I said *defeated,* not beat," she corrected him. "I like that word much better. Do you not think it has a certain pleasant ring to it?"

He rolled his eyes skyward and muttered under his breath.

"Well?" she insisted, "I'm waiting!"

"Fine! You *defeated* me in a drinking bout," he admitted, "but I care little what words you use. Right now the only thing I hear ringing is my skull."

"One day you will realize what it means when I say that I am the daughter of the Goddess of Blood," she informed him. "One day *men* may even discover something which I already know."

"And that is?" he hated to ask.

"That drink goes to your blood before it goes to your head," she declared. "That is why no one can best me at drinking. It has no power over me."

He shot her a sideways look. "Well aren't we special!" he muttered, taking another swig of wine.

"Aye," she agreed, "but I'm not above being generous as well. I can make you forget all about your headache." She grinned and lovingly stroked the battle-ax hanging loosely at her side.

"Humph!" he snorted, "maybe you could end your incessant prattle. That would help immensely."

Sheba replied by silently mimicking him, using broad gestures and an upturned nose to parody his expressions. He shook his head derisively and looked away. The fact was, he couldn't remember even leaving the tavern. The last thing he could recall was seeing several blurry Sheba's sitting across from him at their table. When he had awakened this morning, he was lying on his cot in their room, completely naked.

Sheba had woke him, and she'd slept on her own cot on the opposite side of the room. When he had questioned her as to the cause of his nakedness she'd merely laughed, saying she had stripped him to teach him a lesson. He'd seen her unclothed, so it was only fair that he should suffer the same embarrassment, she had reasoned.

While getting dressed he'd noticed a small cut on his chest, just below the left nipple. Sheba told him that she had given it to him as a reminder. He should be more thoughtful before insulting her in the future. Now he touched the tiny wound with his fingertips and made another mental note not to allow her to out-drink him again.

She noticed him fingering the cut with a look of satisfaction on her face, knowing her point was well taken.

"You have a tendency to think of women as being somewhat weaker than yourself," she commented. "I intend to show you differently by the time we reach my home in Lothair."

"I do not look down on women," he defended.

"Perhaps," she allowed, "but you do not think of them as your equals, even though you claim otherwise. You view us as objects of beauty, to be sure, but I'd wager every piece of gold you own I am the only woman you've ever had for a companion on a journey such as this."

"True," he confirmed, "but you're different."

"Of course I am," she agreed proudly, "but not all of us are the same. Very few women can boast a lineage such as mine. Even so, we are not all servants, trulls, wives and pampered rulers. The women in my land are great warriors."

"There are many women in my land that are fearsome warriors," he replied factually. "It is not unlike your own in many ways, I suspect." He took another pull from his wineskin and adjusted himself on his mount into a more comfortable position.

Sheba gazed at him curiously. "What gods are worshipped in the Sabertooth Tribesland?"

He replaced the stopper on the wineskin and slug it over his shoulder. "They have only one," he replied. "Her name is *Nemontana."*

Sheba frowned. "I've never heard of her," she said thoughtfully. "Do you mean to tell me that they do not recognize any masculine deity?"

"Aye," he replied, "they worship no one but Her. She is the Great Mother of a thousand names. It is She who creates life. They know of many other lesser gods and goddesses, and each may be invoked for aid or advice, and there are many spirits also with whom the people speak, at times. But Nemontana is the Mother of All, and in the Sabertooth Tribes, worship is reserved for her alone."

"And what does she look like?" asked Sheba.

"She is fair to look upon," he answered, "the most beautiful of all. Her hair is long, and black as night. She rides upon a silver chariot which is called *Soma*, and it is drawn by the King of the Sabertooth Tigers, whose name is *Anate*. Her messengers are the owls and ravens, and her arrows of war are like serpents from which none can escape."

"And you yourself worship this Nemontana?" she asked.

"No," he replied solemnly, "although I did call to Her once, as a child, but she failed to answer. So what good is She? The goddess has many other matters that concern Her, so it is wise to trouble Her only when one feels it is absolutely necessary. At least that is what the elders say."

"How do they worship her then?"

"By living," he said flatly. "She created all things, and all life pleases Her."

"So then, would you say that She is a peaceful goddess?" she inquired.

"Aye," he answered.

"But your people are not known for peace," she observed. "They are greatly feared as warriors."

"They love peace just as much as any other people," he replied, "but they are not weak. Freedom is valued above all else, and if they must fight to preserve it, then so be it. Nemontana is strong. When they fight, She is proud, for they fight so that the gift of life which She gave them can endure." His voice grew grim. "The way I see it, the whole point of living is to prove that you are worthy of dying. On that point, at least, I actually agree with the religious dogma of my fellow tribesmen."

Sheba thought for a moment. "Some would contend there is nothing that is worth dying for," she said slowly.

"Aye," he agreed, "but they are afraid of death, and it is such fear that prevents them from truly living."

"How so?" she asked.

"Because of their fear, they place limits on themselves and avoid taking risks," he explained. "Life without risk is boring, and if one lives their entire life in such a manner, they become dead inside."

"You mean spiritually dead," she said.

"Exactly," he replied, "if you are dead inside you cannot enjoy the thrill of living."

She was silent once more, and they rode on for some time before she spoke again.

"Joktan," she said at last, "for a primitive, land your people seem to have a very intelligent structure of belief. It is simple, but honest and true."

He smiled. "A matter of opinion, I suppose. I care little for their religion. Truth is always simple though, and that is the failing of the nations which call themselves civilized and us savages. They think that our people are witless, for our needs and desires are few. We do not build grand temples, for the Earth is the temple of the Goddess. There are no unreasonable laws to restrict us. My people don't live in houses made of brick and mortar. They dwell in small huts that are covered with hides. The walls are made of stones. They have no desire to become an empire, but that does not mean that they have no understanding."

He paused briefly to drink from his wineskin, then passed it over to Sheba. She drank deeply, then tossed it back, and he continued. "I have noticed that in lands were people want much, so too do their gods. The number of gods they worship is vast. With so many deities fighting for recognition----and each one's priests trying to make their god seem more powerful than all the rest----it seems to me that their beliefs only become more and more absurd. But that is just my opinion," he smiled.

They continued their discussion of various beliefs and gods. As they traveled, the Black Mountains began to grow before them, looming in the distance like the dark, jagged teeth of some primeval beast. The sky, still overcast with gray sullen clouds, began to show signs of clearing in places. The weak drizzle of rain that had accompanied them on their departure from Luxantia had since tapered off, and before long it ceased all together.

He reined in his steed and dismounted, then stooped to study the ground. Sheba halted her horse beside him. "What is it?" she asked.

Joktan pointed to the dirt at his feet. "Look at this," he said. "The earth is hard and cracked from the heat of the sun, while right back over there it is still damp and not much farther back from that it is still muddy from the recent rains."

He looked up and surveyed the horizon intently. "It never rained here. The storm started right there," he pointed. "If you look you can see that the sudden end of sunshine and the start of rain has left a definite mark upon the ground. The dry dirt is light colored while the wet part is dark."

His brow furrowed and a troubled look swept over his face. "It's as though something held back the rain, and somehow kept it only over one area."

She followed his line of view from where they now stood, and the difference was immediately apparent. "I agree," she replied, "it's as though someone drew a line and told the rain not to cross it."

Joktan leapt back onto his mount, then stood up upon it's back and peered out in the direction from which they had just come. "On each side of us, as it gets farther away, the line curves. We are standing on the edge of a giant circle," he mussed.

"Aye," she concurred, "and I'll bet you I know what lies at the center of it."

They both looked at each other and answered in unison. "Luxantia."

The hair on the back of Joktan's neck suddenly began to feel as if it stood on end.

"I like it not," he growled, baring his teeth instinctively as he spoke. "It reeks of sorcery if you ask me. I traveled in that foul weather for two weeks." He silently wondered if it had followed him the entire time, guiding him to Luxantia by some mysterious intent, perhaps on account of the golden disk he had carried with him in his coin purse.

"It is not natural, to be sure," she agreed, and her eyes narrowed. "Who would cast such a spell on a little trade town of no concern. And why?"

"I do not know," he replied, "but Luxantia is not so unimportant as it may seem. It is the last town before the Pass of Tirdonath. The pass is the only safe route to the coastal kingdoms. Straltonia guards it well."

He frowned darkly. "There were too many priests of Dhampir in that town."

Sheba laughed. "I was merely a sacrifice. It was you they were hunting."

"True," he replied sourly, "but I doubt they were there only to kill me. They were in Luxantia long before my arrival. No doubt they were doing something of great importance to their kind. I know that they sought a certain fell amulet, which for a time was in my possession."

"You no longer have it?" she asked.

"No," he answered. "I traded it to Paltro for lodgings and such." He spat on the ground in contempt. "It seemed to bring me nothing but ill luck anyway. I have never been more happy to part with a golden bauble in all my life."

"What use do they have for it?" she wondered out loud.

"How should I know?" he snorted. "I know nothing of the Black Arts, excepting that they are evil, of course. Had I left you in that cage, I'm sure you would've seen them put it to some use though."

"So you knew it was a cursed thing?"

"Aye!" he exclaimed, "perhaps not at the start, but the longer I had it--only a fool could have missed it! I suffered every misfortune...."

"And you gave it to Paltro?" she demanded incredulously. "You knew it was evil, and yet you gave it to a man who showed you only kindness?"

"I wasn't completely sure at the time," he defended, "besides, I just wanted to be rid of it. Evil as it may be, I wasn't going to just throw it away. The thing was solid gold! It was a valuable trinket, to be sure. I wanted *something* for it. The jewels on it alone were worth a small fortune."

She glared at him and shook her head. "You ought to be ashamed of yourself! And what may become of Paltro now?"

"I'm sure he won't have it long," he growled. "He probably sold it as soon as I gave it to him. Merchants handle such things often, I imagine. It is no longer my concern."

"Nonetheless, those wretched priests were searching for it, and doubtless they still are. That poor man is in danger now because of you."

"They may think I still have it," he suggested.

"Maybe," she said, "but I think it unlikely. They believe you to be a thief, and thieves sell the things they steal. They'll ask questions. It won't take them long to trace it to Paltro."

"I meant the man no ill at the time, nor do I now," he told her flatly. "If evil comes to him, it is not of my doing. I didn't know those

priests sought it at the time, and there is not a chance I'll return just to trouble him over it now. He was quite happy when last I saw him, so in those regards I have no more concern."

He gave her a sudden judgmental look. "There is also the matter of them capturing you," he said. "You were to be a gift to their god."

"So?"

"I do not know much about their vile religion, but I do know this; they were going to sacrifice you," he replied.

"And your point is?" she asked impetuously.

"They only sacrifice virgins."

Sheba's face flushed. *"Are you implying that I am not a virgin?"* she snarled fiercely. "Who are you to question my virtue?"

Joktan laughed. "I care little about your virtue....or lack there of," he replied, "I merely meant to make a point."

"Pray tell," she growled.

"The priests of Dhampir obviously placed a great value upon you, and it had nothing to do with any sort of wealth which men possess. They chose you for a very specific reason, and went through much trouble, no doubt, to secure you."

"The reason is plain to see," she said tersely, "I am the next Queen of Lothair."

"That is not it," he returned, "there is some other reason, which I suspect you know well enough but have withheld from me......."

"I am the daughter of..." she started.

"Yeah, yeah, the daughter of the Blood Goddess," he cut her off sardonically. "I know. But that is nothing more than a frivolous title."

Her nostrils flared in anger. "Obviously you know nothing about the Blood Goddess."

"True," he granted. "But still that matters little. I am suspicious."

"Maybe I *am* a virgin," she suggested.

"And I am a god."

"No, not a god," she spat, "but you *are* a bastard!" She stuck her nose up in the air haughtily and spurred her horse forward to ride ahead of him, much to his silent mirth.

"You are even more beautiful when you're angry!" he shouted, spurring his horse after her. Her back was turned to him and he couldn't see her face. She made no reply, other than to hold her right hand out behind her back and display her middle finger.

He chuckled to himself. The wench definitely had a temper. That was one fact he knew about her for sure. But she had never yet revealed anything except for the briefest details regarding herself, and even those were vague. What did he really know about this fiery-

trussed she-cat? A queen she might be, although he still had his doubts. She seemed accustomed to giving orders, and she certainly disdained being questioned. Her pale skin was strange to him. The sun darkened the hide of every man and woman alike that he'd ever met, though lately there had been hardly any sunshine. Even so, something inside told him that there was more to her than what she let on, and that bothered him greatly.

The priests of Dhampir would be seeking both of them, but he guessed that they would concentrate even more upon her than on him. They also must have thought her to be dangerous, for it was unusual to imprison and shackle a woman who was to be sacrificed. Normally she would have been bound and gagged, but to go to such lengths to immobilize her was suspicious at best.

What troubled him all the more was that, even though they'd only known each other for a few days, he already felt deeply attracted to her. She was undoubtedly the fairest woman he had ever laid eyes upon, and there were moments when he felt almost hypnotized by the sheer sight of her. The beauty of her face was matched equally by her curvaceous form. Even her hot temper somehow caused him pleasure. He surmised that she was attracted to him as well, but as of yet she had not made it readily apparent.

Joktan desperately wanted her! That he simply could not deny. Even now he would love nothing more than to throw her to the ground and have his way with her; to run his hands and tongue over her voluptuous body. To savor her scent and the taste of her warm, soft flesh....

His thoughts were suddenly interrupted by Sheba's husky voice.

"Look over there," she pointed eastward, and his eyes followed her gesture immediately to a large cloud on the horizon. "Must be a lot of men on horseback to raise that much dust."

"Aye," he agreed, "and they are riding fast."

"To Luxantia, no doubt," she muttered, "but why in such a hurry I cannot imagine."

"They are no priests, if that is your worry," he observed, "I would say they are merchants."

"We have traveled since dawn, and it is now past noon, but at that pace they will reach the town in only a few hours," she commented.

"Caravans are not foolish. In the open plains there is little safety to be had, so they travel quickly. The more obvious they are to all, the less likely they are to be set upon by bandits. If thieves can spot them easily, so too can armed patrols."

"There are few bandits or patrols in this area," Sheba noted.

"Aye," he nodded. "But nonetheless, something tells me it would not have bode well for us if we were to have tarried longer in that place," he said grimly.

Sheba frowned. "Surely you don't think…"

"Yes, I do," he ejected. "In fact, I'm certain of it. Those priests are on the hunt already, and we are the quarry."

"I forgot that you have a price on your head," she replied.

"Maybe you do too," he intoned, shooting her a sideways glance. She averted her eyes to peer once more towards the distant cloud. "We'd best move faster," he advised. "I would feel much better in the mountains, and they are a long way off from here."

Sheba laughed. "You are probably the only person who would say that. The Black Mountains are a dark place."

He merely shrugged. "No one will want to follow us once we are over the first peek."

"I hope what you say is true," she replied.

"We can be sure of it. Men fear that place, and although some might be compelled to venture in a little way in the light of day, few it is indeed who will set foot upon that land after the sun has set," he told her as they started off once more.

"They ride parallel to us," she commented.

"Aye, and if we keep to the hard ground here we shouldn't raise much dust," he assured her.

"Perhaps no one seeks us at all," she suggested as they drove their horses faster over the barren plain.

"Maybe," he allowed, "but we were the only recent newcomers to Luxantia, and it is likely that many of the town folk noticed us leaving this morning." He dug in his heels and his mount surged ahead. "Besides, we were the only people there who were not merchants."

"There were some priests there," she reminded.

"Yes, and we killed three of them, remember?" he replied. "Civilized people tend to frown on such things, last I knew."

With that they ceased their discourse and rode at a steady gallop for several hours. The following day brought them closer to the mountains, and gradually the plains gave way to gently rolling foothills. The grass grew sparse, but the further on they went it gradually thickened, interspersed with small clumps of bushes and the occasional cacti. After another day's ride the small hillocks slowly gave way to much steeper ground, which rose quickly to the base of the jagged peeks beyond.

Here the surrounding vegetation became much more diverse. Scattered clumps of sagebrush and tufts of sweet-grass littered the landscape amongst small yucca shrubs, desert willows, junipers and the odd little twisted cypress tree.

By the fourth day the ground became increasingly rougher, requiring them to slow their pace considerably as they passed over patches of jagged shale and outcroppings of dark colored granite. One sharp stone in a horse's hoof could incapacitate the beast for several days, forcing the riders to walk. Neither of them wished to risk such a hazard.

By late afternoon they approached the base of the lofty peeks, and Joktan brought his mount to a halt. They still had time to spare before dusk crept across the plains. Sheba reigned in beside him, watching as he unsheathed his bow and quickly strung it while gazing ahead to the edge of the forest. No one need explain why men called them the Black Mountains.

Here the last hillocks of the plains ended abruptly against a sudden wall of foreboding trees. Tall pines, spruce and cedars stood like silent guardians of doom, their ancient trunks massive and gnarled. They rose high above, and gigantic bows stretched out from them in every direction, blotting out the light of the sun. Darkness and shadows waited within, and a ghostly mist hovered eerily amongst the trees, brooding, waiting.

Huge roots intertwined and tangled, spreading across the ground like the giant gray tentacles of some nameless ancient horror. A thick carpet of moss covered the ground, and from this grew dark green bracken ferns, broad and tall. Finding a sure footing amid the jumble of roots and dense growth would be difficult at best, for it was nearly impossible to discern what lay beneath it.

He drew an arrow from his quiver and set it upon the bow, holding it in place with his left hand, then spurred his steed forward towards the mountains. Soon they were winding their way through the forest. Cautiously they rode, keeping wary eyes trained about them as they proceeded deeper and deeper into the woods. The forest became increasingly darker and close about them, and it seemed as if even the horses felt claustrophobic in this demon-haunted land.

Joktan led them along the feet of the mountains, choosing to ride through the narrow valleys instead of struggling up forbidding inclines were progress would be much slower. Rocky slopes rose sharply to the left and right, disappearing into an oblivion of swirling mists and menacing shadows.

An unnatural quietness seemed to permeate the woods, and even the birds, if any were indeed present, uttered not a sound. In this unnatural hush their movements seemed almost deafening. Joktan was visibly disturbed, and even the horses seemed to become increasingly uneasy. In all his years of traveling and exploring wild places, he'd never known a mountain area to be so deathly still. Only in the presence of danger were birds and forest creatures silent. He could sense their apprehension, lingering like some unseen yet tangible spirit in the air about them.

Sheba felt it too, as she rode silently behind, and a sudden chill caused her to shudder as goose-bumps rose upon her pale flesh. Out of reflex she drew her sword, feeling slightly less uncomfortable with the cold touch of its keen edge resting lightly across her naked thighs. She was about to speak when Joktan motioned her to halt, reining his steed to a standstill while peering intently ahead into the misty gloom.

"I like this not at all," he growled in a low, throaty tone, searching the forest for some hint of danger. "What do you make of it?" he asked, without so much as a backward glance.

She nodded her agreement, a troubled look upon her brow. "I don't know. It is as though we are watched," she hissed, "or followed." The woman looked about uneasily. "Something is definitely not right."

"Aye," he replied solemnly, "we are being hunted."

"But we have come only a short way into this place," she whispered.

"Regardless, we are being hunted," he replied, "and I'd wager that whatever it may be that stalks this place is no man. It is said that Goblins dwell here." He swung swiftly from the saddle and landed softly on his feet.

"Dismount," he said, his voice low. "These beasts are ill at ease, and they may buck or flee if some fell thing spooks them."

She heeded his advise, and swinging her right leg over the horses back, she leapt gingerly to the ground, the sword still gripped firmly in her fist. Moving to his side like a ghost, she stood gazing into the shadows ahead, then suddenly sucked in her breath. Something had just moved within the mist.

Joktan gave her a knowing look and spoke under his breath. "Every time we move, it moves. Whatever it is, it is wise, for it has been using the sound of the horses hooves to conceal the noise of its own movement."

"Aye," she conferred, "I thought I heard a sound as I alighted off my horse, but it was very faint."

"Let's move on slowly," he said. "Do you see that open spot up ahead?"

She nodded. "It is as good a place as we are likely to find in which to make a stand."

Together they moved on, each leading their mount as they went. Joktan was silently impressed with the way in which the woman handled herself. In such uneven terrain stealth was nearly impossible, yet she made as little noise as he. It was a pity that the horses couldn't move silently as well.

The mist about them seemed to grow denser with every passing moment. By the time they had reached the small space of open ground it had become a thick, blinding haze. Their steeds grew more and more anxious by the second, stamping their feet and snorting angrily. Their nostrils flared and they tossed their heads about violently, eyes growing wide with terror. Joktan bitterly cursed the fearful beasts under his breath.

"I don't think I can hold my horse much longer," Sheba muttered, tugging at the reins in her knotted fist. Joktan was fighting a battle with his own mount. He grunted his acknowledgment.

"We cannot run," he replied, "this accursed fog is too thick to see anything clearly. We must stand our ground, and I see no better place to do it. Strip the gear from your horse, and if she makes a break for it, let her go, or she may trample you in her escape."

Sheba nodded, but at that very instant her horse threw back its head and reared up on her hind legs, ripping the leather reins violently from the woman's grasp. Joktan's horse thrashed furiously, then both beasts bolted into the mist, instantly lost from sight. Briefly the sound of fleeing hooves could be heard, then brooding silence fell once more.

Sheba howled in anger, and a stream of vulgar curses spewed forth from Joktan's snarling lips as he too voiced his wrath. Their outburst was cut short, however, by the most hideous roar, accompanied by the reverberating crash of what sounded like trees being wrenched and snapped asunder. A foul stench suddenly filled the air, so sickening that it seemed it would suffocate them with every breath.

Sheba crouched low, her sword held ready as the unseen peril closed in upon them. Unearthly growls assailed them, nearly deafening in volume and might. With every roar they could feel a gust of putrid breath, and the ground beneath their feet trembled from the sheer malevolence of the creature's fury.

Suddenly the mist came alive before them, as a gigantic form wreathed in fog moved abruptly within the shadows. It came at them with incredible speed. Indeed, so unexpected was its swiftness that Joktan scarcely had time to raise his bow and loose an arrow before it was upon them.

A furious growl broke from deep within his throat as he reacted with animal instinct to the ferocious beast that now attacked.

"Seth and Dagon!" he bellowed, "come out of the shadows and die, fiend!"

He drew back his bow, loosing another shaft, and with a terrifying shriek the visage catapulted towards him like a nightmare spawned in Hell. A giant arm struck him full in the chest, a titanic blow which sent him sailing backwards through the air. He smashed into a tree and crumpled to the ground with a muffled thud, gasping for breath amid the foggy obscurity.

His head swam as he struggled to his feet and tore his scimitar from its sheath, his bow now lost in the pervading gloom. Vaguely he saw a whitish-gray blur rush past, as it raced into the night. It sped away in the same direction their mounts had taken only moments before.

He heard Sheba cry out in rage as he reeled forward, then he swooned and sank to the ground, his head filling with blackness.

How long he'd been out he did not know, but when he came to his senses it was as a result of Sheba dealing him a smart slap to the face. She seemed to be cursing in her native tongue. "Wake up, you imbecile!" she screamed at him.

He made an effort to clear the numbness from his aching skull by shaking his head.

"What the devil…" he muttered incoherently as she buffeted him again. It was a stinging blow, and he covered his face with his hands in an attempt to ward off her assault. His eyes watered and his vision was a cloudy blur as he sought to grab her wrists and shove her away.

"Enough, wench!" he shouted, finally managing to fling her down and stand shakily upon his feet. "What's gotten into you?" he bellowed belligerently at the woman.

She scrambled quickly to her feet to stand tauntingly before him as he rubbed his temples gingerly, his head still groggy and dazed. "What happened?" he demanded. "Last thing I remember, something rushed upon us and I shot an arrow. Then it flung me through the air…."

"The vile creature ran right over us, that is what happened!" she retorted, her green eyes blazing with an angry fire. "I pursued it, but it had great speed, and now is gone. And you smashed your head on this tree and fainted."

She looked exasperated as she made a sudden grab for his tunic and pulled him within an inch from her face. "And for your information," she snarled, "I was trying to make you regain your wits."

"Did you need to hit me so hard?" he moaned, rubbing his jaw ruefully.

"You have a thick skull," she replied, releasing her grip as the fury in her gaze began to subside. Her eyes traveled slowly over his face to fix themselves on his lips. She reached behind his head and wrapped her fingers in his coarse, thick mane, her haughty disposition giving way to an abruptly demure demeanor.

"I'm sure you'll live," she said softly, her voice barely more than a whisper. Joktan was quick to notice the sudden change in her temperament, and if her painful blows had not brought him fully to his senses, the feel of her hot breath on his lips and the closeness of her sleek body pressed against him now surely did.

His loins stirred as his manhood slowly stiffened. He slipped his hands about her narrow waist and grabbed her buttocks, pulling her tight against his hips. How he wanted her! The blood pounded in his head and coursed through his veins like fire. He leaned forward and their lips touched.

Passion surged through his flesh as he locked her lips with his in a savage, lustful embrace. The warmth and wetness of their tongues mingled as they searched each others mouths. He'd wanted desperately to kiss her like this for days, and now his primitive urges seized control like a ravenous fire sweeping through every fiber of his being. Their kiss seemed to last forever, as if time had suddenly stood still, and he kissed her even deeper as his hands explored the sensuous contours of her slender, feminine form.

When their lips parted at last, Sheba gazed longingly into his azure eyes for an instant. Then as if waking from a spell, she suddenly shook her head and pulled herself away.

Forcefully, she shoved him backwards with both hands. The fire that now burned in her stare was no longer one of passion, but of anger. Joktan sensed immediately that her indignation was directed more at herself than him, for she had clearly made the first advance. He smiled and raised his eyebrows, growling softly and baring his ivory fangs as Sheba glowered.

"I see you have regained your wits," she said. "It would be wise to attend to more urgent matters." She turned away, trying to gather her composure once more.

Apparently what Joktan thought to be an urgent matter was not what Sheba had in mind. He stepped back and glanced quickly about. The dense fog was still present, but as for their horses and the mysterious beast which had assailed them, there was not a trace.

Sheba's sword lay upon the ground by her feet, the blade stained crimson with freshly shed blood. "Looks like you got at least one stab at it," he grunted, motioning to the weapon.

She sighed heavily. "I took a swing at the monster right after you nearly loosed an arrow through my head. You almost shot me." She spat the last part out bitterly.

He laughed, his face lighting up with an irrepressible mirth. "Then your head must be smaller than I thought," he quipped, "I never miss."

"Very funny."

"We'd better hole up for the night and sort out our troubles in the morning," he advised. "If we are still followed, it is doubtful anyone could find us in this fog. Tomorrow we shall see what remains of our horses and gear."

"Where do you plan to sleep?" Sheba asked. "This area is much too rocky for my liking."

He thought a moment, then shrugged. "We can rest up there," he pointed towards the tree he had been smashed against. It was an ancient twisted cypress. Its girth was massive, and the branches thick and sturdy. Though most predators would be able to climb it, it would certainly be a safer place to sleep than upon the barren rock beneath their feet.

"Let us hope that no more beasts sniff us out tonight," Sheba murmured as she retrieved her sword and wiped it clean upon the moss a short distance away.

"Aye," he agreed, inspecting himself for cuts and scrapes. "I lost my bow when that thing struck me," he said, peering out into the darkness. "If it is broken, that creature shall surely die."

"We did not come here to hunt strange beasts," she reminded, climbing up the tree. "If your weapon is lost I'm sure you can get another somewhere."

"Not like that one," he lamented. "It was a gift from an elder of my tribe before I left. The wood was aged many years before the bow stave was fashioned from it."

"Whatever," she scoffed from the branches above. "A bow is a bow, I'll warrant. You whine like a suckling child."

He grimaced and bared his teeth. *One thing this wench did not have was a way with words*, he thought, contemplating an angry reply. He decided to bite his tongue, making several obscene gestures instead. On second thought, maybe he was wrong. She did have a way with words, but mostly with insults.

Either she couldn't see his motions or had simply chose to ignore them, for she set about trying to find a comfortable fork in the branches with a satisfied look of victory on her face. He climbed the tree with relative ease, though his body ached from the recent encounter with the beast, and his head throbbed from its recent encounter with the tree.

"By Dagons scaled member!" he cursed under his breath while searching for a comfortable spot amid the lofty branches. "This is the second time in as many months that I have lost my mount in a treacherous land." He'd also spent nearly all his gold in Luxantia, and the small amount that he had left was stowed away on his horse, he thought bitterly. The horse and the provisions it carried were all the wealth he possessed. He doubted that they would ever be seen again.

"Go to sleep," Sheba said quietly. "No use worrying about it now. Whatever that thing was, at least it only wanted our horses. It won't eat our supplies, I don't think." She shifted uncomfortably opposite him. "We can find our mounts tomorrow. I doubt they made it very far. When we discover them we can gather up the things that are not damaged."

"And I shall slay that beast," he promised.

"And that will only delay our travel," she responded. "I do not wish to tarry in these mountains any longer than we need to. This place gives me the creeps."

"It won't take much time," he promised her. "I don't know what manner of fell creature that was, but I do know now that it bleeds. Which means that it can also die."

She sighed wearily and closed her eyes. "Good night, Joktan." She seemed to fall fast asleep within only a few moments.

He closed his eyes too, but even though his body seemed to be at rest, his mind was not. A grim smile had formed upon his lips.

Tomorrow he would find the beast, and when he did, it would have a pissed-off savage and a sharp blade to deal with!

16

Hordo ground his teeth and muttered a curse beneath his wine-tainted breath. Twelve more priests had just entered Luxantia on horseback, and he was none too happy about it. They gave him an uneasy feeling that sent shivers through his bones.

Most priests and acolytes didn't disturb him much at all; just a bunch of deluded fanatics, most of them. And you could always spot a priest a league away; they all wore the same long flowing robes. He suspected that underneath those spacious garments they carried purses full of gold. Their impoverished appearances were probably nothing more than a facade. They most likely carried weapons too.

How he would love to search them just once! If only to abate his curiosity. Then he could prove what frauds they truly were. Forcing a priest to submit to a search, however, was forbidden by law. Only the local Governor had the authority to do such things, for to harass a priest was to elicit the vengeance of his god. While many deities seemed quite powerless at the best of times, Dhampir and the priests who were loyal to him were highly feared in this part of the world, even by followers of other religious orders and sects.

Ten years ago Dhampir had boasted only a handful of devotees, but now his following was growing immensely. This sudden growth was due largely because the priests had demonstrated their power by unleashing arcane forces against an invading army. They had destroyed their foe completely, and had been wise enough to use the occasion to their best advantage. Of course, only the High Priests had performed the feat, and it was rumored that they were the only ones who were able to wield such power, but the lesser priests were under their tutelage, and if one was troubled, the leaders always intervened.

Such circumstances had led to the creation of laws that protected priests from being subjected to searches, but they did not just serve the priests of Dhampir. The laws applied to all priests, so long as they were of an order that was recognized by the King. And no city could charge them an admittance fee, because most priests had taken vows of poverty, though they were in fact quite far from being poor.

It was very rare indeed that one of them ever broke the law or made a nuisance of themselves. However, if a priest did commit an offense, he was dealt with by his own order, and rumor had it that such punishment was often far worse than any court of law could dole out.

Hordo was no Imperial soldier. He was just the local security officer here in Luxantia. There were forty men under his command, not including volunteers if need be, but their chief responsibility was to deal with drunkards and thieves. They enforced the town laws, but they had no real authority outside the walls. He and his men answered to the town's magistrate, who in turn answered to the king's officials in Zebulon. Luxantia had a small dungeon, but it was only a temporary holding cell. Prisoners were picked up once a month and taken to the court in Zebulon to be dealt with.

Dhampir's priests had been coming into town since yesterday in the late afternoon. Most came in groups of six or less, but there had been two that numbered more than twenty. By Hordo's count there were now at least eight score and seventeen priests in Luxantia, including those that were passing through the gates right now.

Neither he nor the gatekeeper Nolan had collected a single copper from any of these wretches, and as far as he was concerned a small fortune had escaped both of them during the last two days. Nolan always charged newcomers a little extra, which was divided between the two of them. The remainder went to the town treasury.

Apparently the priests were coming to Luxantia to celebrate some holy day, supposedly one of which was of great importance to them, but Hordo found it highly suspicious. Luxantia had never hosted such an event as far back as he could recall. An old property on the far side of town had been purchased by them a few years back, and there had been a lot of work going on underground there for some time now. There were plans for the construction of a temple currently in the works, according to the town council, but there were usually no more than a dozen or so priests in town, and they hadn't carried out any further visible construction aside from the excavations.

The fact that each of the new arrivals wore a scarlet lined, jet-black robe signified that they were high priests. Acolytes wore brown. Three high priests had been killed recently. The town officials knew of it, to be sure, and had made it known that they would search for the one responsible. They didn't want any trouble, but Hordo would be damned before investing any of his own time into searching for the killer. These priests seemed to be converging upon the small town en mass. Hordo could do nothing except stand by and watch, but he grew more and more nervous by the minute.

Already he and his officers were outnumbered two to one by these foul men. If they were planning some sort of retaliation for the death of their brethren, there would be little he or anyone else could do to stop it if their numbers continued to grow. He needed to call his men together soon, for things could very easily get out of hand. It would be best to make it seem like there was at least a small armed presence here that could defend the town. Many of the citizens were becoming anxious as well, and with each new group of arrivals it seemed a shadow grew, becoming darker as it hovered over the town. A terrible feeling was now building inside him.

He turned to his scrivener. "Let me know how many more of these priests enter the town at every turn of the glass. I want exact figures," he snapped. "I want to be informed of how many merchants and other travelers arrive, too."

"Aye, sir," the man replied stiffly, knowing his captain was not in a good mood.

Continuing to survey the traffic streaming into town he added. "Send a messenger to the magistrate as well. Tell him that we may be in for a bit of trouble. Only the gods know what folly these vermin have planned."

He turned sharply to another of his men standing close by. "Go round up everyone. Tell them to strap on their swords and whatever armor they have. If you can gather a few recruits and volunteers, then do so quickly. We may need every sword we can find. Hasten, but be discreet."

17

Luena and Glona woke late in the morning, one sprawled out on each side of Paltro. After the previous evenings lovemaking, the two women had been exhausted, sleeping deeply through the night and well past dawn. They had not been witness to the arcane events that had transpired only a few hours before in the room whilst they slept.

Glona, always the first to rouse it seemed, rolled over and groggily rubbed her sleep crusted eyes with the palms of her tiny hands. Propping herself up on one elbow, she reached over Paltro and gently shook Luena's bare shoulder. Luena, never one to rise early on any account, tried in vain to shrug off the others urging hand.

"Leave me be," she moaned, her annoyance obvious. "It is too early." She attempted to roll over to be out of Glona's reach, but to her dismay, her mate was persistent.

"Get up, you fool! If you want to sleep all day then go up to our own room; but we will be noticed here if we tarry longer."

Luena sighed heavily, and Glona watched her pale breasts heave with a sense of delight. The shimmering light of the morning sun played softly upon them as it streamed in through the window above.

"Come on," she insisted. "The sooner we leave, the sooner you can sleep in our own bed. It is much more comfortable there."

"Fine," Luena mumbled sleepily, slowly managing to push herself up into a sitting position at the edge of the bed. "Is Paltro awake?"

"Not yet."

She ran her fingers through her long, silken hair. It was truly a mess this morning! "Better get him up too, then," she said, dragging herself to her feet. "People will start looking for him if the tavern isn't opened up on time." She bent over in search of her clothes. They had been strewn carelessly about the floor last night, and her position afforded the other a revealing view.

"Let me get dressed first," Glona replied, climbing gingerly over Paltro to the opposite side of the bed. "He may awaken and get aroused, and I don't want to have to pleasure him again so soon if I can help it," she whispered in a subdued voice.

"What do you care? It's my turn next," her friend replied, trying hard to stifle her laughter.

"True," Glona agreed with a shrug, "but I would much rather get out of here as soon as possible and wash the taste of him from my mouth with a little wine."

Luena smiled mischievously. "If I remember correctly, the last thing you tasted last night was me!"

"Aye," she replied, "but he is so pungent!" She turned up her nose and twisted her face at the thought as she spoke. "It must be all those spices he eats…"

Luena giggled, quietly amused, then leaned over and kissed her partner softly upon the lips. Her pink tongue flickered briefly before their mouths parted. "You finish getting dressed, sweetie," she coed, "and I'll wake up this big fat oaf."

"Thanks," she said with a sigh of relief while hastily grabbing up the rest of her scant outfit and donning it. The floor boards creaked and groaned as she moved towards the door. As she reached for the latch, she was instantly frozen in her tracks by Luena's startled gasp.

"He's dead!" her horrified scream made Glona's blood run suddenly chill.

"What? Are you sure?" she half whispered in terror, eyes wide with fear.

"Of course I'm sure! I mean….I think I am…" Luena stammered, shrinking back from the bed. "He's not breathing. I pulled back the blankets and his eyes were open and….unmoving."

Glona ran to her side to see for herself, still wondering if maybe Luena was pulling some sort of sick joke on her. Slowly she stooped over the barkeeps rigid form, peering at him intently, then pressed her ear to the cold flesh of his chest.

"He's dead," she confirmed fearfully. "His heart does not beat."

Luena was mortified. Her knees wobbled, and suddenly she sank to the floor. "What are we to do?" she cried as tears welled within her eyes.

"I do not know," Glona replied hoarsely, "but we'd better think of something fast. We may be suspected of killing him."

"Why?"

"Because, dim-wit!" she snapped, "we slept with him last night, remember? We were the last ones to see him alive."

"By Ashtoreth and Dagon!" Luena exclaimed. *"We slept with a corpse!"*

"Yeah," Glona lamented weekly, "I sucked the life out of him!"

"What a horrible thing to say! This is no joke!" she retorted. "We have to get out of here. Who knows who might walk in at any moment."

"The tavern door will still be locked," said Glona, "no one can come in yet."

"Ah!" the other breathed with relief, her face alight with hope. "That gives us time to spare....but not much. He will be looked for soon enough."

"How could he just die? What could have killed him so......" her voice trailed off and the pair sat silent for several minutes.

Suddenly Luena snapped her fingers with a click, and in the stillness of the room the sound was nearly deafening. Glona jumped. "I've got it!" she proclaimed with a devious smile.

"What? What have you got?"

"A plan!" the other replied so excitedly that she was almost shouting. Glona raced to cover the woman's mouth with her hand. "Quiet!" she hissed, "you'll be heard if you don't shut up. Do you want us both to die as well?"

"No!" her friend responded, lowering her tone.

"Listen up then. Those two barbarians, the wench with red hair and the savage; they left town, did they not?"

"Yes," Glona hesitated, a little confused. "At least they were planning on it first thing this morning. Paltro made sure their things were all in order last night."

"That's right," the other woman replied, "and I'll wager that if you check their room you won't find them. They were very anxious to leave, and no doubt did so in a great hurry."

"But we would have heard them come into the room," Glona countered.

"No, imbecile!" the other barked at her. "Of course they didn't kill the fat pig. No one did, he just died. But only we know that."

"So?"

"So we'll make it look like Paltro was murdered. We take what we can that is of worth, and get all our things out of here. We'll go back to our own room and everyone else will think that those other two killed him. They won't suspect us of anything. We've been here for years, but they were strangers, and the whole town is suspicious of them as it is."

The light went on in Glona's eyes as she finally realized what the other was saying. "I love you!" she squealed, embracing Luena violently with childlike exuberance. "You are so brilliant!"

"Pull yourself together, girl," Luena snapped, "we haven't got all day. Search the room quickly for anything of value."

"And what about him?" the other asked.

Luena turned to face the bed, a long, narrow dagger gripped tightly in her pale fist. "Don't worry about Paltro. I'll take care of him," she replied, and plunged the bronze blade into the barkeeper's chest.

Quickly they searched the room, finding several wooden boxes that had been hidden beneath the bed. Most contained gold and silver coins, and a few were filled with gems and precious stones. Spilling out the contents of one of the smaller boxes, Glona let out an excited squeal. She held up a golden disk, set with brilliant jewels and inscribed with strange looking symbols.

The pair studied it for a moment in awe. It was truly a finely crafted treasure, and neither one had ever seen it's like before.

"Where do you suppose Paltro got this?" Glona whispered, mesmerized.

"I don't know," Luena replied, "it's beautiful! And it looks as though it was made to be hung on a chain."

"There is a small fortune here," the other commented, casting her eyes greedily over the pile of coins and costly baubles.

"Aye," agreed Luena. "Let's get all of this back into the boxes. We've got to get it to our room before we are found out!"

18

The heat was suffocating. High overhead, the blazing sun scorched everything beneath its searing gaze. Water was fast becoming a most precious commodity, and tempers were growing shorter by the moment. Already there had been a dozen or more fist fights amongst the men. Most had been over water. If an oasis was not found soon there would almost certainly be a mutiny, for the patience of the troops seemed to be directly related to their supply of the life-preserving liquid. The majority of the water and wine skins they carried with them had been emptied by sundown the night before.

What had started out two days ago as an orderly column of fighting men had now degenerated into a long string of weary, sun burnt travelers. It was no easy task to keep the thirst of a hundred soldiers satisfied on these dusty, windswept, desert plains. And marching non-stop for two days and nights did not help matters either. The men were tired out. Luxantia was a sixteen day march from Zebulon, and Skeltar had hoped to make the journey in half that time. He now realized that it would take much longer than he'd intended.

The Hakon Desert showed little mercy to those who tread it's barren sands. This was the northern region of the dessert. Had they needed to cross any further to the south, the mission would have certainly failed already. Still, Straltonian troops traversed these inhospitable places regularly. Why should it be so difficult now? Perhaps the amulet itself was working against him….

Inside the lurching carriage, at what had been the center of the small army only days before, an angry Skeltar sat fuming, lost deeply in his thoughts.

"What a fool!" he muttered, clenching his fists tightly into bony little balls. "How could I have been so stupid as to ask the King for one hundred men who were both *good and expendable in the same breath?* Small wonder he sent me the number I asked for so quickly. He does not care if they all perish, for obviously they are far from the elite professionals I requested."

He parted the curtain that covered the window beside him and surveyed his failing troops. Each man he saw trudged slowly on, their heads hung low in exhaustion. Some had stripped away their armor the day before, and it was hard to imagine any of them being capable of putting up much of a fight. If they were attacked right now they would be struck down with ease, indeed almost willingly. He knew just as well as any that they needed some rest, but there was precious little time to waste. They could sleep once they arrived at Luxantia.

The horses suffered too, and had slowed their pace considerably. Their well-maintained coats were now matted with dust and sweat. If the poor beasts were deprived of water and rest much longer they would start dropping off as well.

Skeltar closed the curtain tightly over the window once again. His bitumen eyes were seething with anger, for he cared not if every man and beast outside his carriage burnt to a crisp. That he loathed them all was a fact he tried very little to conceal. After all, he was the most feared wizard in all the western lands, and soon he would be the most powerful mage the world had ever seen.

However, he *did* need these puny imbeciles to help him secure the amulet he so desired, and without them his chances would be greatly lessened. Without the amulet he would be just another wizard, for it was the key to gaining untold might. But he needed the woman too, for without her the ritual could not be completed. The *Book of Kethros* was very clear about this. Few women in this part of the world were descended from such ancient bloodlines, and Sheba would not be in the lands of the Westermarch much longer, that much he felt certain of.

So for now, at least, he had no choice but to look after the needs of his little army, an army that he now believed to be composed of the dregs of King Xalton's Imperial forces. He snorted in disgust. The more he scrutinized them, the more expendable they seemed to be. And the more he loathed them.

Inside his carriage Skeltar was unaffected by the blistering heat. He was not yet able to control the weather outside, but that ability would be withheld from him only for a short while. Soon he would be able to cause even the elements of nature to cower at his voice. He could already feel the arcane power of the amulet he sought, and every passing minute brought him closer to it now.

The temperature inside his carriage was a different matter all together. Controlling it was mere child's play, a talent he'd mastered when he had still been a fledgling acolyte. At present it was cold enough that his breath looked like thin wisps of smoke in the small compartment in which he sat. He was quite comfortable in the near-freezing chill air, but the time had come to venture out into the wretched heat. The troops needed an example, something that would motivate them and get them back in line. He could use magick on them, a spell that would enable the men to endure the rigor and exhaustion of a forced march....

He reached up with a bony hand and tugged violently at the cord hanging from the roof over head, signaling Cral to halt.

Captains began barking orders to the weary soldiers as the creaking wheels of the carriage ground to a sudden stop. No sooner had it ceased to move than the door was flung open and the glowering wizard appeared. His dark hood was drawn up over his head to shield him from the burning rays of the sun.

Very few men present could actually see the sorcerer's face, but that made little difference. So terrible was their dread of him that just his presence and sudden appearance was enough to silence their grumbling and complaints. Not a one of them, with the exception of Cral, had ever laid eyes upon Skeltar before this moment. It was a well known fact that in all the western lands, there were very few people who had ever seen the mage's face and lived to tell of it.

Now the stern faces of the soldiers were painted in fear as the wizard seemed to glide out from the carriage and move toward a large gray rock that jutted up from the dusty ground not far away. It looked as though it had sat here for centuries. Once jagged edges were now rounded and polished smooth as glass by the frequent dust storms that wreaked havoc across the plains year after year. It seemed odd that no one had even noticed the massive stone before Skeltar had began to move in it's direction.

Once he had reached the rock, the mage stopped and stood motionless for several moments, resting his frail right hand upon it's polished surface. Then turning to the troops, he signaled to the chief officer to come forward. The man had sat silent upon his dark brown steed, and now spurred his mount forward to within a few paces of the wizard. He said nothing, but his eyes vividly portrayed his contempt for Skeltar.

Now the wizard spoke for the first time since his appearance. His voice was a dry, rattling hiss that carried easily in the heavy air to the ears of the anxious soldiers watching intently.

"Your men need water," the mage stated matter-of-factly.

The officer's parched lips were cracked and swollen from heat and thirst, but his reply was clear. "They will die without it. The water we stowed at the oasis two days ago is now gone."

Skeltar peered up at the man, his mouth twisted tightly into his ever-present sneer. "Which man among them has been the most insubordinate?" he inquired.

The officer thought for a moment. "That would be Trascus," he replied flatly.

"Then bring this man to me," Skeltar commanded.

The officer gazed coldly at the hooded mage. "This is not the time or the place for demonstrations of discipline," he advised. "These men have traveled both day and night without rest. The heat of the sun burns upon them like an oven. Few men would not complain in such circumstances as these."

Skeltar's black eyes seemed to smolder in their sockets. "Then you would take his place?"

The man glared at him, then turned to his captains. They had drawn the men up into loosely formed lines and now stood looking on in silent apprehension.

"Bring me Trascus," he snapped. "Now!"

There was a brief commotion among the troops as the lesser officers laid hold upon the man and shoved him roughly to the front of the column. He came begrudgingly, and they prodded him forward with the gleaming points of steel-tipped spears. Within moments he stood shaking before the wizard. Sweat ran down his pockmarked brow, caused not only by the desert heat, but fear as well.

Trascus was a large, burly man, broad in the shoulders, deep in chest and of a stocky build. His dry lips parted as he squinted in the bright mid-day sun, revealing numerous chipped and missing teeth.

Skeltar studied him silently, then turned to the chief officer. "Is this the vagabond of whom you spoke?"

The man swallowed hard. "He is."

"And this man has been disobedient to your commands, knowing full well that your orders come directly from me?" asked the mage.

"That is correct," he replied weakly, his anger plainly evident.

Skeltar turned once more to Trascus and peered at him from beneath his hooded robe, but his eyes had suddenly lost their evil glare. "Why have you been so insolent?" he asked quietly.

The man was taken aback by the wizard's change in tone, and a glimmer of hope began to grow in his dust-caked eyes.

"I am thirsty," he replied meekly. "I have not had a drop of water since yesterday. I asked only for a drink! I had no intention of causing trouble, nor do I want any." His voice was appealing, almost pleading for sympathy.

"He lies!" the chief officer growled. "This thief stole water twice today from his mates."

The accused made no comment, averting his eyes and staring glumly at the ground at his feet. The wizard thrust a hand into the folds of his dark robe to produce a small bronze flask.

"Have a drink," he said, offering it to Trascus, and man's face lit up instantly. He snatched it up quickly and held the flask to his lips, emptying the contents in one long, desperate draught. He shook the last drop into his mouth, then handed the empty container back to the wizard.

"Thank-you! Thank-you very much, sir wizard!" he gasped gratefully to Skeltar. "You are a very good man."

The mage gazed at him silently for an instant. No one had ever called him a good man before. This was truly a first! He rested a hand lightly upon the man's shoulder. Trascus started to speak once more, but Skeltar pressed a skeletal finger against his lips.

In a thin, piercing voice he intoned. "*A drop of water for a drop of blood, and a drop of blood for a well of life.*"

Trascus was confused, and the wizard turned to the chief officer of the troops. "Tie him down to the rock," he hissed his command, the rattle returning again to his loathsome voice.

"What? But....wait! What are you doing? I thought you said.......wait!" Trascus pleaded as soldiers hurried forward, taking hold of his arms and dragging him kicking and screaming toward the giant stone, seemingly oblivious to his cries. Hastily they lashed his wrists and ankles to the top of the rock with rawhide cords, while Trascus struggled desperately to no avail. His cries for help and forgiveness went unanswered by all those present as they waited in anxious expectation.

Skeltar fixed his evil stare once more upon the chief officer. "Give me your sword," he demanded.

The soldier shook his head in refusal. "I am the only man who wields this blade. Not you, nor anyone else."

"Very well," the wizard replied, and he almost seemed to smile, a fact that made the soldier move uneasily upon his mount. "Get down off your horse and stand by Trascus."

The man made no move at all, but sat motionless upon his steed in silent defiance, his eyes seething with hostility. The wizard noted the challenge in his gaze, and knew that the officer plainly despised him. He accepted the affront without a word or the slightest outward sign.

Trascus had now ceased his struggles, and he too had fallen

silent, sensing another confrontation about to ensue. He seemed to know that it's outcome held his life in the balance. As for the mage, he was well aware that if this officer would not obey his command, none of the troops would either, and they now waited in hushed anticipation.

Suddenly the wizard closed the distance between himself and the chief officer. He moved so quickly that, to those who watched, it seemed as if he disappeared from where he had just stood and reappeared instantly beside the soldier's horse. He laid a bony hand upon the muzzle of the officer's mount and peered into its eyes, stroking the beast's nose almost lovingly.

"This is a magnificent beast you ride," he hissed with the usual sneer, "but riding is effortless. Maybe you would feel your men's thirst more truly if you traveled upon your own two feet."

"I know their need for water well enough. I have already told you that we will die without it very soon," the man grated between clenched teeth.

"Yet I have offered you water, and you refuse it," replied the mage. "Your King is a very long way from here. His orders to you were to obey my command, to the death if need be. But thus far, you have been just as obstinate as Trascus here. Perhaps your men only reflect the attitude which by example you yourself have displayed."

The officer felt his mouth become dry under the wizard's stare, and his discomfort was obvious to all. *How dare you rebuke me in front of my men!* he thought silently, but he dared not voice the words. The mage seemed to know what he was thinking.

Trying hard to salvage what was left of his pride, the captain now made a desperate attempt to sound more dignified. "I did not realize that you had my King's best interests at heart, sorcerer," he rasped.

Skeltar's eyes became thin, angry slits. "You do not realize because you do not think!" he retorted, and his tone could not have been more demeaning. "The life of your King will be decided by the success or failure of this journey. If his best interests were truly your first priority, then you would undoubtedly be much more cooperative."

The wizard now directed his gaze at the officer's mount, which he had been gently stroking all the while. He spoke to the man while staring intently at his beast.

"You do not need such a creature to carry your weight. It makes you lazy."

Slowly he waved his sinewy hand in front of the animal's eyes. *"Sleep,"* he intoned with a ragged hiss. *"Sleep and do not wake."*

The horse froze instantly. It didn't fall, but remained standing, yet in every respect it seemed quite dead indeed. The beast stared ahead unblinking, it's eyes glazed and lifeless. The officer cried out in surprise and leapt fearfully from his mount, and the sudden movement caused his horse to sway unsteadily from side to side. Then finally, it toppled over upon it's side, stiff and rigid.

The man stood silent for a moment, at first as if in disbelief, but this soon gave way to undisguised anger. The troops seemed to gasp at once in shock, and now a slight murmur rose from their midst.

The officer turned on the wizard, his hand reaching instantly for his sword, then thought better of it. He set his shoulders square and raised himself up to his full height. For a brief moment he glared at Skeltar, but there was something inhuman in the wizard's gaze and it terrified him immensely. Nonetheless, for a moment his eyes brimmed with hate. Then the soldier turned and strode resolutely toward the helpless Trascus. With a violent jerk he tore his blade from its scabbard.

Trascus, suddenly realizing his final moments were close at hand, abandoned his pleas for help and now began to pray in earnest to every god and deity he'd ever heard tell of. His lips moved feverishly as he beseeched the gods to spare his soul from certain death.

If the gods truly heard his cries, they chose not to answer.

His dark eyes bulged wide within their sockets as the officer raised his glimmering sword, awaiting the sorcerer's command. His hands searched and clawed desperately as he sought in vain to free himself of his bonds. Tiny rivers of sweat trickled down his brow, and his voice was now nearly a whisper as he continued to beg for some sort of divine intervention.

The officer clenched his teeth, his lips pressed tightly together. This was murder. It was unjustifiable, and without conscience, but his own life was a very precious thing as well, above all else. He closed his eyes, as if gathering his strength, then once more stared at Skeltar, waiting for a signal. Perhaps the wizard was merely testing him? Maybe he wouldn't have to kill Trascus at all!

To his dismay, the wizard nodded, and the gesture was punctuated with an urgent command. "Now!"

He could hear his own heart pounding in his ears as he flexed his muscled thews, his sword held high overhead. He glanced down at Trascus and their eyes met.

"I don't want to die!" Trascus whispered hoarsely, mortal terror cracking his voice.

"Nor do I," the officer replied, and he swung his blade with all his might.

The razor edge cut a gleaming arc through the air with a swoosh of finality, slicing cleanly into Trascus' midsection and biting into the stone behind him. Blood gushed forth like a fountain, showering the rock and earth. The captain's face was painted in the warm, crimson spray, while the contents of Trascus' stomach poured out upon the ground in a steaming pile of gore and entrails.

His body was severed into two pieces, and for a short while they twitched and spasmed, the lower half upon the ground and his upper half still suspended upon the rock. His eyes slowly took on the gaze of the dead, and with a rattled hiss, the man's final breath escaped through his lips, a look of horror frozen upon the features of his face.

No sooner did he die than the ground began to shake. It trembled like the slow rumbling of an earthquake, and the stone on which Trascus' upper body was still bound suddenly split into two halves with a deafening crack, rending his halved carcass asunder.

Before the officer could even mobilize his feet to move, a great blast of air burst forth from the earth beneath the stone, followed by a column of water that shot skyward with a mighty rush. It rose high above before falling back to the earth, at once drenching all those who stood nearby.

The abrupt change in the troops was extraordinary. Their looks of shock and surprise now turned to joy. They seemed to instantly forget about their butchered comrade, shouting in excitement and slapping each other on the back as if they had been the ones who had caused the fountain appear. Men scrambled madly to get close to the rock, from which a quickly growing steam of cool water bubbled up from the bowels of the earth and flowed out upon the dusty plain.

Angrily, the chief officer made his way toward Skeltar, closing the distance rapidly amid the hubbub and confusion.

"I did what you asked!" he shouted above the deafening roar about them. "I did what you asked! Now give me back my horse."

But alas! Skeltar had already read his thoughts. He glared at the man from beneath his heavy hood, then turned his attention toward the animal's unmoving form. The officer halted his steps and turned his gaze in the direction of his trusty stead just in time to see it burst into flame, and before his startled mind could grasp what was happening, the fire disappeared. It left behind only the blackened outline of his horse and a smoldering mound of ash.

Oddly enough, no one else seemed to take notice of the arcane blaze, so occupied were they in their efforts to quench their thirst. Skeltar once more turned his evil stare upon the captain, and the man's legs suddenly became numb. He slumped to the ground, unable to move. Instantly the wizard stood above him, seeming to tower high against the brilliant sun. As he fixed his gaze intently upon the man, the officer felt as though his will to resist was swept away in a sea of dread. His ego and pride faded, and in their place all that remained was humility and fear. His strength was utterly gone.

He looked about him. Everything seemed to move in slow motion, without any sound. The fountain of water was now winding it's way out into the desert, cutting a muddy trench across the parched and barren land. Of the accursed fire which had virtually vaporized his mount, nothing could be seen. He felt confused, and the impossible feats that he had just witnessed seemed surreal, as if part of some terrible nightmare from which he could not awaken. Any resolve he once had was now shattered.

He was startled by the touch of the wizard's foul hand upon his sagging shoulder, and the sights and noise around him suddenly rushed in like a thunderous wave of chaos. It jolted him violently back to his senses. He rose slowly to his feet, staring at Skeltar intently, his face void of expression. The garish orbs of the mage peered back at him victoriously.

"This could have been avoided, had you obeyed my command as soon as it was given," the wizard said in a low voice. "I trust further such examples will not be necessary in the future?"

The officer nodded the affirmative.

"If there *is* a next time, you will perish in like manner as your beast of burden," he continued. "Do you understand me?"

"Yes," the man replied flatly.

"Good," the mage intoned. "Now then, get your wits about you. You have a company of soldiers to command, and you cannot do it in such a mindless stupor."

The man's eyes suddenly lit up, and he snapped rigidly to attention. "Yes, my lord!" he responded loudly. "What are your orders?"

"After the men have drank, stow as much water as you deem necessary. It will give them strength and vitality in abundance. Already much precious time has been lost. We must resume the march immediately."

"Yes, my lord," the officer replied.

The wizard seemed to almost smile as he turned toward his carriage. As he reached the door he paused and turned to the officer, whose eyes had been fastened upon his every move.

"Keep your men in tight formation from now on," the mage commanded. "There may be trouble ahead of us, so be alert. I don't like surprises. I am a generous man, and although you may find it hard to believe at the moment, I *will* reward you for faithful service," Skeltar said. "But fail me again, and my wrath shall be terrible indeed."

"It was a small misunderstanding," the soldier replied. "It shall never happen again. You have my word."

"Very well, then," the wizard replied, "now carry on with your duties, Brutus."

19

Joktan awoke before dawn with a start, shifting uncomfortably on the branches of the tree in which they slept. His legs dangled loosely from his perch, and the familiar tingling sensation he now felt told him they were asleep, the circulation cut off by the combination of knotted branches and the weight of his body pressed against them. Slowly, he forced his feet to move and wiggled his toes, and as the blood rushed back it felt as though he was being pricked by a thousand tiny needles all at once.

As he waited for the feeling to pass he wondered just how long they had been asleep. Surely it could only have been a few hours. If he could just see the sun, he would be able to estimate fairly well, but the dense forest blocked his view and allowed only dim light to filter through the foliage and leaves. Taking this into consideration, he judged that they had slept longer than he'd thought.

He peered through the greenery at Sheba, who slept motionless close by. She had wedged herself tightly between two large limbs, her head resting against the gnarled trunk of the ancient cypress, her hands clasped together between her thighs.

Even in the early gray of the morning he found her beauty striking. Though she was covered in dust and grime from travel and the events of the night, she was a picture of tranquility and comeliness. He marveled inwardly at the rugged grace and elegance she exuded. Rarely did one see such perfect symmetry in a woman's features and feminine proportions.

It struck him that this was the first time he had seen her sleep, and a warm smile crept across his lips. He felt a strange mixture of wonderment and attraction mingled with the carnal flames of lust, and once more his loins stirred, reminding him of just how desperately he wanted her. The memory of the woman's naked body glistening with sweat only days before roused his passion and thrust it to the surface of all his desires.

His thoughts would have continued on in this direction if it were not for the tingling sensations in his legs. As the blood began to flow to his extremities, feeling began to return as well, and now it felt as though something was crawling up the side of his right calf. Something with many little legs.

Instinctively he moved to swat at it, then stopped his hand abruptly, deciding to see what it was before striking out. It proved to be a wise decision indeed! A sudden chill ran up his spine as he beheld what, at first glance, appeared to be the biggest spider he had ever seen.

This was no ordinary arachnid, however. It was grayish-brown and black. Its body was comprised of large two segments, like that of a spider, but it was the size of a dinner plate. It had a shell like a crab, but with the texture and look of the bark from a cottonwood tree. The thing had six segmented legs, much like a crab as well. All were plated in the same shell-like armor as it's body, and each one was over a foot and a half in length. Tufts of coarse hair protruded around each fissure of the horrible creature's shell and the joints of each appendage. It held out two massive, jointed pincers.

Two pairs of huge ant-like mandibles, the size of a man's finger, clicked together before the thing's fanged, slimy maw as it stared at him intently from black, beady eyes that glistened like glass in the morning light.

For a brief instant Joktan gaped at the thing in horror. He had heard of tree crabs before, but never had he actually seen one. They were much more grotesque that the stories could have possibly described.

If such tales were to be believed, one thing was certain; these creatures had a lust for flesh. It was said that they could strip every shred of meat from the body of a man in the matter of hours, leaving only his bones behind. They lived in colonies, some numbering several hundred each, and were very aggressive. It was also said that such creatures used their giant pincers to crush bones, extracting even the marrow of their unfortunate victims. By the look of the thing's long, sharp mandibles, being bitten by one would certainly be very painful, though he'd heard they were not poisonous like other creatures such as scorpions.

At the moment Joktan was not of a mind to find out first hand. Reaching slowly for his dagger, he unsheathed its shiny blade and extended it threateningly toward the armored crustacean. There was no response.

That's odd, he thought to himself. He'd expected some sort of reaction from it. He waved the blade back and forth, and still the creature sat motionless, but there seemed to be intelligence in its faceted eyes.

Joktan was about to pull back his arm when suddenly a mighty claw snapped out in a flash and seized the dagger's steel blade in a vise-like grip. So quickly did it move that it startled him and he jumped, nearly falling from his perch in the tree and feeling immediately foolish.

He withdrew his dagger, but the crab had an iron grip on it, and was obviously not about to surrender its grasp. He lifted the dagger into the air, and the crab held on tenaciously, allowing him to get a closer look at it as he held it up for inspection. He was familiar with sea crabs, and this creature was very similar to them in many respects. It occurred to him that other crabs were quite delicious when boiled, and he began to wonder if indeed these things were as well.

The crab held on with all its might, gripping his blade relentlessly. It's other appendages, some nearly two feet in length, thrashed wildly about in the air, and he now noticed small horned, bony barbs that protruded along each of its spidery legs. He was uncertain of how to get the thing to release it's hold.

Rather than thump it against the trunk of the tree, he simply let go of his dagger, watching the crab fall through the air before smashing into the rocks on the ground far below.

Swiftly he descended from the tree limbs to retrieve his blade and see what damage the fall had done to the strange crab. It had landed on it's back, but to his amazement the thing still held fast to his dagger as it sought to right itself.

He stooped to pick up a rock and dealt the crab several stunning blows, in an effort to convince the creature to relinquish it's grip, but instead the thing merely tightened its grasp.

Maybe this is how they kill people, he thought aloud. *They steal their blades from them.*

He picked up the dagger with the crab still attached and strode to the nearest tree. Cocking his arm back, Joktan swung the crab against the ancient cypress, but it still would not let go.

Holding the creature against the tree trunk, he grabbed a second blade and drove the point through the crab's head and into the tree. It's back was against the cypress, but its exposed underside looked as well armored as the rest of it. Though the thing was now thrust through and pinned to the tree, still it would not give up it's grasp on his dagger.

Joktan stood back to admire his handiwork, somewhat amused by the creature. He'd heard several stories about these things and of how dangerous they were, how they hid in trees during the day and descended at night to feed. Sometimes the creatures hunted in large numbers, and when they did so they were capable of taking down animals as big as deer and mountain sheep. This particular crab was helpless at the moment, but it looked truly horrible, and he shuddered to think of encountering a large group of them all at once.

As he studied the strange crab he began to wonder if they were edible. He'd not eaten since yesterday, and he suddenly felt famished. This thing might be dangerous, but it was also beginning to look tasty as well, and a few more of them might make a delicious feast for a hungry savage.

From out of nowhere a battle-ax swept past his head and bit deep into the tree. It lopped off the crab's pincers with a crunch, and the creature fell to the ground, it's segmented legs thrashing wildly.

Instantly Joktan whirled and dropped to one knee. As he turned he reached over his back and tore both swords from their scabbards, drawing them in one smooth, fluid motion. The sword in his left hand he held ready to ward off an attack, the other to strike out at the unseen foe.

To his surprise, the attacker was Sheba. She'd been awakened by his struggles with the crab, and had came up behind him unawares while he had stood examining the thing as it hung from the tree.

"Scare you?" she asked huskily, raising an eyebrow slightly. A sly smile played upon her luscious lips, and a spark of humor twinkled in her eyes.

Joktan rose, returning his swords to their sheaths as she strode past him and wrenched first her ax, then his dagger from the tree.

"You shouldn't sneak up on me like that," he growled, feeling rather embarrassed.

She handed him his dagger, holding it by the blade. "Did the little crab overpower you?" she asked coyly.

"Of course not," he replied. "I was just getting a closer look at it. I have never seen such creatures before."

Her smirk said that she wasn't buying his story, and he could feel his cheeks beginning to grow warm.

"You can only eat these things if they are boiled alive," she said. "Otherwise their meat will make you sick."

Joktan stuck his nose up in the air, still feeling a bit foolish. "Who would want to eat such a loathsome creature?" he snorted contemptuously. "I was merely trying to get a better look at it."

"I see," she replied, walking away from him toward a nearby tree. There was another, much larger crab clinging to it. Sheba took hold of its shell and wrenched it free, then turned to Joktan, holding the tree crab out in front of her for him to see. It's legs were nearly three feet long and flayed wildly about, trying in vain to get a hold on her.

"This one is much nicer, don't you think?" she asked, as the thing's massive pincers snapped in the air dangerously close to her face. It required a great deal of effort for her to maintain her grasp on the thing, and she now held it with both hands.

Joktan said nothing, but from the look on his face it was plain to see that he was mortified. He had not been afraid of the tree crab when it was skewered upon his dagger, but she was holding it in her bare hands! This one was very much alive and did not appear to enjoy being played with. He took a step back.

"Here," she offered. "Would you like to take a look at this one? They are quite sluggish during the day. It is the time when they are normally asleep."

He stifled the urge to scream at her to drop the foul creature, and instead tried to act unconcerned. "That is interesting, but you can keep it."

"Oh, please, but I insist!" Sheba smiled, and to his utter horror she tossed it at him saying, "Here, catch!"

"What the devil..!"

The crab sailed hideously through the air straight at him, it's legs flailing and trashing menacingly. Joktan freed his sword and swung with all his might, and the sharp steel clove the crustacean asunder in mid air.

"What's gotten into you, wench!" he bellowed, hacking the creature into several more pieces with his broadsword while it struggled upon the ground. "Have you lost your senses?"

Sheba burst into a fit of laughter. "Really, Joktan! It's only an oversized bug!" she replied. "Goblins are said to be quite fond of them, or so I've been told."

He glared at her angrily and sheathed his sword. "I am no goblin, in case you haven't noticed, and these overgrown bugs, as you call them, are not to be toyed with, woman!" he retorted. "Your games are not amusing."

"I was only teasing!" she said, suppressing her mirth, "you mustn't be so serious all the time. That will teach you to wake me so early." She glanced down at the two dead tree crabs on the ground. "It may have been unwise to kill those things," she frowned.

"They are of no concern now," Joktan muttered.

"Not these two, at least," Sheba replied. "However, they are very small, and we have scarcely entered into the mountains. Mature tree crabs tend to stay further in, preferring the darker valleys. From what I've been told, they tend to hunt in vast numbers."

"Do you have a point, or this just more of your endless prattle?" Joktan was still very much annoyed.

"If others of their kind discover these ones that you killed, they may come looking for us."

"I highly doubt it," he snorted. "I myself would be much more concerned about running into Goblins. Unlike these mindless creatures, they can actually think."

"I wouldn't be so sure….," she started.

"Why don't you make yourself useful and help me find my bow," he interrupted. "It must be around here somewhere."

"Find it yourself!" she ejected, "you're the one who lost it."

Joktan muttered a curse beneath his breath and set about searching for his weapon. After a few moments he located it in a patch of dense underbrush. It appeared to have survived the previous night's melee without suffering any damage, which relieved him immensely.

"We'd better locate our mounts," he said presently.

"Aye," Sheba replied, studying the ground near her feet. "Look over here. I do not know what sort of creature we battled last night, but it has huge tracks."

He hadn't noticed the tracks earlier, but now as she drew his attention to them he wondered how he could have missed such obvious signs. They were monstrous in size, nearly four times the width of a his hands and twice as long.

"What sort of beast leaves such a mark on hard soil?" she mussed softly.

"I don't know," he replied, "but I think we shall soon find out if we stay here much longer."

"I concur," she said. "We need to get moving."

Joktan grunted his agreement, and soon the pair set off in search of their horses. Following the trail left behind by the mysterious beast was an easy matter, for it had torn up the ground and disrupted everything in its path during the night. It must have received at least one serious wound during their brief encounter, for it had lost quite a bit of blood along the way.

As the morning wore on the two worked their way through the dense growth of the woods, doggedly following the trail left behind by the beast. It wound up along the mountainsides and through deep ravines and gullies. Just before mid-day they reached a place where the ground abruptly dropped away, a shear cliff that plummeted downwards for several leagues. At the bottom of the cliffs the rocks were sharp and jagged, and upon these rocks far below them lay the broken carcasses of their horses.

"They must have ran headlong over the edge," Sheba guessed as they peered down from above. "Even the horses were blinded by the fog. They stampeded off into the darkness in blind terror and couldn't see the cliffs."

"Aye," Joktan replied, "but it looks like the beast that pursued them dove over the edge too, for it's tracks go straight, and don't turn off anywhere."

"We'll have to find a spot to climb down," Sheba sighed heavily. "I had a lot of gear on that steed."

"So did I," he replied, "although there may not be much left to salvage. It is a long fall from here."

Silently the two of them studied the surrounding terrain, searching for the best possible route to the bottom of the chasm. Descending the shear rock face would be no easy task, and Joktan cursed himself for not carrying at least one coil of rope on him instead of on his horse. It took several hours to finally reach their mounts, and by that time the sun was already starting to set.

The place where their steeds had fallen had definitely been discovered by either the thing, which had attacked them, or some other beast, for the rocky ground was strewn with pieces of flesh and bone. The supplies and gear, which had been strapped securely to their mounts the night before, were now scattered in every direction.

Together they scoured the area for whatever they could find that might still be salvageable, but most of their supplies were now ruined and destroyed. Many of the things that they found to be still intact and serviceable would have to be left behind. There was a limit to the amount two people would be able to pack on their backs, and after stowing away what they could, they set off once more in search of a safe place to spend the night, for darkness had now fallen.

They walked away along the foot of the cliffs. In one spot they found a shallow cave, a small scoop in the rock wall. It wasn't much, but it did offer a little bit of shelter and would allow them to defend themselves if necessary without having to worry about guarding their backs.

They unloaded their burdens and spread out their cloaks upon the stony ground. While Sheba lit a small fire, Joktan began gathering armloads of wood with which to feed it, and soon the small flicker of flame was a roaring blaze. He feared that whatever had assailed them the previous night would return once more, and Sheba felt likewise. They decided to gather enough wood to feed the fire and keep it blazing all night long.

No sooner had they done this than they began to hear a rustle moving through the trees and underbrush. It seemed far away at first, but as they listened it grew steadily closer with frightening speed. Something was moving quickly through the dense forest, and it was headed straight towards their small encampment.

Joktan looked about them, sizing up their surroundings. "We should gather together enough big stones to make a ring around us," he said thoughtfully. "At least that way the ground on which we stand will be clear of obstacles and we will be less likely to trip and fall if we must make a stand here tonight. It will also place a small barrier between us and the foe, along which we can pile even more wood. If we are attacked we can set it on fire."

Sheba agreed, and they set to work immediately, building a low semi-circular ring of boulders and stones that arced out from the rock wall and enclosed their small cleft in the cliff. All the while the sounds in the night kept getting closer, and the two of them worked at a frenzied pace, heaping branches and deadfall upon the ring of stone.

The noise in the darkness was now almost upon them, but it was not the sound of some giant predator. It was more akin to the rattle of thousands of dry branches against each other. It grew in volume until it was a terrible din, and as they drew their weapons and braced for a fight, Joktan turned to Sheba.

"Take a log from the fire and light the wood about us!" he told her, snatching up several flaming branches and tossing them onto the heap. She quickly followed his example, and within moments the fire spread around the circle of stones and sprang to life. The wood was dry as tinder, and soon a great wall of flame several feet high surrounded them. Amid the crackles of the blaze the racket about them suddenly ceased, and an eerie hush fell within the shadows.

"What manner of evil awaits us?" Joktan muttered, drawing an arrow and notching it to his bow.

"I don't know," Sheba replied, "but it must not have been expecting fire."

As they peered past the light of the flames into the blackness of the night, something began to move round about the circle, and with sudden horror they realized what it was. Thousands of armored, jointed legs clambered over each other in the shadows, as a wall of anxious tree crabs surged into view, their massive pincers snapping menacingly with anticipation.

"Say hello to your oversized bugs!" he growled. Judging by the look in her eyes, she did not find them so harmless anymore.

"They will be deterred by these flames for the moment," she replied grimly.

But as the two warriors looked on countless more tree crabs leapt into the light. The creatures climbed on top of each other, and within moments a great wave of the spidery things surrounded the protective ring of fire. Some threw themselves wildly against the flames, screaming hideously as they slowly burned upon the glowing embers. They clawed desperately amid the searing coals, seeking to escape the roaring fire, but their plight did not appear to have any effect on the rest of the bloodthirsty horde. Strangely, it seemed to drive them further into a violent frenzy, and suddenly they began to leap into the air above the flames.

Joktan cast his bow aside and tore his broadswords from their scabbards as a huge crab now hurtled towards him through the air, it's legs and pincers spread out wide and flailing. Each appendage was nearly as long as a man's arm, and he struck out savagely as the terror fell upon him.

His blade sliced the creature's shelled body in half, and he reeled as two more sailed furiously toward him. Their hideous screams made his flesh crawl. He slashed at them desperately as several more leapt across the fire, their mandibles clicking menacingly back and forth.

Sheba shouted with rage and ripped both her axes from their sheaths, turning to meet the foe. She cut a swath of death in the air before her, and the ground about their feet was showered with severed appendages and slimy ooze as the pair fought to hold the dreadful creatures at bay.

Both she and Joktan knew that they would not be able to fend off the attack for very long. Soon they would be hopelessly overwhelmed by the horrid nightmare, but knowing this only hardened their resolve. They responded to the onslaught with brutal fury, slashing madly as the hellish bugs began to swarm over the blaze.

Joktan was beginning to think that all was lost, when suddenly the tree crabs broke off the attack as abruptly as it had begun. To both he and Sheba's utter amazement, the creatures fled into the darkness, scrambling in seeming desperation to abandon the fight. Their eerie shrieks and screams were deafening as hundreds of the terrified tree crabs receded into the darkness from which they had come.

Amid their cries another sound could now be heard.

It was that of branches and trees being snapped and broken and thrown about, and it was accompanied by a thunderous roar.

Sheba dealt a final blow to the last of the crabs that had leapt over the fire, splitting it's blackish gray shell in two, then paused to listen to the noise which grew steadily closer. She glanced over at Joktan with an exasperated look, a battle-ax held tightly in each fist.

"What horror is this new foe, that even these foul bugs flee in terror before it?" she asked, bewildered.

He shook his head grimly. "I have no idea, but it looks like we shall soon find out, like it or no."

Sheba studied her axes, as if making a decision, then quickly returned one of them to the scabbard and drew her scimitar. Joktan heaped the remainder of the wood onto the fire, then armed himself once more with his bow. The hard shells on the tree crabs would have deflected his arrows. Perhaps, he hoped, this new assailant would not be so well protected.

He didn't have to wait long to find out.

The dense fog that had encompassed them the night before now billowed forth from the shadows, and a familiar stench followed close behind. It was enough to nearly make them gag, so foul and loathsome was the smell of it. The tumult was almost upon them, and the very ground shook from the weight of the monster's footsteps.

Suddenly a massive form burst forth from the darkness. It was wreathed in smoky tendrils of fog which obscured portions of it's body and head, but it towered above them some thirty feet in height.

It halted briefly before the fire, a giant, beastly visage. It's shaggy, gray hair was filthy and matted, and a gust of putrid breath assailed them as it shook it's mane and let loose an earth-rending roar. It lowered it's head as it bellowed, spewing a spray of foam and slaver upon them from an enormous gaping maw rimmed with dreadful, elongated fangs. Fearsome claws protruded from huge bear-like feet, and upon it's skull grew terrible twisted horns.

The mighty blasts of reeking air that issued forth with each thundering roar fanned the fire like the bellows of a blacksmith's forge, and the flames sprang to life about them, hungrily licking at the wood added to the blaze moments before.

Lesser men would have cowered and fainted at the sight which greeted the pair, but such was not the case with Joktan. Already during his short life he had battled numerous beasts and monsters of every kind, and this new threat was just another foe to be conquered and destroyed.

He stood unflinching against its wrath, resolute and sure. The tree crabs had numbers on their side, but this beast had only it's size. True, it had managed to knock him senseless the previous night. It had robbed both of them of their horses and ruined most the provisions and supplies as well, but now the moment for vengeance had come, and he would not be beaten by a mere beast.

It scarcely had time to step forward as Joktan loosed half a dozen arrows in rapid succession. Each one found its mark, tearing through the enemy's mated chest with deadly fury and sinking deep into it's thickly muscled flesh. With an awful sound the beast let out a ferocious snarl and charged through the flames, scattering glowing coals and embers all about them. Joktan answered the cry with one of his own as he fired three more arrows and unsheathed his sword.

Sheba screamed insanely and stepped forward to meet the foe, her sword and ax held ready, gleaming in each of her hands. The stench of burning hair filled their nostrils as the fire licked at the beast's coarse hide and the hot coals burned the leathery soles of its gigantic feet. Angrily it fell upon them, swinging with giant hand-like paws. Joktan dodged the attack, slashing at its legs as it sought to rend him with deadly talons.

Sheba circled the beast and leapt high into the air, thrusting her sword downwards with all her might into its flank. Blood gushed from the wound, and it turned swiftly, attempting to rake her with its claws. Joktan snatched up his bow and shot another arrow, aiming for the thing's mighty neck. The beast reared up on its hind legs and squealed in pain, clawing desperately at its throat. Several more arrows flew through the air as the savage wielded his bow with expert skill, and the creature growled angrily as each one sank into it's flesh.

Suddenly it stooped forward, swinging widely at Joktan, and one of its horrible talons tore through the fabric of his tunic. It ripped painfully across his chest, but so terrible was his bloodlust that he hardly noticed.

He staggered back from the strength of the blow, then regained his footing and charged ahead between the creature's corded legs. Raising his sword high above his head, he struck with all his might against the huge muscles and tendons, severing them completely. They beast lurched forward, partially hobbled, then crashed to the ground with a terrible roar.

As it struggled to rise it lashed out viciously, clawing at anything within its reach.

Sheba snatched up a burning branch from the fire and flung it at the creature, and instantly it's matted fur began to smolder and burn. It rolled about upon the rocks, swatting at the flames, but she wasted no time. Quickly she grabbed another burning stick and hurled it at the foe, then several more as Joktan worked his way around the crippled beast toward it's huge head, slashing and thrusting with his sword as it thrashed wildly upon the ground.

The creature was truly terrified by the flames that burnt it's hide and flesh, and it's terrible black eyes were now filled equally with fear and wrath. For an instant it had forgotten about Joktan and his sword on account of the fire, but that was all the time he needed. Thrusting mightily, he buried his sword to the hilt in the nightmare's ribcage. It snarled in sudden agony and struck out madly as a spray of crimson blood gushed forth, but Joktan leapt nimbly away and drew another sword.

At the same instant Sheba dealt the beast a harsh blow with her ax, then thrust her sword into its side. The blade stuck between its bones and was torn violently from her hand. She hurled the ax at its broad skull in rage, screaming vulgar curses. It spun through the air and smote the creature between the eyes before becoming lost in the clangor.

The beast reached for her, and one of its talons pierced her leg, then it hastily recoiled as two more arrows struck it in the neck. It turned on Joktan with a malevolent shriek, stretching out a monstrous hand and seizing him by the leg. He lost his footing and tumbled onto his back as he was dragged roughly across the jagged rocks toward the infuriated beast. It lifted him high into the air, holding him upside down and shaking him violently. He slashed at the creature's arm with all his might, but it tightened its hold on him relentlessly.

While the beast was distracted, Sheba closed in on it from behind, a battle-ax held high. It opened its massive jowls wickedly, drawing Joktan closer to it's dripping fangs just and she brought her weapon down hard against the side of the beast's hairy neck. The ax ripped through hide and hair, rupturing the beast's jugular. A fount of blood erupted, and it released Joktan abruptly.

He dropped onto the creature's matted torso, drawing a dagger as the foe clutched at it's own throat, gasping air and choking on it's own virulent blood. He thrust his blade into its stomach and wrenched it sideways, opening up the beast's abdomen from side to side. The enemy writhed in desperate agony, and Joktan was hurled to the ground as it's bowels spilled forth in a steaming pile of slimy gore and filth.

He lay there for a moment, nearly senseless and fighting for breath amid the horrible cries of the wounded monster. Slowly he rose and glanced about, searching for Sheba. He spotted her nearby, sprawled out upon the rocks. She was attempting to get up, but the dense fog obscured his vision and it was difficult to know for sure if she was all right.

Taking up his sword once more, he turned grimly toward the enemy.

With renewed strength and brutal fury he approached the beast as it lay upon the ground. He stood above it defiantly and raised his sword, then struck with all his might. The sharp steel sliced through cartilage and flesh with a sickening, yet reassuring sound.

The creature's severed head hit the ground with a hollow thud. It's body twitched and shuddered, then slumped lifeless onto the rocks at his feet in a pool of steaming blood. He plunged his blade into it's chest and moved it about, opening up a gaping hole, then reached inside the cavity with both hands and tore out the monster's heart. Gore rilled down his arms as he held it in his hands, and strangely, the fog that had accompanied their foe now rapidly dispersed. Within a few more moments it was completely gone.

Joktan turned and cast the creature's heart into the fire. It sank into the embers, sizzling as the flames slowly consumed it.

Suddenly Sheba was standing by his side, and he was amazed to discover that she had survived the battle unscathed. Together they sat down on the carcass of the beast to catch their breath. Remembering the wound she'd received when the beast had clawed her, he looked at Sheba.

"How's your leg?" he asked.

"What do you mean?" she replied.

"I thought the beast wounded you."

She moved her leg so he could see for himself. "I'm perfectly fine. It merely tore my boot."

To his amazement there wasn't even the slightest scratch on her skin, although the upper portion of her boot had been ripped away entirely.

"I must've been seeing things," he murmured, but he was sure that his eyes had not deceived him. How could this be? He thought to question her further, then shrugged his shoulders, choosing to forget about it for the moment. At the present he was just glad that she was not injured, for both of them could have been easily killed by the terrible beast.

He looked about the place, surveying their surroundings. The remnants of their supplies had been scattered all about during the battle, and a wineskin lay nearby. To his surprise it was still intact. Joktan picked it up, uncorked it and drank deeply, then handed it to Sheba. She accepted it gratefully.

"Well, I must say," she said looking at him, "you really know how to show a woman a good time, Joktan! Judging from the last couple of days, I can't wait to see what manner of surprise you have planned for tomorrow!"

20

Paltro's strange and untimely death had caused no small amount of unease in Luxantia. Most of the townsmen regarded it as an evil omen. "It is a curse," some said, "he brought it on himself for keeping company with that peculiar savage and the woman with red hair."

"Aye," said others, "and both appeared in town after that terrible storm started. Perhaps they were brought here by the storm itself!"

The township quickly decided to hold a meeting to determine the fate of the tavern owner's possessions. It seemed that the portly man had lacked any family members or next-of-kin. He'd made no provisions for his tavern in the event of his demise, but that was fairly common. Luxantia was, and always had been, a town of merchants. While the more wealthy members of the community usually took care of such matters, it was not by any means customary, and in the case of Paltro it came as no great surprise.

Generally, people who owned taverns had family of some sort, and they would take possession of their relative's property after their death, as well as make the necessary funeral arrangements. The right to receive ownership of a dead family member's property was rarely contested.

However, since no one knew of any relatives in this situation, the Open Arms Tavern was immediately put up for sale. Any one could buy it if they had the money, for it would be sold to the highest bidder. In a town of merchants, that was always the easiest way to get rid of property and still avoid a lot of unwanted hassles.

The tavern had been built in a prime location, being one of the first buildings one passed when coming into town, and everyone knows that location is everything when opening up a business. But recent events had cast a shadow of superstition on the tavern, and by and large, merchants were usually a very superstitious lot indeed!

That being the case, when Luena and Glona announced their interest in buying the place, their proposal was met with great surprise, for no one had imagined that two whores could ever afford such an expense.

However, after the town officials had verified their considerable wealth, their bid for ownership was met with only the slightest resistance. In fact, it almost seemed like everyone was relieved to see the pair purchase the place.

Caravans would be arriving soon, and wealth would pour into the little town as it filled with travelers from abroad. It was not good to have an establishment such as the Open Arms Tavern sitting vacant and deserted, for that would look suspicious. All the townsmen were afraid to buy the place, believing that whatever had befallen poor Paltro would come after them as well. Merchants were generally a superstitious lot.

So within two days of the barkeep's death, the Open Arms Tavern was purchased by the two trulls for one thousand pieces of gold. The only proviso was that it would have to undergo a change of name, and that it should also be re-opened as soon as possible. The town officials did not want to have to deal with any relatives of the deceased laying claim to the tavern and causing a dispute in the future. With business picking up lately in Luxantia, the sooner the tavern was re-opened, the sooner Paltro's death would be forgotten. And of course there were the expected remarks, such as perhaps the tavern could now be called the Open Legs....

Luena and Glona promised that, should any of Paltro's relatives come to lay claim to the tavern, they would simply pay them in gold to go away. This pleased the officials greatly, for being merchants, they saw any peaceful solution to a problem as a welcome one, so long as it cost them nothing themselves.

So it was that the two trulls took possession of the tavern. Renovations were begun immediately, with a multitude of carpenters, masons, laborers, and various other craftsmen being hired to refurbish the building inside and out. It would take at least three weeks to complete the work, but nonetheless the tavern would remain open for business during the daylight hours.

The tavern was renamed *The Palace.* The old weathered sign out front came down, and a new one was hoisted up in it's place. Luena and Glona oversaw the changes personally, making every effort to keep things moving along as quickly as possible.

They no longer wore their usual revealing attire; they now

dressed in clothes made of exotic silks and linens, and wore gold and silver jewelry. In this way they hoped to effect an air of importance and wealth, even though certain of the more costly craftsmen were rumored to be at least partially paid for their labors in sweat and flesh.

Today the two women flitted about from place to place, busily helping customers while trying to keep up with the workers that were renovating the rooms above the tavern. Business was far from hectic, as most customers preferred doing their drinking in an establishment that was not under construction.

Still, it took a vast amount of time and energy just to look after the numerous craftsmen that were constantly coming and going.

Just before noon the women took a rest, seating themselves at a table close to the bar and sharing a flagon of good wine. As they sat gloating over the recent turn of events, the tavern door was thrust open and a group of strange, cloaked figures silently stepped inside.

There were four of them in all, and for a time they stood perfectly still. Their dark robes hung almost to the floor, obscuring their feet. Each had his arms folded in front of their chests, hands thrust into their sleeves. The hoods of their cloaks cast dark shadows across their faces, obscuring their features. All that was visible were their mouths and noses. They were priests, worshipers of the god Dhampir.

Luena tugged at Glona's arm and motioned toward the queer group, a quizzical look upon her heavily painted face.

"Did you send for them?" she asked, keeping her voice to a whisper.

"No," she replied similarly. "I thought you might have, though for what reason I cannot fathom."

"Well I didn't!" snorted Luena, shooting a disdainful look at the newcomers. She was visibly agitated. "Let's see what they want. They don't look like paying customers at any rate."

Glona nodded her agreement, and getting to their feet, the pair made their way through the piles of rubble and materials strewn about the tavern. As they approached the group of hooded figures, they assumed an air of dignity that only a few days before they would never have dared.

"Welcome!" Glona smiled broadly as they drew nearer. "You must be lost, for it is not often that priests come here."

One of the priests stood a few steps in front of the others; apparently the spokesman of the lot.

"Good day, madam," he replied dryly, his face still obscured by the thick, coarse, fabric of his heavy cloak. The tone of his voice was flat, lacking the slightest trace of warmth as he continued. "We come in peace, to wish you good fortune with your newly-acquired establishment, and our sincerest regrets for the recently deceased."

He looked up slightly. "We understand he was a...friend of yours?"

It was more of a statement than a question, and one that immediately unsettled the two women.

"And who might you be?" Luena demanded, a look of indifference in her eyes.

"I am Shoto, a mere priest of the one true god," he answered.

"Well, Shoto," she replied haughtily, "we knew very little about the previous owner, may Hecate bless his poor soul. Obviously you have been ill informed." She glanced at Glona hastily, then went on. "We had what you might call a *working relationship* with the man."

"He let us conduct our business here for a fairly hefty monthly fee," Glona interjected coyly. "I believe that he saw us as a way to bring in more customers." Her pink tongue flickered briefly over her lips licentiously, and she gently touched a pale hand to one of her breasts. "Tell me, are you sworn to celibacy, Shoto?"

The priest peered at her, unmoved and clearly disinterested.

"I care not about Paltro's relationship with you," he sneered. "We have come in regards to another matter."

"Oh?" Luena raised an eyebrow questioningly.

"There were two strangers here a while back," he said coldly.

"Perhaps you could be more forthcoming," Glona laughed. "This *is* a tavern, after all. There are countless strangers here every single day."

Shoto glared at her briefly; his patience was wearing dangerously thin. Choosing to ignore Glona, he fixed his stare upon her companion.

"One was a man, a savage from the northern lands. The other was a red-haired woman with pale skin."

"What of them?" asked Luena.

"They killed three of our brethren," the priest replied. "We would be willing to pay handsomely....in gold....for information about them." His narrow eyes widened just a touch. "I believe that your relationship with *that* is a more passionate one, no?"

The woman's icy gaze melted instantly, replaced by the lustful sparkle of greed. She turned to Glona, and nether one needed to say a word, for they both knew instinctively what the other was thinking. She turned once more toward Shoto, her face a living portrait of sensual desire as she spoke.

"My dear priest," she purred, "you have no idea just how

passionate I can be!" She stared intensely into his eyes. "How much gold are we talking about?"

Suddenly an unseen force seemed to grasp her by the neck. It felt like a serpent, coiling itself around her pale throat tighter and tighter. She let out a stifled gasp, and her hands sought to tear away whatever it might be that was slowly strangling her, but to no avail. Her full lips began to turn blue, and panic instantly filled her eyes as they began to bulge from their sockets grotesquely, her face a mask of terror. She felt her feet leave the floor as she was lifted into the air, and kicked her legs in vain, attempting to strike out at Shoto by whatever means possible..

Glona looked on without moving, frozen with fear, as her partner fought against the malignant power and struggled to breath. An arcane power held her rooted to the floor.

"The games are over, wench!" Shoto hissed horribly. "The mere fact that you are a whore-- a common trull who sells her flesh to the highest bidder-- gives me a very good idea of just how passionate you can be when the price is right."

The invisible force released it's deadly grasp, and she shrank back in fright, gasping raggedly for air.

"I did not come here today to deal in insults," he continued evenly. "I came for information, and to offer you gold for it as well. Time is of the essence, and you have wasted plenty of it already. Perhaps I have been too generous, for I could end your life right now."

Luena slowly recovered herself. Suddenly she wanted nothing to do with these vile priests. What a fool she was! She should have listened to her instincts and sent them away when she'd had the chance. *But what about the gold?*

The truth was, she didn't care what became of the two strangers. They had left town days ago. Everyone in Luxantia thought they were trouble in the first place, and maybe if Paltro hadn't have been so quick to befriend them, he would still be alive. She knew that she would have to tell Shoto what he wanted to know; he would get it out of her and Glona one way or another, and if they refused, he would be sure to do it in a very unpleasant fashion, that much was certain.

In the end, no amount of gold was worth dying over; she decided to answer his questions. At least that way he would leave, and the whole thing could just be forgotten.

"How much gold were you offering?" It was Glona who spoke, and Luena looked at her as if she was insane. She glanced around, noticed that several of the workmen were now standing nearby, and understood the reason for her partner's sudden courage.

"That depends on the quality of the information you can give us," replied Shoto.

"We do not know where the two you speak of were headed, but they left many days ago," Glona informed him.

Shoto shook his hooded head. "That much we already know. You will have to do better."

Luena had an idea. "I overheard something about Endrakana, now that I think of it. We might even have some of their clothes," she offered.

Shoto's eyes lit up. "Clothing, did you say?"

"Aye," she replied hastily, lowering her voice, "but there are too many people here right now. We don't want everyone in town thinking we are loose tongued. It would be bad for business."

"I understand," the priest replied, "but that is your concern, not mine. I suppose your death might be just as detrimental."

"You must leave now," she said guardedly. "Come back later tonight and I will have them ready for you." She paused, then added, "but be sure to bring plenty of gold with you, else I'll burn every stitch of them. And no funny business, or I'll fetch the city guards. Nobody threatens me in my own establishment."

"Very well," replied the priest, "tonight then. But I warn you, do not toy with me further. It would not be a healthy decision."

21

"Cave dwellers," Joktan muttered, hunkering down behind a rough line of boulders for concealment. He peered intently around the side of a large basalt outcrop to get a better view.

"Aye," Sheba whispered, "there must be ten score of them, too."

He grunted his agreement while attempting to get comfortable amid the mountain ruble on which he lay.

Their horrifying encounter with the tree crabs and the dreadful hairy monster had been several days ago now, and although they had traveled a considerable distance since, the pair were yet well within the boundaries of the Black Mountains.

The going had been painfully slow and arduous. The terrain thus far had been as treacherous as any Joktan had ever traversed.

Countless times they had been forced to backtrack in search of more passable routes after hours of strenuous climbing, only to find their way blocked once more.

He now estimated that it would be at least two more days before they were out of the Black Mountains, provided there were no further delays, but in this accursed land, it seemed that delays were unavoidable.

Twice they had been set upon by packs of gigantic, rabid wolves since battling the terrible beast which had killed their horses. In the valleys they'd encountered even more tree crabs, as well as enormous serpents and deadly scorpions over three feet in length.

They had been forced to battle monstrous spiders while passing through dense forests in the lower elevations, arachnids whose jointed legs were longer than a full-grown man. And just yesterday he had been attacked by a pair of Sabertooth grizzlies while attempting to traverse a perilous rockslide.

The only creatures that they had not encountered thus far were

Goblins. According to many rumors the Black Mountains were filled with them, but so far, they hadn't seen anything which confirmed such rumors.

Each passing day brought with it some new, deadly foe, and now the prospect of having to battle an army of cave dwellers did not bode well with him at all.

At the moment, they were near the summit of an immense mountain. He had chosen to climb this one in particular because it rose higher than any of the neighboring peaks, and it would afford a commanding view of the surrounding land. From this lofty position they could survey the terrain through which they had traveled thus far, and it offered an excellent vantage point from which to plot their next course.

The sun shone brilliantly overhead, a welcome relief from the gloom and darkness of the forbidding forest in the mist-shrouded valleys below. A refreshing breeze wafted over the mountainside, and the air was clean and pure.

At this elevation, vegetation was sparse indeed. Aside from rock tripe, lichens and moss, only the occasional juniper managed to grow here. The land was a jumble of jagged rocks and massive boulders, making travel excruciatingly slow, and stealth was difficult at best. His hands and legs were scraped and bloodied, although amazingly Sheba had suffered not even the tiniest scratch.

Up ahead the land became much more green, as the barren rock gave way abruptly to mountain grasses and meadow flowers. Both he and Sheba hoped that perhaps the going would be a little easier from now on.

Because of the lack of forest cover, they had refrained from lighting a fire for the past two days, eating only the dried rations they had been able to salvage from the remains of their unfortunate mounts. Once they were clear of the mountains and in more hospitable environs, he planned on securing a good, hot meal.

Sheba had slept by his side the last two nights, and this morning he had awoken to find her snuggled up close behind him. He had been struck by the coolness of her touch; her skin felt as cold as ice. He reasoned that she slept with him for warmth, but inwardly he hoped that she desired something more. So far, every time they had begun to get close she'd pushed him away, and his frustration was mounting more and more.

They had not imagined the possibility of encountering humans in this area. Sheba had noticed them first, pulling Joktan violently to the ground. Now as they studied the horde ahead of them, she voiced her thoughts aloud in subdued tones.

"They all carry spears, so they must be warriors. Or hunters. I see no women or children."

Joktan nodded. "They look like hunters to me, too. I have never encountered cave dwellers who were not hostile." He cursed silently. "In this foul place, I cannot imagine this lot to be any different."

"Then you have seen their kind before?" she asked.

"Aye," he replied, "many a time I have seen them---and fought them. They are crazy, not really even men. Their ancestors were apes, or so I've been told."

"Apes?" Sheba laughed.

"That is what my people and many others believe," he replied seriously. "Cave dwellers have no wisdom. They don't really even have much of a language. Their speech is mostly grunting. They sound just like the hairy apes of the northlands, and they make a lot of motions to each other in much the same way."

"Yet they have enough wits to know how to fashion spears and throwing devices for themselves," Sheba observed, peering furtively towards the horde.

"True," he allowed, "and they'll kill you with them if they see you, or beat you to death with their clubs. They are very strong, and that is not the worst of it."

"Oh?" she eyed him, curious.

"They eat the flesh of men. I have even seen them eat their own kind." A dark shadow seemed to pass over his face. He shook his head, as if trying to dispel some dreadful memory that he would rather not recall at the moment. "And they were still alive."

Sheba stared thoughtfully at him a for a moment, then suddenly her face lit up and she smiled humorously. "Maybe they are your ancestors, Joktan!" she exclaimed. "They sound an awful lot like you!"

"Humph!" he snorted in disgust, then returned his attention to the figures moving across the mountainside ahead.

"It looks as though they have killed something, but at this distance it's impossible to tell what that might be," he mussed aloud. "It's big though, whatever it is."

"Who cares?" Sheba replied. "I just want to get out of here. I will be glad when these mountains are far behind us," she sighed wearily. A cool breeze swept over the mountain and tossed her flame hair wildly about her shoulders and over her back.

"My sentiments exactly," he agreed, "if we but had our mounts we could make a break for it and ride right over them." He silently began to string his bow.

She pushed a long strand of hair out of her face. "Obviously, that isn't an option, is it?" she replied, sounding somewhat annoyed.

Joktan mimicked her and rolled his eyes skyward, and Sheba, who had been watching the cave dwellers, turned just in time to catch him. Her gaze narrowed.

He smiled broadly at her, his ivory fangs gleaming in the morning sun, then turned once more to study the horde. "We must give them a wide berth," he advised presently. "I have noticed in the past that such folk seem to have poor eyesight. But their sense of smell and hearing are quite keen."

He looked at Sheba grimly. "Stay low. If we crawl slowly we can use the rocks for cover, and this moss will help make our movements more silent, provided we are careful. They are not aware of us yet, so for the moment, the advantage is ours."

She nodded and he motioned to her. "You go first."

Sheba glared at him. "Why me?" she growled apprehensively.

Joktan smiled, a mischievous sparkle in his azure eyes. "Because," he said slowly, raising an eyebrow, "I think I shall enjoy the view!"

Sheba flushed. "Has anyone ever told you how childish you are?" she retorted. "All you care about is your loins!"

"That's not entirely true," he countered with a sheepish grin. "It is *your* loins which have occupied my thoughts of late!"

Her green eyes widened in surprise. She had not expected such a response.

"This is not the time or place for such talk," she scolded haughtily, "and while you dawdle away our precious time, the chances of passing around these brothers of yours undetected grow less and less."

"Very well, wench," he chuckled, "I will lead the way."

He looked about quickly and spotted another large boulder some fifty paces ahead and to the left, then pointed it out to her.

"I will head for that rock. You just keep a bit of distance between us and stay as low as possible. And don't crawl on your knees. Spread your body out flat, and crawl along on your hands and toes."

"What…?"

"It will keep you lower to the ground, and give our enemy less to see," he replied. "Watch me, then follow my example."

Sheba nodded her consent. "Get on with it then," she replied throatily. "Once you are several paces out I will start behind you."

But Joktan had already dropped to the ground and begun to crawl forward. Sheathing her ax, Sheba crouched low and prepared to follow.

22

Upon arriving at Luxantia, Brutus ordered his men to set up camp outside the town's wall. Skeltar had made it very clear that they were not to lodge within, and now the soldiers sat huddled around fires recovering from the arduous journey they had just completed. They had made it to Luxantia in just nine days, traveling at a speed that would have ordinarily caused even the hardiest of men to collapse with fatigue.

Somehow the water that the wizard had magically produced in the desert had given the soldiers inexhaustible reserves of strength and endurance, but now that they had finally arrived at their destination, the relentless pace of the march was taking it's toll.

The night was calm and peaceful, but amid the cluster of canvas tents the soldiers were sullen and weary. The liberal rations of wine and mead----purchased from the local taverns and dispersed throughout the camp---- failed to lighten their spirits. Their bones ached, their muscles throbbed painfully, and before the sun had dipped under the distant horizon sleep had overtaken them.

Even in sleep, however, they found little comfort and relief, for their dreams were horrible nightmares, filled with all manner of loathsome monsters and fearful horrors, aftereffects of the sorcerous water they had drank in large quantities during the long, unending march.

Now a grim-faced Skeltar sat silently, alone in his darkened room. The only light that shone was cast by a lone, black candle on the wooden table before him, a taper made from the fat of a long-dead pubescent child.

The various articles of his sinister art had been laid out purposefully, so as to form a series of shapes and magickal figures. In the midst of these was placed a gold-rimmed mirror on an iron tripod, the size of which was not much larger than the open palm of his gnarled hand.

The mirror was the object of the sorcerer's present fascination, but it was not his own reflection upon which he bent his gaze, for this mirror cast no such image.

Instead, the scene portrayed in the spell-laden looking glass was of a different man. He was accompanied by a woman, some place far away, and they were quickly making their way down a lush, green mountain slope towards the tree-covered hills and valleys below.

Skeltar cursed silently as the picture began to shimmer, then became hazy. He snatched up a small vial of arcane liquid, uncorked it, and dribbled a few drops of the substance upon the surface of the mirror, reciting an ancient spell.

Slowly, the image came back into focus once more.

The woman was traveling at a short distance behind the man, and it was apparent that they had recently been involved in some sort of battle, for there was blood splattered upon her lithesome form. As the wizard watched her stride along, the blood smeared upon her pale flesh seemed to gradually disappear, as if the very pores of her ivory skin were absorbing it.

Seeing this brought a sneer to the mage's parchment features. *"If only that savage knew what manner of woman she is,"* thought Skeltar. *"He would try to slay her himself!"*

The beast from beyond the void had failed to kill the northland cur with whom the she-devil had recently taken a fancy to. Skeltar had worked hard to conjure that beast, to draw it out from beyond the veil and set it loose upon them. Such creatures were extremely difficult to control at close range, not to mention from a distance, bumping along in a horse drawn carriage no less! But once summoned they would remain confined in the area to which they had been sent.

They were terribly bloodthirsty beings with insatiable appetites and lust for flesh. One had to ensure that they were well fed to keep them bound under his power for any length of time.

Such a hellish beast should have torn the savage limb from limb, but some other power seemed to be at work about him. It should have captured the woman and held her prisoner until he could retrieve her from it. Why the beast had failed, the wizard was not sure, but now it was apparent that other avenues would clearly need to be employed if he was to somehow subdue her.

Nonetheless, the beast had delayed their journey and slowed their progress, so his efforts had not been a complete disaster.

And yet, with every passing moment Sheba was moving father away. He had much more traveling to do in the near future. They needed to be slowed down even more, but how? Wounding the woman was futile; she healed much too quickly. The tribesman could be wounded easily, or at least so it would seem, but events were proving otherwise. Indeed, he was becoming quite a bothersome fellow. There was something about him though, something very familiar...

Skeltar had a new scheme in mind, but it required the use of a special parchment, an accursed variety fashioned from human skin. In his haste to leave his castle, he'd forgotten it in his private chambers, but he would surely need it now to accomplish the working at hand.

He greatly disdained the priests of Dhampir, but he also knew that they could furnish him with the parchment he desperately required. He also knew that their reason for being in Luxantia was much the same as his own, so it might be possible that he could work out some sort of arrangement with them, an exchange that would be mutually beneficial. Besides, they would be much easier to deal with if they were to consider him an ally instead of a meddling interference.

It will be an efficient rouse to gain entrance to their chamber...

The mere thought of it made him nearly wretch in disgust, but Luxantia was too small a place for him to set about trying to procure such parchment the hard way. It would also mean that he would have to wait even longer, until the Mother Moon was in her dark phase, which would not be for another two weeks. Also, the parchment had to be made from the skin of a newly born child, and there were not very many of those to be had in a town as small as Luxantia.

Skeltar sighed heavily, then gathered up his cloak and extinguished the candle on the table, leaving the room in sudden darkness. As he exited his chamber and locked the door behind him, he noticed that his servant Cral was nowhere to be seen.

Come to think of it, he'd been shirking his duties for far too long, and especially so since they had arrived in Luxantia. The mage made a note of this as he turned down the corridor leading toward the stairs. Cral would have to be dealt with very soon.

As Skeltar moved silently down the street, a dark, shadowy form followed closely at his heels. It had the shape of a large, black dog.

Just now Cral was not thinking of his master at all. Indeed, Skeltar was the farthest thing from his mind, for at the moment he was busily engaged in eyeing up the two women sitting at the table beside him.

It had been a long journey to Luxantia, under constant, unforgiving heat that had sun burnt his skin and left him with a tremendous thirst. Skeltar had not planned on feeding his faithful servant either, for throughout the entire trip Cral had been forced to go without anything substantial in the way of food.

Now that his thirst had been quenched with a generous amount of wine and his stomach was filled with fresh roasted fowl, he was seeking to satisfy still yet one more desire, and that was for Luena and her slender partner, Glona.

At the table, one woman sat across from him, the other at his side. That the pleasure of both could be bought with gold was obvious. Cral had overheard their conversation with Shoto, and while he knew that his master would want the same information which the priests had sought, at the moment he could not have cared less about the two adventurers who seemed to so intrigue everyone else around him.

Cral had grown tired of playing the subservient role of late. His entire life, since meeting Skeltar, had been one of catering to the needs and whims of another. It was time that someone looked after *his* desires for a while.

At first Luena and Glona had flatly rejected him, but now as he produced a bulging leather purse, their demeanor changed markedly. He placed it in the center of the small table, open just enough for them to see that it was filled with gold and silver Straltonian coins.

"How much money are you willing to part with?" Luena asked.

"All of it," he replied.

She smiled sensuously at him from across the table, and he felt

Glona's hand slide slowly up his thigh.

"For that much gold," Luena said, "you could have both of us for the entire night."

"That was the idea," he replied as Glona's hand gently caressed the growing bulge between his legs. Cral had never bedded two women at once before; indeed, it had been a long time since he'd had a woman at all. His master usually kept several goats, however, to be used in his black rituals. Often times Cral used them to relieve his sexual urges and frustrations.....

Luena hefted the purse, and Cral's hand shot across the table, snatching it from her grasp. He was not anxious to part with all his money so quickly.

"You get the money *after*," he growled lustily, "not before."

Glona continued stroking him gently. "Why don't you give us half now and the other half later, big boy?"

Cral would have objected, but just at that moment Glona's fingers slipped beneath his trousers. They encircled his hardened shaft, squeezing it firmly, and her hand moved slowly back and forth. It was enough to cause a viscous droplet of fluid to ooze from his manhood....enough to lubricate the friction of the whore's grip upon his aching shaft.

"You drive a hard bargain," he moaned, as erotic sensations quickly mounted within his loins. He could feel his heart racing in anticipation....

"No," Luena smiled and leaned close, whispering as the pair slid to their feet. "It looks like you will be the one doing that!"

She slid out of her seat and pulled him to his feet, and together the trulls led him across the tavern, one woman on each arm.

All thoughts of his master's wishes were driven from his mind as he was guided up the stairs to the floor above. Tonight would definitely be a night to remember!

24

From the far corner of the room, seated alone at a small table, Brutus watched with interest as the threesome made their way up the stairs to a room above. His cloak was pulled tight about him to obscure his identity in the dimly lighted tavern.

He waited until they were gone, then hastily made his exit, heading towards Skeltar's lodgings on the other side of town. He didn't stop until he had reached the wizard's room, and when his knocking went unanswered, he turned and put his back to the door. He felt sure that the mage could not have ventured out very far. Sometime soon Skeltar would return.

A twisted sneer played upon his lips. He could hardly wait to see the wizard's face, to tell him what his faithful servant was up to. Cral had it coming anyway. He was a creepy little lout if ever there was one. If the wizard killed him outright, no one would morn his passing, of that the soldier was certain.

25

Joktan and Sheba had been working their way slowly over the rocky terrain, crawling from one boulder to the next as silent as a pair of ghosts.

They were nearly past the cave dwellers now, and with a little luck, would soon be able to put some distance between themselves and the primate horde. The though brought a feeling of satisfaction to Joktan as he inched stealthily ahead.

A quick glance behind told him that Sheba still followed not far away, although from her gestures and the look on her face, he knew that she was quickly losing her patience.

He smiled to himself because of this as he continued to crawl forward. He understood her impatience very well. If she had her way, he knew that Sheba would much rather just stand up and run for it instead of sneak painfully over the jagged rocks.

Moving along in this fashion became tiring very quickly. His muscles were aching already, and he knew hers were most likely feeling just as exhausted too. He sympathized with her completely, but not just because of their slow progress.

He knew there was no honor to be found in skulking about, and a little bit of swordplay would certainly loosen up the tension in his burning thews. But at the moment the two of them were vastly outmanned, to say the least, and taking on the entire horde would be utterly foolish indeed. The cave dwellers had superior numbers, and a skirmish between them would be short lived at best.

As he reached the next boulder he suddenly noticed that the wind had changed direction, and he cursed silently. Their scent would be blowing directly towards the horde, a thought which made him more than a little uneasy.

He and Sheba would have to stay close together now, for it would be easy for them to become separated if they were attacked at the moment. Sticking close together had one major drawback though; it would make the two of them much more noticeable.

He looked back and saw that Sheba was still in the open some thirty or so paces away. He motioned for her to catch up to him. As he waited, the tribesman wondered silently what the cave dwellers were up to; he hadn't heard them for some time now, and they had been making a lot of noise before. He knew that he hadn't yet passed around the creatures, so something had to be amiss.

Abrupt silence always made Joktan wary. It was the most unnatural sound that one could ever hear in the forest and open wilds. He recognized it as a sign of danger. Perhaps this was because most forest creatures knew when a predator was on the prowl. Or it might have been due to some ancient, subconscious alarm that was more akin to the primitive instincts of these cave dwelling primates than he could possibly realize.

Joktan raised himself up on his hands to peer about, and instinctively ducked as something flew swiftly past his head with a swoosh, glancing wildly off of the rocks behind him. He did not need to look too far to know what it was that had nearly brained him.

Nearby lay a short spear, it's roughly hewn shaft broken from the violent impact against the stones beside him, and instantly he knew why the cave dwellers had grown so suddenly still.

Both him and Sheba were now being hunted by the ape-men. Already an arrow was notched and his bow drawn as a large stone whipped dangerously close past his head. It struck the ground with a solid thud behind him even as another nearly caught him in the leg.

He glanced back at Sheba just in time to see her impale one of the primates through the chest with a long dagger. The man-beast stood frozen for a moment, his bone club held high overhead, then collapsed. Sheba withdrew her blade and raced toward Joktan as fast as her legs could carry her, leaping to one side and then the other as stones and spears rained down all around.

Several more ape-men were rushing upon them. They were less than twenty paces away and closing fast. Black eyes flashed with savage frenzy and drool foamed from their barred, yellowish teeth.

His first arrow struck one of the attackers in the chest, and a mere second later his next shaft took another through the throat. The apes were only a few paces from them now, and Joktan swiftly notched four more arrows and loosed them in rapid succession.

Each one found it's mark, the steel tips tearing through flesh and bone and hide, but so close were the attackers that the arrows didn't stop. They went right through their victims and into those behind them, so that four arrows took seven foes screaming to the ground.

The cave dwellers were stunned, and halted abruptly. Apparently they had never seen such a weapon, and it so surprised them that for a brief moment they stood still, gaping at their fallen comrades and the shafts which protruded from their dying bodies. Further still was their amazement when several more of their number slumped lifeless to the ground, these being the ones through which the arrows had passed before striking the primates behind them.

All this happened in the space of only a few seconds, however the bow and arrow were weapons of Joktan's homeland, and those fleeting moments were enough for him to fire off a dozen more shots, all of which wounded or killed their intended target.

The beastly horde's awe quickly turned to horror, and they turned suddenly to flee, shrieking in terror as they ran madly across the rugged slope.

Joktan seized the moment, loosing arrow after arrow as he and Sheba now pursued the enemy. Within just a few minutes over a score of the cave dwellers lay dead or dying amid the jagged rocks, their blood staining the alpine vegetation darkly.

He had not expected so easy a victory, and silently thanked the gods as he looked about. A dozen paces away, Sheba was wiping blood and gore from the blade of her battle-ax. The ground about her was littered with corpses and steaming entrails, as she stood triumphantly with her weapon brandished menacingly. From head to toe, her body was covered in blood.

The fact that the woman seemed to be unharmed did not strike Joktan as being strange, but what *did* give him pause for thought was the number of bodies which lay strewn about her. There were nearly twice as many as what he had slain so far, and she was armed with only an ax, not at all the weapon of speed and distance that his bow was.

Such a feat bordered on something more than simply superb fighting skills, and Joktan wondered at it silently as Sheba strode toward him. She seemed unconcerned by what she had done, as if it were nothing at all. Her long hair blew wildly over her shoulders and face, and blood was splattered liberally across her attractive features.

"We had better move quickly!" Joktan told her as she approached. "Those things will soon regain their courage and come back twice as mad."

"Aye," she agreed, smiling broadly, "although I was just beginning to enjoy myself!" She paused to wipe her face with the back of her hand, a strange smile playing upon her lips.

He wasn't sure now if it had been his archery that had sent the primates fleeing. Perhaps it was the swift and terrible butchery which Sheba had unleashed so suddenly upon them.

Together the pair made a run for it, hoping to put as much distance as possible between themselves and the shaggy hared apes, but as they ran, Joktan's mind was churning.

Never before had he witnessed such single-handed slaughter. Never before had he seen one person kill so many foes with such ease. What manner of woman was she? He didn't know what it was, but something was tugging at his mind, as if trying to tell him something that he needed to urgently know, but he just couldn't seem to put his finger on it.

He now knew that the woman could handle herself in battle. Hell, she could fight as well as any man he'd ever known--quite possibly as well as himself--and he was good.

Yet she was without doubt the most beautiful woman he had ever seen.

As they ran, the rocks gave way to more moss and grasses, and soon they were moving quickly down the other side of the mountain towards the valley far below.

And from somewhere far, far away, an eerie laughter was carried upon the wind, and two evil eyes watched as the pair disappeared into the trees that grew farther down the slope.

Upon the plains of Gershom,
The grass grows tall and green,
An endless sea of deepest emerald,
Swept by summer breeze.
The hills fall from the mountains,
Rolling south and to the east,
Upon which wondrous creatures roam,
And pasture there in peace.
But distant on horizon,
Black legions swarm the sky,
And beating wings swirl screeching,
Like demons from on high.
Whilst birds of prey and jackals,
Lay claim about their prize,
The butchered merchants vainly flail,
As vultures peck their eyes.
A band of brigands turn their backs,
Upon the dying prey,
And ride seeking new travelers,
In fading light of day.

----Excerpt from an ancient Keddishyan scroll.

The sun was slowly making its ascent into the morning sky, and although it would still be several hours before mid-day, the temperature on the Keddishyan Plains was nearly suffocating.

Tall grasses covered the land, swaying in the breeze like waves upon an unending sea of green. Small hills rolled out as far as the eye could see, dotted by occasional clumps of brush and stunted trees. Here and there a cool, shallow stream splashed a meandering path across the undulating expanse.

Upon these plains great herds of bison, aurochs, antelope and fallow deer roamed in countless numbers, their ears twitching at insects which buzzed about them as they fed lazily upon the lush abundance of the land. They were joined from time to time by smaller herds of elk, wild sheep, gazelles and zebras.

These roving herds were followed closely by lions, leopards, cheetahs, jackals, hyenas, wolves and a multitude of other predatory beasts that hunted and fed upon the weak, sick and unwary.

In the sky above, ravens, vultures, and other fowl circled tirelessly, the sound of their cries carried on the wind as they searched for carrion, waiting for a fresh kill and their next bloody prize.

The Keddishyan Plains were also home to many small, nomadic tribes of people known as *Plainsmen.* They were peaceful for the most part, living in tents, and herding sheep and goats. What they could not produce for themselves they purchased by bartering with the merchant caravans that traveled through the plains over the many trade routes crisscrossing the land.

Such wandering tribes had their own laws, customs and beliefs. Due to their small numbers and meager needs, tribal wars were practically unheard of. But that is not to say that violence perpetrated by men did not exist here, for there were other predators who roamed the gassy hills of these wild plains.

Brigands and thieves, cutthroats and bandits, outlaws all, and fugitives from justice; such men also traveled the grasslands, preying upon merchants and other sojourners. They were bloodthirsty and brutal, often fighting amongst themselves for leadership and control, and today one such band in particular was carefully keeping watch on an ever-nearing cloud of dust that was moving quickly over the hills.

Numbering some twenty men in all, they lay concealed on their bellies in the tall grass, just beyond the crest of a gentle rise. Each man had the look of a starving hyena; lean, ragged, and unpredictable.

All bore the scars of sword and dagger, and the permanent marks of the Imperial whip etched indelibly across their backs. Such scars were a constant reminder of the many crimes they had committed in other lands. Some were tattooed with the mark of execution, obviously having escaped some cruel fate before arriving here with others of their ilk. There were even a few who sported lopped ears and notched nostrils, the customary mark of convicted villains in many lands.

Most were armed with long, crescent-shaped swords called

swaltas, as well as an assortment of dirks, daggers and broadswords. The cloud of dust they were watching had appeared suddenly on the horizon and was now moving towards them with great haste.

The leader of the brigands was a large, heavily muscled brute with red matted hair. It clung to his neck and shoulders in a greasy, tangled mess. His name was Jrasseph, and his large, protruding eyes were dark brown, brimming with malice and cruel greed. He was a veteran of the plains, and his exploits had made his name a legend among outlaws and merchants alike.

He wiped the sweat from his glistening brow with a dirty paw, studying the approaching horsemen. Well he knew that it was uncommon for travelers to move so quickly through this land, and he judged that they must be ether heedless of danger or on some urgent business, for to risk drawing attention to themselves by raising such a large cloud of dust was very foolish, even for bandits.

It was strange that someone would travel so quickly on such a hot, dry day. The occasional flash of sunlight glinting on steel told him that the oncoming group was definitely armed, and they were not soldiers, for soldiers always traveled in much greater numbers, and at a vastly slower, more wary pace.

At any rate, horses were a highly valued commodity on the plains, and even if these travelers did not carry some other form of wealth, their mounts would make a decent prize indeed.

Jrasseph didn't even question the outcome of a skirmish between his band of villains and the approaching group; his men outnumbered the newcomers two to one, and they were all well seasoned rouges. He turned and barked his orders in a gruff, defiant tone, and they grinned wickedly at each other in anticipation.

Every one of them was eager to draw fresh blood, for it had been several days since they had last encountered anyone at all. Bandits grew restless easily. Their livelihood was dependent upon constant action, and periods of inactivity were fraught with quarrels and dissension. Men like Jrasseph held onto their positions of leadership by managing to keep the attention of their men focused constantly upon the next raid--the next kill.

Now they quickly mounted their steeds and waited for his signal, swords drawn and held ready, taking care to stay out of sight just beyond the crest of the hill.

Minutes seemed to pass like hours, and when their leader's signal finally came, they burst over the hill in a storm of dust and noisy cries.

The newcomers instantly reigned in their mounts, forming a tight circle, each one facing the brigands as they were swiftly surrounded. These men had seen much in their days of lawless living upon the plains, but they were not prepared for what they now beheld.

For as the dust settled about them, they realized that the riders were not men or even merchants. On the contrary, they were all women. There were eight in number; each wore high leather boots and leggings of chained mail and scale armor. Their loincloths were made of silk, and from waist to neck, each woman wore a tunic of fine steel mail.

Even more startling was that all of them were women of exquisite beauty; long hair, voluptuous breasts and lithe bodies. The grime of travel did little to lessen their comeliness, and in truth, these brigands had never before seen such beautiful women in all their lives.

Each carried a sword and dagger, sheathed in gold and encrusted in jewels, and each held a crossbow firmly in their hands, cocked and ready for use in an instant. These crossbows had been fashioned curiously, however, with two pairs of limbs and two triggers each.

Jrasseph suddenly felt uneasy. There was no fear in the eyes of these women, and they gazed confidently at the brigands with the cool, steady stare of well-trained soldiers, sizing up their foe and preparing for battle.

As brigand leader studied them he noticed that each crossbow was fastened to it's owners saddle by a leather strap, so that it could be dropped to hang alongside by their legs when not in use. Such weapons were rare on the plains, and were considerably expensive; he had never before seen crossbows like the ones these women now had trained upon him and his men. At least three of these lovely maidens carried two such weapons apiece.

The woman who seemed to be their leader had jet-black hair. It cascaded down her sleek back to fall just above her rounded buttocks. Her eyes matched the color of her mane, but the corners slanted toward her temples slightly. Jrasseph carefully chose his words before addressing her.

"Why travel you so quickly," he asked, as if truly concerned. "Be you pursued?" He acted as if he did not notice the weapon which she held firmly, pointed at his chest.

"Did you see a cloud of dust behind us, wasteland dog?" the woman retorted hotly, her black eyes sparkling with menace.

"Well, no," Jrasseph replied nervously, taken aback by the woman's total lack of fear. "But it is a shame to see such good mounts driven so hard in the summer heat."

"Never mind the horses," one brigand spoke up. "'Tis a shame to see such beautiful women roaming about these parts without the company of men, so far from home and all….."

"Aye," said another, turning his head to the side and spitting out his tobacco. "I say it is they that should be driven hard!"

"Hold your tongues!" Jrasseph silenced his men with an angry stare, then turned his attention back to the woman who had spoken.

"What is your name, wench?" he barked gruffly at her.

"I am Chia," she informed him flatly. "You and your flea-infested mates now block my way." Her slanted eyes narrowed angrily. "Be off with you this instant!"

Jrasseph threw back his head, roaring in laughter. "Such commands you give….and a woman no less!" His grin revealed several chipped and blackened teeth.

His men joined in raucous ridicule while feasting their eyes upon the women with wicked lust. Crude comments ensued while their leader glared at Chia, and there was no warmth in his gaze. It seemed obvious that this wench cared little for small talk, and his hand moved instinctively to rest upon the silver pommel of his sword.

"Mayhap I should teach…." He started.

"Mayhap I should kill you and leave your corpse for the buzzards," she snarled.

Instantly a quarrel flew through the air. It was a mere blur, so fast did it fly, and it appeared to have sprouted as if by some form of magick from between Jrasseph's bulging eyes. A trickle of blood began to run down his face.

His laughter ceased abruptly, and he sat for a moment as if frozen upon his mount; then slowly he slumped forward and pitched head first to the grass below. The tip of the quarrel protruded from the back of his skull as the weight of his body impacting the ground drove it forcefully through his head. His nerves twitched briefly, then his body went limp. He was dead.

No sooner had Jrasseph begun to fall from his saddle than Chia fired upon the next closest of his mates. Her second quarrel buried itself deeply in another brigand's chest. The man stared at in shock, then toppled sideways from his horse, clawing desperately at the shaft. Bloody foam began to spill from his lips as he struggled upon the ground, and as if some unspoken signal had been issued, the other seven women began to fire their weapons in unison.

Quarrels sped through the air, each one expertly finding its mark, much to the horror of the stunned bandits. One moment they were sitting comfortably upon their mounts, the next they were falling from their saddles.

Within the space of but a few seconds, a total of sixteen brigands lay dead or dying upon the ground. Their mounts stood still, as if unaware of what was happening about them, and the four remaining brigands looked on in dumb-founded shock and surprise.

Chia and her companions sprang into action, charging through the pile of corpses against the last of their surviving foes.

One man raised his sword high overhead to strike as two women rushed upon him. The one on his left drove her blade through his midriff as the other woman's broadsword sliced deep into his side, laying bare his lower ribs. The brigand's entrails spilled out over his saddle and splattered to the ground.

He fell screaming, staining the Keddishyan grasses red with blood, his eyes wide with terror. The other three bandits died just as quickly, easily overpowered and slaughtered mercilessly by the women whom they had though to be their prey, and within moments, the battle was over. The women hadn't even suffered a scratch, and of the bandits, not a one survived.

Chia and her companions dismounted, swinging swiftly from their horses and landing lightly upon booted feet. Hastily, they wrenched their spent quarrels from the corpses of the brigands, cleaning each one on the clothes of its victim before returning it to the quiver.

Then with the efficiency of an elite military unit, they ensured that all of the brigands were truly dead by loping of their heads, one by one. This completed, they stripped the horses of their packs and saddles, then turned them loose to roam the plains unencumbered.

With that, each woman remounted and dug in her heels, galloping once more into the same westward direction they had been traveling in before the brief encounter.

27

Joktan and Sheba had made good time during their descent from the Black Mountains. They reached the foothills without further incident, and the cave dwellers did not pursue them. Nonetheless, the pair remained ever wary.

They traveled through the foothills now, a land of broad forests and gentle brooks fed by mountain glaciers and icy springs. The plant-life was lush and vibrant here, and flocks of blue jays, sparrows, finches and wrens sang and chirped loudly as they flew from tree to tree and fluttered amid the undergrowth and bushes. Every now and then the familiar tune of a red-breasted robin could be heard somewhere nearby, and farther off in the distance the occasional woodpecker drummed a relentless beat.

The abundance and vibrancy of plant and animal life that flourished here contrasted sharply with the dark, foreboding mountains and valleys through which they had just passed. Clean, clear streams splashed off toward the south, and both Joktan and Sheba found these to be immensely refreshing.

Their food supplies had ran out quickly in the mountains, and Joktan had taken down a young buck with his bow on their first day here. The fresh venison satisfied their empty bellies, strengthened their weary bodies and lifted their spirits greatly.

As they traveled the pair crossed over the Gershom border, heading southward over the Tulmac Plains along one of the many trade routes that ran through the region. The Keddishyan Plains lay to the east of the Tulmac, while to the west lay the southern reaches of Bezakzia, a land dominated by dense forests and rugged mountains.

This land was new to Joktan, and presently they slowed their pace as the mountains receded into the distance behind them. Traveling by foot was tiring, and neither of them felt a need to hurry.

Any previous pursuers would almost certainly have given up the chase by now. Both felt sure they had not been had followed through the mountains, for that region was well known to be a dreadful place. Very few people would ever think of setting foot in there, and in truth, they themselves had had a rough enough time getting through those treacherous peaks as it was.

Not one to be given to superstition, nor deterred by it, Joktan trusted in his skill with a sword for safety from every unknown. That is not to say he hadn't felt an overwhelming sense of dread within the depths of the mountains; it had truly been a dark and terrible place. But now the jagged peaks were fading farther and farther into the distance, and this new land was so full of life and beauty that the shadows of the Black Mountains seemed as if they'd been nothing more than a passing dream.

Sheba was familiar with these parts, having traveled through this land a few years before, and she informed him that, on foot, they were now only about six days journey from a small town. There they would be able to purchase horses and more supplies before continuing south.

Joktan hadn't told her yet just how little gold he now had left in his purse. He still had the obsidian skull that he'd stolen from the dead priest in Luxantia. It had been stowed away in a pack on his horse. Somehow it had survived the fall over the cliffs in the mountains. He hoped that perhaps he could sell it in the next town. Even so, there was no way that he could afford to purchase a horse. There had been no signs of other travelers thus far, but he was secretly hoping that they would encounter other sojourners soon. If so, he could relieve them of their mounts and travel with greater ease.

True, it wasn't the kindest thing to do, but it had happened to him several times before, although in the end the thieves had been more than happy to return his horse to him!

He smiled grimly at the thought as he strode along, and Sheba gave him a queer look, noticing his expression but not being privy to the source of his amusement.

"What are you thinking?" she asked him presently.

"Just that my gold is in short supply," he replied. "I have only that stone skull that I robbed the dead priest of when I found you. I'm thinking maybe we should just rob the first hapless travelers we meet and steal their mounts."

"I have plenty of coin left," she frowned disapprovingly. "There is no need to resort to reaving."

Joktan shrugged. He had endured many torments at the hands of the civilized men. Robbing them of a couple horses seemed trivial by comparison.

As they traveled on the forest gave way to the open plains, and a sultry breeze swept lazily over the land. The grasses grew tall as far as the eye could see, and farther out from the foothills, the terrain gradually became more even. The hills here were not nearly the size of those through which they had just come; they were more like gentle, sloping knolls, and as the pair continued, the land became progressively more flat and featureless.

Suddenly from behind them there came the sound of rushing movement in the grass, and Joktan wheeled to see several ostriches charging toward them at a furious speed.

He'd never seen such creatures before, and immediately thought them to be attacking. Their size was incredible, as was the speed at which they ran. Their long legs obviously had great strength, covering an enormous distance with every stride. The necks and heads of the giant birds bobbed and swayed from side to side as they quickly closed in on him. They had massive beaks, and the huge claws on their feet looked truly dangerous.

Joktan glanced at Sheba. She too seemed to be as shocked as he by the shear size of these monstrous birds, for she just stood there, simply watching, without making the slightest move to defend herself. In that brief moment Joktan thought she seemed almost fascinated by the over-grown turkeys. How could she have slaughtered the cave dwellers so brutally, only to stand frozen before these misshapen chickens?

He wasn't taking any chances.

With lightning speed his bow was drawn, the feathered shaft of his arrow touching his ear as he drew and took steady aim. In an instant the arrow flashed towards the bird closest to him, striking the thing squarely through its feathered breast.

Twice more he let loose his arrows, hitting the same bird with every shot, and still the strange creature hurtled at him headlong, it's pace and stride unbroken. *Did these things not die?*

They were nearly upon him now, and Joktan flung his bow to the ground, drawing both of his trusty broadswords. The steel blades dazzled brilliantly in the sun as he braced himself to strike.

But to his utter amazement, they did not attack at all. Instead, they charged right past him, as if he wasn't even there, narrowly missing him and Sheba in the process. As the lead bird rushed by, Joktan swung his sword, lopping off its head, which was relatively small compared to the rest of it's unusually huge body.

He turned to watch as the things sped away, and it was several moments before the bird he had shot and beheaded finally lurched and crumpled awkwardly to the ground.

Now Joktan realized that the ostriches had not intended to attack him and Sheba at all; they were attempting to flee some foe which pursued them. His blue eyes narrowed as he quickly scanned the direction from which the ostriches had come.

To his utter annoyance, it suddenly dawned on him that Sheba was practically doubled over in a fit of laughter, and he scowled angrily at the woman, which only made her laughter all the more intense. She was bent over, clutching her stomach, nearly hysterical with mirth.

Apparently, she has lost her senses, he thought, snorting in disgust as she finally fell to the ground, her entire body shaking with unbridled glee.

"Have you never seen an ostrich before?" she managed at last.

Joktan ignored her, focusing his attention instead on locating whatever it was that had frightened the birds so badly.

He felt its presence before even he saw it.

The very ground beneath his feet began to tremble at the coming of the beast. Sheba's laughter ended abruptly. In an instant she was on her feet, a battle-ax held tightly in each clenched fist. Joktan thrust both swords into the ground before him and armed himself once more with his bow.

In an explosion of fury, the monster burst into view, charging toward them at nearly the same speed as the terrified birds fleeing before it.

Its head was immense, some four feet in length. The creature's jaws were big enough to swallow a man whole, and it's slavering lips were rimmed with long, white, pointed teeth, each one the length of a grown man's hand.

The monster's broad, bulging neck was nearly as long as Joktan was tall, and heavily muscled. Its front legs were relatively small, compared to the rest of it's body, and ended in paws that looked more like three-fingered hands than feet. These fingers ended in talon-like claws, several inches in length.

The beast stood erect on it's hind legs, which were huge and bowed outward slightly. Joktan could not have reached around them with both arms.

Its tail was like that of a crocodile, nearly fifteen feet long. From the tip of this tail to the top of its terrible head, the beast was covered in black and dark green scales that glittered in the sun like polished plates of steel.

The beast towered some twenty-five feet above the ground, glaring about with dark eyes that shone brightly with intelligence and malicious intent.

It halted some thirty paces before them, and even at that distance they could smell it's awful breath. It reeked like a battlefield littered with moldering corpses under the burning mid-day sun.

The beast had not expected Joktan and Sheba to be there when it had broke into view, and it looked as though it were trying to decide whether to continue after the ostriches or face this new-found foe.

Joktan's mind worked quickly, trying to recall everything he had ever heard about such beasts. He'd seen them in the past, during his adventures in the land of the Bear Tribes, but only from a distance, which he now preferred much more than his present vantage point.

"Ballagor," he muttered, remembering the name that the Bear Tribesmen had given these fearsome predators. It meant simply, *"big death,"* clearly an understatement if ever there was one. He had also been told that these beasts hunted in pairs, a fact which he now considered with no small amount of unease.

The ballagor suddenly let out a hideous roar, it's massive jaws opening wide, teeth and fangs gleaming like scores of deadly knives. As it vented its wrath, it threw back its head violently, as if uttering its battle cry to the gods themselves.

As of yet no other such beast had appeared to join in the attack, and Joktan hoped that this one was a loner. He raised his bow and took aim, and the thing began to move slowly toward them, as if trying to decide upon the best approach.

It was thinking--Joktan could see it plainly in the monster's eyes--and he was sure that its mind was working every bit as fast as his own.

Cautiously it circled them, and they in turn circled it as well, maintaining the tenuous distance between them.

The ballagor lifted its right foot and slammed it back down against the ground, then stepped forward, expelling a noisome breath of putrid air. Its nostrils flared contemptuously, dripping with moist, slimy ooze.

Joktan let loose an arrow at its massive chest, and it shattered against the creature's steely scales. It snorted angrily at him, then cocked its immense head to peer at Sheba, slaver dripping from its horrible jaws.

The moment was not lost on Joktan.

He aimed higher and loosed another arrow at the beast. It struck the creature in the eye, and the ballagor bellowed painfully as a black, tar-like substance erupted from the wounded socket and streamed down the side of its hideous face. He had the beast's full attention now, and it roared wildly before lunging toward him in a sudden, dreadful rage.

Joktan shouldered his bow and tore his swords from the ground, then charged to meet his foe. Savage instincts surged through him in a wave of holy wrath as he met the attack with a throaty, barbaric cry.

A civilized man might have fled across the plain in blind terror for his life, but Joktan had never been civilized. The rage now suddenly coursing through his veins was more akin to that of the beast he fought than to that of any mortal man.

The ballagor was upon him in an instant, and Joktan flung himself to the ground as razor sharp incisors snapped shut in the air, where only a second before his head would have been. The beast twisted and bent it's huge head down low, and Joktan struck out at it furiously. Massive jaws slammed down on the sword in his left hand, ripping it from his grasp and shattering the blade like a dried-up twig.

He jumped and rolled between the beast's giant legs, thrusting and slashing powerfully, wielding his sword with both hands. The creature moved with blinding speed, and Joktan darted away from it just in time to avoid being squashed beneath one of its gigantic feet.

Sheba flanked the monster, and it lunged at her in retaliation, bellowing its fury with a spray of slaver and foam. Her ax tore into its broad neck, and blood erupted, spurting from the wound. She leapt back and swung once more as the beast snapped at her, exposing two rows of jagged incisors. Her ax slammed against it's closed teeth. The steel edge shattered several of the monster's incisors, enraging it all the more.

It jerked back it's head and let out a piercing, painful cry, then with terrifying swiftness it lunged at Sheba. She avoided the attack, darting just beyond its reach before striking back with a flurry of vicious blows.

Meanwhile, Joktan had been searching for a soft spot on the underside of the creature, and in that instant he thrust his sword upward. The tip slipped under the hard, protective scales, and he threw his full weight into the blow. His sword sank to the hilt into the belly of the beast, and a foul stench filled the air about him as he wrenched it from side to side and ripped it free. The ballagor shrieked in agony as gastric juices poured from the gaping hole in a fountain of filth and blood.

Joktan thrust his blade into the wound once more, and griping it with both hands, drove it across the broad girth of the ballagor's belly with all his might. Sharpened steel sliced through tender flesh and sinew beneath the scaled surface of the behemoth's stomach, opening a jagged gash through which intestines and gore burst forth and gushed upon the ground.

The fury of the beast was unimaginable. It contorted grotesquely and threw back it's head, screaming to the heavens in pain and wrath with it's massive jaws open wide. Joktan retreated in a shower vile spray, and the beast lowered its head and roared violently at him, a cry filled with unimaginable hatred and rage.

Joktan's sword rilled crimson. He twirled it up into the air and caught it in his hand. Firmly grasping the blade, he cocked his arm back and flung the weapon straight into the open mouth of the roaring monster. The tip struck the back of the creature's throat and sank deeply into the soft, pink flesh, and it screamed even more insanely than before, but this time it's cry was filled with fear and terror.

Sheba ran toward Joktan as the beast lurched and crashed to the ground. It thrashed desperately, slowly choking on the unyielding weapon lodged firmly in it's throat.

"Give me an ax!" Joktan shouted to her above the ear-splitting din of the bellowing monster.

"Joktan! Look out!" Sheba cried, tossing him the ax in her right hand, then drawing her scimitar.

The ballagor struck out with its mighty tail, and Joktan was swept off of his feet. He hurtled through the air and slammed into the ground, gasping for breath. His head spun and he struggled to rise as Sheba launched another assault upon the foe.

Before Joktan had time to move, the creature struck him again, and the sharp spines on it's tail gashed his legs and torso. Pain shot through his body in excruciating waves.

He fought desperately for air and clutched the handle of the ax fiercely as the beast swung its tail at him again and again, seeking to smash him into the earth with every savage blow. His vision was blurred, blinded by dust, as the beast flailed at him relentlessly.

His heart raced and blood pounded in his ears. He was vaguely aware of Sheba howling angrily, as if at a distance. He struggled to his feet and staggered sideways as the beast's barbed tail lashed dangerously close to his head.

Through a blinding haze of dust, he saw the beast writhe in agony as Sheba buried her battle-ax into its ribcage. So vicious was the blow that the entire head of the weapon tore through both scales and flesh with seeming ease, becoming embedded deep within the ballagor's side. It stuck there, between the bones, and as she tugged on the handle in an effort to rip it free, the beast screamed thunderously and rolled from side to side. The ax was wrenched from her hands and she fell backwards into the grass, crying out in surprise and indignation.

Joktan surged forward, teeth bared in a ferocious snarl, the ax gripped tightly in both hands. There was a flash of steel as he swung with all his might, then the crunch of fractured bone as the blade smashed into the beast's massive skull. The whole side of its head was caved in from the sheer force of the blow, and the creature suddenly ceased its struggles. It lay there unmoving and stunned, but the bloodlust was now flowing wildly in the savage's veins. He smote it brutally, smashing the ballagor's head into a bloody mound of splintered bone and mangled flesh. It's huge body shuddered, then went limp; at last the ballagor lay dead.

Joktan stepped back to catch his breath, his chest heaving from exertion, holding Sheba's ax loosely at his side. Within a few moments she joined him, and together they rested while the blood of the slain beast spread slowly across the ground, staining the grass and congealing thickly in a steaming pool around the creature's carcass. The warm smell of the carnage was sickening.

"By Ashtoreth's tits!" Joktan exclaimed, "that was a worthy foe!"

"Aye," Sheba agreed, "but I would not care to fight too many more of these beasts."

"It smashed one of my short swords," he panted, "and the other is lodged in its throat. It too, is broken now."

"Which is why I prefer axes," Sheba remarked wryly. "They are much stronger."

Joktan caught his breath, then handed her back her weapon. Drawing his broadsword in silence, he plunged the blade deep into the chest of the beast, opening up a gaping hole though it's scaled flesh, and removed it's heart. The steaming organ was the size of Joktan's head, and he held it almost reverently before presenting it to Sheba.

"Do you want half?" he asked her sternly, blood dripping from his hands and running down his arms. "You helped kill it."

Sheba stared at him, a puzzled expression on her finely featured face. "And what on earth am I to do with it?" she replied, the disgust in her voice undisguised. "Surely you don't intend to eat such a foul thing!"

Joktan was obviously surprised at the woman's reaction. "Of course I do!" he returned. "It would be an insult to such a valiant foe and a dishonor to the gods if I didn't."

He gazed at her grimly. "If you eat the heart of this beast, you will absorb its strength and part of its spirit. It will also give you power over it's kind, and you will always be victorious in future battles against them."

"I presume that this is some backwards custom of your people," she snorted derisively, casting a loathsome glance at the bloody prize. Joktan grinned wickedly and nodded in the affirmative.

"We do not hold to such barbaric notions in Lothair," she said.

Joktan frowned, growling disapprovingly, and with a reluctant sigh, Sheba finally agreed.

"Very well. If it makes you happy, I will oblige you," she said haughtily, "but don't think I'm going to make a habit of it in the future."

Joktan smiled and bared his fangs, pleased at last with her decision. He cut the heart in half with his dagger and thrust it toward her, and Sheba reluctantly accepted. He tore into the flesh with obvious relish, and after a few moments Sheba gingerly bit off a small mouthful of meat and chewed it hesitantly. Joktan nodded and grunted with pleasure, then set about devouring his portion, and when he'd eaten nearly half of it, he placed the remainder upon the beast's chest and stood wiping the blood from his face.

Sheba followed his example, relieved that she was not expected to consume all of the heart she had been allotted. She placed the rest of her share beside Joktan's, then turned to him.

"I thought you were going to eat the whole thing."

"Oh no," he replied, "it is as much of a dishonor not to leave a portion for the gods."

He wiped at the blood on his face with the back of his hand, which was not much cleaner at the moment. Sheba eyed him humorously.

"I had no idea you were such a devout man," she commented with a smirk.

"No, I'm just hungry!" he replied with a grin. "It was not so long ago that my people ate the hearts of all their enemies. As recently as my grandfather's time, such things were still done."

Sheba looked at him with mock sincerity. "Your people have become much more civilized since then, I see."

Joktan missed her sarcasm. "Oh yes!" he enthused, oblivious to her sarcasm. "Our enemies remember such times even today, and my kin are feared greatly in our land, though now they eat only the hearts of animals."

"Oh, I see," she replied mocked. "Your race has made great progress."

"My people are a proud race!" Joktan retorted, finally sensing that he was being made fun of. "They do not forget their past, and would still feast upon the hearts of their enemies with pleasure."

"That somehow does not surprise me!" she scoffed, but she smiled warmly.

The pair gathered up their weapons and quickly cleaned them as best as possible, then sat down amid the swaying grasses to rest and eat before moving on. Joktan's legs were badly cut and scraped from having been whipped by the beast's spiked tail, and presently Sheba set about cleaning his wounds, despite his objections. She produced a small vial of dark liquid, and dabbed a few drops of it on each cut before bandaging them with strips of cloth.

"This is a very potent healing ointment," she told him as he watched her skeptically. "It is a potion used in my homeland, and it will cause your wounds to heal fast. I made it before we left Luxantia."

"It looks like dark colored blood," he told her, wincing as she applied a few more drops to one of the deeper gashes on his calf. Sheba smiled, but made no further comment, other than to tell him to sit still and quit moving around so much.

Joktan liked her closeness. He could smell the scent of her, and his loins began to stir as he studied the woman's features. Her fiery hair hung down over her shoulders and breasts as she worked, and as he watched her the breeze blew it to one side, affording him a revealing view of her cleavage. She caught his stare out of the corner of her eye and smiled coyly, but made no effort to obscure his view. Instead, Sheba leaned further forward and pushed out her chest, emphasizing her endowments all the more, and her hands began to slowly move up his leg and thigh.

Impulsively, he reached out and touched her full lips with his fingertips, and their eyes met. At that moment, all the passion and longing, all the lust that had been building inside of him like a storm since the moment they had first met, overwhelmed him.

Suddenly he grabbed Sheba and pulled her roughly to him, pressing his lips to hers. She yielded to his embrace, grabbing his hair and returning his kiss with desperate passion. He could feel her tongue against his fangs as each of them explored the warm wetness of the other's mouth, and his manhood grew and stiffened within the confines of his clothing. Slowly his hands began to move over the curves of her shapely body, and he fell back onto the ground.

Sheba straddled him, her hair spilling down over her shoulders and cascading about her body like fire, glowing vibrantly in the sun, and he felt her touch the hardness of his throbbing cock. He tugged anxiously at her clothing, stripping it away, and caressed her large, firm breasts in his hands. She responded by moving forward against him, her pink nipples hard and erect.

She moaned softly and wrapped her arms around his shoulders and back as he sucked on them, moving the tip of his tongue in circles, massaging her nipples within his mouth. Sheba tore away his loincloth, and her fingers closed around the thickness of his aching shaft. Her hand moved gently, up and down, causing the lust inside him to burn uncontrollably. How badly he wanted her!

Joktan rolled over and threw her onto her back upon the ground with a throaty growl. He sucked on her breasts while slipping his hand downwards, along the side of her stomach and hips, between her thighs. A sudden surge of excitement raced through him as he felt her wetness on his fingers.

He kissed her lips again, then began to move his kisses lower and lower along her naked body, following the direction in which his hands had traveled, and Sheba spread her legs in anticipation. He paused briefly, to lightly brush the tip of his nose against her shorn pubic mound and savor the musk of her aroma, before burying his face between her trembling, milky thighs. Joktan slid his hands beneath her buttocks and pulled her body tight against his waiting mouth.

How long he had waited for this moment, to taste her wetness!

Sheba's moans of pleasure drove him wild as she surrendered to the strokes of his tongue between her moist lips. He explored her, and the soft folds of her womanhood opened like the petals of a rose in the warmth of the morning sun, glistening with drops of dew.

Her cries grew louder as he sucked on her swollen clitoris and flicked his tongue about urgently, manipulating her senses, and causing her passion to grow more intense with every skillful touch, worshipping at the altar of her femininity. She gasped in surprise as his finger slipped inside her, gently probing her warm, moist slit, and then her entire body suddenly stiffened and shuddered.

He felt her contract inside, and Sheba closed her eyes and screamed in ecstasy as she burst into violent orgasm. The sensation burned through her like flames of raging fire; it rose like a tidal wave in the depths of her being before crashing wildly upon her, sweeping uncontrollably through every part of her body. It was as if lightening flashed behind her lids; she wrapped her slender fingers in Joktan's thick mane, grinding her quivering mound even harder against his face, against his mouth, and the soft warmth of his tongue between her folds.

As Sheba's throws subsided, Joktan moved upwards, kissing her deeply while kneading her heaving breasts. His face was slick and wet, and she could taste her own essence upon his lips. Her body now moved with his eagerly, wanting, needing, and she nipped at his neck with her teeth.

He positioned himself above, then entered her. She helped guide him with her hands, and his cock slipped in slowly, while he fought back the all-consuming desire to plunge into her as hard and fast as he could. She sucked in her breath sharply and moaned as he sank deeper and deeper inside her, inch by inch, allowing her time to envelop him inside of her, time to truly feel the length and thickness of his aching shaft.

At first his strokes were slow and steady, but soon he was no longer able to control himself, to restrain his desperate need to make her his. He drove his cock into her, faster and harder and deeper with every thrust, and Sheba arched her back and clawed at him madly, completely lost in the moment.

As he pounded against her like an angry bull, he felt her muscles tense up around his stiff shaft, and he knew instinctively that she was on the verge of cumming again.

She could feel his cock grow even harder inside her, and knew that he was fighting the urge to release. As she gazed up at him, Sheba saw a look of surprise sweep over his features, and she knew that he couldn't hold it back any longer. She moaned and moved her hips faster against him, in rhythm with his frenzied thrusts, and suddenly she felt her own sensations rise within her, and she cried out desperately as her body tensed in anticipation.

In that moment, as both of them trembled on the brink of orgasm, Joktan growled savagely and sank his fangs into her neck. Sheba gasped in shock as his sharp teeth tore through her soft, pale flesh, and she felt her blood flowing into his mouth. Then both of them burst into orgasm, surging against one another like ocean waves crashing violently upon a rocky shore.

Time seemed to stand still, as each rush of ecstasy coursed through their bodies in successive waves, and Joktan thrust hard and deep one last time as his manhood erupted, pumping hot inside of her, filling her with his essence.

His teeth sank deeper into her neck, and as the salty warmth of Sheba's blood began to fill his mouth, a cacophony of strange images and feelings swarmed uncontrollably into his mind. They were visions that were not his own, of dense, steaming jungles and rugged mountain peaks, lush valleys, and forested hills, but it was all somehow different. The world was different. There was a glow of light that seemed to shroud every living thing. It was a breath-taking image, of a pristine world filled with life and vibrancy, as if the Gods themselves walked and lived there.

He saw a meadow, and in the center of it a figure stood within a circle of stones. The form was that of a woman, and it shimmered with an ethereal radiance that drew him closer, pulling him toward her. She had long, golden hair that spilled in thick waves and ringlets from her head down past her buttocks, shining like silk in the light of the summer sun. Her face was like that of a goddess, more beautiful than any woman Joktan had ever seen, and her lithe form was well proportioned. Her skin was the color of burnished bronze, and she wore silver armbands, bracelets and anklets, and a curious necklace strung with amber and jet beads, but she wore nothing else.

She stood with her legs spread slightly apart, her arms raised in the air as she faced toward the north, her large, firm breasts heaving as she spoke some ancient tongue long since forgotten by men. But she was not of the race of men; this Joktan knew instinctively. As she stood within the circle, the wind blew back her silken tresses to reveal pointed ears.

She was an Elf!

The scene changed, and a man approached her. He stood tall and strong, and he too shone with the same radiance as the Elven woman. He had large wings that spread out about him as he strode to her. They were feathered, like those of birds, yet they also emitted the same ethereal light that shone about him and the woman so brightly. He was a Watcher, and Joktan marveled at the perfection of his features and the strength this man exuded. He felt a mysterious connection to this man, this Watcher, but the scene was gone before he could examine the feeling further. He watched as the pair embraced, then sank to the ground and made love with wild abandon.

Once more the scene changed. The Watcher was gone, but now strange men crept stealthily towards the woman. They resembled men in shape and form, but their bodies were covered in fine scales, glistening in the light of the fading sun. They charged upon the woman, and Joktan looked on in horror as they raped her.

He sought to release his grip on Sheba's neck, but something held him there and he was plunged into a world that he could not recognize. It seemed as though he were flying high overhead, looking down upon the world from the sky, but the scene had changed again, and now the sky was darkened by clouds of black smoke and ash. Grisly scenes of moldering corpses swept into view, bodies of the dead heaped high in countless mounds upon endless plains; men, Elves, Dwarves, Goblins, Trolls, and creatures too hideous to describe, all of them slaughtered and rotting in a sea of festering gore.

The Earth was stained red by rivers of blood and dark pools of rancid decay. The air was foul and putrid. It stung his eyes and burned like acid inside his nostrils. Death and destruction permeated everything he saw, and with it a feeling of hopelessness and despair that was so immense it seemed to consume his very soul.

He saw frightening storms rage through the heavens, hurling blinding bolts of lightening amid deafening bursts of thunder, and his senses reeled from the intensity and violence of the chaos. Great fires swept across the world, destroying every living thing in their path and leaving behind only desolation and smoldering ash.

And far off in the distance of this visage he began to sense the presence of something that was utterly malignant and terrifying. It pulled him closer against his will, and soon a terrible form loomed before him, a shadow far darker than the darkest night, more black than the deepest pit, and evil beyond the vilest torments of Hecate's hell. Never in his life had Joktan experienced the feeling of true fear, but in that moment it engulfed him, and it seemed as though he was being slowly and mercilessly suffocated.

The image faded, replaced only by a myriad of feelings, thoughts, and what seemed like ancient memories, but not those of his own kind. They were the memories of another race, in the dim past of now forgotten ages, as well as those of Sheba herself.

Memories of great joy and sadness, of relatives, friends, lovers, and foes. His mind was bombarded with thousands upon thousands of such images, and while some seemed to last a lifetime, all of them raced through his mind within a matter of seconds, but they were as tangible and real as the waking world in which he lived.

In the distance he heard a scream, then suddenly the images he beheld were gone, and he was once more on the plains, lying upon his back amid the tall, swaying grasses. His senses were distorted, his mind disoriented, his body soaked and dripping with sweat as he lay there, chest heaving, heart pounding wildly.

Sheba lay next to him, upon her back as well, her eyes closed. There was a painful expression on her face, and her breasts swelled as she gasped raggedly for breath. The sleek curves of her beautiful body glistened with perspiration, and her fiery hair was a tangled mess. He stared hard at her for a moment, confused and unsure, his brain still swimming from the sensory overload he had just experienced only a few short seconds before. There was much more to this woman than he could have ever guessed, and his mind filled with questions.

Who was she? *What was she?*

At last Sheba opened her emerald eyes, but her face was stern as she studied him. There was a strange, far-away look in her gaze, then finally she spoke.

"You should not have bitten me," she admonished him, "and you certainly should not have drank my blood."

Joktan shook his head. "I didn't mean to, it just sort of happened. I couldn't let go....and then the visions began. It was as though I was lost....or in another world."

He wasn't sure exactly what to say to her. He felt strange, as if his mind had traveled to another place, somewhere far away, and it was still out of sync with his body.

"I know what you saw," Sheba said softly, rolling onto her side to look at him. "I saw it too, for it was the memories of my people."

"I have never experienced such a thing before," he confessed. "My body is tingling even now, like a fire is coursing through my veins. I feel dizzy.... almost drunk......"

He stared knowingly at her. "Ever since we met, I knew there was something different about you, something I just couldn't put my finger on. And I have always known that you have not told me everything, that you've withheld certain details about yourself from me from time to time, and that's fair, for there are many things about me and my life that I have also withheld from you." His eyes held hers for a moment, then he looked away. "But I was not prepared for this."

"How could you have been!" Sheba replied. "And if I would have tried to explain it to you, would you have ever believed? Even now you are unsure about what you saw, about what you *felt*, and it is plain to see you are unsure about me."

Joktan sighed wearily. "No, you are right, of course, and it will probably take some time for me to sort out my feelings."

"Are you frightened?" Sheba asked quietly.

"Of course not!"

"It is all right if you are, Joktan," Sheba smiled. "I'm not like any other woman you have ever been with, and I can tell that at this moment you want to know who I truly am, for although you thought that you knew me, what you imagined was not entirely so. This you have seen simply by drinking my blood."

She drew closer and wrapped her pale arms around him, her head resting on his shoulder. Joktan could feel her heart beating in her chest, and he put his arms about her and held her tightly to him.

"I like who you are," he said, "it is *what* you are that perplexes me, but still I am not afraid. I feel a connection to you that is hard to describe. It wasn't there before, but now I sense it. Something familiar, yet ancient and powerful in such a way that even I do not understand."

"You saw much....far more than you should have," Sheba replied. *"You drank much more than you should have.* It was not just the memories that exist within my veins which filled your mind. When you bit me, your feelings washed over me like a wave, and combined with our orgasms, it was a powerful moment. You have the gift of sight, though I get the feeling that you have never really known until this moment." She frowned, studying his face.

"Aye," Joktan confirmed, "a gift from my mother, no doubt."

Sheba looked him in the eyes. "Or your father."

Her words struck him suddenly, like ice-cold water on a hot summer's day. It was as if they awakened some forgotten knowledge deep inside, some secret that he had once known but now couldn't quite recall. For a brief instant he struggled with it, but his mind was still swimming from the visions he had seen. He had enough to think about for the moment.

The feel of her naked body pressed tight against his was reassuring. Her womanly scent upon the gentle breeze filled his nostrils and awakened other feelings as well. Sheba sensed it immediately, and her hand slid down to touch his arousal.

His voice was a low, throaty rasp when he finally spoke. "I have wanted you since the moment I first saw you," he said, "hanging by your wrists in that big, brazen cage!"

"I know!" she laughed softly, "and the truth is, I've wanted you this whole time as well! I just didn't want to admit it to you," she confessed.

"Why not?"

"Because," Sheba replied, "in my land, women are warriors, not playthings."

"You are still a warrior," he said earnestly.

"Aye," she agreed, "and I could best you any day!" Her eyes sparkled with good-natured humor.

"Don't count on it!" Joktan snorted. "I've fought many warriors, and as I told you before, I never lose."

"Do not be so sure of yourself, Joktan," she taunted him. "After all, you *are* an uncivilized savage. Everyone must lose *sometime."*

"Aye," he rolled over onto his back and stared up at the sky, laughing heartily. "And lose they shall. *To my blade!"*

He sat up again and grew serious once more. "We must talk more about this, about what I saw, but we have tarried too long in this place already."

"Aye," Sheba agreed, "let us gather up our things and be off. We can talk as we travel."

"O.K.," he replied, "but before we do I need to have you one more time."

She looked down at his stiff manhood and smiled pleasantly.

"So I see!" she purred, licking her lips.

28

Within the narrow alleys,
The dregs of men await,
Unwary prey who hapless tread,
Like sheep to wolfish fate;
Daggers hiss like serpents,
Thieves slither at their backs,
To sheath steel blades in human flesh,
Then scurry off like rats.

----An old rhyme from Escalon.

Luxantia lay silently sleeping in a shroud of darkness as the priests of Dhampir gathered in their underground chamber in preparation for their nightly ceremony to their dark god. There was a feeling of dread in the air this night, however, for one of their more esteemed members had been recently slain. The very mention of it made many of the priests feel uneasy. It was very rare indeed that such danger was able to penetrate to the very heart of their sanctuary, in any of their numerous locations of worship.

So it was that when Skeltar entered and made his presence known, he was greeted with an equal mixture of shock and apprehension. He was renowned as a powerful sorcerer, with a reputation for shunning human companionship, preferring the

solitude of his gloomy castle.

In truth, both parties shared many common interests, chiefly the pursuit of arcane knowledge and supernatural power, but Skeltar possessed abilities far more dangerous than what even a thousand Dhampir priests could ever hope to muster by combining all their abilities at once. It was a fact that the priests here tonight were keenly aware of.

The wizard's icy gaze made even the oldest priests shudder with trepidation; his black, liquid eyes seemed to bore right into their very soul. It was as though something else peered out at them from behind those unearthly orbs--something ancient and unspeakably dreadful; something far from human.

His stare could reach right into their minds, probing the deepest recesses of their beings. Nothing could be kept hidden from him for very long. Indeed, it was physically painful to even try. And the thoughts which Skeltar could speak to them, without saying an audible word, were in themselves the very definition of terror. They carried with them an inescapable feeling of utter defilement and violation.

When the wizard finally spoke, the sound of his lifeless voice was like the dry rattle of a rattlesnake's tail. His words were uttered quietly, but every ear present could here them with absolute clarity.

"I have come in peace," the mage intoned, lacking any visible trace of emotion. "We share common interests, it would seem." His cold eyes swept the room slowly as he added, "mayhap we could help each other."

Adhra, the Chief High Priest, stepped forward to face the mage. "What could we offer one such as yourself, great wizard? Surely your power is sufficient already."

"True," Skeltar agreed arrogantly, "but it has come to my attention that you seek a certain woman and her companion. I too, plot their capture as we speak. I know that you had the woman here as a captive, for this I saw from my keep. I also saw the savage she travels with. You should know that I watched as he slew one of your brethren in this very room."

Adhra's forehead wrinkled in thought. "It seems very little escapes your sight," he replied acidly. "I find no pleasure in the thought of being spied upon."

He glared at the wizard intently, but even his many years of experience in the black arts were no match against the evil of this wicked mage. As he stared into the eyes of Skeltar, a horrible apprehension swept over him like a dark, malignant shadow. It felt as though his intestines were being slowly tied in knots. Adhra quickly averted his gaze, an act which in itself required all the power at his command.

"For what purpose do you seek the woman?" he asked, his voice scarcely more than a whisper.

"That, of course, is my own business," answered Skeltar coldly. "You don't really want her all *that* badly." He was using the voice of power, a hypnotic means of arcane suggestion. The priest of Dhampir wasn't even aware of it!.

"You do not really even need her at all," he continued, carefully gauging the inflections in his voice. "She was merely another sacrifice, just one of countless others."

His dark eyes fixed upon the high priest, unmoving. "It is the savage whom you truly seek. The one who defiled your temple but a year ago, and who recently killed one of your members."

Adhra felt like he was being lulled into a stupor. He tried to shake the feeling, but it was impossible. Skeltar's words were sinking into him like a barbed and baited hook. He realized too late that there was nothing he could do to stop it.

The wizard paused. "I have a gift for you," he said slowly after a moment of intense scrutiny. "Call it an act of good will."

Adhra's eyebrows raised in a questioning expression. He was clearly surprised. "And what is this gift, if I may be so bold as to ask?"

"Why, my very own apprentice!" Skeltar replied with a wry, creepy smile. "A far better sacrifice to your dread god than some common, worthless whore."

"We care little for the whore." Adhra was startled by his own response. *What am I saying?* He wondered silently. *She is of utmost importance!*

"That's right," Skeltar droned on. "She is of little use to you. You would rather have my apprentice. *Your god would rather have him too."*

"Yes....our god would rather have him too," the priest responded mechanically. "And in return?"

"In return I ask that you give me the woman, to do with as I please. You can have the savage as well, and in this way we both get what we seek."

Adhra struggled desperately to counteract the force of Skeltar's intrusive, piecing stare. "We do prefer to give our God women as gifts," he managed, summoning every last ounce of willpower in an attempt to break Skeltar's mental grasp. Some part of him wanted to tell this conceited mage exactly where to go in no uncertain terms, but the mesmerism was too strong. It held his mind in an iron grip, and he was incapable of uttering a refusal.

"The one of which we speak has already been anointed as an offering to our lord Dhampir. These are things we must consider."

The wizard frowned. He knew it must have taken an enormous effort for Adhra to reply in such a way. The priest was trying to break his spell by using phrases that were not direct refusals. Skeltar smiled inwardly. He knew this game all too well. He willed his mind deeper into that of the priest, flooding his consciousness with an overwhelming stream of images so blasphemous and obscene that Adhra impulsively took a step back.

The priest felt at once debased and defiled. His mind began to drown in a cacophony of diabolical torments. It seemed as if a demonic hand were prying at the locks on the vaults of his reason and sanity. Madness swept through him like a black swarm of flies on a festering corpse. He felt his stomach turning and struggled valiantly not to wretch----but overriding every other horror of this telepathic assault was an inescapable mental command to yield or die.

"Your God would be more pleased with the life of one who reviled him, than with that of a trull." Skeltar was telling him now. "After all, this barbarian stole a sacrifice that was intended for Dhampir himself! Consider what you must, but remember that time waits for no one, Adhra, not even those of us who seek the ancient glory and it's power! Accept my proposal, and you shall have your sacrifice on the morrow, just in time for the offering to the Sisters of Mercy in their dark lunar aspect. Do we have a bargain?"

"I must confer with my brothers; we make no decisions without complete agreement," he said hastily. "But this savage of whom you speak managed to steal an object of value from us as well as our sacrifice. It is the Face of Death, and we desire to have it back in our possession once more."

"Very well," Skeltar allowed, releasing his hold over Adhra's senses.

The priest shook his head suddenly, as if awakening from a nightmare too horrible to describe. He felt his faculties returning, like a breath of refreshing air, but he was also aware that a seed had been planted somewhere in his subconscious mind. Fear surged through him anew.

The wizard smirked knowingly and nodded, increasing Adhra's unease all the more. "There is another matter that I must attend to for King Xalton, but I am missing one of the final ingredients necessary to complete the work. Once this task is done, I shall be free to devote all of my powers toward capturing the woman and her companion." He gave the priest an inquiring glance. "Maybe you could help me, as a sign of good faith on your behalf, of course."

Adhra smiled. "What is it you require?"

"Nothing, really," Skeltar replied, "just a small piece of sacred parchment on which to write a spell. I have an abundance of it within my castle, but that is a long way from here."

So, even a mighty sorcerer can still forget things! Adhra wondered silently why Skeltar would openly admit to making a mistake. He wanted to refuse, to laugh in the wizard's withered face, but something deep within forbade it. When he spoke his response seemed foreign, as if someone else were speaking for him and he was listening from a distance.

"We will send you the parchment when the star of Regulus is overhead tonight."

Skeltar knew that the priest wanted to defy him. He sensed the inner turmoil this was causing him----the war now being waged deep within Adhra's soul as he discovered the inevitable futility of resistance----and he gloated triumphantly. If the priest thought this was the worst of it, he would be in for a terrible surprise!

"Very well," the mage replied thinly, "but do make haste. I would like to get on with this business as soon as possible."

With that the wizard turned and moved quickly away, mumbling something incomprehensible under his breath as he went. Adhra let out a sigh of relief as he watched him disappear into the shadows, but an eerie shiver fingered at his spine when he suddenly realized that Skeltar's feet were not touching the floor. It was as if the sorcerer was being pulled toward the direction in which he wished to move.

"How does he do that?" he priest muttered to himself as the wizard passed out of sight.

Skeltar sneered crookedly as he made his exit. It was a curse which he'd mumbled as he had turned to leave. In a few hours Adhra would be stricken with the worst case of boils and hemorrhoids anyone had ever seen.

"The Elven woman you saw, standing in the circle of stones, she was the mother of my kind," said Sheba, sweeping her hair away from her face with a pale hand. "Her name was Aradia, and she was the most powerful Elven witch to ever lived."

"And the Watcher?"

"His name is Uriel," she replied. "He is the Guardian of the Northern Watchtower, a place of power called Uriel's Keep, and he is also the father of my race."

"You speak of the woman as if she no longer lives," Joktan commented, "yet you refer to the Watcher as if he were still alive."

"Aye," Sheba replied, "the things you saw took place very long ago. Uriel yet lives, but Aradia nearly died during childbirth. She now slumbers in the Garden of Ellyllon, the resting place of the Elven Queens."

"So they were lovers, then," he surmised aloud.

"That they were," she sighed. "It was to be a glorious event, the union of two immortal bloodlines, both ancient and powerful."

Joktan frowned. "Such things were forbidden in ancient times."

"Quite true," she replied, "but only amongst the race of men. The union of men and Watchers led to the birth of giants, the Nephilim. They were a terrible race, bloodthirsty and cruel, and most human women died giving birth to them. However, such unions were not forbidden among the Elves, for they were and still are immortal, and pure souls. But the union you witnessed was different."

Joktan couldn't help thinking of his own ancestry, of the fact that his father was a Watcher, and of the Elven blood which he now knew flowed through his own veins. Had his birth been forbidden as well?

"The union of Aradia and Uriel was for a grand purpose," Sheba continued. "It was to give rise to a new race, a race that possessed the power and magick of both bloodlines, but one which would also live amongst men. This race would live to protect the world against the power of the Black Scroll."

"So your people are this race of which you speak?" asked Joktan curiously.

"Yes," she replied, "but we are few in number."

"Obviously not that few, if you have your own kingdom," he returned.

Sheba laughed. "We are the rulers of the Lothairians, but the people who inhabit the land are of the race of men. They are a beautiful people, with skin the color of burnished bronze. They are our protectors, for very few know the things I am telling you, and in truth, only my mother and I remain of our kind, and she will soon cease. We are not truly their governors, though, for they have their own Queen, their own rulers. We are the secret they live to protect."

"So you are not really a princess," Joktan said, "yet you call yourself a ruler. A future Queen."

"My mother is Queen at the present time, and I shall take her place upon my return," she explained.

"The people of our land called themselves Lydians long ago, and we lived among them. They knew of our origins, for they were friends to the Elves. Their rulers also knew why we were created, and they promised both the Watchers and the Elves that they would protect us, and keep our existence and our purpose a secret."

She fell silent for a while, and Joktan didn't press her to continue, for he was lost in contemplation. What chance had brought the two of them together? If what Sheba said was true, and he knew inside himself that it must be, then both of them had been fathered by Watchers and birthed by powerful witches. Joktan's people were dying out, their lands now being taken over slowly but surely by the more civilized kingdoms to the south, and Sheba's people were now gone, for all intents. And what was this Black Scroll of which she spoke? He had never heard of it before.

Her words broke in upon his thoughts. "My mother and I are of the strongest bloodline of the Lothairians. We are direct descendants, and we are the last of our kind. We were once the rulers of the Lothairians, that is why she is the Queen, and I am soon to take her place and title. But before I am truly Queen, I must give birth to a child of my own, for it will be impossible afterwards, and when I cease to live, my race will be forever gone."

Joktan was confused. "I don't understand. Why will you not be able to give birth after you are Queen?"

Sheba looked away into the distance, and a painful expression suddenly swept across her face. Her voice shook with anger when she spoke.

"You saw the rape of Aradia. The reptilian star people, the ones who defiled our race and brought the curse upon all our kind," she said bitterly. "They were the *Morashi,* the ones who desecrated the Earth. When they raped our mother, their seed was mingled. It corrupted the union of Aradia and Uriel, and has been the bane of our existence ever since."

"I still don't understand."

Sheba looked at him then, and there was a fire burning in her eyes such as he had never seen before. Although her voice was soft and measured, the light in her eyes was that of pure rage. "The bloodlust!" she said. "The Morashi lived long lives, but they were not immortal! They polluted our bloodline at it's very conception, and we have been forced to live with it ever since."

The small town of Makron was really nothing more than a glorified village, but it was the trade routes crossing through it which had made it's population increase so rapidly over the last thirty years.

Makron had no walls or defenses. There were no soldiers loitering about in the taverns, waiting impatiently for some unseen uprising or attack. Tradesmen of every kind set up make-shift shops in the myriad tents that lined the dusty byways and narrow streets, causing the small town to look more like a carnival than a center of commerce.

Traveling caravans, adventurers, bandits, nomads and wandering mercenaries passed through Makron with little notice. It was rare for anyone to stay very long, for the town had little to offer those intent on making a quiet home for themselves. Here the greatest demand was for the mending and repairing of broken equipment and clothes, and even the tradesmen who plied their talents never remained in Makron for more than a few months before moving on to larger cities where their professions would be in greater demand. For the most part, their absence was never noticed.

When Joktan and Sheba strode into town, their arrival caused little more than a sideways glance in the crowded streets. After securing lodging in one of the few wooden buildings amid the endless maze of canvas shops, they made their way to the nearest bathhouse to wash away the dust of travel and grime of battle.

Feeling much refreshed, Sheba located a tavern where they sat down to a welcome meal of boiled vegetables and roast boar, served in an unleavened trencher. It was complimented by a generous supply of watered-down ale, a local variety made from fermented barley and certain roots indigenous to the region.

It had taken them the better part of six days to reach Makron on foot, and the canvas above their heads provided a much-needed reprieve from the blistering heat of the mid-day sun. The occasional gust of wind made it flap noisily like a giant sail. The large poles that held up the roof swayed and shook violently, straining the thick hemp ropes that had been used to hold them securely in place.

Once their meal was finished, Joktan set out to locate two trustworthy mounts. He had very little gold left now, and even with what Sheba had given him, his purse was empty by the time he had purchased new steeds. A few coppers and three silver pieces were all that remained of the considerable amount of wealth he had possessed only a couple of weeks before. While he stabled their mounts and readied them for an early morning departure, Sheba set off to secure provisions for the next leg of their journey.

Joktan's idea of shopping for food was usually just a matter of picking out which member of the herd to kill, so he had wisely decided it would be best if Sheba handled the bartering for their victuals. As well, he wasn't very picky when it came to filling his stomach, and this way there would be no chance of him packing food which Sheba might not care for. He wasn't too sure what type of fare she preferred, but Joktan he was fairly certain that she wasn't fond of such delicacies as raw hearts torn still beating from chests of wild beasts.

As he wandered the town, he stopped to talk to several merchants. He had hoped to sell the obsidian skull he had taken from the dead priest in Luxantia, but it seemed no one was interested. All who saw the skull grew fearful, and one merchant in particular became so distraught that he threatened to draw his sword if Joktan didn't take it away immediately. Soon he gave up trying to locate a buyer.

When he had first stolen the skull, he had also taken a curious-looking curved dagger, which he yet carried, thrust beneath his belt. The thought of selling it had briefly crossed his mind, but after seeing the way these merchants reacted to the obsidian skull, he surmised that such a move would be unwise.

The byways were filled with strangers from many lands, and as he wandered about he noted their diversity of dress and speech with interest. After meandering aimlessly about the town for some time, he turned back toward the tavern where they had eaten a few hours before. Sheba had chosen it as a rendezvous point.

By now he was a considerable distance away, so he chose a shorter route, via a series of narrow alleyways that wound through the endless rows of canvas tents. It was beginning to get dark out, and most people preferred the busy streets instead of risking the dangers of a shadowy alley. Joktan, however, was accustomed to such places and the perils that frequently prowled them, so he fearlessly struck out for the tavern through the by-ways without so much as a second thought.

Suddenly a man stepped out from the shadows, a long dagger held tightly in his dirty, knotted fist. Joktan stopped short, just in time to feel the point of a second blade pressed firmly against his back.

He could not see the assailant behind him, but the man facing him grinned wickedly as he approached. He was missing several teeth, and a deep scar ran down one side of his pockmarked face. It started just above his eye and ended at his jaw.

Instantly Joktan was on guard. The villain before him stepped confidently, waving his dagger from side to side, the steel blade flashing ominously in the shadows.

"Those be nice swords you carry, outlander," he grated at Joktan with a sinister sneer. "I'll be having them, and your purse too!"

The tribesman froze, and the man moved closer. He could smell the slovenly stench of his body odor, sweat mingled with ale and strong drink.

"Don't try to be courageous, stranger," the thief warned, "or you'll be skewered from behind as well as by me."

"Aye," Joktan muttered with a sigh, as if to comply with their demands. "I reckon my gold will do me no good if I am dead, though I have precious little of it to be sure."

Both men laughed. "You are wise, my friend," the one in front said evenly, "now hurry it up, or it shall not go well for you."

Joktan raised both hands in the air. "Don't hurt me," he said, trying his best to sound scared and defenseless. "Come but a little closer and I'll give you what you seek."

He felt the pressure on the blade at his back ease slightly, as if the man behind him had relaxed. These cutthroats were sure of themselves. Too sure. It was what he was waiting for.

In that instant Joktan spun to the side. He grabbed the assailant behind him by the hand holding the dagger, clamping his own hand tightly over that of the villain's while his left hand grasped the mans elbow. Before his foe had time to move, Joktan turned his wrist inwards and pulled down violently on his elbow, bending the man's arm and plunging the dagger deep into his throat. In the gloom of the narrow walkway he could see a look of shock and terror upon the dying man's features as blood frothed about the hilt of the dagger and spilled down over his chest.

Joktan spun around once more, maintaining an iron grasp on his attacker while using his body as a human shield, and the thief who had spoken thrust his blade at him. The dagger stabbed deeply into the back of the man's own comrade, and Joktan released his hold and dropped to his knees. There was the familiar rasp as his sword cleared the scabbard and he thrust with deadly speed.

His foe let out a sharp, piercing cry as he was skewered through the thigh, then screamed again as Joktan wrenched his blade free. The thief grabbed painfully at his wounded leg and sank to the ground as his would-be victim rose to his full height, and there was a desperate, fearful look in his frightened eyes.

It was a look of indescribable surprise, of anguish and horror, and of sudden dread; it was the wide-eyed panic of one who has suddenly realized that they are about to die. His own blood dripped red upon him from the sword held high above, and trickled down his face as sharpened steel flashed in the darkness.

In the next instant it was over.

Joktan's blade slammed into the thief's neck, just above the shoulder. The man crumbled under the weight of the vicious blow, nearly decapitated. A tiny shred of flesh was all that held his head to his body, and it lolled grotesquely to the side in a growing pool of dark blood.

Suddenly the impact of what had just transpired struck him. He had moved with blinding speed, far exceeding his normal ability. It had taken him but a few brief seconds to dispatch these ruffians, and he had accomplished the task so quickly that neither one of them could have ever had a chance of defending themselves.

As he gazed down upon their lifeless corpses, a powerful bloodlust began to swell within him, such as he had never felt before. The act of killing had brought with it relief and satisfaction, but the sight of their blood congealing in the dust aroused another feeling in the pit of his stomach, and it wasn't that of revulsion. Instead it was a hunger, a thirst he desperately desired to quench.

He closed his eyes for a moment. It felt as though his head were spinning, like he was slightly drunk. He was confused, but at the same time, his senses felt keener than they had ever been. He could hear sounds that would have normally been much too faint to perceive, like the gentle scurrying of a shrew some thirty paces further down the alleyway. He shook his head to clear it and glanced down at his feet.

"Try to rob me, will you!" Joktan growled at the corpse with an angry kick, before wiping his sullied blade on the dead man's clothes.

He glanced about to see if his brief fight had been noticed, but the walkway was deserted. He knew, however, that it would not be long before the bodies would be discovered, and he did not want to be present when they were.

Sheathing his sword, he snatched up the purses of the two thieves and hefted them; they were fairly heavy, a fact which pleasantly surprised him. He transferred the contents of the two coin purses into his, casting the empty pouches away, before disappearing silently into the gloom.

He hurried along for a few minutes, turning into one narrow alley, then another, just in case some unseen witness was following him, for one could never be too certain. After traveling rapidly for several more minutes, he ducked into another walkway on his right and suddenly stopped short.

In the middle of the alley were four bodies, all men, piled in a heap. Curiously, Joktan drew nearer, glancing furtively into the darkness of the night. All was quiet and still, save for the rustling and flapping of countless tents in the gentle breeze that swept across the plains and the indistinct voices of drunken men babbling incoherently somewhere down the nearby street.

After a closer look, the cause of their demise became plainly apparent. Their throats had been torn open, but these were no sword wounds. It looked as if it had been done by claws. Each man was armed with a sword, yet none had drawn their blade in defense, for all of their swords were still sheathed. The ground should have been covered in blood, but strangely, not a drop could be found, neither on their clothing nor in the dust about them. And stranger still, he discovered, not a one of the men had been robbed. Each man still had a full purse of coins tied securely to his belt!

The small hairs on the back of his neck stood on end, and instinctively his hand sought the reassurance of steel. What sort of evil foe had these dead men encountered, an enemy that could kill four armed men before even a one of them could draw his a blade? What could kill without leaving the slightest trace of blood? Since none of them had been robbed, it was obvious that they had not been attacked for their money, though he quickly decided to relieve them of it now, seeing as they would have no further use for it.

Joktan stared at the corpses a moment longer, trying to make sense of it all, looking for some sort of clue that could tell him something about the nature of the foe these men had encountered. He found nothing, sensed nothing, except a growing feeling of uneasiness deep inside. He had to get away from here, and he had to do it fast. Those voices down the street were getting closer now, and if he was spotted here, he would be suspected of murder and the entire town would be after him.

He scooped up the coin purses of the murdered men and stowed them away, then rose swiftly and hurried into the night like a shadow drifting silent in the dark. He moved quickly, careful not to let himself be seen of heard, blending into the gloom. Upon reaching a main throughway, he slowed his pace to a brisk walk until he eventually arrived at the tavern where he and Sheba had agreed earlier to meet.

He entered, pausing to allow his vision to adjust to the illuminated interior, and spotted Sheba. She was seated alone in the far corner of the tavern, and he quickly made his way around the crowded tables to where she waited, casually sipping a from a flagon of wine.

She smiled warmly at him, and in an instant the adventures of the evening vanished from his mind as he stared into her emerald eyes. Her hair shimmered like fire in the soft glow of the oil lamps that hung from the poles overhead, and his gaze wandered briefly, down the contours of her graceful neck, halting for a moment on her pale breasts.

"It's about time you showed up," her voice interrupted his gaze, and he looked up to see her grinning brightly. Her usually pale cheeks seemed to have a ruddy glow. "The men in this place act like I am the only woman they have seen in years."

Joktan returned her smile. He'd noticed the way the other patrons were eyeing her when he had been making his way over to her. "Likely," he chuckled, "you're the only real woman they have laid eyes on for some time." He studied her for a couple seconds, then added, "the only one that matters, at least."

"How sweet!" she replied demurely, pushing a flagon towards him across the table. He accepted it gratefully, taking a long draught. It was surprising how thirsty a man could feel after a just a little bit of killing.

"Of course," he teased, "it could be that these men think you to be a trull!"

Sheba shot him a fiery glare. "If you had not returned just now, I might have gone searching for you amongst the whores!"

Joktan laughed heartily, then grew serious. He leaned over the table toward her, and when he spoke, it was in a subdued tone.

"I was detained by a pair of cutthroats," he informed her, "and I also saw a strange sight, such as I have not encountered before."

"Oh?"

"Aye," he nodded sternly, before giving her an abbreviated account of what he had seen on his way to the tavern. She listened quietly as he told her of how he had not been able to find a single drop of blood on the murdered men, and of how their throats had been so viciously ripped apart. When he had finished his tale, he took another draught of wine and looked at her gravely.

"All of this leads me to believe that some evil stalks this town tonight. Even a beast leaves it's victims bloodied. At first I thought that those men's throats had been torn open by claws, but now, after thinking about it more," he shook his head, "I think that something or someone simply took a huge bite out of them." He took another swig of wine. "What it could be, I do not know. We must be wary."

Sheba raised her eyebrows thoughtfully. "We are in a strange place, in a strange land. It sounds as if something drank the blood of those men. At least, that is the only logical conclusion, is it not?"

"Aye," Joktan agreed. "I thought likewise. Even though it sounds crazy, it is the only explanation."

"We should not spend too long here," she said, glancing around the room. "If there is one such beast on the prowl, it would be wise to assume there are others as well."

Joktan shook his head agreeably. "I think we should leave right now!"

"What?" Sheba exclaimed. "We have only just arrived! I want to stay till morning. I'm not afraid to spend the night in this place, and if some bloodthirsty fiend attacks us, I am quite confident that we can protect ourselves. Chances are, whatever did this won't come looking for us. It obviously lurks in the back ways, and this is a very big town. There is nothing to fear at the moment."

"I am not afraid!" Joktan growled indignantly. "I fear nothing, but I also know that there is something amiss here. It is not right, and I don't think it is natural either."

"I don't care!" Sheba declared flatly. "I have been sleeping for over two weeks on the barren ground, with bugs and spiders and tree crabs and....whatever else! I want to sleep in a bed tonight, with blankets and pillows and fresh, clean straw, and I'll be damned before I run from anything just because it kills unwary idiots and drinks their blood."

Joktan glowered at her from his side of the table. He was very clearly displeased, and he uttered a string of profanities under his breath in his native tongue before addressing her again.

"Very well," he consented at last, "but we leave in the morning at dawn."

Sheba's face lit up suddenly, and that pleasant smile played once more upon her features. "Good then, it's all settled!" she announced merrily. "Now let's enjoy ourselves for the evening, shall we?"

Joktan shrugged his shoulders and sighed heavily. How foolish of him to be so cautious, so superstitious! It was plain to see that Sheba was unconcerned, at least for the moment. He knew that he had a tendency to be overly cautious at times; maybe this was one of them. He looked over at her and thought about it. Maybe what he truly needed was a good nights sleep. Maybe what he really needed even more than that was a taste of her wetness! A night of wild, drunken sex would definitely make him feel much more relaxed, and by the looks of things, she already had a head start on him in the drink department!

"Maybe you're right," he said to her with a grin. "I'm going to get some more wine, and we are going to get drunk."

"Now that sounds like a plan!" Sheba laughed.

"Aye," Joktan agreed. "And then I'm going to take you back to our room and do some very naughty things to you!"

The riders had been traveling at a relentless pace across the plains, but now they brought their mounts to an abrupt halt. The road before them was blocked by the carcass of a massive beast, the likes of which none of them had ever seen. It's scaled sides and stomach had been torn open, and there were numerous gashes all over its heavily muscled frame. Flies buzzed about the rotting hulk by the thousands, swarming to feed and breed in the vile stench of rot and decay. Crows, vultures and ravens fought incessantly for supremacy over the carnage.

While their horses stood panting raggedly in the scorching heat, the riders dismounted and carefully studied the remains of the strange and terrible looking beast. There were definite signs of a struggle, and each of the eight women began to scour the area around the carcass for further clues as to what had occurred here. They could well imagine that the battle had been a desperate one indeed, for such a creature must have certainly put up a terrible fight.

"This Leviathan has not been dead for very long," Chia observed, turning up her nose and making an awful face. The overwhelming reek made the air about them almost unfit to even breath. "The hyenas and jackals haven't gotten to it yet."

She turned to her companions. "Shyla, Brashi, look around quickly. The rest of us will continue on down the road a ways."

"As you wish," Shyla replied, "we will not be long."

Chia pushed several strands of loose hair away from her face, tying them back into a pony tail behind her head, then addressed the others. "Keep an eye out for more of these beasts, and look for other corpses as well. It may be that whoever slew this thing did not live very long thereafter."

With that Chia and five of her warriors remounted and moved off down the road, while Shyla and Brashi searched the area for anything that might be of interest. Finally satisfied, the two remaining women reclaimed their mounts and galloped away. A few leagues further down the dusty road, all eight riders met up once more and halted to confer.

"What did you find?" Chia questioned Shyla as her horse chewed on the grasses that grew tall around them.

"We found several broken arrows, a broken sword, and some bloody strips of cloth," the other replied, holding out the various items for her inspection. "There was also another sword, but it is lodged in the mouth of the beast."

"I do not recognize these type of arrows, though," Brashi informed their leader, a puzzled expression on her exotic features. "They seem to be northern, but that is all I can surmise. Perhaps they were purchased from an arms dealer and then re-fletched at some later date."

"What makes you think they were fashioned by a northerner?" Chia asked, handing the items back to Brashi.

"Well, the fletching is done with sinew, while most civilized people use strong, waxed thread. Whoever did it cut the feathers fairly wide, not as slender and sleek as those we would use in the southern kingdoms. It is done this way in the north lands, not just on arrows, mind you, but on javelins and short spears as well."

Chia smiled, pleased with her companion's observations. "The man traveling with the daughter of the Blood Goddess is said to be a savage from the northlands. Judging from what you have just told me, I would guess that it was he who slew this beast. It is not common to find northerners in this area, and we know that he went south from Luxantia through the Black Mountains, so it is safe to believe that he passed through here not long ago."

"Well, that is most encouraging, for there is one other detail which I have not told you yet," Shyla said.

Chia turned her attention toward her blonde trussed comrade. "Do tell."

Shyla couldn't help but crack a smile. "There were two distinctly different sets of foot prints in the area of the kill. One was obviously that of a man, but the other was smaller, more slender. More like ours."

"So it was a man and a woman," Chia deduced. Anything else?"

"Yes," Shyla replied. "It was, as you guess, a man and a woman, but from the way that the grass was matted down nearby the kill site, it would seem that they wrestled with each other for a while. They certainly rested there, I'd say for several hours at least. I know this sounds strange, but it is the only conclusion that I can reasonably conceive of from the signs left in the grass."

Chia's features furrowed in thought, then she looked at Shyla. "Why would they wrestle? It makes no sense."

"My thoughts exactly," Shyla concurred, "but perhaps they were not wrestling at all. If it were two men, I could see it. But a man and a woman, traveling together as companions----I think they could have been engaged in something of a more personal nature......"

"Right after battling a Leviathan? I would find the very thought of it repulsive myself," Brashi interjected. "I mean, all the blood and guts and gore----the very stench of it all, not to mention the mess----its unthinkable!"

"Did you notice anything else of importance?" asked Chia.

"Well, that is another strange thing," Shyla replied. "A little further from the kill site we found several dead ostriches. They had been shot with the same sort of arrows as was used on the beast, so obviously the same person killed them as well, but once again, I cannot fathom why someone would kill such a bird for no reason. They were left to rot just like the beast."

Chia pondered this for a moment. "Some things that are easy to deduce; others pose a great mystery. Forget about the ostriches and the wrestling for now. Those details are probably inconsequential at this time. But even so, from everything else you have noticed we can ascertain at least one thing that seems certain."

She paused, gazing seriously at her companions. "We now know that two people passed through this area; a man and a woman. One is from the northern lands. They came from the direction of the Black Mountains, and at least one of them can fight extremely well."

Shyla nodded her agreement. "We also know that the town of Makron is situated not far from here. It is closer than any other civilized place. If I had just journeyed through those cursed peeks and fought a huge beast, possibly getting wounded in the process----I would definitely head for Makron. I would want to rest a while and purchase victuals before continuing on my journey, so that is where we must go next. But we must travel quickly, for they will not tarry there too long."

My dreams smolder to ashes,
Warm Summers burnt to dusk;
My gleaming helm of youthful Spring,
Now lies riven in rust.
My hopes have fled unbidden,
Leaves borne on Autumn's wind;
Dark shadows slowly lengthen,
As Winter's chill creeps in.

-----Excerpt from the *Chronicles of King Xalton*

King Xalton lay exhausted upon his floating bed, fatigue overshadowing his frail form like a gray and ghastly specter. Weariness grew steadily upon him with every passing day. It took all of his strength just to go about his daily duties and routines. The flesh sagged from his aching bones like a hanged man from the gallows, his once toned and firm physique now soft and flabby from decay.

Only a few weeks ago he could have enjoyed the pleasures of ten women in a single day, with energy and strength to spare, a fact that the virile king was quite proud of. But it had been nearly twelve days since he had last bedded one of his beauties, and that one woman had left him feeling spent and exhausted. Now as his vitality slowly slipped away, the king doubted if he would ever again enjoy such carnal pastimes before choking out his final breath.

Today he had summoned another wizard to the palace, a mage renowned in the lands far to the east, albeit little known in all of King Xalton's vast domains. His reasoning for doing so was simple; it had been over sixteen days since he had sent his elite female warriors to locate the strange woman who supposedly held his cure, and as of yet the whereabouts of both the red-haired wench and his warriors was still unknown.

As for that cursed sorcerer Skeltar, it had been even longer since his departure to Luxantia, and as far as the King could surmise from the few, brief messages he'd received, the wizard was far from returning with a cure anytime soon.

That the untrustworthy wizard had a complete squadron of the King's Imperial soldiers at his command did not bode well with him. What Skeltar was truly up to was anybody's guess, and the King grew more and more uneasy about it every day.

He wondered too what had become of Brutus. He was a dedicated soldier, with awards and decorations of valor to prove it many times over. He was also an extremely motivated man, a fact that caused the king to retain a certain measure of wariness towards him. Brutus would still be a lower general if his bitter rival Marcus had not died so unexpectedly. Many times King Xalton had pondered it, and although Brutus was an exemplary soldier, Marcus had been possessed of a quality which, try as he might, Brutus could never hope to match or attain. The King strongly suspected that Brutus had played a clandestine role in bringing about the untimely death of the one he'd envied so much, an outstanding general who'd had the most impeccable character of any man the King had ever known.

That was why he'd selected Brutus to accompany the wizard Skeltar to Luxantia. Brutus had few friends, and even fewer family members. Even his women never stayed with him for any real length of time. In spite of his few redeeming qualities, his death was not likely to be mourned.

Due to the nature of the mission--and the one who led it--he'd sent only those who were expendable, and Brutus was one such man who fit the bill.

As well, King Xalton had never been the type of man to place all his eggs in one basket, and if a sorcerer under his employ happened to be keeping his Royal Highness in the dark, it stood to reason that the king should employ another mage. This second wizard could retrieve any information which Skeltar might be concealing for his own arcane intents, while providing some added protection for the king at the same time. It was never a good idea to hire a wizard to do your bidding, for they could rarely be trusted at the best of times. There was always an ulterior motive.

However, to fight or kill a wizard was a dangerous task indeed, and not something to be taken lightly. To slay such a foe, one would need to be able to counter any spell or evil that he might summon against you, and only another wizard was capable of accomplishing such a feat.

Such were the king's reason for seeking out another mage, and now that very wizard stood humbly before him, his head held low in a respectful posture. King Xalton motioned to be moved to the edge of the great pool, and as several of his naked maidens propelled him forward, he studied the newcomer curiously.

His clothing was comprised of a pair of long breeches that covered his feet, a loose fitting tunic, and a long, flowing robe. All were crimson, spun from the finest silk and embroidered with golden designs of eastern astrology and magickal symbols. A broad belt made of thick, black silk wrapped around his waist several times and tied in front in a square knot.

The wizard wore a most peculiar type of boots; the soles appeared to be fashioned from soft leather, but were split in the front, so that the big toe of each foot was separated from the rest of the toes. The tops of these boots were made of a heavy cloth that was wrapped around the calf and leg and was held securely in place by strong cords. These cords were made of black, braided silk, and thin silver wire had been woven into them for decoration. To these cords, several small, magickal amulets were attached here and there, for what purpose, only the wizard himself could say for sure.

His head was shaved bald, except for a long black braid that protruded from the back of his head and reached nearly to the ground. It was tipped with a silver spear point, quite curious indeed. The diminutive man had a long, gray, goatee-type of beard that hung down past his chest on each side.

His name was Quan Chang Xu. King Xalton had heard about him from one of his personal guards, the one whose name was Chia. She had often spoke of this strange little man, and believed him to be the most powerful wizard in the world.

King Xalton had actually sent for Quan Chang Xu before summoning Skeltar to his chambers, but it had taken a very long time for the mage to journey from his home in Zhenya to the palace in Straltonia.

The King was not a very patient man, and he had decided that the eastern mage likely wasn't coming. So he'd sent for the closest wizard he could find at the time. Now as he considered the course of recent events, he wished inwardly that he had waited just a little longer.

The wizard was silent for a long time before addressing the king, so long, in fact, that King Xalton almost began to wonder if maybe the mage hadn't fallen asleep on his feet. When he finally spoke, his voice was low and wavering. He had a curious accent, much like Chia's, but with a different tinge to it. The king imagined the man to be far older than he appeared.

A brightness shone from his slanted eyes, a gleam of light not unlike that of untamed youth, full of vigor and warmth. Simply just peering into the wizard's steady gaze produced a calming effect, making the king feel instantly at ease.

"Your problems are many, Oh King," the little man said softly, and there was kindness in his voice. "More intricately woven that the web of a spider. When I first received your request, I wanted to help, but was already employed by the Emperor of my homeland in Zhenya's Golden City. I made my journey when my work was complete, and have arrived here now."

The wizard paused. "For two full cycles of the Mother Moon have I considered your request," he motioned as he spoke, "and as I traveled to meet you your problems grew even greater about you. This I saw from far away, for nothing is hidden from my sight, your Highness."

The wizard gestured, seeking the king's approval to be seated. "I am an old man, as you can clearly see, and even my staff grows weary of supporting me at times!" he chuckled humorously.

This granted, he accepted a glass of wine from one of the king's women nearby and made himself comfortable before continuing to speak, sitting cross-legged on a large, soft cushion. He admired the lass, then glanced at the king with an impish smile.

"Now where was I?" he asked, almost as if he where talking to himself. He frowned and began scratching his glistening, bald head with his long, gnarled fingernails. "I am truly sorry, but I must confess she distracted me for a moment…."

"Oh yes!" he exclaimed suddenly, and his face lit up once more with a pleasant glow. "I was explaining why I could not get here sooner. For not only was I delayed in service to my own king, but the season of snow and ice rests upon my homeland at this time of the year, and it makes travel quite cumbersome and slow," he smiled good-naturedly. "Even for wizards!"

As he spoke the wizard produced a silver cylinder. It was elaborately engraved with magickal symbols and encrusted with glittering jewels. He carefully removed the cap and pulled out a piece of white silk, then spread it out a small table that had been placed before him by his apprentice.

Upon this cloth was drawn what appeared to be an astrological chart of the heavens, but it didn't resemble anything the king had ever seen. He was familiar with the common zodiac symbols, the crab, scorpion, the archer, and so forth. But this chart bore a tiger, a snake, a ram, and even a chicken! There were other creatures depicted on it too, accompanied by a strange form of writing and numerous arcane symbols.

"I will tell you what I have seen, that your knowledge may be increased," Qua Chang Xu informed him softly, placing a small jade amulet in the center of the chart. He moved his hands over the surface of the cloth, just a hairs breadth above it, chanting and moaning with his eyes tightly closed. After a few moments the wizard fell silent, then at last he spoke, though his eyes were still closed.

"I see a young warrior, not yet a man. He has the teeth of the tiger, and is a great fighter, even in the ways of my people, something very rare in this part of the world," he mused.

"He has found favor with the gods. You seek him out even now, but others do as well."

The mage was silent once more, as if listening intently to some unheard voice, then suddenly he looked up at the king in genuine surprise. His voice held an edge of excitement as he continued.

"You already know this man! Or at least you have dealt with him before, for there is a price on his head by your Royal Decree."

King Xalton's brow furrowed, deep in thought. Then he nodded, finally remembering an event that had transpired some time back. It seemed like long ago--or was it? Why, it was only a year ago!

"Yes," he replied to the wizard. "I do recall such a warrior, only if my memory serves me correctly, he was to be executed as a thief."

The mage was silent as the king thought a few moments longer.

"That's it!" he said at last, snapping his fingers loudly. "He broke into a temple to rob it. He was then thrown into the dungeon awaiting death, but he escaped. Only person to ever do it too, I might add. He killed over two score of my Imperial Guardsmen! The dungeon was bathed in blood by the time he was gone."

The king looked quizzically at the wizard. "What does that villain have to do with my illness?"

Qua Chang Xu smiled wisely. "You shall soon see!" he declared, withdrawing another stone amulet from a secret fold in his silken robe. This one was fashioned of opal, and it dazzled brightly as he placed reverently upon the silk chart. After a few more moments of chanting and moaning, the wizard raised his head and addressed the king.

"You seek a woman, believing her to hold the cure to what ails you. At this time she travels to her homeland, and that man travels with her. This woman journeys to receive a crown."

After a brief silence the mage added. "She can cure you, although to be completely healed you must take back the blood you gave to another. A great power awaits this woman. She is both death and eternity, and you have been mislead into searching for her, to fulfill the wicked desires of another man. You must treat her well when she arrives, and if you harm her companion, great misfortune will befall you."

Now the wizard held out another small stone in the palm of his hand. It was uncut, appearing to be a piece of jet. He paused, then placed it upon the cloth beside the other two stones and sighed deeply.

"This is your ailment. It is also the one who seeks to kill you. He desires to kill not only you, but the woman too. In time he will try to slay the young warrior as well. He is a wizard, such as myself, but he knows only evil, and his mind has been twisted and polluted by the black arts. He desires to wear your crown and to seat himself upon your throne, till the whole world cowers and trembles at his feet. He is in league with darkness, and if left to his devices, he will plunge your kingdom into a time of unfathomable evil and torment."

"I knew it!" exclaimed the frail king, his sunken eyes bulging with sudden rage. "I should have never summoned Skeltar to my chambers!"

The mage gazed sternly now at the king. "You should not have given him of your blood, for that is a symbol of your life and mortality." His voice shook, and his face became grave and concerned.

"You are in terrible danger, Oh King, and even now death waits, impatient to snuff out your life," Qua Chang Xu intoned seriously. "There is another, in league with Skeltar, who conspires against you, but the image is shrouded and vague. This person's identity is obscured from me at the present time by sorcery, a disturbing thing indeed, for it is someone close to you--someone you trust. It is imperative that you conduct yourself with the utmost caution."

King Xalton cast his eyes away and stared off at the far corner of the room. His mind was working hard to comprehend what the sorcerer had just told him. Who was this other person, the one he trusted? How could he have ever been so foolish, to have listened and given aid to a wizard who sought to kill him? And take my throne? I'll be damned before that happens!

He looked at the little wizard helplessly, as if pleading for his life to some higher power. "What can I do?" he asked plaintively, his voice filled with hopelessness and despair.

The wizard smiled, and touched the king lightly upon the

shoulder. "You have already set into motion the events which will lead to your recovery, though as yet you do not know it. It seems some god in heaven has shown you favor, and for that, you should be ever thankful. Hope yet remains." He gazed kindly at the king for a few brief moments, then his face became serious once more.

"Skeltar will turn your army against you if he can."

"I feared as much," the king admitted ruefully. "Can you kill Skeltar?"

The eastern wizard shook his head. "No, my Lord, I cannot. It is not my destiny. However, there *is* one who can, and he is already on his way. I will aid him to the full extent of my power."

"Are you not the most powerful wizard in the East?" King Xalton demanded. "Why not kill this fiend yourself and be done with it?"

"It is a dangerous thing, to touch evil," replied Qua Chang Xu. "Because I too am a sorcerer, it would be easy to become corrupted by his darkness, through even the slightest contact. Skeltar has defiled himself, from an early age. He has also performed the foulest rites, and these things have polluted not only his body, but his eternal soul as well."

"I still don't understand," the king snapped impatiently. "I did not summon you to play games. I want him killed."

"And he shall be!" the wizard cried, "but I swore an oath before the gods; I swore that I would never spill the blood of another living soul, and I cannot--*I will not*--break my oath, for that is the first step down the path of folly." He shook his head resolutely.

"I will aid you in defeating Skeltar, but I will not shed blood. Another will do that. I will keep you alive, but make no mistake, my Lord, his knowledge of the black arts is profound. The spell that he has placed upon you cannot be broken unless one of two things happens first."

"And those are?"

"Skeltar must release you from the spell, and I doubt he will do that. Or, he must first die, in which case his evil hold upon you will be broken, and your health will return once more."

"Then what is your counsel for me at this time?" the king sighed heavily.

"When the young warrior and his companion arrive, this is what you must do. Follow my words exactly, and you shall recover and become even stronger than you once were. But know this; if you fail to head my advice, and do not act as I now advise, you *will* die."

The king's brow furrowed deeply at the words of the mage. It seemed to him that he had heard this same speech before, only not from an eastern wizard, but from a more local one--Skeltar.

Brutus strode through the darkened streets of Luxantia, a look of triumph drawn firmly across his weathered features. It would be a glorious night indeed!

If Skeltar had been surprised to see the soldier guarding the wizard's door upon his return, he had concealed it perfectly. And once Brutus had informed the mage of Cral's activities, Skeltar had paid him handsomely in gold before sending him out to capture the slothful apprentice.

Now, as the soldier made his way silently through the town's deserted streets, the weight of the coin purse hanging from his belt gave him a sense of even more wealth to come, for Skeltar had paid him more in this one night than Brutus usually earned in a month of service to King Xalton.

He was now in charge of personally guarding the wizard, as well as for carrying out any wishes that Skeltar saw fit. Surely he would be looked upon with fear and dread, for he was now the guardian of the most powerful sorcerer in all the lands of the Westermarch.

No longer would he be just another guardsman for another whimsical king, fighting dangerous battles and marching for endless months to some far-flung, dung hole region of the King's empire, all the while getting paid meagerly in silver to risk his life for naught. Though Brutus had not taken kindly to being assigned to the wizard's service at the start, he'd had plenty of time to think things over lately, and it seemed that serving the wizard was much more rewarding than slaving for the king.

Xalton was an ungrateful master, and Brutus now felt resentful of the loyalty he had given to the king for so many years.

True, Skeltar was prone to fits of sudden, terrible rage, and even to a soldier such as Brutus such moments were truly terrifying. But they usually only occurred when the wizard's commands were not followed correctly, and being a man accustomed to authority, he could respect that. He was also a man that seized a good opportunity when it came along, which generally wasn't very often.

Tonight, however, he'd seen his chance and taken it, and now he was much richer because of it. No soldier was paid as highly as what Skeltar could offer, and the first installment now hung heavily at his hip by a leather thong.

Only moments before, in the wizard's darkened chambers, he had recanted his allegiance to the king and swore an oath to protect and serve Skeltar, faithfully and exclusively. He had promised to uphold his end of the bargain unquestioningly. The wizard had required a few drops of his blood, obtained easily enough by a small cut on the soldier's chest, just slightly below his heart.

Skeltar himself had made the incision with a strangely shaped knife, some sort of dagger. He had then mixed Brutus' blood with some wine in a glass and consumed it in one single gulp.

Brutus had little faith in gods and spirits, so when the mage had required him to swear that his immortal soul would forever serve Skeltar, he had done so without a moment's hesitation.

"Let the dead worry about their souls," he thought, *"the living need gold."*

He turned down another dimly lighted street, stepping quickly to the side to avoid a mound of horse manure. He was about to carry out his first assignment for Skeltar the Great, and as he ducked into a doorway he slowed his pace, making his way through the crowded room to the stairs in the far corner. Silently, he climbed the stairs leading to the upper floor, a cruel smile twisting his lips.

Cral lay upon his back on the sweat-soaked bed, the glistening bodies of the naked whores lying limply beside him. Such erotic pleasures as he had experienced this night were a rare occurrence for one such as himself, and he breathed in deeply, savoring the aroma of the women's juices, still wet and sticky upon his face.

Both of these whores had been impressed by the length and thickness of his manhood. They had moaned and screamed in pleasure as he impaled them upon it, driving it deeply into their soft, pink flesh, until at last his seed was finally spent.

As a pool of dark red liquid spread slowly across the floor's marble tiles, Cral's thin lips twisted into a hideously evil grin. His mind replayed the terrified expressions that could still be seen, frozen upon the faces of the trulls. In the end, he had impaled them upon something else as well.

He had driven his dagger to the hilt between their heaving breasts, amid their throws of orgasm. First he had stabbed Glona, while she straddled his face between her naked thighs; then he killed Luena. She didn't even see it coming until the final moment, for she had been facing the opposite direction, her hips bucking desperately upon his throbbing erection. He had held her tightly against him, his arms pinning hers to her sides, then slowly sank the blade of the dagger into her chest as she screamed in horror and fear.

As she died, he had let her body slump forward, face down upon the bed, his manhood still buried deep inside her dripping mound. He'd paused briefly, surveying the scene, listening to his heart pound loudly in his chest, feeling the adrenaline rush through his veins; then he had adjusted his position behind Luena's lifeless body and continued to use her. He drove into her furiously, his hips slamming against her buttocks, making a loud smack that echoed in the stillness of the chamber with each successive violent thrust as he sodomized her bluing corpse.

She had refused to let him take her this way, saying it wasn't proper, it wasn't right. Glona had allowed him to enter her from behind, but Luena would hear none of it.

Their blood was now soaking into the feather-filled mattress beneath him, gradually congealing against his own naked flesh. He could feel their bodies begin to cool and stiffen as he lay between them, and as he touched them with his fingers he felt a sadistic sense of pleasure, once more becoming slowly aroused. But he felt so tired now. He touched himself and began to entertain thoughts of using the whores again, but his eyelids kept closing, and each time it became a little harder to open them. Then sleep overtook him, and his twisted mind began to dream the dreams which only madmen and demons know, unspeakable acts and fantasies, vile, despicable, depraved.

All the years he had spent in close proximity to evil, the countless nights being tormented by the spirits that dwelled within the wizard's keep, the gruesome deeds he'd performed at the command of his master; they had all taken their toll upon him, twisting his mind and polluting his sanity. Cral was unaware of the influence, unknowing of the effects of living each day so close to darkness.

He roused, and his mind drifted lazily, watching the shifting images cast by the sputtering tapers nearby. Shadows danced upon the ceiling and crept like phantoms down the walls, like specters risen from the unearthed graves of restless, butchered saints.

Suddenly the door burst open in an explosive crash of splintered wood. To Cral's startled horror, Brutus strode swiftly towards him across the bloody chamber floor. A bared Straltonian short-sword was held firmly in his massive, meaty fist, gleaming menacingly in the gloomy interior like a spike of silver death.

The guardsman halted abruptly, his eyes sweeping over the grisly scene in startled disbelief. Seizing the moment, Cral sprang into the air. He leaped from the blood soaked bed, ripping his dagger from between Luena's rigid breasts and lunging at Brutus insanely.

"Get back to your post, soldier!" he grated, "and forget what you see here if you value your worthless life!"

Cral held his slender dagger out before him, but his hand trembled, and Brutus stepped lightly toward him. His heavy blade was held steady and firm, ready to strike.

"I don't take orders from swine like you!" he growled through clenched, white teeth.

Cral lunged at him, whipping his blade from side to side, attempting to close in on the soldier.

"Obey me now or die!" he spat. "When Skeltar hears how you

broke into my room and killed these whores, he will be greatly displeased. When I tell him of how you then sought to murder me, he will use foul magick on you, and you will suffer terribly. You'll wish you had listened to me, that you were never born!"

Brutus stood unmoved, his face contorted with contempt. "Skeltar sent me to capture you."

"Is that so?"

"Aye," he confirmed dryly, "that it is. He has plans for you, but I'm sure you've already figured that much out, having been his slave for so long."

"I am no slave, dog!" Cral retorted.

He lunged again, slashing wildly with his blade, and the soldier rushed to meet him, his mighty sword flashing as it arched through the air.

Cral thrust his dagger at Brutus' throat, but the warrior parried it with a smashing blow that sent the weapon clattering across the room. Cral cried out in fear and leapt backwards, attempting now to put himself beyond the reach of the soldier's sword, but his feet suddenly slipped on the bloody floor. He crashed to floor, his arms flailing uselessly in an attempt to break his fall. Blood splashed into the air as he collapsed upon the marble tiles, and in an instant Brutus was upon him.

He placed his knee between Cral's shoulder blades and shifted all his weight onto it, pinning the scrawny servant helplessly to the floor. Within moments he had his hands tied tightly behind his back.

"I would love to kill you right here," Brutus leaned down to rasp in his ear. "I would mingle your blood with that of these wretched whores, save for the fact that Skeltar wishes to keep you alive."

"Ah!" the other proclaimed, "that is because I have served him faithfully for so many years. *That's_loyalty!* But then, you wouldn't know anything about that, would you?"

Brutus jerked him to his feet and shoved him toward the door.

"Skeltar would never hurt me!" Cral said tersely, as if trying more to convince himself than the soldier.

"We shall soon see about that," Brutus retorted, "and if not he, than surely I, but you should know one thing more as well."

Cral turned to look at him. "And that is....?"

The soldier was grinning wickedly. "You've been replaced."

"Replaced?" the captive echoed. "Bah! Replaced by whom?"

Brutus spun him around and shoved him once more towards the ruined door as he snarled his reply. "You've been replaced by me!"

Darkness had fallen swiftly upon Makron, rolling out the heavens like a jewel-studded scroll. Amid the brilliance of the twinkling stars, the Mother Moon shone full and bright, but the Sisters of Mercy could not be seen. In their place was only blackness, a space void of light in a sky filled with gleaming radiance, and it was an eerie sight to behold.

Joktan lay stretched out upon a straw bed in the room he and Sheba had purchased for the night. The two had retired rather early, leaving the tavern filled with drunken men to seek out the privacy of their quarters at the inn.

When they had first entered the room, Joktan had drawn the heavy wooden bolt across the narrow door, while Sheba lighted a tallow taper at a small table in the far corner, opposite the bed.

He had watched her undress, revealing the sensual curves of her womanly form silhouetted in the dim, flickering glow of the flickering candle's flame. His eyes feasted hungrily upon her body, and his arousal grew steadily as each piece of her clothing was stripped away.

Hastily, Joktan joined her on the bed. Their lips met, tongues touching in deep, exploratory kisses. Sheba's hands drifted slowly over his body, down to his manhood. Her fingers closed upon it firmly, caressing him with smooth, even strokes.

He'd held her pale breasts in his hands, fondling them gently before nuzzling them between his moistened lips. Her soft sighing pleased him as he sucked then into his mouth and flicked the tip of his tongue across them, gently nibbling on them with his teeth as they became turgid and erect.

Soon his fingers sought out the softness between her thighs, and as he rubbed her there his fingers grew moist with her wetness. He slipped one inside of her as she pulled him down on the bed, moving his hand in rhythm to the motion of her swaying hips.

Her hair spilled over his chest as she kissed his nipples and worked her way down, until he could feel her hot breath upon his throbbing manhood. A sudden jolt of pleasure surged through his body as her warm lips closed around the head of his swollen shaft, and her hand stroked him faster as she took him deeper and deeper into her mouth.

For an instant, he'd thought he could feel something sharp against him, but amid the incredible sensations of pleasure he was also feeling, he quickly forgot about it. She teased him with skillful movements of her tongue, and as her mouth and hands moved faster along the length of his manhood, his excitement grew more and more intense. She sucked harder, and he stiffened even more, aching and yearning for release.

He wound his fingers into her hair and his hips rocked in unison with her oral urging, moving back and forth within the warmth of her throat and mouth. His heart raced and his breathing quickened; he moaned uncontrollably, then exploded, his manhood pumping violently as she sucked out every last drop of his viscous, milky seed.

Sheba giggled playfully, moving up to kiss his lips, and once again their kisses were deep and wet, but now they were mingled with the familiar iron tinge of blood--*his* blood.

She squealed with delight as Joktan threw her down unto her back and roughly grabbed her legs, spreading them widely apart.

He buried his face between her pale thighs and opened his mouth over her pubic mound. Her scent drove him wild, and as his tongue began exploring the soft folds of her femininity, her wetness glistened upon his lips. Sheba pressed herself against him, grinding her hips into his mouth, and she could feel the cool smoothness of his fangs brushing against the softness of her lips. Each time his tongue moved about her swollen clitoris it felt like an electric shock surging through her body, driving her closer and closer to the height of ecstasy, and her involuntary moans grew in volume and frequency, causing his tongue to move even faster.

He slipped one of his fingers inside her; she wasn't expecting it, and it caught her off guard! She could feel it slipping slowly in and out of her, probing her gently, and combined with the unrelenting strokes of his tongue, it drove her over the edge. She cried out as she burst into a tremendous orgasm, her body convulsing with each successive wave of pleasure that swept through her, hot and intense.

Suddenly she felt his teeth pierce her skin, just above her pubic mound, and as her juices flowed into his open mouth, so too did her blood. His fangs sank further into her flesh as his tongue continued to manipulate her, and she could feel her blood flowing faster as he began to suck once more. Some part of her wanted to stop him, but he was still fingering her slit, still massaging her clit with his tongue, and she didn't want the pleasure to cease just yet because she was on the verge of coming a second time...

She sat nearly upright as her body hurtled into the throws of another orgasm, and as it slowly subsided, Joktan withdrew his fangs. He had to struggle to break free, for some part of him frantically hungered for more. Each drop of her blood was like a drug, more intoxicating than any wine he had ever savored.

Sheba lay back upon the bed, gasping for air as her breasts heaved with each desperate breath, and he moved towards her, as if to kiss her. The images and visions combined with such powerful orgasms were exhausting, and she desperately needed to recover her strength. But Joktan wasn't ready to stop.

He wrapped his arms around her, pulling her head to one side, and sank his fangs deep into her neck. Instantly her blood began to flow yet again, and she gasped uncontrollably as he continued to drink. Each beat of her heart sent another rush of blood into his mouth, and with it the visions swarmed into his mind. They overwhelmed him, possessed him....and made him lust for more.

He used his knees to spread her legs apart and hold them there with a throaty, guttural snarl. Sheba yielded, her claws tearing into his arms like deadly talons, and suddenly she gasped as the entire thickness and length of his rock-hard manhood penetrated her completely. His strokes were deep and merciless, pounding against her so forcefully that her entire body was jolted forward with every powerful, relentless thrust. The bed rocked against the wall as he plunged his throbbing cock into her soaking femininity again and again.

Every time his hips slammed into hers the motion stimulated her sensually, and combined with the feelings he was arousing as he drank her blood, the sensations of pleasure were too much to resist, and suddenly she felt another orgasm swell and course through her body, more intense and violent than the ones that had preceded it.

Her flesh felt like it was on fire, her blood roared in her ears; it felt like thunder was crashing all around her.

Joktan released his bite and threw his head back, his aching manhood erupting inside of her, and they clung to each other desperately until their passion finally subsided. Then they collapsed upon the bed, their bodies soaked and stuck together with sweat from their exertion.

Now both man and woman slept soundly, the humid aroma of sex and sweat hanging thickly within the tiny room. The taper had long since burned itself out, but the silvery light of the full Mother

Moon found it's way in around the edges of the heavy curtain which had been drawn down over the window, causing shadows to play upon the walls like serpentine specters in the darkness.

Unbeknownst to the sleepers, a beam of light suddenly appeared upon the wall at the foot of their bed, thin as the silk strands of a spider's web. It started out near the ceiling, then slowly ran vertically down to the floor, creating a line of golden light that seemed to come from inside the very wall itself.

Within moments in began to grow, like a glowing crack within the wall, until soon it was nearly a cubit in width, bathing the room in golden radiance as brilliant as the noonday sun. From within this light a vision appeared; a woman of great beauty, pale of skin, with long, dark, voluminous hair that spilled down about her breasts and ended near her waist. A scanty halter of silver scale mail barely concealed her large, rounded breast; they strained within it's constricting confines, threatening to burst out at any moment. A thin strip of black silk attached to a small chain around her waist and ran between her thighs, narrowly covering her feminine mound.

Boots of black, polished leather rose halfway up her thighs, and these too, were decorated and embossed with silver in intricate, swirling designs. She wore silver armor that covered only her arms and shoulders. Each arm-piece was adorned with vicious looking silver horns, several inches long, and beautiful jewels glittered brightly, set of by elaborately engraved patterns similar to those on her boots.

There was a circlet upon her forehead that was also wrought of silver, from which a horn protruded above each temple, and a silver band fastened around her neck; it was embedded with faceted jewels and featured a golden emblem in the front, created with the same craftsmanship and cunning as each of the other accouterments she wore.

The woman stepped into the room, and the light that shone through the wall disappeared, but she was yet shrouded in a pale, ethereal aura that seemed to radiate from her very flesh.

Without the slightest sound, she moved to the side of the bed. Joktan stirred and started to rise, reaching quickly for his sword even in his sleep, but the figure reached out quickly and waved her hand before his face. She spoke, and the sound of her voice was like the wind blowing gently across the plains.

"Sleep, young warrior," she whispered, "sleep well, and deep. Do not be troubled."

He fell back to the bed, fast asleep, as if under a spell, and the woman turned her attention to Sheba, who was now sitting up beside

her slumbering comrade. Her emerald eyes focused on the womanly figure nearby.

"Mother?" **she asked, rubbing her eyes with her hands before looking up at the woman once more.** ***"What are you doing here?"***

The dark passageway was lit only by the flickering light of torches, and Cral's heart pounded madly in his chest as Brutus prodded him along with the point of his sword. He lurched forward, nearly stumbling over his own feet in fear. Perspiration ran down his face in rivulets despite the coolness in this underground hall, and the anxiety he felt inside was so great that he could scarcely manage to breathe.

Skeltar was leading the way, and although the wizard had not spoken a single word to him since his capture, Cral was convinced that his life was in jeopardy. He trembled uncontrollably as he struggled ahead. He had no visible bonds, but there was no need for ropes or chains to restrain him. Skeltar had cast a binding spell upon him, and he could only move in the direction in which the wizard willed him to go. Even so, the spell was so powerful that his movements were difficult and pained.

He knew that some terrible punishment awaited him, and he wondered just how severe it would be. Surely the wizard would not kill him outright, not after all these years of loyal service, but on the other hand, if Skeltar was truly furious, death would probably be a much better end than whatever the wizard might have in mind for him. Skeltar was cruel, brutal, and unimaginably evil. Cral's stomach felt suddenly queasy, and he started to wretch. He slipped and fell to his hands and knees, but Brutus yanked him to his feet again and mercilessly shoved him ahead.

"Move it!" the soldier barked.

Cral cringed, and Brutus dealt him a harsh blow, sending him reeling forward. The servant cursed at him bitterly and continued on, muttering under his breath. It was plain to see that the muscled man of arms behind him had found favor with his master, and although Cral had never liked him much to begin with, it nonetheless caused him hate the soldier that much more.

The floor of the passage through which they went was covered by at least a foot of water. The sound of their footsteps sloshing along echoed hollowly through the foul, musty air. Rats swam past them now and then, and Cral stared after them in wide-eyed terror. His master frequently called him a rat--a name the poor servant deeply despised--and he had always loathed the scurrying vermin intensely.

The only member of the trio that seemed to move with ease was Skeltar, and he glided silently along the surface of the murky water. It looked as if his feet didn't even touch it, and this bothered not only the servant, but Brutus as well, albeit the latter appeared not to notice.

Soon they halted before a partially open door. Beyond this, the passage opened into an immense cavern, and Adhra, Chief High Priest of Dhampir, emerged from the shadows to meet them. Cral nearly screamed in fright at his sudden appearance, but Skeltar merely nodded in silence. The priest glanced quickly at the party before addressing the mage.

"The wizard has kept his word," he intoned, his voice devoid of all emotion.

Skeltar moved to the side, and Brutus propelled the trembling servant forward with an urgent jab of his sharp tipped sword. Adhra gestured with his hands, and four acolytes rushed to lay hold of Cral. He cried out and screamed in protest, but they made no reply. He was drug to the great cage in the center of the room and roughly tossed inside.

The binding spell was now broken, and he clawed and struck out at his captors, but to no avail. They shoved him to the cold stone floor. Three of them held the servant still while another ripped the clothing from his body with a sinister grin. The ruined garments were wadded up into a ball and cast outside, then the priests hastily exited the cage. The door slammed shut with a metallic groan, and a heavy chain run through the bars secured it along with several large, rusty locks.

Brutus looked on with amusement, and the wizard turned to Adhra. "I believe you have something for me," he hissed, extending a gnarled, bony hand.

"Ah, yes!" The priest replied. He clapped his hands sharply, and another priest joined them, a small wooden box held in his arms. He handed it to Adhra with a slight bow, who in turn gave it Skeltar.

"Just as you requested," he intoned. "Sacred parchment, encased in the carcass of a black male cat, according to the ancient laws."

"Of course," the mage replied, opening the lid to inspect the contents for himself. Satisfied, he closed it up and instructed Brutus to carry it for him. The soldier accepted the parcel hesitantly.

"Our business is done, for the time being," Skeltar informed the High Priest of Dhampir.

"Yes," the other responded, "but would you not care to witness this offering to our Lord?"

The wizard almost seemed to smile. "I wouldn't miss it for all the power in the world!"

"Excellent!" said the priest. "And if I may, it would be most beneficial to place your guardsman by the door."

"As you wish," the wizard consented.

"We have the outer doors secured, but it would be prudent to set you as a watch in here, to guard this inner sanctum. We wouldn't want any intruders," Adhra explained to Brutus.

"I understand," the soldier replied. "It will be an honor."

"Then take your position," the priest told him, "and kill anyone who enters. There must be no interruptions."

Unknown to all those present in the room, Skeltar had never before witnessed the summoning of a god, not to mention one so greatly feared as the dark lord Dhampir. It was not something that the uninitiated were permitted to see, and although he was well aquatinted with the black arts, he had never been offered the opportunity to partake in such a rite. For a rogue wizard, this was indeed a rare treat.

It was common practice to sacrifice humans to deities in many parts of the world, but Dhampir was different. The cage in the center of the room was proof of that. It was gigantic, and had been moved into the chamber piece by piece before being assembled. It would have taken a score of men just to carry each bar down into this subterranean vault.

This cage was not merely designed to restrain the sacrifice--ropes and chains could do that easily enough, in addition to spells of binding. This cage had been built to restrain something much bigger--and something far more dangerous. It was created to restrain the god Dhampir himself, to protect these priests from their dreadful god.

The bloodlust of Dhampir was unimaginable, and once triggered, unstoppable. There were legends about him, dark legends, of horrible and unspeakable atrocities, and it had taken centuries of trial and error before his worshipers had finally discovered the proper materials and spells that would hold their god at bay.

By now Cral had given up on trying to persuade someone to help him. He knew he was doomed, and was now desperately searching in vain for a way to escape from the monstrous cage. His naked body was still covered in the dried blood of Glona and Luena, and the master he had served day and night for so many years watched on in silent fascination, unmoving from where he stood.

The priests gathered silently, forming a circle around the perimeter of the room, maintaining a safe distance. The lesser priests joined hands and began to chant an incantation that sounded more like a dirge, while the adepts drew a line between the cage and all those present with white chalk, moving in a counter-clockwise direction. Adhra held a wand in his left hand and a long, two-edged sword in his right. As his brethren drew the line, he walked before them, reciting the words of power to cast the magick circle.

"Hear ye, Guardians of the realms of the dead," he called out in an unearthly tone, "I Adhra, Servant of Dhampir and Chief of his High Priests, Master of the Arts of Wisdom, do cast this circle of protection, for the benefit of myself and all those present, as we offer this worthy sacrifice to our Lord Dhampir."

"Sacrifice?" Cral's shrieked in horror, his eyes bulging hideously in their sockets.

Adhra raised his wand towards the captive. "Be still!" he commanded, and instantly, the servant fell silent.

The priests finished drawing out the line on the floor, then retreated to join the lesser priests, while Adhra continued to walk the circumference of the circle they had made, his wand pointing down at the powdery white demarcation.

His voice boomed within the stone chamber, resounding off the walls and ceiling with a preternatural quality that instantly sent chills down the spine of the soldier guarding the door.

"I conjure ye, O circle of power, to be a boundary of protection, between those of us gathered here this night, and the realms of the mighty spirits, yea, even that of our dread Lord Dhampir. Thou shalt contain this night the power that I raise within thee, and that power shall be our Lord, King of the Legions of the Dead, known by many other names, but to us as Dhampir. I circle thrice, according to the ancient laws, and conjure thee in the name of our Lord. Thus is this circle cast."

He raised his sword to point at the ceiling. "As above," he intoned, then lowered it to the floor, "so below." Adhra stamped his right foot abruptly. "This circle is sealed."

"So mote it be," the lesser priests droned in perfect unison.

The chalk line began to glow, and from it burst an iridescent light. Another priest stepped forward to stand at Adhra's side. He carried a brazier of smoldering incense by a thin, golden chain in his right hand, and a golden tripod in his left. Together they strode to the eastern edge of the circle of light, and Adhra stood solemnly as his companion set up the tripod and placed the brazier upon it. He returned to join the other priests, and their leader drew a symbol upon the floor, then raised his sword.

"Spirit of the East, Creature of Air, I do summon thee now to witness this rite, and guard this circle of power," Adhra intoned. "Come now by my command!"

Suddenly within the smoke of the incense a form began to appear, accompanied by the sound of a mighty, rushing wind. It was dark and gray, a horrible site to behold, and reached nearly to the roof of the great cavern in which they stood. It bent down to peer at the priest with ghastly eyes.

"I have come at thy command!" The chamber reverberated with the sound of the spirit's voice.

Adhra acknowledged the visage by bowing his head. "When this rite is done, thou shalt be released, to return to thy abode in the east," he informed the spirit before moving to the northern edge of the circle.

Once more he was joined by another priest, this one placing a caldron of salt on the floor before them. He rejoined his brothers, and the High Priest drew several arcane symbols on the stone floor, then raised his sword in the air.

"Spirit of the North, Creature of Earth, whose abode is upon the Seat of Power; I do summon thee forth, to witness this rite, and to guard this circle of power. Come now at my command!" Adhra cried out, and almost instantly a form began to appear.

The spirit came with a frightening roar. It was not of smoke and mist like the one preceding it, but solid, as if carved out of some ancient, living stone. It stood tall and fearsome, and the ground shook as it took its designated place at the circle of light. It peered down at the priest, who seemed insignificant before it, and it's eyes burned like the embers of a blacksmith's molten forge.

"Why do you trouble me, meddling mortal?" the spirit bellowed, it's voice deep and resonating.

Adhra stood tall and before the spirit, and there was not the slightest hint of fear on his solemn features as he made his reply.

"Obey me now, according to the ancient laws!" he cried, "and thou wilt be released to return to thy realm in the north when this rite hast been done. But thou wast created to serve the call of the wise, and obey my voice thou shalt!"

The spirit appeared none too pleased, but obeyed the priest nonetheless. "Very well, priest of Dhampir!" it grudgingly obliged. "Make haste with thine affairs."

Adhra bowed his head respectfully, then strode to the western portion of the circle, accompanied again by another member of his sect. A bowl of water was placed upon the floor, and they spoke in an ancient tongue while sprinkling salt into it. Adhra touched his wand to the mixture, uttered an incantation, and stirred the contents several times, while his assistant returned to his place with the lesser priests.

The High Priest raised his sword into the air as before and cried out. "Spirit of the West, Creature of Water; Come forth by my command, to guard this circle, and witness the rite I shall perform! Hear my voice and make thy presence known!"

All was quiet and deathly still; then, as if from a distance, a faint sound could be heard. It grew steadily in volume, becoming a thunderous din within moments, like angry waves breaking upon a rocky shore in the midst of a hurricane's wrath.

When the spirit appeared, it's form was liquid, spilling into the room like a raging torrent to tower above the priest. Its color was like that of the sea, a bluish-green column of swirling chaos. Shapeless at first, it quickly coalesced into the semblance of a massive dragon and took its appointed place at the edge of the circle.

"Thou hast called, and behold! I have come!" the spirit addressed the priest, the sound of it's voice like that of a raging torrent.

"Thou shalt be released when this work is done, to return to thy abode in the Eastern Realms. Till then, thou shalt remain, according to the ancient laws, to add thy power to this circle, and to guard against the glory of our dread Lord," Adhra informed the demon.

"I find no pleasure within thy bonds of magick," lamented the visage. "Nonetheless, I shall lend my power to your rite; see that thou keep thy word."

Adhra bowed his head respectfully, then made his way to the southernmost part of the magick circle. As before, another priest moved forward, this time placing a golden lamp upon the floor. It was filled with oil, and the assistant lit it with the flame of a torch before returning to his previous position.

The High Priest raised his sword, as he had done in the other quarters of the circle, and his voice boomed within the stone cavern.

"Spirit of the Southern Realms, Creature of Eternal Flame; I do hereby summon and stir thee. Come forth by my command, and lend thine energy to this sacred rite!"

Without warning, the air in front of the priest suddenly exploded into flame. Adhra was thrown backwards upon the floor by the sheer force of the spirit's arrival. It rose upon its hind legs to its full height, a giant reptile wreathed in billowing smoke and living flame. The fire snapped and crackled like a blazing inferno, and several of the lesser priests stepped back involuntarily, their foreheads glistening with perspiration on account of the intense heat generated by the frightening specter.

"Thou hast called, and thus I have come, I who am King of the Salamanders, to lend mine energy to thy rite," hissed the creature, as Adhra quickly gathered himself up from the floor and stood before it. "What is thy bidding?"

"Thou shalt witness this rite as I have already declared," he answered with authority. "And thou shalt guard and protect all those gathered within this room before the glory of our God."

"As you wish," replied the spirit. "But my time is sacrosanct. See that thou hasten to perform thy work, that I might be released once again to my own Realm in the South."

Adhra bowed. "So shall it be."

Now the High Priest strode to the door of the great cage. He threw back his head and raised both arms into the air, his wand in his left hand and the sword in his right, both feet slightly apart and planted firmly.

"Now is the hour when mortal flesh shall witness the splendor of our great and terrible ancient Lord!" he cried out. "Now is the hour of the coming of our Lord. Beware, and tremble before him! For he shows mercy to none, and his strength is awesome to behold!"

"Blessed is he that offers the sacrifice of blood, according to the laws of old. For within the blood of mortals is found life eternal, and it is to our Lord as the nectar of the holy lotus blossom is to the honeybee! Thus have we gathered this night, in the sacred hour, and cast this circle of power, and thus do the creatures of the Four Realms lend their energy to our desire!"

"So mote it be!" the lesser priests responded, as if on cue.

Adhra sheathed his sword, then thrust his hand into the folds of his robe and produced a tiny vial. It was shaped like a human heart, and was fashioned of amethyst crystal. He opened it and held it up before the captive in the cage.

"This is the water of life, consecrated to our Lord." He flung the contents at Cral, and as it slashed upon his face the stench of urine filled his nostrils. His eyes watered and burned as the liquid trickled down his forehead and cheeks, and he shrank back in terror, wiping at it desperately with his frail, trembling hands.

"I anoint thee, in the name of the Eater of Souls, in the name of our God, Dhampir," Adhra intoned. "May the darkness of his Glory purify your mortal body. May your spirit nourish His hunger and quench His awesome thirst. May your soul be acceptable in His sight, that He might imbue us with his power."

One of the other priests moved to Adhra's side, bearing a brazen ladle and a bowl of steaming blood.

"As the ram is sacred to our Lord, so too is it's blood, as a symbol of his essence. With this sacrament I cleanse your body," the High Priest declared, splashing it liberally upon the captive. One by one the remaining priests came forward, repeating the words Adhra had spoken, then dousing Cral with a ladle of blood before resuming their place along the perimeter of the room. Their victim cowered on the floor of the cage, sobbing in anguish as they soaked him. When the last priest had emptied the contents of the bowl upon him, Adhra turned to face his brethren. He unsheathed his sword and motioned with it.

"As it is below, so may it be above."

"So mote it be," the lesser priests replied.

"I, Adhra, High Priest of the one true God Dhampir, do call unto thee in the cloak of the midnight hour. Hear my voice and answer! Be ye conjured in the name Al-Khafiz, the Abaser! Be ye conjured in the name Al-Muzil, the Destroyer!" Adhra's voice rose in volume and power as he recited the archaic incantation, while the lesser priests chanted monotonously in some long-forgotten tongue.

The air within the confines of the cage grew swiftly cold and frigid, and Cral shivered pathetically in the icy chill that now surrounded him. His breath came in ragged gasps as he hyperventilated, and when he breathed out it hung like a white fog in the space about him.

"Be ye conjured in the name of Al-Mumit, the Killer! Be ye conjured in the name of Az-Zarr, the Distresser! I summon ye forth, from thy abode beyond the mighty river Nar Marratu, whose gatekeeper is Ne-Gab. Ye ancient consort of Lamashtu, be thou stirred within the shadows, He whose name was once known as Shamash!"

A sudden tremor violently shook the chamber, rending the stone floor beneath the metal cage in which Cral cowered, opening a gaping hole that plunged endlessly down into darkness. The smell of burning sulfur and tar issued forth from this abyss, and the captive choked and sputtered within the cage, gasping frantically for air. His feet slipped through the bars of the cage floor, and he scrambled desperately to the side of his prison in an effort to position himself as far away from the hole as possible.

The quake sent many of the lesser priests sprawling on the ground, and although Brutus held his sword firmly in both fists, he had the look of one about to flee. As for the others, Skeltar appeared unconcerned, and Adhra continued the ancient conjuration, his voice gaining even more fervency and passion than before.

"He who seized Asakku and overwhelmed Alu, I call ye out of thy fearsome abode! On this night, while the Sisters of Mercy are overtaken with darkness and shadow, I call thee forth into the world of flesh and blood, the dwelling place of mortals, to feast upon the soul of this worthy offering, and show us thy power without delay, as we await thy dreadful and most holy presence!"

The lesser priests were now chanting. "Come forth! Come forth! Come forth!" Adhra motioned to them for silence, and they ceased abruptly. Not a sound could be heard within the chamber, save for the sobbing servant within the cage, and an atmosphere of anxious expectation filled the room. Though no one moved or spoke, their fear was just as tangible and real as the cold stone beneath their feet.

Suddenly the ground shook, and a black column of thick smoke burst forth from the abyss. It was accompanied by a thunderous, inhuman roar, a sound so sinister and dreadful that nine of the lesser priests fainted, collapsing in a heap upon the floor. The other priests made no move to help them, for it was not permitted; they would be attended to after the rite was completed. But the effect it had upon them was readily apparent, and many now trembled uncontrollably.

Adhra was quick to notice their terror, and addressed them hastily, his sword pointed at each man's throat in turn. "Better it be that thou fall upon this blade, then witness this rite in fear!" he shouted above the din. "Steel yourselves by my command!"

Billowing smoke filled the cage completely, broiling and churning as if it had a life of it's own. The putrid stench of burning, rotted flesh assailed them, and Cral began to vomit uncontrollably.

A horrible form suddenly took shape within the gloom. The lesser priests fell prostrate upon the ground in fear, and Adhra's voice was a hoarse whisper as he knelt in awe upon the floor.

"Behold our Lord! Behold Dhampir!"

Cihuacoatl, the Goddess of Blood, smiled and sat down at the edge of the bed, reaching out to touch Sheba gently with a pale and slender hand.

"Merry meet! I have come to warn you, my child," she whispered in the darkness.

"Warn me of what?" Sheba demanded groggily.

"That you are followed by the priests of Dhampir….."

"Again?" she exclaimed. "I thought they were far behind us. They ought to have given up by now."

"The priesthood seeks the life of your companion. They have made a pact with an evil wizard named Skeltar. They have sworn to capture both of you, and they have promised Skeltar to deliver you to him in exchange for his aid in capturing your friend."

"Why?" Sheba wanted to know.

Her mother motioned towards Joktan. "The priests seek him out for several reasons; he plundered their temple, killed many members of their sect, and stole you from them. Those reasons alone would be enough to warrant them hunting him down, but there is something else which has caused them to seek him out with great zeal."

"Pray tell," said Sheba, suddenly curious.

"When he rescued you, he also stole several items of value. Most of them were of little religious significance, and he sold them before departing on this journey, or so I would imagine. One object yet remains in his possession, however, and to the priests of Dhampir….it is priceless."

"He has told me of no such trinket," she frowned, "and I believe he has been honest with me so far……"

"Aye," her mother replied, "but perhaps he has not spoken to you about it because he is ignorant of the object's true worth."

"What are we talking about then?" Sheba asked.

"It is called the 'Face of Death.' It is a piece of obsidian stone, crafted into the shape of a human skull. It is far more than just another bauble."

"Wait.....I remember it now!" she muttered thoughtfully. "It was sitting on the table. The priest had been looking at it right before Joktan killed him."

"It is they key to communicating with their vile god," her mother informed her. "The priests have a saying; *'To speak to god, one must first look upon the Face of Death.'*"

Sheba ran slender fingers through her tousled and matted hair. "To tell you the truth, I had forgotten about that thing completely."

"The priests haven't, I assure you."

"That may be, but we left them behind in Luxantia. That was some time ago, and we will be leaving this place at dawn. I cannot see how they should pose a threat to us any longer."

"Don't be so naïve!" her mother asserted. "There are many of them, and temples to Dhampir are everywhere these days. They can find you easily enough, and that makes them extremely dangerous."

"Fine!" Sheba snorted, "We'll just have to be careful for a while. Besides, they are not fighters. I killed three of them in Luxantia, and they died easily enough."

"Listen to me!" her mother nearly shouted. "You might be able to fight them a few at a time, but you will not be able to stand against them in large numbers. They will use the black arts to capture you, and you are not yet ready for such a test....nor is he!" she pointed at Joktan's sleeping form.

Sheba scowled at the floor in silence.

"The priests know nothing about you, but the wizard is no fool," her mother continued after regaining her composure. "He knows about the legends. *He knows our secret!* He will drain you of your blood, and as for you body, only the gods know what despicable designs he has devised. You must leave here immediately, while it is yet dark."

Her daughter made no reply.

"Do you understand me?" Cihuacoatl prodded.

Sheba nodded in agreement. She knew her mother was right, and staying here too long might spell disaster for her and Joktan both.

"I'll wake him when you leave. It will still be dark for several hours," she mussed. "We'll be far away from here by sunrise."

The older woman breathed a sigh of relief. She knew, more than anyone else, just how stubborn her daughter could be at times.

"You cannot bring the Face of Death to Lothair. It *must* be disposed of--it will endanger the lives of all who live in our land."

"I will see to it that it is gotten rid of," she promised.

"Promise?"

"Yes, mother," Sheba sighed, somewhat annoyed by her mother's persistence in pressing the issue. "I promise."

"Take care that you do not damage it. It is a foul thing, this obsidian skull, possessed by the darkness of a degenerate and unholy god. The Face of Death is a very unique object--to my knowledge, no other of its kind exists. It once belonged to a powerful goddess, in an age all but forgotten. It was never intended to be used by men. Ages have come and gone, fading into the mists of legend and half-remembered fables, yet this cursed stone still contains a portion of Dhampir's evil, the results of constant use by the twisted souls who carry out his bidding. That is why it must be disposed of with the utmost care."

"So we must hide it."

"Aye," the Goddess confirmed, "in a place where the priests cannot find it. And it must be done soon. I will try to learn more about it in the meantime."

"Why don't you dispose of it?" Sheba asked.

"I can't. Even just touching it would be dangerous for me," her mother replied. "I feel too keenly. The bloodlust is strong in me. It would pollute my senses."

"I'll take care of it then," Sheba resolved.

"Very well. There is one other matter you should be aware of," her mother added. "A band of women is searching for you. They are excellent warriors, and you will soon meet. There are eight of them."

Sheba looked exasperated. "More pursuers? I'm almost afraid to ask what they want…."

She laughed softly. "They are on a king's errand. They do not seek to harm you in any way. Rather, they desire your assistance, and I believe that you should lend it to them. You may do as you like, of course," she added quickly, "but I believe that destiny guides them to you."

Sheba sighed, and suddenly she felt very tired. "I just want to go home."

"I know," her mother replied.

"I wish you visited me more often, too."

The Blood Goddess nodded. "I understand, and I wish that it were feasible. I come as often as possible, but much of my time is taken up with other concerns."

"It seems like centuries since I last stood beneath the great oaks of Lothair. The sweat smell of wisteria blossoms upon the autumn breeze; the sound of the wind rustling through the branches of the shitim-wood groves; the enchanting songs of the Elves, making their way down to the Crystal Spring. How I used to love the music they made! Their voices always sounded so pure and haunting." She gazed into her mother's eyes as tears welled up within her own.

"Sometimes I fear I will forget such things, or that I will never live to see them again!" she whispered, her voice trembling with sorrow.

Her mother took her into her arms and held her tight against her breasts. Her embrace was comforting, reassuring. Sheba closed her eyes, and then suddenly she felt a strange sensation come over her. It was warm and soothing, almost healing in a way, but at the same time she sensed an incredible strength and power, unlike anything she had ever known. It coursed through her body, through her very flesh and bones, and instantly her tears were gone. In their place was a knowing beyond all human explanation, and she heard her mother's voice inside her head. It was soft as the wind, but at the same time there was a potency that underlined it that could not have been equaled in even the mightiest roar.

"Drink and be strong."

She looked at her questioningly, uncertain. *"I've never.....it isn't time yet..."*

"Of course it isn't! Not for that, anyway.....," her mother replied telepathically. "But there is still much you must do before your return--*before you are Queen!"*

She continued aloud. "You need more strength. The feeling you have just experienced was an energy which you yourself possess, but were never aware of until this moment. I didn't impart it to you, I merely caused you to become conscious of it, but from now on it will grow stronger within you, if you but concentrate on it and nourish it, like a newborn child. It is the gift of sight, but also much more than that. It will guide you in times of uncertainty, and give you clarity of thought and will."

"Many other gifts and abilities lie within you, waiting to be awakened, each of them unique, and powerful beyond compare. Some you will master very quickly, while others may take many years--you almost have to grow into them, so to speak."

"Why did you not speak of these things before?" Sheba asked curiously.

"Because it was not time for you to know this until now. You needed to develop more emotionally and spiritually before these powers were awakened, for they are not to be taken lightly, nor used without first having complete control of your feelings. The consequences could be disastrous."

"And how do you know this?" she inquired.

"My senses are acute. I commune with energies that exist in realms which natural human perception cannot espy. Soon you too will begin to become aware of these energies, and once you are perfected, you will feel them as close as I am to you at this very moment. Until then, you must endure many trials. There are tests to pass, battles to fight, and victories to be won. And there are others whose destiny must intersect with your own. They will have an impact on your life, just as you will on theirs. For some, this will be fortuitous, though for others it may be far less pleasant. Nonetheless, these things must come to pass before you are made Queen."

Sheba listened intently to her mother's words. They had very rarely spoken of such matters before, and when they had it was only in passing. She had never fully realized the extent of her mother's abilities and power. Since childhood she had heard people refer to her as a Goddess, and for some reason that had never seemed the least bit strange. She had never questioned it, taking for granted that the title was simply something that came with the Queen's crown. Now, for the first time in her life, Sheba understood why her mother was venerated as a Goddess, and though this new realization filled her with a sense of wonder and curiosity, something else deep inside of her recoiled in fear.

Cihuacoatl sensed this instantly, a fact that made Sheba suddenly uneasy.

"Do not be frightened, my daughter," her mother's tone was reassuring. "When I first learned of these things from my mother, I experienced the same emotions that you are feeling right now. Fear is a natural response when facing the unknown, but that which seems mysterious to you presently will one day be so familiar that it will be difficult for you to imagine ever having lived without it. Tonight you must take the first step onto the path that leads to perfection."

"And what is this *perfection* of which you speak?" she asked. "What does it entail?"

"I cannot give you those answers," her mother laughed quietly. "You must discover them within yourself."

"Why?"

"So that you will not falter at the brink of glory! You must take the final leap with absolute faith and conviction, and that can only be accomplished when you know with every part of your being that what you must do is absolutely necessary. There is a price to pay for immortality, and make no mistake; one day you *will* be immortal. But even greater than that cost is the attendant responsibility, which you must accept as well."

Suddenly her mother's face darkened. She averted her eyes, and the two of them sat there in absolute silence for what seemed like an eternity before she continued. When she began to speak, her voice shook with pain and remorse.

"I was perfected much too soon--*I was so young!* It wasn't my fault, nor the fault of anyone else. It was merely the circumstances at the time," She smiled wistfully. "There are some things even a goddess cannot control!"

Sheba listened, waiting anxiously for her to continue.

"I had not yet mastered my emotions. I simply wasn't ready for it at all, on every level. But it had to be done; there wasn't any other choice."

Their eyes met, and Sheba had never seen her mother look so grieved as she did at that moment.

"I made such terrible mistakes! There are so many things I should have never done!"

She shook her head remorsefully. "But such are the dangers of not knowing."

Sheba was stunned. She had never seen her mother this way before. Cihuacoatl, the Blood Goddess, the mighty Queen of Lothair, the immortal! She wondered what others might think if they were to see her in such agony. She looked so frail, so weak and burdened--*so human*!

Another expression suddenly swept her features, as if lost in her own thoughts, her own memories. "Did you know that they used to worship us? Not out of fear and dread, but out of love! People venerated us. To them we were wise and compassionate--the physical embodiment of the Great Mother Goddess."

Sheba watched as her eyes became hard and her voice rose in anger. "But I changed all that!" she snarled bitterly. "Oh, I *wanted* to be good and just, but my power was so strong! I had no control, no wisdom--no restraint! The bloodlust overwhelmed me completely. Now they fear me. Blood Goddess, they call me! She who brings the slaughter! The Terrible Queen! How could I have made such foolish mistakes? Now we are the terrible secret, the ones who protect, but must be feared."

Sheba couldn't bear to see her mother in such pain. She threw her arms around her and held her tightly, and for a while they sat there in the dark as the Goddess wept. She knew there wasn't anything that she could say that would change the way her mother felt. There were no words of comfort that could magically erase such sorrow.

Her mother touched her softly. "That is why I have been so

careful with you. I don't want you to have to learn the way I did. I don't want you to make the same mistakes. I gave birth to you much too soon, but as I said before, that was how it had to be at the time. But so much of my wildness and passion was thrust upon you during conception, I feared that I would never live to see you become perfected."

She smiled broadly, and her face lit up with a radiant glow. "You have made me so proud!" her mother beamed. "You are my only daughter, and in you I am well pleased! There are no words to describe how much I love you, and because I am your mother, I fear constantly for you as well, and all of this should prove one thing to you above all else; we may not be human, but neither are we deities, nor gods, nor devils. We can make grievous errors even after perfection. Thus it is vitally important to develop your abilities and powers before the final act. If they seem to overwhelm you now, rest assured, they can destroy you later. Power without restraint is true abomination."

"You have passed many trials, but the most difficult ones remain to be faced, and face them you must. There are many other abilities that lie dormant within you. They must be awakened, and only my blood can do this."

She held out her wrist and suddenly it began to bleed, as if cut by some invisible blade. "Drink, and be made strong. Awaken the slumbering gifts, and taste the glory which is to come!"

Something inside her told Sheba that there was no other way, that it must be done. She was accustomed to drinking blood. It was the only way to gain strength, and each crimson drop that spilled into her mouth brought with it indescribable bliss. It nourished and empowered her, and it ignited an erotic fervor to which nothing else could compare! Yet the thought of drinking her own mother's blood was revolting.

She fought the urge to turn away and pressed her lips to her mother's pale flesh. It was like no other blood she had ever tasted. Scarcely had it touched her tongue when a force swept through her that was more powerful than she could fathom. It overpowered her senses, causing her to swoon and collapse upon the floor.

"I cannot!" she gasped desperately. "It is more than I can bear!"

The Goddess laughed gently and lifted her onto the bed. "You have done well," she whispered. "The power is strong within me. I could not have drank as much as what you have when I was your age."

She glanced over at Joktan's sleeping form. "You have given him much of your blood," she stated factually, but also with approval.

"He is insatiable," Sheba remarked wryly. "I fear he has drank too much."

"His destiny is linked to yours, as is his lineage," her mother informed her. "He also has many trials to pass, but it is a good match. I have spoken to Uriel about him. He is the one."

"Are you so certain?" she asked doubtfully.

"Definitely!" the other assured. "He is still young, and already he possesses great strength--much more than he knows. He may bring hope to many, though he is still quite impulsive."

"I am fond of him," Sheba blurted.

"I can tell," Cihuacoatl replied. "And the feeling would seem to be mutual. Just remember who you are....and what you will have to do."

"I know," she sighed, studying Joktan as he slept beside her.

"He will be the last of his kind," her mother said quietly. "But also the first."

Sheba's brow furrowed thoughtfully. "I think he knows that on some inner level. From what I understand, he has spent very little time with his people, yet he often speaks of their customs and traditions."

"He is unique among them," Cihuacoatl informed her. "He senses that they will one day be gone, and some part of him seeks to preserve their ways, if only just for his own sake--to satisfy his own sense of belonging. But because he is different from them as well, he doesn't seem to fit in when he is in his homeland. He is searching for something. He feels restless within, and it makes it difficult for him to stay for very long in any one place. He thinks it is merely the lust for adventure, but in truth, it is a quest, and it will lead him to his destiny."

"Nonetheless, I have come to like his company," Sheba told her.

"That's good," her mother smiled, "for as of this night, you are pregnant with his child!"

Suddenly a form emerged from within the billowing haze. It was accompanied by a tremendous roar that shook the cavern like an angry burst of deafening thunder. Huge chucks of stone fell from the ceiling, smashing to bits upon the floor, and three of the lesser priests collapsed, knocked senseless by the rain of debris.

All eyes were riveted in fearful awe upon the cage as the smoke swirled and slowly dissipated. The specter was monstrous, nearly fifteen feet high. It's body glistened like blackened steel, it's skin transparent and smooth as smoked glass. The corded musculature and tendons beneath were readily apparent in the eerie glow that filled the room.

Its feet resembled those of a dragon. Each foot had four toes, from which protruded dreadful-looking claws that were nearly the length of a man's forearm, gleaming like polished jet.

It stood on two massive legs, powerful, and thickly muscled. A long, bony tail trailed out behind it, undulating menacingly, and the tip of it looked like the blade of a short sword. It was slightly curved and razor sharp.

The horrific creature's torso was similar to that of a man, as was most of it's upper body, except that it had four long arms, two on each side of it's broad chest. It's mighty thews stood out in bold relief within the gloom. Four disproportionately huge, three-fingered hands reached out and laid hold upon the bars of the cage, displaying deadly talons that matched it's claws in length and color.

As the entity moved about, it's muscles bulged and rippled hideously, and the floor trembled from the shear weight of its footsteps. Cral still cowered at the side of the cage, overtaken with fear and terror, his hands covering his face. He shivered uncontrollably, and as Dhampir closed in on him he forced himself to peer up at the horrible god's hellish face. The poor wretch spread his fingers apart just enough for a quick, furtive peek.

He immediately regretted it.

What he saw was a nightmarish mixture of man, beast, and demon. Fanged jaws, rimmed with rows of white, serrated teeth opened wide. Slimy, viscous ooze dripped down upon him sickeningly from the gaping maw, drenching his head and face. Two molten eyes glared grotesquely from sunken sockets. The fist-sized orbs seemed to broil with rage and malevolence, a primordial hatred which struck some subconscious cord within the man, greatly increasing the intensity of his terror. Cral shank even further against the side and bottom of the cage, too frightened to beg for mercy, to mortified to scream.

The demon had horns like a ram; they were gray, curling forward, the tips pointing slightly outwards. Behind and below these were its ears. Each one was considerably small in proportion to the rest of its sizable bulk.

Dhampir expelled a powerful blast of yellowish-colored air. His nostrils flared angrily, like a raging bull in rut, and a rancid vapor filled the space about him, reeking of brimstone and decay.

While most of the lesser priests present in the room moved further away, Skeltar drew closer, attempting to procure a better vantage point. He eyed the dark Lord with obvious fascination, without the slightest hint of fear.

The wizard had often wondered what manner of devil this god might truly be, but never before had he been afforded the opportunity to witness such a demon in the flesh. There were many ancient tales of similar entities, all of them brimming with horror and dread. There were just as many names ascribed to them, the most common of which was *"incubus"*.

The priests started chanting another baritone dirge, and Adhra's voice rose in an arcane incantation. He asked that their sacrifice be found pleasing by Dhampir, while his god stared down at the helpless captive servant with sinister intent. Indeed, he was so interested in Cral at that very moment, he scarcely acknowledged the High Priest and his companions.

His enormous phallus began to grow even larger as it slowly stiffened. The organ was the size of a thoroughbred stallion's. Small, bony horns protruded in two rows along its entire length, pointed and sharp. They were slightly curved, like the steel barbs on a fisherman's hook, and as thick and long as a man's forefinger.

The demon reached out and grabbed Cral, pulling the terrified servant close and lifting him into the air. Dhampir's black, forked tongue dripped with putrid mung as it flicked out at the mortified captive's face, licking off the blood that was dried and caked upon his skin. His breath bore the stench of rotting flesh and feces, and the helpless man gagged in revulsion.

Dhampir grasped Cral's hand tightly, guiding it down to his engorged sex organ, forcing him to stroke it. The man's eyes looked as though they would bulge out of their sockets, and suddenly he began to struggle desperately, realizing what the demon had in mind.

"No*!*" he screamed in terror. "*This isn't happening! You're not real!*"

But the demon was real, and it mercilessly slammed him against the bars of its spell-laden cell. With a terrible clawed hand, it turned him around to face the priests and his former master, who now watched anxiously beyond the confines of the cage. And while the pitiful servant sobbed and pleaded incoherently, Dhampir positioned himself behind him, moving his awful phallus into place with slow, deliberate intent.

With a violent thrust of its massive hips, the nightmare suddenly drove its barbed member deep into the hysterical servant's rectum. Cral screamed hideously as the demon began to pump back and forth inside of him, clutching desperately at the side of the cage. Each time Dhampir withdrew his massive phallus, his victim's shredded flesh and mangled viscera clung to the rows of bony spikes along its length.

Cral's tortured screams caused even the priests to shudder in frightful reverence, and as the pain became too great for his senses to comprehend, he began to lapse in and out of consciousness. Still the demon continued raping him, holding its prize firmly in place against the brazen bars of the mighty cage.

Dhampir's orgasm was accompanied by a terrifying roar, his head thrown back in unholy ecstasy. The demon paused briefly, as if savoring the euphoric feelings of sexual release now surging through it's ghastly form; then it moaned eerily and resumed raping the Cral's broken and mutilated body.

Slavering jaws opened wide as the dark Lord sank his teeth into Cral's skull. The top of his cranium was torn away, revealing his cerebral tissue. It was pale and bloody, steaming in the chill temperature of the cavern, and the demon's serpentine tongue lapped at it hungrily. It ripped off the servant's entire head with one enormous bite. Cral's esophagus flopped grotesquely from Dhampir's dreadful maw as its horrible teeth ground his bloody skull into tiny pieces.

The entity gnawed at Cral's flesh while it's enormous phallus plunged in and out of his twitching corpse, then it threw his carcass to the floor and savagely devoured it. The onlookers were silent as their bloodthirsty god feasted upon the man's mangled carcass. All remained prostrated upon the floor in fearful worship....all except for Skeltar.

The mage actually moved closer, scrutinizing the demon called Dhampir as it gorged itself with hellish delight. To the rest of those present in the cavern, however, it seemed like an eternity had passed before the grim sounds of tearing flesh and splintering bone finally ceased.

The demon rose to his full height and shook the bars of the cage furiously, glaring out upon his trembling servants. His evil glare swept the room, then came to rest upon Adhra, who stood unflinching before his god's molten stare. He addressed the High Priest in an ancient tongue, his voice a low, rumbling snarl.

"You dare to toy with me, priest!"

"No, my Lord," Adhra replied calmly.

"Then why have you offered me this man, instead of the woman I was promised?" the demon demanded angrily.

"Soon, my Lord," Adhra responded. "This offering was but a small token of our gratitude."

Dhampir grimaced and snorted forcefully, his nostrils flaring wide with each foul breath. "You have lost the Face of Death."

"It was treacherously stolen from us, Oh Great One," the priest defended. "An uncivilized savage broke in to this sacred place. He desecrated it, spilling the blood of your faithful servants. He robbed and killed your priests. When he left he took the woman, and the Face of Death went him."

The demon roared menacingly, baring its terrible teeth. "You must find all three!"

Adhra bowed his head humbly. "Even now, my Lord, we seek them out, and soon they will be within our hands."

Dhampir's gaze once more swept the room, this time settling upon Skeltar.

"Who are you?" The demon demanded, but now he spoke in a different tongue, even more ancient and obscure. Adhra clearly didn't recognize it, but he could easily see that the demon's attention was now directed at the wizard instead of him, and the priest became visibly distraught.

Skeltar moved closer, peering back at the evil god from beneath the heavy hood of his fibrous cloak.

"I am Skeltar, the sorcerer," he replied in the same, blasphemous tongue. "It is I who provided you with this sacrifice. The man was my very own apprentice."

"Yet you do not bow before me!" the demon observed.

Skeltar was unmoved. "I bow to no one, least of all some ancient demon who aspires to be a god."

Dhampir's eyes narrowed, and he suddenly burst out in a furious roar, causing even Adhra to fall to his face on the floor in fear.

"You are nothing!" the demon raged. "You are mortal, but I, I am forever! I walked upon the Earth when the kings of old fought the bloody wars of Kethros! It was I who led his armies of Goblins into battle and bathed the Earth in the blood of the living, and even then I was worshipped by the race of men! They fell on their knees before me in fear and awe, men like Therion, wizards far more knowledgeable than you shall ever hope to become!"

"And yet a simple little cage, with a few arcane inscriptions placed upon it, can imprison you with ease," Skeltar sneered scornfully.

"You are but an incubus, a lesser creature whose existence is dependent upon the blood of mortals. You were created by the abominations wrought by men, not by some god or devil in the depths below. If these imbeciles who worship you so devoutly were to cease with their prayers and sacrifices, you would gradually diminish. Your life would fade into the eternal emptiness of the great abyss."

Dhampir snarled and shook the cage threateningly, but the wizard continued, without concern.

"How long have they conjured you?" he demanded knowingly, "how long have they offered you mortal blood, but always just a taste? And how many more centuries shall you endure, craving desperately for enough blood to become strong again, enough to walk the Earth once more as in the days of old of which you speak? Yet knowing all the while that you shall never see that yearning fulfilled!"

The demon glared diabolically, but he was listening intently to every word. "Say on, mage."

Skeltar laughed harshly. "I am not so foolish as these idiots who ignorantly fear you! You have no power over me, and as to the extent of my knowledge, do not be deceived, for there are few living who can equal my wisdom."

"You are arrogant," Dhampir spat. "Surely, if you are as wise as you claim, you would know that I would never deign to submit to you, nor any other mortal man. I appear when conjured by these priests because of the blood they offer me. If it were not for that, their rituals would be null and void."

The wizard smiled smugly and stepped closer to the cage, his tone even and chill. *"But serve me you shall!"*

"Like the spirit dog that follows at your heel? *Never!"* the demon roared defiantly. "Come but a little closer, so I can feast upon your blood!"

Now it was the mage who laughed, and although it was not nearly as terrible as that of Dhampir's demonic mirth, it yet caused even Adhra to back away in sudden dread.

"Let me tell you of my knowledge," Skeltar sneered triumphantly. "I forced my servant to swallow a spell, written with Dragon's Blood and Vervain upon parchment of Olibanum, in the appropriate hour. It is an ancient curse and binding--*I'm sure you know of what I speak!"*

The demon grimaced and the mage continued with wicked glee. "After my servant ate it, the talisman became a part of his flesh, and in your greed, you have eaten his corpse completely. It is now within your body."

He paused for a moment, allowing the full weight of his words to fully sink in.

"I am now your master."

The demon realized suddenly that he had been tricked, and his wrath was unimaginable. In vain Dhampir tried to free himself from the cage, his arms flailing futilely in the air, attempting to lay hold of the sorcerer and tear him to pieces, but it was useless. His screams were deafening as he vented his indignation.

"I bind you in the presence of these Four Eternal Guardians," Skeltar gloated maliciously. "You shall perform my bidding when you are summoned. When you hear my voice, you shall answer speedily, for by the blood of men you exist, and by the blood of my apprentice, I claim power over you!"

"No!" Dhampir roared, shaking the bars of the cage with all his strength. "I am not some familiar to be tamed. Do not attempt to harness me! Release me now, for I shall not serve you!"

Skeltar raised his frail hand and pointed at the demon with a gnarled, bony finger. "By the power within me, by the power of the Four Guardians, I bind you in my service, and serve me you shall! Toy with these priests as you see fit. Let them continue to worship you, to offer sacrifices to you, but be thou ever mindful from this day forth of whom it is you truly serve! They will keep you strong for me, so that when I call upon you to do my bidding, you will be able to perform it without fail. I shall give you your hearts desire, but only for as long as you serve me."

"How shall you do this?" the demon inquired hotly.

"When the time is right, I shall conjure you. When you hear my call, you will come, but not to be kept bound behind bars like a prisoner, nor to follow at my heels. I shall lose you upon the sons of men! You will taste their flesh and drink their blood until you weary of it, both you and your minions with you as well!"

Dhampir's expression changed. Now he seemed somewhat pleased by Skeltar's promise. He glared eagerly at the wizard. "How long must I wait? Release me now!"

"Now is not the time," Skeltar responded tersely. "I will call on you when all is ready. But for the moment, you must give me one of the horns of thy phallus."

"Why?" Dhampir growled bitterly.

"That is my own business," snapped the wizard. "Do as I say, or I shall leave you to wither away in the abyss for the rest of eternity, and you will never taste the blood of mortals again."

The demon looked no longer pleased, but resentfully obliged, breaking away one of the sharp barbs that protruded from his horrible sex organ. He tossed it to the wizard.

Skeltar then turned to Adhra and sneered. "Have you nothing more to say to your god?"

The priest shook his head. He was confused, but somehow he also seemed to understand that the mage had tricked him. At the same time he could plainly see how easily Skeltar had taken control of the demon, and this new knowledge frightened him immensely. *What power did this wizard possess, that even the god Dhampir would submit to his will with such apparent ease?*

Skeltar faced the demon once more and motioned with his hand. "Be off with you!"

Dhampir scowled at the wizard angrily, then in a sudden burst of flame and smoke he disappeared into the floor. The chamber grew cold and silent as the grave.

Without acknowledging anyone else in the room, Skeltar turned and moved quickly to the door where Brutus waited. The guardsman's face was white as ash, and in spite his best efforts to control his fear, he trembled visibly.

"Did you seal off the room where the two whores were slain?" Skeltar asked him thinly.

"I did." The soldier's voice shook when he spoke.

"Very good, then," his master hissed. "Take me there at once!"

Brutus nearly leapt through the door, so eager was he to leave the chamber. He had witnessed many frightening things during his career as a soldier, but none could compare to what he had saw this night. Somewhere inside of himself he knew that it would haunt him for the rest of his life.

Together they exited the chamber, leaving Adhra and his fellow priests to banish the spirits they had summoned and close their magick circle.

As Brutus led the way along the darkened streets of Luxantia, the horrors he had witnessed in the underground chamber continued to replay themselves inside his head. He had seen many battles during his years of service in the Straltonian army, and the atrocities of war had long ago lost their effect upon him, but the things he'd been privy to this evening could not be so easily repressed. It took all of his willpower to drive them from his mind, and still the sickening knot in the pit of his stomach remained.

It seemed to take only a few moments to reach the Open Arms Tavern. The Tavern itself was empty, and he quickly led the wizard up the stairs to the apartment above in silence. As he opened the door and stepped aside, Skeltar addressed the soldier with a rattled hiss.

"Stand guard here in the hall."

"As you wish," Brutus replied, offering the torch to his master with a trembling hand. Skeltar noticed the soldier's anxiety immediately. Indeed, he'd been aware of it since the moment the pair had left the chamber of the priests. He accepted the torch, then laid a skeletal hand upon the man's shoulder.

"You cannot serve me if such terrors fill your mind," he intoned.

"Do not worry, master," Brutus replied. "What I saw down there...."

"You have not seen such things before, I know," Skeltar said, "and what I do now, I do not for your peace of mind, but for my own. You must have your wits about you to serve me properly."

The mage placed his hand upon the soldier's head. Brutus stood as if rooted to the ground, unable to move, as he felt a sudden burning sensation begin to wash over his mind and body. It was accompanied by a pale yellow light, a glow that overwhelmed his senses so completely that he instantly forgot about the events he'd witnessed altogether. It seemed like an eternity had passed before the wizard removed his hand, but when he did, the soldier's mind was more at peace than ever before in his life.

Brutus stood rigid and unmoving. The tranquil feeling that engulfed his senses slowly subsided. When it was gone, all that remained was an emptiness, a void within his mind where not a single feeling existed. The horrors he'd seen had vanished, but so too had everything else. It was as if he had no emotions whatsoever. No guilt, no fear, no love. In their place was only a sense of duty, an unwavering commitment to fulfill his master's every word without question.

"You will serve me faithfully," the wizard commanded. "You shall know no fear, no pain, and no remorse. Greed and lust shall compel you, but above all, loyalty to my word. I fill the emptiness with these things. Do you understand?"

Brutus nodded in the affirmative.

"Very well," Skeltar said. "Now wait here till I return."

His master disappeared inside the room, and it was some time before he reemerged and stepped into the shadowy corridor. He held out his palm to the soldier, displaying a small, circular disc of solid gold. Jewels glittered brightly from their settings upon it, and a faint glow seemed to radiate about the object eerily. Skeltar stared at him briefly, as if in thought, then he spoke.

"This is what we came to Luxantia for. In the morning we shall return to Zebulon."

Brutus nodded, and the wizard continued. "I am going to my quarters now, but inside of this room lies much wealth for the taking. You may choose what you please, for I have no need of such trivial things. Once you have taken what you desire, divide the remaining portion amongst your soldiers."

"As you wish, master," he replied hollowly. "You are most generous."

"Remind your men of that when you give them their share," Skeltar returned flatly. "Remind them how much better my wages are compared to those of their frivolous dying king."

"I will," Brutus assured him.

"Before you plunder this room, however, you must lead some of your men back into the chamber where the priests are gathered. You must seal them all into the cavern. Secure it and leave. Report to me when you have done this."

"Yes master."

"Do not kill any of them! Is that clear?"

"Yes master," Brutus responded once more.

"Good then. Don't forget to advise me when this is done."

Skeltar made to leave, then turned back to him again. "And one more thing," he added. "When you have looted the room of all that is of value, burn it."

"Burn it," the soldier echoed.

"Yes," came his master's voice. "Do it just before sunrise. Start the fire on the lowest level and the rest of the building will fall as it burns. It will give these annoying townsmen something to do."

Brutus peered into the room. "I will do everything as you command," he said, turning back to his master. To his surprise, the hallway was empty. Skeltar had already left.

Makron lay far behind them when at last the sun began to rise. Sheba roused Joktan from his sleep as soon as her mother had left, and under cover of night, they had stolen two horses and fled the town.

They spoke little, spurring their mounts toward the south and quickening their pace with the approach of dawn. Joktan led the way, following a trade route, but instead of staying on the road, he had chosen to ride through the grass beside it. In this way he hoped to avoid raising a tale-tell cloud of dust. It would of course make tracking them a breeze, but at the moment they needed speed more than anything else.

Neither he nor Sheba were desirous of attracting attention to themselves, especially since they were riding stolen horses. They were yet in northern Gershom, and bandits were numerous throughout this land. Such villains preyed heavily upon unwary travelers, and those that journeyed in small numbers were easily overwhelmed and slaughtered.

Joktan estimated that it would take them at least ten or twelve days to reach the River Thule, the northern border of Lagash, provided there were no unexpected delays. He knew very little about that land, except that it was where the plains ended and the forest began.

Sheba had told him that south of Lagash lay the nation of Kahsdim, a land comprised of numerous city-states, each with their own king and all tenuously allied together, forming a loosely-knit nation. Kahsdim was governed by a council, at which each of the states were represented by their king. Dissention and discord ran rampant, and fighting amongst states was incessant. These warring factions never seemed to be able to reach an agreement for any real length of time, and only when the land of Kahsdim was invaded by neighboring kingdoms did they temporarily halt their fighting to fend off the larger threat.

To make matters even worse, sometimes a state would ally with an enemy nation in an attempt to destroy one of it's rivals, creating still more resentment and mistrust within Kahsdim's governing council.

Such a situation was rumored to currently be the case, and it was whispered that one of the Kahsdimitte states had allied with Mahalla, the nation which bordered Kahsdim to the southwest. Very little was known about Mahalla in the northern lands, for the eastern ranges of the Mountains of Erdulette separated them. To the best of his knowledge, there had never been a war between a nation of the Westermarch and a southern kingdom.

Joktan knew that it would be difficult at best to travel through those lands if they were indeed at war with each other. They were sure to be spotted by scouts from roving armies. If they were not killed or captured, they were certain to be consigned into service by one side or the other.

In light of this, he had decided to continue southeast once they were safely within the borders of Lagash. From Lagash they would cross into Korava. Seaports were numerous along the coast, and they could easily board a southern-bound ship, thus skirting the two warring countries completely. Traveling by sea would be faster, too. There were some very treacherous mountains beyond Kahsdim.

They began at the shores of the Tethys Sea and ran northwest, creating a natural border between several kingdoms. On the north side of these lofty peaks lay the lands of Kahsdim, Lagash, and the White Dessert, a desolate and barren waste of endless shifting dunes. On the southern edge sprawled the nations of Mahalla and Mjolnir, the fabled western kingdom of the Dwarves.

The Mountains of Erdulette formed the borders of Mjolnir, which was divided into two nations--one of mountain-dwelling Dwarves, the other of those who lived in the forest. Legend maintained that they were ruled by a beautiful Queen who's name was Morrana.

She was said to be a *Skadi,* the most powerful witch to have ever lived among the Dwarves. All this was merely hearsay, of course. But it was also said that the Dwarves had built a great wall of stone that ran along the entire length of the Mountains of Erdulette. If such a structure actually did exist, it would certainly be very ancient, for it was said to have been built during the time of the great wars which had ravaged the Earth during forgotten ages long ago.

In any event, this wall was rumored to be fiercely guarded and patrolled, and although Joktan fancied the idea of meeting a Dwarf in the flesh, he did not desire to meet scores of them if they were heavily armed and unfriendly to boot.

As the morning wore on the pair slowed their pace, allowing the horses to move at a steady trot. The sky was clear and blue, dotted by little clusters of small white clouds that looked like tiny clumps of wool. They drifted lazily in the gentle breeze, disappearing over the horizon as the sun warmed the grassy plains. By mid-day the temperature had become stifling, forcing them to slow their pace further still.

Presently Joktan reined in his mount, halting just beyond the crest of a large knoll. Sheba did likewise, noticing the frown that had settled upon his darkly tanned features. He peered intently back in the direction from which they had come, and the woman's eyes followed his gaze. A brief glance was all that it took for her to ascertain the source of his concern.

"Riders," Joktan muttered tersely, pointing toward a small cloud of dust far back in the distance toward Makron. Though it looked tiny from their present vantage point, both of them knew that it was in reality quite large.

"They've been following us for some time now," he rasped thinly, "and they must be in a hurry, else they would be more mindful of the dust they are raising."

"Aye," Sheba agreed, "at that speed they will overtake us within a couple of hours, provided their horses hold out."

"I'll wager there are at least a dozen of them, maybe more," he said shortly. "They obviously don't care if we see them, which means that they don't consider us to be a threat. I would say they're well armed."

Sheba pursed her lips and began surveying the surrounding terrain. She was looking for a good spot from which to make a stand. Joktan read her thoughts, but a brief perusal of the landscape revealed what he already knew; there was no place in their immediate area that would prove ideal. Their present position, he determined, was about as good a spot as they were going to find.

"We'll fight here," he decided. "It's not the best patch of grass, but I reckon it doesn't much matter. These hills all look the same to me, though this one drops down quite steep. There was water flowing through here recently." He indicated down below, where a dry streambed could still be seen easily enough. The once-muddy soil was now cracked and broken from the scorching summer heat.

"We may be able to out-run them if we make a break for it now," Sheba suggested. "We are well ahead of them as it is." The previous night's conversation with her mother still weighed heavily on her mind, and she wasn't thrilled about the prospect of fighting a battle against such numbers on open ground. The look on Joktan's face, however, made it clear that he shared none of her apprehensions.

"I'll not run," he declared, teeth clenched. "I do not know why they would be after us, but if it's a fight they seek, I'll give it to them." He swung out of his saddle, landing squarely on his feet, knees bent slightly to absorb his weight. No sooner had he hit the ground than his sword was drawn.

"Besides, the way I see it," he said, "they're riding hard. In this heat, horses become exhausted very quickly. By the time they reach us those mounts will be ready to drop. Our own beasts are in need of rest as well. If we wait and stand our ground, ours will be ready to run again, if in the end we must, while theirs will be as good as dead."

Sheba shielded her eyes from the sun with a pale hand and studied the riders in the distance. Her eyesight was far keener than Joktan's--or any other man's for that matter--another ability she had inherited from her mother. There was a good chance that these horsemen were not pursuing them at all, that perhaps they were merely in a hurry to reach some unknown destination which simply by chance lay in the same direction she and Joktan happened to be traveling. Something inside her said otherwise, however.

With each passing moment the riders grew closer, and as she reflected on her mother's recent visit and urgent warning, an unexplainable feeling of danger began to grow within her, accompanied by something else; a sense of *knowing* that had never been there before. Was this also a gift from her mother, a latent ability which the Blood Goddess had caused to awaken during her brief visit the night before?

She closed her eyes and concentrated on the horsemen, clearing all other thoughts and distractions from her mind, allowing the feeling to become more clear and focused. It was as though she could actually perceive the *intentions* of the riders. She opened her eyes quickly and turned to Joktan.

"There are sixteen of them."

He turned his head and peered out across the plains. "Then you have the vision of an eagle, for I see naught but a cloud of dust."

"I can see things at a distance more clearly than most people," she replied. "I see them in my mind. And not only can I see them distinctly, I can feel their intent--don't ask me how-- but I can."

Joktan studied her face for a moment, but if her statement surprised him, he didn't show it. He simply shrugged his shoulders. "We should stake our horses down into this little gully," he gestured. "We have some time to spare, and they are tired out. If we rub them down with some grass, they will be rested when we need them again."

"So you still intend to fight?" Sheba inquired.

"Of course," he replied matter-of-factly.

"But there are eight times more of them then us!" she exclaimed. "These are not cave-dwellers. And as you said, they may be well armed, with more than just clubs and stones."

Joktan nodded his head agreeably. "It will be a good battle."

Sheba shook her head derisively as he lead his horse away. "*Savages!*" she muttered under her breath. "Small wonder there are so few of you left!"

He ignored her remark. "Their horses will be useless when they get here. That will be in our favor."

"Really?" Sheba's returned sarcastically. "So what exactly is your plan?"

"We will rest our mounts, while waiting for the riders to close in. We can wait up there," he pointed to the top of the hill. "Just below the crest where they will not see us. Once they are close, we'll stand up and show ourselves, then run back down here. They will charge us, and I will shoot at them with my bow. Before they close in I will aim for the men, and once they fall upon us, I will shoot for their mounts. "

Sheba looked incredulous. *"That's it?* That is your battle plan?"

Joktan shook his head seriously. "Pretty much. I figure I'll be able to pick off close to half of them before they fall upon us."

She stared at him in disbelief. "That has got to be the worst battle plan I have ever heard of!"

"Do you have a better idea?" he growled, gritting his teeth.

"As a matter of fact, I do!" she exclaimed. "I don't have a problem with letting our horses catch their breath--we have little choice as it is. But I think that afterwards we should ride like the wind and get out of here."

"I like my plan better," Joktan growled darkly. "We will face them sooner or later. Right now we can see them coming."

Sheba turned her back on him and set about tethering her mount, emerald eyes blazing just as brightly as her red hair in the glaring sun. "You obviously didn't see the other riders that are closing in upon us from the north," she ejected caustically. "Shall we butcher them as well?"

Joktan frowned. "What other riders? I saw only one group from the west."

"Oh, so now you have second thoughts, do you?" she retorted.

"Where are they exactly?" he demanded, ignoring her blatant

sneer and running back up the hillside to see for himself.

Sheba stormed up to him near the crest of the rise and pointed across the plains. "The north, just like I said."

He scowled at her momentarily. The truth was, he hadn't noticed a second group of horsemen. As he studied the rolling expanse of endlessly waving grass, he began to think that the woman was simply putting him on out of spite. If there were more men approaching, why hadn't she said something earlier? Still, she might be telling the truth….

"How many do you see?" he asked presently.

"At least six or eight," she replied thoughtfully, but her eyes were closed. "They ride through the grass like us, instead of on the road, and they are moving fast."

Sheba faced him, and her features softened. "In all honesty, I cannot see them either, but I can sense their will. It is bent on us without waver."

He sat down in the grass, considering what she had said. "How long have you been able to feel such things?"

Sheba found a comfortable spot nearby and sank to the ground with a sigh. "Only just now," she confided, "though it seems as if I could have had this ability my whole life. Something has changed inside of me--it's hard to explain or describe. Perhaps that is why I feel so edgy."

Joktan fell silent. She could tell that he was mulling over what she had told him. A slight smile tugged faintly at the corners of her mouth. Sometimes he was easy to read, but there were other times--like right now….

"I slept fitfully last night," he spoke at last. "My dreams were dark….and yet……intriguing."

"My sleep was also troubled," Sheba muttered. She considered telling him about her mother's visit, then changed her mind. Now was not the time, she decided.

"Tell me something," he asked.

"What?"

"Did you kill anyone in Makron last night?"

Sheba stared at him silently, then the corners of her mouth tuned up slightly in a coy smile. "I may have."

"Either you did or you didn't," he said flatly. "From that look on your face, I'd say you did."

"Fine," Sheba admitted, "but if I harmed anyone, you can rest assured that it was for good reasons."

"I am merely trying to figure out why anyone would be pursuing us," he explained. "I killed a couple of cutthroats, but I doubt their death could be traced back to me."

"These riders travel with purpose," Sheba surmised. "They definitely have a reason, and I doubt that it has anything to do with the death of a couple worthless thieves."

"Do you remember the crystal skull I stole from the dead priest in Luxantia?" Joktan asked suddenly. "It was made of obsidian...."

"I remember."

"Well," he continued, "I tried to sell it in Makron, but no one would buy it."

"So you still have it then?" she asked.

"Aye," he replied, "but that is not all."

He stood and withdrew a dagger from his belt, holding it up for her to see. The sunlight glinted off the long, curved blade as he offered it to her. "This was the knife they intended to kill you with."

Sheba had completely forgotten about the strange weapon. The blade was a narrow crescent shape. It was razor sharp, and made of hard, black iron. The knife was clearly a ceremonial instrument, for the handle, which was made from a dark colored wood, was engraved with arcane symbols. She quickly handed it back to him.

"You can keep it," she shuddered. "I doubt it has any value. Besides, it gives me the creeps. It looks like a bolline."

"What's a bolline?" he asked.

"A knife used in magick ritual," she replied. "They usually have a white handle. Many witches and wizards use them, but their primary use is for cutting herbs and roots and what-not."

"I doubt that this one was fashioned for such mundane purposes," he surmised.

"I agree," she replied. "As you said, it seems likely that they would have cut my throat with it."

"It may yet be of some use," he replied. "There could be priests of Dhampir in Makron. I should not have tried to sell the skull. Everyone knows that most merchants are loose-tongued....." He paused. "Would you like to see it?"

"See what, the skull?"

"Aye," he replied. "It's on my horse."

"No thanks," she declined. "That blade bothers me enough as it is. I have no wish to look upon the Face of Death, though I've been meaning to speak to you about it."

"What did you call it?" he asked with a sudden frown.

"The Face of Death," she replied. "The priests of Dhampir have a saying. *To speak to god, you must first look upon the Face of Death."*

"How do you know this?" Joktan inquired.

Sheba sighed heavily, then looked at him. "You said that your sleep was troubled last night?"

"Yes," he replied, "but I fail to see…."

"That is because my mother was in our room."

"Your mother?" he looked surprised and at once suspicious. "I saw no one, but even so, isn't she supposed to be in Lothair?"

"Aye," she answered, "but the Blood Goddess has many powers, and one of them is the ability to leave her body. When she does this, she can travel vast distances in a mere heartbeat."

"Such things are not uncommon," Joktan said. "My mother could do that as well."

"I'm sure she could," Sheba replied softly, "but there is one difference. My mother can become physical once she reaches her destination."

"I'm not sure I understand," he replied.

Sheba thought for a moment. "Say I was her," she explained slowly. "If I wanted to go to….I don't know……lets say the Golden City of Zhenya, for example. I would relax myself, maybe by laying down or something. Then I would *will* my spirit to travel to the Golden City. I would imagine it in my mind, and then simply go there."

"You yourself can do this?" Joktan asked skeptically.

"No!" she laughed. "I'm saying that my mother can, but that is not the end of it. Once her spirit reaches the Golden City, she can then cause her physical body to materialize there as well. That is how my mother travels. That is how she came to be in our room last night."

Joktan's brow was furrowed in thought. He'd never heard of such a thing before. "One thing is yet not clear to me," he told her. "How did she know you were in Makron, of all places. And how did she know which room to find you in? That makes no sense to me."

"Easy," Sheba replied. "She has a connection to me. She can locate me anywhere, no matter how far from home I may be."

"And she does this often?"

"No," she said. "Only occasionally, if she feels I may be in danger."

"And she feels you to be in danger now, is that it?" Joktan reasoned.

"Yes," Sheba sighed once more, relieved that he seemed to finally understand.

"So that is why you were in such a hurry to leave Makron this morning," he muttered.

"Yes," she replied. "My mother's warning was urgent. She

knows you have the skull--the Face of Death--and she also knows that the priests of Dhampir are looking for it. I didn't have time to explain all this to you earlier this morning, and I wasn't sure if you would even believe me if I did."

"Last night I dreamed that a woman was standing in our room," he recalled. "In the darkness I didn't know who it was, and I reached for my sword, but she touched me and told me to go back to sleep." His eyes studied her face intently. "Now I know that it was no dream."

"She was concerned about me," Sheba said, "and you are quite correct. It wasn't a dream. My mother came only to speak to me, and she couldn't stay long, so she cast a spell on you to make you go back to sleep."

"I do not appreciate being toyed with," he replied uneasily. "She should have spoke to me as well."

"And I agree with you," Sheba assured him quickly, "but I had no say in the matter. My mother does as she sees fit."

"But you are not the one with the skull," he said tersely.

"True," she allowed, "however, we are traveling together, so whatever dangers lie ahead for you await me too."

Joktan looked off into the distance. "Those riders are much closer now," he observed. "They will be upon us soon." He turned to Sheba once more. "I am trusting my life to you. Promise me I have nothing to fear from your mother."

Sheba rose to look him squarely in the eyes. "My mother will cause you no harm," she said earnestly.

"She knows that I am fond of you, and it pleases her. You have nothing to fear. I swear it."

"Are you certain of this?"

"Absolutely!" she replied. "My mother thinks we are a good match for each other."

He returned her gaze in silence, and for several moments they stood there, staring at each other. Her beauty still mesmerized him every time he looked deep into her emerald colored eyes. Sheba drew close and kissed him, and the touch of her lips felt reassuring.

"So what should I do with the skull?" he asked.

She told him everything her mother had said about the Face of Death, and when she had finished he looked at her gravely.

"I should have never taken that thing, but at the time I thought I might be able to sell it."

"The priests of Dhampir seek not only the skull, but me as well," she told him. "They want to sacrifice me to their foul god, but you already know as much."

"Of course," he replied. "I'm sure they want to capture me, too. I robbed their temple in Zebulon, killed many of their brothers, and stole you from them in Luxantia." He smiled broadly. "They will certainly want to punish me."

"Well, I killed some of them in Luxantia too," she said. "And yes, I also killed a few in Makron last night, just before meeting up with you in the tavern." She gave him an impish look. "I couldn't help myself!"

"I suspected as much," he confirmed. "So it would be safe to assume that the men closing in upon us now are priests of Dhampir."

"It would make the most sense," she agreed. "The thieves you killed would not raise enough concern to warrant sending out a party to pursue us."

"Then I shall enjoy this fight all the more!" Joktan rasped through clenched teeth.

Sheba gazed toward the horsemen, noting their position, then turned back to him. "My mother wanted you to know one more thing."

"What is it?"

"That there is a wizard after us also," she said. "He is seeking to capture me, for what reason she did not know, except that he has discovered who I am. My mother claims that he has agreed to aid the priests in capturing you, and in exchange, they will turn me over to him."

Joktan frowned. "The priests were going to sacrifice you when we met. Their reasons for capturing me are obvious enough, but I am merely a thief to them. Why would they make such a deal, when you have already been consecrated as a sacrifice to Dhampir?"

"It does seem strange, doesn't it?" she replied.

"Maybe I'm wrong," he started, "but if I were those priests, I'd be curious as to why a wizard places such great value upon you. Do you remember when we left Luxantia, how I said that the priests had a specific reason for choosing you as a sacrifice?"

"When you questioned my virginity?" Sheba shot back with a laugh.

"Exactly," he smiled. "Perhaps the priests know about your ancestry. That might be why they captured you in the first place."

Sheba pursed her lips. "So if they knew about it before, why would they want to give me over to him now?"

Joktan looked at her grimly. "They don't. The priests have simply allied with the wizard as a means to an end, so that they can capture us more quickly. Perhaps they intend to break their bargain with him after we are caught. They would then have not only their sacrifice, but the thief too."

She though for a moment. "You could be right."

Joktan suddenly became curious. "Did your mother know the wizard's name?"

"Yes," she replied. "I believe she said his name is Skeltar."

Joktan froze. "*What did you say?*" His voice was nearly a whisper.

"His name is Skeltar," Sheba repeated, giving him a queer look. Hearing that name made his pulse quicken, and his own mother's words echoed in his mind.

"His name is Skeltar. Head for the south. You will not have to search for him. He will soon find you."

40

On raven wings of shadow,
Death stalks from the plain,
Dawn grins gray and grimly,
Upon the wreckage of the slain.
Bloody hues of sunrise,
Unveil the ghastly scene,
Heaped high amid the ruin,
These ashes once had dreams!

----Fragment of the Straltonian Book of Kings

Darkness held Luxantia in a suffocating grasp, like a noose on a hanged man's neck. Black clouds broiled overhead, obliterating the pale light of the moons and stars. The streets were now deserted, the townspeople having retired for the evening hours before to the safety of their homes.

In the underground chamber where the priests of Dhampir were gathered, however, sleep would not be found this night. All was chaos and confusion as the they struggled desperately to escape. A few sat huddled upon the floor against the cold stone walls praying fervently to their god, as the rest of the priests threw themselves at the heavy wooden door, trying in vain to break it down and force it open.

The few objects within the room they used as battering rams, but despite all efforts, the doors held fast. There was no hope for escape, and panic spread throughout the chamber like contagion. Soldiers had rounded up the priests beyond the doors and cast them all into the chamber, sealing it up from the other side.

Although none of them could seem to figure out why they had been shut up like this, all knew beyond a doubt who was responsible for it. At first the High Priests had attempted to force the doors open by the use of spells and words of power, but all of their arcane methods failed miserably.

The torchlight began to grow dim, and shadows crept in about the room like demonic talons clawing at their prey. The flames sputtered and died one by one, and soon the stone vault was engulfed in a profound and impenetrable blackness.

The High Priests made futile attempts to calm everyone down, but their efforts were useless. Fear of the unknown became suffocating, the darkness overwhelming, and soon they too despaired, joining those who had long since given up hope upon the floor. Some muttered incantations beneath their breath, others cried out desperately to Dhampir for release.

The air became close and heavy, filled with the smell of sweat, and the vile stench of Cral's macabre remains within the cage became overpowering.

Presently the floor beneath them started to tremble. The walls began to shake, and the reek of burning sulfur slowly crept into the room. Fear quickly turned to terror, for all were familiar with the horrible odors that now assailed them. The temperature in the chamber began to increase, rising to a frightening degree. The floor shook violently, and bits of stone and debris began to fall from the ceiling high above.

Suddenly the vault was filled with a thunderous roar. The pitch black became brighter than day as flames of living fire leapt into the room from somewhere far below. The priests shrieked in fright as the great cage in the center of the chamber dropped downward, becoming instantly lost in a bottomless abyss of smoke and flame.

The priests shrank back from the gaping hole and pressed their backs to the cold stone walls. Their fear was now tangible; the heat in the room became unbearable and suffocating. They choked amid the vile stench of burning brimstone, watching in horror as huge clawed fingers reached up over the lip of the opening,

Black smoke billowed forth from the abyss, and suddenly Dhampir stood before them. His face was dreadful to look upon as the dark lord threw back his head and furiously announced his arrival with a hellish howl. His jaws dripped with venomous ooze, and fanged teeth gleamed like sharpened ivory daggers. The priests cowered fearfully against the walls, then fell on their faces before him, trembling uncontrollably as they begged for mercy. This time there was no cage to imprison him, no bars to keep him at bay, and he stared back at them with wickedly, eyes brimming with malevolent glee.

His priests fell silent, knowing there was no escape from their terrible god, and in the next instant he was upon them, clawing, ripping, tearing, devouring. The chamber resounded with cries of terror and desperate screams as Dhampir began to feast upon them one by one.

In the confusion of the melee Adhra pressed his back against the wall. His lips moved fervently, reciting an incantation few of his order had ever learned. Amid the fires of burning brimstone and the black smoke swirling throughout the room, no one noticed his body disappear into the stone.

Dhampir's long, deadly, tail flicked menacingly through the air like a sword-blade on the end of a bullwhip, impaling and disemboweling. He lunged this way and that, clutching at the terrified priests with all four hands, his talons closing around their bodies tightly, crushing the breath from their lungs before his slavering maw closed over their heads, decapitating their writhing bodies in a single, monstrous bite.

His hunger was endless, his thirst for blood unquenchable, and within moments the priests were gone, devoured feverishly by the horrible god they had so foolishly dedicated their lives to serving. Dhampir stood and gazed about the chamber intently, his blazing eyes searching for some shred of human remains that had been missed or overlooked amid the mayhem of his slaughter. The floor was soaked in blood, the walls splattered with gore. The dark Lord spoke in unearthly tones, and the blood upon the floor began to flow towards him in tiny streams. As it reached his feet it disappeared, absorbed into his body like water on a dry sponge.

The room resounded deafeningly with evil laughter as he strode to the doors and flung them open with a gesture of his clawed hand. The heavy crossbars that had been used to barricade them from the opposite side splintered and burst into matchsticks.

Dhampir peered down the passageway that led up to the street, then turned back to the abyss and roared into the flames. Instantly hordes of dark, loathsome creatures began swarming over the lip of the chasm and pouring into the chamber.

Their bodies were elongated, nearly four feet from end to end. Their abdomens were covered beneath in thick armor shells, between which an oily substance oozed. They had six legs, jointed and covered in rust-colored barbs, the rearmost long and powerful, built for leaping. The foremost were armed with pincers for clutching, ripping and tearing flesh from sinew and bone.

Their heads were horned and nightmarish. Huge black eyes gleamed darkly like polished obsidian orbs from their misshapen faces. Serrated incisors clicked together like deadly knives, and steel-like mandibles moved anxiously in demonic anticipation. A pair of scaled wings folded over the backs of the hell-spawned locusts. They resembled like the wings of dragonflies, rustling eerily as the creatures fluttered about. The translucent wings were much too weak and small to be used for flight, serving only to help propel them quickly over short distances.

Some of the creatures sported long, curving tails tipped with a venomous stinger. These were the legions of Hel itself, born in the dark pits of the Underworld where even devils fear to tread.

"Tonight we feast upon the sons of men!" Dhampir declared to his hellish minions. "Come forth! Glut yourselves upon them, and be strengthened, for my time of bondage is at an end, and behold! What mighty things I shall do!"

With an awful noise the locust creatures surged through the open door. They clambered over one another in a dizzying frenzy fueled by the lust for living flesh, racing up through the tunnel and spilling into the deserted streets. They gathered moment like an angry torrent, swarming out upon the slumbering town, and the hapless citizens were unaware as the horde boiled up around them in the blackness of the night.

Dhampir followed them, much too tall to stand up in the narrow tunnel. He dropped to the ground and scurried up the passage, using his hands and feet to claw his way up to the streets above.

Suddenly the town began to spring to life, as the groggy citizens awoke from their dreams to find themselves embedded in a nightmare from which there was no waking, no escape. Screams of horror filled the night sky, back-lit by broiling smoke and tongues of fire as the demon horde eagerly sought their prey amid the flames that quickly spread throughout the town.

41

Hordo awakened with a start.

What the nine hells was that? His heart beat quickly in his chest as he sat in the darkness upon his bed, listening to the sounds outside his quarters. He threw back the blankets and got to his feet, reaching for his clothes. Suddenly the floor shook violently, and he lost his balance, thrown sprawling upon the rough wooden floor. Was that a scream he heard?

The guardsman hurriedly finished dressing and snatched up his sword. A knock at the door made him whirl instantly, blade drawn in readiness.

"Who's there?" he called out briskly.

"Sir!" came the fearful reply from outside. "We are under attack!"

He recognized the messenger's voice at once as belonging to his second officer. Hordo drew back the bolt and sheathed his sword. "Where are the rest of the men?" he demanded.

"They await you in the guardhouse," the guardsman responded quickly. His face was twisted with panic and fright in the flickering light of the torch he held tightly in his fist.

"Get hold of yourself, man!" Hordo barked gruffly.

"Yes sir!" the man replied, his voice shaking as he spoke.

"Hurry now," Hordo said. "Lead the way to the others."

They quickly made their way down the long corridor to a flight of stairs, below which the town guards had already assembled and were waiting anxiously. As Hordo neared the bottom his lieutenant, a squarely built veteran of many border wars, stepped forward quickly.

"Report, Rowlov!" Hordo barked. "What is our situation?"

"Fires have broken out in several places throughout the town, sir. I sent out five men to discover the cause, but so far they have not returned. The people are in a panic."

"Where did the fire start?" Hordo asked.

"Near as I can tell, over by the lake. The old warehouses are engulfed in flames, and a few have already collapsed." Rowlov's expression was grave.

"Two weeks ago this town was a swamp, and now it is dry as a tinderbox," Hordo muttered under his breath.

"Aye, sir," Rowlov replied. "We have little time."

Hordo nodded grimly, then faced the rest of the men under his command. "We will head for the lake. Each of you bring a bucket. Once we get there we will divide up into groups and form a chain, starting at the water's edge. Hopefully we can contain the fire before it gets too far out of hand, but we must act swiftly!"

Within moments all was ready, and with Hordo and Rowlov at the lead, they filed out of the guardhouse and turned down the street toward the lake. They had gone only a few blocks when Hordo brought them briskly to a halt.

"What is it?" Rowlov asked tensely, as Hordo drew his sword.

"There is something amiss," his commander responded. He pointed to an old building a block away. "Did you see that?"

"Aye," Rowlov confirmed darkly. "It seems as though there is something moving upon the walls."

"Just shadows, nothing more, but nonetheless...the fire may be a diversion," Hordo grated. "Something does moves along the ground, at the far corner down there."

"Why would any one attack Luxantia?" Rowlov wondered aloud.

"Who can say," said Hordo, turning to his men. "Draw your swords!" he ordered loudly. "We may be fighting more than just fire this night!"

He turned back to Rowlov. "Take ten men. Go to the soldiers camp outside the wall.... their Captain's name is Brutus. Tell him Luxantia needs their aid, then meet me at the lake. Any volunteers you can scrounge up along the way will be greatly welcome too. Understood?"

"Yes sir," Rowlov answered. "We are most fortunate to have a detachment of the King's soldiers so close at hand. Consider it done."

"Go quickly!" Hordo said.

Rowlov turned and selected his men. "We go to the soldiers outside the gate," he told them quickly. "Keep your eye open for any sign of attackers."

Hordo paused as Rowlov led his men away, then he turned back in the direction of the lake. "Follow me!" He called out over his shoulder, starting out once more.

As they rounded a bend in the street they were met by a mob of desperate townsmen. They ran past Hordo and his volunteers, nearly blind with fear and dread. The citizens were screaming incoherently in horror, trampling over his men as they fled toward the main gates, and Hordo called out to the frightened men now rushing by.

"Men of Luxantia!" he shouted. "Turn back and lend a hand to fight the fire!"

His cries went unnoticed, and Hordo reached out and grabbed a local merchant by the tunic as he rushed along with the throng. The man's face vividly portrayed his terror.

"Will you not help us save Luxantia from the flames?" Hordo bellowed mightily.

The fellow struggled desperately to break the guardsman's hold upon him. "It is not the fire we flee," he shrieked. "The creatures….!" The merchant stammered something unintelligible and tore his tunic out of Hordo's grasp before dashing away.

As he ran he called back over his shoulder. "You'll run too when you see them….!"

Hordo grouped his men into a tight formation and turned in the direction from which the town's folk fled. He stepped on something that wriggled and squirmed beneath his foot and pitched head first into the street. He swore angrily, hearing the familiar squeal of a sewer rat, and one of his men drug him to his feet as several more of the vile rodents scurried over him. A large rat clawed up his leg, and he swatted it away with the blunt side of his blade before crying out to his men and charging ahead.

"Quickly, men!" he yelled. "To the lake!"

Only five more blocks! he told himself, forcing his legs to move even faster. Suddenly he stopped dead in his tracks, and two of the men behind him tripped over each other as his company of guardsmen abruptly came to a halt. Hordo's eyes grew wide in disbelief as a wave of horrible creatures swelled around the next corner and rushed upon them. Never before had he seen such hellish-looking things, and both he and his men stood staring, shocked and bewildered, as the massive locusts came at them in a raging storm of wings and mandibles.

The horrors were nearly upon them by the time Hordo had regained his senses. His sword flashed as he held it high and screamed at the top of his lungs.

"To arms! We won't be able to outrun them! Draw your swords and fight like men!"

In another instant the creatures were upon them, their legs clawing and kicking, wings fluttering and twitching, pincers moving with blinding speed and fury. Hordo slashed wildly at the horde, his sword a blur as he stabbed one through the side of it's grotesque head, then struck out viciously at another as it lurched toward him, it's pincers snapping dangerously close to his throat.

His men, knowing that there would be no escaping the monsters, drew their swords and fell to, shouting and striking out insanely at the foe.

"To me!" cried Hordo, attempting to gather the guardsmen into a tighter group. "Damn the fire! Our only chance is to get to the lake," he shouted. "And pray these creatures cannot swim!"

Not all of the creatures were attacking. The larger portion of them flew past and overhead, chasing after the fleeing residents of Luxantia as they made a frantic dash to the main gates of the town. The hell-spawn seemed to somehow know that the unarmed citizens would be much easier prey. Many of the hideous bugs caught fire as they swarmed after their quarry, and high-pitched squeals of pain rose eerily above the din and confusion of the night.

The creatures launched themselves at the men wildly, leaping high into the air and landing heavily on top of them. Hordo managed to bunch his men together, and slowly they worked their way down the broiling street. The locusts fell back a little, and he drove his men into them relentlessly. His small company becoming an island of gleaming steel, rising and falling in a boiling sea of flailing appendages and beating wings.

One of the guards screamed in agony as he was dragged away into the midst of the horde. The sound of his terrified voice quickly faded as the creatures piled around him. They fought amongst themselves, quickly tearing his body to pieces, and the taste of human blood drove them into an even greater frenzy.

Another man cried out helplessly as he fell beneath a tangle of legs and pincers. His screams sent a chill through the rest of the guards, but nonetheless served to encourage them to redouble their efforts and fight back twice as hard.

By this time the fires had spread throughout most of the town, and Luxantia as a whole was engulfed in hues of crimson, orange and yellow as the fire danced upon the rooftops and licked hungrily up the walls of the old, weathered buildings that comprised the larger portion of the settlement. The buildings were bone dry, and hungry waves of rolling flames spread with frightening speed from one structure to the next. Columns of black smoke billowed up into the night sky, silhouetted by the brightness of the crackling inferno. Burning timbers and beams collapsed and crashed into the streets, sparks and embers spraying about them brilliantly.

Hordo's company had their hands full battling the overgrown insects as it was, but now the fire made their going all the more perilous, and three of his men were crushed, buried beneath the weight of crashing debris. Judging from their dying screams, it was hard to tell which was worse; death by being torn limb from limb amid the locusts, or being burned alive. Hordo though he would almost prefer the first, but he was of no mind to surrender his life just yet.

He thrust his sword as a pair of nightmarish mandibles slammed shut only inched from his face. The blade pierced the creature through the neck at an angle, the tip protruding out the back of it's ugly head, and he wrenched it free just in time to impale another as it fell upon him, it's pincers clawing at his cloak.

His clothes and armor were covered in gore, a dark, oily sludge that seemed to ooze from the bodies of the horrors. He ducked to avoid getting splattered in the face by more of the filth as a guard on his left lopped off a head, then slashed out savagely as another creature rushed in to attack him.

His company had nearly reached the lake, but only a handful now remained. They had suffered some serious losses, yet they continued to fight valiantly, in spite of seeing many of their number die horribly, ripped apart by the army of angry demons.

The creatures were awful to look upon, but they were not possessed of any great amount of intelligence. Their only motivation was the lust for living flesh. They fought solely by instinct, and many of the them shied away from Hordo's company after feeling the sting of sharpened steel. Flames that swirled about them, burning the locust too, and many of them turned on each other in a feverish attempt to scramble away from the searing heat and blinding smoke.

As they fought their way to the safety of the water, the foe's numbers seemed to diminish considerably. Within thirty paces from the edge of the lake, the locusts had disappeared, and Hordo urged his men to hurry. All hope of putting out the fire had been crushed. His men were now too few and the fire too great to battle such a blaze. Soon the spot on which they now stood would be hotter than a blacksmith's forge, and if the fire didn't kill them, they would surely suffocate from the intensity of the heat and the smothering smoke. Only in the water would they be able to survive.

Suddenly a terrible roar filled the air and Hordo spun about. Instantly he was filled with a fear so overwhelming, that for a moment he couldn't even move. He felt his legs refused to respond, his heart thrummed in his chest, and a creature far worse than any horde of locust turned toward him.

It's eyes burned brighter than the flames that spread around him. Its huge arms were thickly muscled and covered in scale-like armor, it's face more terrifying than any nightmare he had ever dreamed. It opened its dreadful mouth and grinned grotesquely. Shreds of meat and bloody tissue were plainly visible, the remains of the demon's last victim, caught between its terrible fangs.

Hordo knew that he alone would be no match for this new demonic foe. It would take the combined efforts of all the men he had left to bring this fearsome creature down. As it moved towards him, he tried to call out to his men. At first his voice failed him, his words coming out in a jumbled gasp that was barely audible. His lips felt numb and swollen, his tongue unresponsive. As the beast came closer his voice returned, and he shouted to the remaining guards.

"To arms! To arms!"

He glanced back quickly to see his guardsmen scrambling desperately for the water, and his heart instantly filled with rage, realizing that they were abandoning him.

"Come back and fight, you cowards!" he bellowed as they splashed into the lake. "Stand your ground and fight with me, or by Mithra's tits, I'll gut you myself!"

Clearly they didn't care.

Already several of them were wading out into the water. He shouted at them again, even louder, but they would not listen, for they too had seen the monster. Hordo turned to glare grimly at the visage, and the rage he felt inside him grew beyond description. His knuckled turned white as he clenched his sword with a vise-like grip, his eyes narrowing with resolve and defiance.

"I have not fought through flames and monsters to be foiled by you in the end," he growled. "Come meet my sword!"

Dhampir strode closer, his eyes filled with malevolence and hate. He reached for the guardsman, and Hordo swung his blade with all his might. The beast blocked the blow effortlessly with one of its massive, talon-fingered hands, then clutched Hordo by the waist and lifted him up into the air. It stared at him for a moment, a few seconds that seemed to last a lifetime. So tight and powerful was the creatures grip upon him that all movement became impossible. He felt a vile substance drip from its partially open mouth and trickle sluggishly over his face.

"You are a brave man," the demon intoned.

Hordo's mind raced deliriously. *The beast can talk! Surely it will kill me any moment now!*

"No, I shall not," it said, in answer to his thoughts. "And I am no beast! My name is Dhampir. Have you heard of me?"

Hordo tried to speak, but his lips refused to move.

"Well speak up, mortal!" Dhampir commanded. "Are you

familiar with my name?"

"Y-y-yes," Hordo managed. *Mithra be damned! Not only can it talk, but it reads my mind as well!*

"Yes, I can read your mind. It is no great feat, trust me," Dhampir said thinly. "And Mithra shall be damned soon enough, along with every other god in heaven!"

"What do you want?" Hordo whispered in horror. "Kill me and be done with it!"

"You shall not die this night," Dhampir replied. "You will be a witness. You will tell the world that I am coming, and I will be no man nor wizard's slave."

"I don't understand," the man responded fearfully. "I am no wizard, and I don't know of any either."

Dhampir gripped him tighter. The breath was crushed from his chest, and Hordo struggled desperately for air.

"On second thought, you do look mighty tasty!" the demon replied, surveying his victim with renewed interest.

From out on the lake Hordo heard the voices of his men, those who had deserted him to flee across the water. Now they were crying out to each other in terror, and he discerned by the sound of their thrashing about that they were in some sort of mortal danger. The demon gazed out over the lake briefly, then directed his attention once more to Hordo.

"Your men have just met some of my other children," Dhampir informed him without expression. "So you see now that the lake would have provided you no refuge in the end."

The fiend tilted its head slightly, listening to the town guards as they were slaughtered by the creatures swarming around them in the lake. The water boiled about them as long, slimy tentacles wrapped themselves around their bodies and pulled them down beneath the surface. Serpentine forms moved like eels through the churning water of the lake, and the surface suddenly became red with blood.

Hordo shut his eyes tightly. Perhaps this is a dream! He told himself silently. Any minute now I'll wake up, safe and warm in my bed. Soon the screams of his men were gone, and he opened his eyes to find the demon still staring at him intently. The guardsman's face twisted in terror, and Dhampir grinned maliciously. With a free hand he laid hold of Hordo's left arm.

"Do you like music?" the demon asked him suddenly.

Hordo stared at him, confused. "Music?"

"Yes," Dhampir responded. "Does it please you?"

"I....I guess so," the man replied haltingly.

"Well!" Dhampir slavered. "Either you do, or you don't." He

glared at Hordo menacingly. "Now which is it?"

"Y-yes, I…I do."

The demon looked pleased. "You mortals have such a wide variety of music. I once found it interesting, but it has been ages since I last heard the strains of a lyre or a harp. Now that I have returned, I doubt it shall give me much pleasure. Do you have any idea as to why that is?"

Hordo shook his head weakly. The stench of Dhampir's putrid breath made him sick.

"Your instruments have no souls," the demon continued. "Even your singing is contrived at best. There is only one type of music that I enjoy. There is only one song that is truly filled with passion."

He glared at his captive. "You will sing it for me now."

"I am no singer," Hordo gasped. "I'm a guardsman."

"Oh! But I have such faith in you!" Dhampir enthused. His grip on Hordo's left arm tightened. With a sudden jerk he ripped off the guardsman's left arm, tearing it free from his body at the shoulder. Blood spurted from the joint in a crimson arc, spraying in the air like a fountain of gore. The pain was excruciating, and Hordo screamed in tortured agony.

"Yes!" exclaimed Dhampir. "That's it! That is the song I've been longing to hear!"

The demon turned in the direction of the main gate, striding casually through the carnage of Luxantia while the fires raged about him. As he walked along, he ripped strips of flesh from Hordo's broken body and thrust them eagerly into his mouth. In this manner he slowly devoured the man while making his way through the ruined streets to the main gate on the other side of town.

Outside the palisade wall of Luxantia, Brutus prepared to ready his men for battle. He knew that they would need a reason to do what must be done, some explanation that made enough sense to them that they would feel that it was not only justifiable, but necessary as well. On his right hand side stood the dark forbidding figure of Skeltar, his heavy hood concealing his features from open view.

"The priests of Dhampir have used their foul art to unleash a terrible plague upon this town," Brutus informed them. "It is such an evil malady, that even the slightest touch by those who are smitten by it will be enough to infect you."

"I was in town just this afternoon," one of the soldiers offered. "I saw no such plague."

"Of course not," Brutus responded harshly. "The evil sickness did not fall until after the setting of the sun. Such are the ways of these accursed priests." He spat upon the ground as if to punctuate his reply.

He paused, knowing that they were watching him closely. Rarely had Skeltar appeared in front of the them since leaving Zebulon, and now with the wizard standing beside him, Brutus knew that he had their undivided attention. If the mighty Skeltar was personally attending such a briefing, it must truly be important indeed, and an anxious hush fell over the troops.

"Too long have these priests intimidated our country with their black arts," Brutus postured. "Too long have they brought famine and pestilence upon our good land, and wrought pain and suffering upon the poor and wealthy alike. If they have conjured such a disease upon this little town tonight, it won't be long before they cast some spell on us as well."

His words instantly caused the soldiers to become greatly disturbed. It was just the sort of response he'd anticipated.

"I say we kill them all!" one of the soldiers growled murderously.

"Aye," said another. "My sword has seen only sand and dust since we left Zebulon."

"Here, here!" agreed a stout man of arms in gray scale mail. "I thought this mission would involve bloodshed and loot, but so far all I have done is sit by and watch my blade rust in the sheath!"

"Silence!" Brutus shouted fiercely, and the talking ceased abruptly. "Now listen up! Our leader Skeltar has been given charge by the King to do as he sees fit, and he will deal with the priests of Dhampir. Everyone knows that swords fail miserably against the foul magick that these damnable priests wield against our land. But praise be to Mithra that the most renowned and powerful wizard in all of the Westermarch stands with us on this night, to destroy these workers of the profane with the very arts they use against us!"

A hearty cheer went up from the men, and Brutus waited for a moment until their voices died down.

"The priests shall be his concern, but ours will be the ones who have been smitten by this loathsome plague. You must not let any of the inhabitants of this town escape alive, else they will flee to some other place and afflict all those they meet."

"You want us to kill the town folk?" a soldier asked in surprise.

"Every man, woman and child," Brutus confirmed. "There is no other choice, unless of course you wish to fall prey to the sickness that rots their flesh and bones even as we speak. Their fates have been already decided by the priests of Dhampir, and none of them shall live long enough to see another sunrise. Our swords shall show them more mercy than the horrible death which awaits them."

"Even so," one of the captains objected, "killing unarmed civilians is a dirty task. Would that I could but get my hands on just one of those priests, I'd hew his black heart from his chest with my poniard."

"I understand how you feel," Brutus agreed grimly. "There is no honor in slaying the innocent, but better they be dispatched quickly than linger for hours in torment. On the other hand, you are all soldiers, to the last man. It is nothing that you have not done before, except this time the pay is much better!"

"By Mithra's teeth!" one of the men exclaimed. "I'll kill whoever I must if it is a matter of them or me! I'll face my enemy standing and die by his sword willingly, but I'll be damned before I'm taken by some fell plague!"

More murmurs and curses broke out amongst the men, and presently Brutus held up his hand, motioning them to quiet down.

"Enough!" he shouted authoritatively. "We haven't much time. Already the citizens have lost their minds and are storming the gates. Harden your hearts! Fight like men, and leave none alive! You have all been paid well, with the gold and jewels that Skeltar gave you earlier tonight. That gold was taken earlier from the treasury of Dhampir's priests. Now it is time for you to earn your keep!"

The soldiers roared their enthusiasm. The clank of steel on steel filled the night, and with military precision they quickly strapped on breastplates and bucklers, gray mail and shining steel helmets, drawing up into a tight line that bristled with spear points and gleaming sword blades bared for battle.

Brutus rode down the length of the formation on a great stallion, his armor shining, the bright red plume on his helm trailing behind him, and the eagle upon his breastplate striking fire from the glow of the flames that now swallowed up the town. His steed's hooves drummed a beat of death upon the hard-packed dusty earth as he shouted out orders to the captains of ten, giving last minute instructions before the melee ensued.

"I want every second man to draw his bow. The rest of you take up defensive positions with your shields and spears. We will cut them down with a hail of arrows when they rush out of the town, and when the gap between us is finally closed they shall fall upon a wall of spears! Make no mistake; it is a grim night indeed. A bad night to be a peasant or a priest....but a good night to be a soldier!"

It took little effort for Rowlov and the men with him to reach the gates of Luxantia. So greatly did the frightened mob of citizens press about them as they fled across the town that the guardsmen were swept along inescapably in a veritable human sea. If Rowlov had changed his mind and attempted returning to the place where he and Hordo had parted company, it would have been virtually impossible.

The sight of eleven guardsmen heading toward the main gate along with everyone else did little to assuage the fears of the town folk. On the contrary, it only served to lend fuel to their fears, and they rushed on all the more desperately than before. Women floundered amid the madness, clinging to their young, vainly seeking to prevent them from being trampled mindlessly underfoot. The dirty streets were carpeted thickly with the crushed and broken bodies of fleeing rats. The vermin outnumbered the other residents of the town nearly ten to one. They bit and clawed as a thousand booted and sandal-clad feet pummeled them mercilessly into mangled, bloody pulp.

Amid the panicked dries of the throng, Rowlov heard the voices farthest behind suddenly increase in volume and terror. He thought instantly of the dark shadows he'd seen creeping along the wall and swarming down the crooked alleys, and wondered silently if perhaps those strange shapes were responsible for the horrified screams that now reached his ears.

The gates stood open wide up ahead, and he was swept towards them inexorably. He scooped up a child that had been separated from her mother and carried her in his massive hairy arms. The tot was too frightened to cry, her mind too young to comprehend the horror that swelled about them, and she dug her tiny fingers into his skin as he moved ahead.

Past the wooden gates the mob streamed out in every direction, rushing toward the line of steel-helmed soldiers that had drawn up just beyond the outer wall. The armor-clad men stood their ground stolidly, watching the crazed citizens of Luxantia sweep like a raging torrent in their direction. Before them at the far end of the line Brutus sat mounted upon a black warhorse, his face expressionless, and to his left stood a darkly robed and hooded figure.

The captain raised his sword and held it high above his head, then peered down at the shrouded form of the wizard, awaiting his command as the frightened mob drew nearer by the second. Rowlov halted, peering intently about the scene as his men drew up around him. He set down the child, telling her to seek out her mother, then espying Brutus, he started forward again, making his way quickly to him through the panic driven throng of helpless men and screaming women.

He was only some thirty paces from the line of soldiers when he heard Brutus shout a command, and he looked up just in time to see the soldier's arm fall, his gleaming short-sword held out before him. For one long, desperate moment he stood there, startled and numb, his mind realing, unwilling to accept the treachery his eyes confirmed to be true. He watched in horror as the soldiers set arrows to bowstrings, drawing back and taking aim upon their helpless victims, the citizens of Luxantia.

Suddenly Rowlov turned to face his men, his eyes burning with anger, his lips twisted into a grim snarl of rage.

"Draw your swords!" he rasped as his own leaped from its scabbard. "The soldiers intend to kill us all, guards and townsfolk alike!"

His men stared at him dumfounded, and as the first volley of arrows fell hissing among the throng a flood of vulgar profanities issued from him and he barked once more. "To arms, dogs! Draw your swords and die like men, for no safety will be found here this night!"

Then he turned and stormed upon the soldiers, not waiting to see if his men followed or fled behind him. Upon the ground lay the dead and dying, feathered shafts protruding from their bodies as they writhed in agony, the dry dust of the plain drinking their blood like a thirsty sponge. He bounded over the fallen and swarmed upon the soldiers like a howling storm, his sword cleaving a circle of death about him.

One soldier, caught off guard as he reached over his shoulder for another arrow, looked up at the last instant to see Rowlov's blade sweep in. The man's eyes still blinked in confusion as his head rolled upon the ground and his body fell away in the opposite direction, a fountain of blood spurting from the place where his head had been only moments before.

Seven of the remaining town guardsmen joined Rowlov, and as

he slashed a hole through the line of soldiers they rushed in to fill it. Their blades fell and rose in the angry rhythm of death whose meter their fearless leader set before them and now maintained with brutal fury.

As Rowlov's desperate men rallied to his side, the soldiers drew their swords and met them with military precision, the likes of which no mere town guard could hope to match. In the matter of minutes the guardsmen were dead, their bloody corpses scattered and butchered upon the ground, but Rowlov yet stood, his voice rising deliriously above the din of the chaos about him, his blade weaving a pattern of gore and slaughter.

"Come on, you traitorous sons of whores!" he yelled, his eyes wild and insane. His blood roared like thunder in his ears, bloodlust coursing through his veins and driving him on as soldiers fell away beneath the frenzy of his blade.

He felt the sharp sting of steel as a soldier slashed open his left shoulder, and he reeled to met the man in a spray of sparks as their blades crashed together. The soldier struggled hard to parry and block as Rowlov delivered a series of powerful blows, driving him to his knees.

An arrow stuck the guardsman, piercing his battered armor from behind as his sword fell, cleaving a soldier's upper body into two bloody pieces. He lunged back and swung his blade just in time to swipe a hurled spear out of the air, then staggered forward red-hot agony rushed through him. Another soldier had struck him from the side, his sword thrusting through the unprotected spot where his breastplate buckled to the armor on his back. Rowlov gathered his strength and forced himself to his feet, but a devastating blow clove his helmet in half and sent him sprawling upon the ground.

His vision blurred, blood flowing into his eyes and down his head from an awful wound, and he peered up to see the massive form of Brutus standing above him, sword held firmly in his knotted fist.

"Well done!" Brutus allowed. "You have fought admirably, as good as any trained soldier I've ever met. Never have I seen so many soldiers die at the hand of a single man."

"Coward!" Rowlov spat, blood frothing from his swollen lips. "You are nothing but a worthless traitor!" he sputtered. "Had I but thirty good men, I would carve your soldiers to pieces. I'd cut your head from your shoulders and leave your corpse for the buzzards!"

"Aye," replied Brutus, "I doubt not that you would try, and a mighty effort you would surely make of it too," he agreed. "But in the end it would be the same--and I would stand as I do now, with your blood dripping from my blade, and you, dying like a dog at my feet."

Rowlov looked about. They were in the midst of chaos. Unarmed townsfolk screamed hideously as solders fell upon them without mercy, sword and ax falling just as swiftly upon men as women and children. Arrows rained upon the scrambling people like a hailstorm of death, and they fell to the earth convulsing in pain only to be ran through by steel-tipped spears and pikes. They tried to turn back into the town, but the gates were now closed. Skeltar had sealed up the town with his arcane powers, thus protecting his soldiers from the hell-spawn that fed upon human flesh within.

"The King shall hear of this!" Rowlov foamed bitterly. "My captain shall send him word, and your treason will bring you to the gallows."

"Ha!" laughed Brutus, "the King shall indeed hear of this, for tonight we march for Zebulon. In a week or so it too shall fall, and King Xalton will beg at Skeltar's feet for mercy, for none can withstand the might of the wizard and his power!"

Rowlov glared at him, his breath coming in short, stabbing gasps. The carnage that surrounded him seemed surreal, like a scene from a nightmare from which escape was impossible and death inescapable.

"Finish it! Swing your sword and slay me. If you have not the courage to be a man, at least let me die as one!"

The guardsman reached for his sword, and one of the solders moved in to strike him down, but Brutus held him back. "You had your chance to kill this man when he charged the line, and you failed. See how many he has taken with him?" He shoved the soldier away harshly. "Join the others in killing the innocent."

While Brutus had been chastising the soldier, Rowlov had managed to climb to his feet, and now he stood, wobbling and swaying like a tree in the wind, awaiting the final blow of the forester's ax. His fingers wrapped around the handle of his sword like talons of iron as he tried to summon enough of the strength that yet remained within him for one last powerful blow.

As Brutus shoved the soldier, Rowlov lifted his sword. He turned toward the guardsman as he began to swing, his blade cutting a deadly arc that was aimed at the Captain's helmed head. Brutus somehow managed to raise his own sword, but he had been caught off guard, and his parry was weak. Rowlov was a powerfully built man, and even though he stood upon the threshold of death, his blow carried twice the force of most fighting men.

Brutus cursed violently as their blades smashed together. He fell back and his short-sword nearly fell from his grasp as Rowlov's blade slammed down upon his plumed helmet. The guard faltered for a brief moment, stumbling forward, attempting to gather his strength again, but that mere instant was all the time that Brutus needed to strike back. He thrust his sword with all his might, and it plunged into the guardsman's chest and sank to the hilt. He stared at the man for a few seconds, then in one fluid motion, he pushed Rowlov off of his blade and swung it in a circular path that severed his head from his neck in a single stroke.

Rowlov's body shuddered, then collapsed upon the corpse-strewn ground, his head falling heavily, eyes glazed over with death.

Brutus slung the dead man's blood from his blade and strode back to his mount, and all the while Skeltar peered out at him questioningly from beneath his hood, as if waiting for an explanation or response.

"If you want something done right, you have to do it yourself," Brutus offered coldly. He felt a trickle of blood run down his face.

"Yet you have been cut," Skeltar retorted, then shrugged. "Perhaps you will be more careful the next time."

"There won't be a next time," Brutus replied dryly. "The man is dead by my hand, though a better soldier I have rarely met....except maybe for Marcus."

"There will be a next time," the wizard insisted. "And a better warrior you will meet than the guard you fought tonight. A warrior who shall be far more formidable than your old friend Marcus ever was."

44

The horsemen spread out into a wide "V" formation and bore down upon them at break-neck speed. Dust billowed into the air as their horses careened ahead, white lather foaming from their mouths and splattering back along their sides as their riders urged them on relentlessly.

Joktan turned to peer into the distance one last time before the fight began. He could see the second group of riders now quite plainly, and they too were closing in at an alarming rate.

Sheba armed herself. Holding her shield firmly in the left hand and an ax in the right, she assumed a battle stance and faced the enemy with a grim look of determination.

"They wear the garb of priests," she growled.

"Aye," Joktan agreed, "it would seem our assumption has proven to be correct."

"The other group of riders will be here soon," she said. "I did not expect them to move so quickly." Sheba looked at him seriously. "I know that we are both good fighters, but this is a bit much. Our situation grows desperate."

"I happen to like our situation," he growled.

Sheba shook her head and muttered a curse, while Joktan drew an arrow from his quiver and notched it to his bow.

The horsemen were still some hundred paces away when he fired his first shot. It struck the lead rider's mount in the chest, and the wounded beast crumbled to the ground in a cloud of dust, sending its rider flailing into the air with a sudden scream.

His second arrow fell short, missing completely, as if an invisible shield had been erected between himself and the riders.

"Mithra be damned!" Joktan cursed angrily. "That arrow should not have missed!"

He drew another and let it fly. The arrow flew straight and true, nearly a blur as it sped toward its intended mark, but at the last instant it glanced wildly away. Although it failed to strike a priest, the horse nearest him was not so protected, and the shaft tore into the steed's front shoulder. The wound was far from fatal, but it succeeded in maiming the animal just enough to make it stagger and fall behind. It disappeared in the cloud of dust, and Joktan turned to Sheba.

"They shield themselves with sorcery!" he spat. "If you cannot kill the riders, take out their mounts."

Sheba nodded resolutely. "Such magick requires focused concentration. I'll take the left flank, you take the others." she grimaced. "If we can break their line and rattle them a bit, then perhaps the spell will be broken."

The horsemen were now within thirty paces and closing fast. In unison they lowered their spears and fell upon them, the steel points gleaming brightly in the sunlight. Joktan shouldered the bow and drew his sword.

The rider that had now assumed the lead position closed in, his spear bobbing up and down with the motion of his horse as he held it level with Joktan's chest.

Joktan stood his ground, unflinching as the priest bore down upon him. Then suddenly he let out a hideous war cry and charged at the on-coming foe, his sword held high overhead with both hands.

The man held his spear firmly poised to strike, but at the last instant Joktan parried the weapon with a vicious side-ways cut. His blade smashed into the haft of the spear. It splintered as he crouched low and swung his sword in a continuing arc that severed the tendons in the front right leg of the attacker's horse just above the knee. The beast bellowed in pain as it surged past him, toppling headfirst into the grass. The rider was thrown from his saddle, his arms flailing as he hurdled over his mount and crashed to the ground, unable to rise.

Another rider tried in vain to clear the first man's steed as it thrashed madly, attempting to regain it's feet, but to no avail. His mount was caught by the beasts kicking legs. The horse tripped, sending the rider to join his fallen comrade in the grass. The man struck the earth hard, his head twisting back grotesquely as his neck snapped.

The dust momentarily blinded Joktan. He rose to his feet and spun around just in time to see Sheba throw down her shield and leap into the air. She jumped so high that she cleared both her attacker and his mount. The woman turned as she leaped, landing neatly behind her foe astride his steed. An instant later her ax clove the man's head clean from his neck. His twitching corpse slumped from the saddle, becoming lost to sight in a spray of blood and cloud of dust.

The line of riders now split into two groups as they neared the crest of the hill, each circling around in the direction from which they had just came. Joktan knew that they would ride in a circle, rejoining for another assault. He decided to test Sheba's theory, loosing two arrows as the enemy sought to regroup and charge again. Two priests screamed, lurched from their mounts, and hit the ground. Joktan smiled grimly, satisfied that the spell was broken, and took aim again.

A third rider cried in agony as an arrow pierced his left leg. The barbed point ripped through his calf and buried itself deeply in his steed's ribcage, pinning him to his horse and causing the beast to stampede uncontrollably. The priest clung frantically to the reins before loosing his grip and falling from the saddle. The wooden shaft snapped and he fell to the ground, clutching his useless appendage.

Sheba spurred her mount toward another priest, leaping from her steed onto his as she drew near, an ax in each hand. The man tried to turn in the saddle to defend himself, but it was too late. One of her axes smashed through his cloak, opening up a gaping hole in his side. The other came down upon the back of his neck, and he pitched sideways from his mount, blood streaming from his wounds.

Another rider turned toward her, his spear raised high for a powerful thrust. She hurled an ax at the man, aiming for his chest, but he quickly reined his mount to the side and ducked. The ax spun past him, striking a fellow priest's horse in the side of its neck. The beast bellowed in terror and began bucking furiously, sending it's master sprawling in the grass.

By this time the other man had closed in upon her, and he flung his spear with all his might. Sheba swung to one side just in time. It whipped past her, falling harmlessly and becoming lost in the haze of dust that engulfed them. She pulled herself upright once more just as the attacker's mount slammed into her steed. Her ax was lost, knocked out of her hand by the jarring force of the collision, and Sheba fell backwards. She struck the ground, sputtering and coughing on account of the dust as she struggled to her feet. Through the haze of battle the robed form of a priest loomed before her. His dark robes billowed about him as he raised his sword high for a powerful downward stroke and rushed in for the kill.

Sheba threw herself to one side, evading his swing and maneuvering herself behind him. Before her attacker could react, she grabbed his head with both hands and wrenched it back. The priest's neck snapped with a sickening crunch, and she quickly reached around in front of him, grasping his windpipe. Her fingers closed upon his esophagus, and with an angry snarl she tore his throat open and flung his corpse to the ground.

She swept her long hair back with a bloodied hand and drew her sword, then turned to meet the remaining attackers. "Who dies next!" she cried, the bloodlust burning like fire in her veins. To her surprise, a low voice answered from somewhere behind her.

"I'll accept your challenge," a sinister voice intoned, and she spun to meet her adversary. A priest, armed only with a thin, black wand, stood fearlessly before her. He swept back the hood of his dark cloak to reveal a shaven skull as Sheba stepped toward him.

"Come and meet your god!" she snarled, lunging at him with her blade.

He raised his right hand and pointed the wand at her, and instantly a bluish-white bolt of light leapt through the air. Sheba gasped in shock and dropped her sword as the arcane blast smote her in the chest. An electrifying jolt surged through her body, and she sank involuntarily to her knees. Searing pain overloaded her senses. The priest moved closer, summoning another powerful bolt of energy and directing it at her with the wand. A brilliant flash struck her forehead, danced over her flesh like lightening, and she collapsed upon the ground.

Her muscles convulsed uncontrollably. Agony far beyond anything she had ever known shot up her spine and coursed through her limbs. She lay there helplessly, fighting for breath and unable to move, as the priest came closer, his lips curled triumphantly.

"I have already met my God," he sneered. "Now it is your turn!"

His voice seemed to come from far away as Sheba struggled to rise. An overwhelming ringing sensation filled her ears, and her vision blurred. Everything around her seemed to move in slow motion. Pain gripped her body like fingers of steel, and she realized with horror that the priest was laughing at her, raising his hand and aiming the wand, preparing to summon yet another devastating blast of sorcerous power.

Anger suddenly welled up from deep within her, a fearsome rage more profound than she'd ever felt possible. How she wanted to kill him! She desperately wanted to see him writhing in agony, to hear him screaming in torment. Sheba glared at the priest contemptuously as her hatred swelled, building within her like the fury of a volcano. Her vision began to clear as indignation filled her heart, and the thought occurred to her that she wished she could watch him burn. Somehow her voice returned, and Sheba opened her mouth and venomously hurled her animosity with a violent roar. The abhorrence she felt became so complete that it seemed to encompass the totality of her very soul, and now she focused it upon him intensely. How satisfying it would be to watch the flesh melt from his bones!

The priest faltered, becoming confused. He glanced about uncertainly and dropped his wand as black smoke began to wisp from the sleeves of his robe. His expression changed to that of horror as a dark haze of noxious smoke suddenly billowed forth around his feet, and he began to scream.

Joktan parried an attacker's sword, then thrust him through. He wrenched his blade free from the dead man's chest and heard Sheba's angry cry.

Amid the dust of battle he turned just in time to see the priest burst into flame. As he flailed in terror, Sheba regained her feet and sent him reeling to the ground with a devastating kick. She signaled to him that she was all right, then swept up her sword and rejoined the melee with a visceral howl.

He ducked instinctively as a spear sailed past his head, then whipped around, plunging his sword to the hilt in another priest's midriff. Blood gushed thickly from the wound, and the man's eyes bulged in disbelief. Joktan withdrew his blade and swung again, cleaving the priest's head asunder with a mighty blow. The man slumped lifelessly into the grass as three more took his place, and Joktan eagerly rushed to meet them in a flurry of deadly steel.

Another quickly joined them. This priest hurriedly uttered an incantation, making a gesture with his hands, and instantly Joktan was dealt a jarring blow that sent him staggering backwards. He nearly swooned, fought to clear his head, and raised his sword as they moved in on him.

"Vermin!" he bellowed angrily, slashing at them with his sword. His stroke bit deeply into the nearest priest's shoulder and the man shrieked as blood pumped into the air.

"Why can't you fight like men?" Joktan raged.

An unseen force struck him again, this time even harder, and he felt his legs nearly buckle beneath him. His arm went numb and he lost his grip on his sword. Desperately he tore a dagger from its sheath and hurled it with all the strength he could summon. The blade buried itself to the hilt in the victim's chest, but the man seemed to hardly notice.

Joktan threw yet another dagger as a third devastating blow swept him off his feet and tossed him through the air. He crashed to the ground, stunned and gasping raggedly for breath. His eyes were caked with dirt and blood, blurring his vision as he slowly pulled himself up and reached for a blade. He scarcely had time to hurl it at the nearest foe before the next arcane blow struck again.

It slammed into his head with tremendous force, sending him reeling to the ground. He fought for consciousness as darkness swarmed into his mind. Pain flashed through his temples, and his muscles spasmed and convulsed uncontrollably. His savage instincts swelled, driven by anger and determination, the will to not only survive, but retaliate against his attackers. He pushed himself up once more with a barbaric roar. Sheba saw his peril and made towards him, but was cut off by two more robed attackers. Her fury was unabated, and she met them with a fearsome, bloodthirsty cry. She raised her sword high above her head, preparing to strike, when suddenly both men stumbled forward, then toppled to the ground. From each man's back protruded a pair of feathered shafts. She lowered her weapon, looking about in startled surprise.

She saw Joktan rise, still dazed from the power of the arcane force that had smashed him senseless, and felt a wave of relief. His attackers were all dead, lying in a heap several paces away, each of them sporting feathered shafts that looked very much like those which protruded from the backs of the two priests at her feet.

Dust swirled heavily in the air, making it impossible to breathe or see clearly. She hastened to join him, keeping a watchful eye for any sign of further attackers.

"I've taken some powerful blows before," Joktan managed, "but by Dagon's scales, that beat them all!"

Tenderly he touched his side; when he withdrew his hand it was covered with blood. A look of concern swept over Sheba's face, then quickly vanished when she realized that it was not his own.

She gazed about them nervously. "Have your senses returned yet?" she asked.

"Aye," Joktan replied, obviously shaken. "They were using some sort of wizardry against me."

"Tell me about it," she muttered darkly.

He smiled broadly. "By Mithra's left breast, that was a good fight! I could have finished them off without your help, though."

She was peering past him. "I didn't kill those ones," she said distantly.

"Well if you didn't slay them, who did?" he asked, rubbing the sides of his bloodied head gingerly.

Sheba raised a bloody hand and pointed over his shoulder.

"They did."

45

Back in his tent, Skeltar carefully unfolded a piece of black silk and spread it out upon a small wooden table. In the flickering light of tallow tapers placed purposefully about the room, he studied his prize excitedly.

The golden talisman gleamed brightly, the jewels upon it twinkling like small stars in their settings.

The Seal of Kawisu!

He held a withered hand over the talisman, then stroked it ever so lightly with his finger. He could feel the dark power it exuded, and reverently the mage leaned over to inspect it more closely. He knew that this was a genuine piece of the fabled Black Scroll, but still he wanted to be absolutely sure. He poured over the object intently, examining every etching, every arcane symbol, the placement of the jewels that glittered hypnotically from their settings. A beautiful bloodstone was fastened in the center of the talisman. He stared at it even closer, then sat up straight in surprise.

The Eye of Nischoaz! Obviously someone who was familiar with the legend had found the stone and placed it there themselves!

This was an unexpected stroke of good fortune, for the Eye--the jewel mounted upon the piece--had to accompany the Seal in order to for it to be used properly. He wondered what had befallen the one who had found the Eye and placed it upon the Seal. He held up the talisman and stared at it once more. The bloodstone had been engraved with the Zodiac Sign of Leo, the Lion.

This is it! he thought, peering at the object in near disbelief. *I've found it at last! This is the object for which I have been searching all these years! With this I can locate the others. Piece by piece I will assemble the Black Scroll. But in the meantime its power will yet serve me well!*

He sprang from his chair and sought out a small chest. It had been hidden carefully beneath his bed, and it overflowed with numerous manuscripts and ancient looking texts. He rummaged through them hastily, then his patience failing, he overturned the chest upon the bed and spilled out the contents.

Quickly sorting through them, he snatched up a small piece of parchment that had been rolled up like a tiny scroll. Unrolled, it fit neatly in the palm of his hand. Upon it could be seen a strange script, an ancient form of writing that had not been used for ages, save for a few knowledgeable wizards and those immersed deeply in the Black Arts like himself.

The Key of Amon! Few knew that it even existed, yet he had kept it hidden for nearly ten years, safe within this little chest. It had once belonged to another sorcerer, one who had been completely unaware of its true purpose, of its true power! Skeltar had carried it beneath his robe from the steaming jungles of Ramaya.

Now I have not only the Key of Amon and the Seal of Kawisu, but the Eye of Nischoaz as well! Three pieces that make a whole, three pieces that will lead me to the rest of the Black Scroll and the ultimate power!

He carefully stowed away the object, then set about gathering up what few belongings he had within the tiny room. His time in Luxantia was at an end. Now he would head back to Zebulon. But first he would need to test the power of the Seal of Kawisu. A small experiment, perhaps, just to be certain that it was not a forgery.

He moved over to the window and gazed out across the horizon. *Somewhere out there, beyond the Black Mountains, was the Daughter of the Blood Goddess.*

He would need to capture her soon if all was to go as planned, and she was slowly slipping out of his grasp. He frowned darkly. *Yes,* he thought finally, *a small experiment just might prove to be very beneficial indeed.*

Joktan turned as eight riders slowly emerged from the dusty haze. They had approached unawares, and were now spread out before them in a wide semi-circular line. Amid the chaos of battle he had completely forgotten about the other group of horsemen they had seen approaching from the north.

"More priests," he thought, but then his jaw dropped in surprise.

They were all women. While each one appeared to be of differing origin, all were possessed of rare and stunning beauty. He stared at them in dumbfounded amazement, closed his eyes tightly and rubbed and with a bloodied hand, then opened them once more to gape in disbelief. Was this a mirage, a hallucination brought about by the force of the unnatural blows he'd received only moments before?

Suddenly another explanation sprang into his mind. Could this be a trick, some sort of fell magick cast upon them by the priests of Dhampir? Perhaps they were not women at all, but priests, waiting for a moment, allowing the spell to take hold before rushing upon them once more. Joktan's growled in disdain as his scimitar rasped from it's sheath. He stepped forward, preparing himself for another assault, and Sheba quickly moved to stop him. She placed her hand on his shoulder and pulled him back.

"Don't," she whispered urgently. "They are not attacking."

"Maybe not yet," Joktan replied, drawing her attention to the crossbows each woman held trained upon them. "This could all be an illusion."

"Trust me," she insisted. "Look at your feet."

He glanced down. The bodies of three priests lay there, each with one or more feathered shafts protruding from their backs.

He glanced back at Sheba skeptically as one of the newcomers separated herself from the rest of her companions and came toward them. She rode cautiously forward, then reined her horse to a halt and lowered her weapon.

"Greetings!" she called out loudly. Her voice had a heavy eastern accent.

"Stay where you are!" Joktan ordered roughly. The woman was truly beautiful, but her eyes had the look of a seasoned warrior. She was too well armed for his comfort.

"We come in peace," she assured him, motioning to her company to lower their crossbows. "We saw your struggle and thought we might even the odds a little."

"For that we thank you," Sheba spoke up. "In truth, we were greatly outnumbered from the start."

The woman tethered her crossbow to the saddle, then dismounted and walked toward them. She had long, jet-black hair that flowed down to her hips and seemed to gleam in the warmth of the afternoon sun. The others with her quickly followed their leader's example, and together they approached, flanking the woman in an orderly line to her rear. A few paces away they halted, studying both of them appraisingly.

"My name is Chia," their leader announced.

Sheba glanced at Joktan's drawn sword disapprovingly. Reluctantly, he returned it to the scabbard with another low, disapproving growl, and she turned back to the woman who had spoken.

"You may call me Sheba," she informed her graciously. "My companion's name is Joktan. He hails from the land of the Sabertooth Clans."

Chia nodded. "In truth, we have been searching desperately for you. We are servants of King Xalton, Ruler of Straltonia, and we are come to request your assistance in a most urgent matter."

Sheba's heart skipped a beat. *These must be the women of which my mother spoke!* she thought. 'On a king's errand….'

She studied them thoughtfully before she responded. "What possible assistance can I provide?" she asked. "You all look like skilled and competent warriors. My blade would be of little benefit."

"If it is possible, I would rather speak to you in private," Chia replied.

Sheba smiled. "Anything you must say to me, you can say to Joktan as well, Chia. He is my companion, and we are bound to each other by an oath of blood. There are no secrets between us."

"Forgive me," the woman apologized. "I did not know if….." Her voice trailed off as she stared at Sheba, her eyes growing wide with sudden fear. Sheba's body had been soaked in blood during the battle, and now it seeped into her skin, as if being absorbed by the very pores of her flesh. Joktan had been quick to notice it too, but he had said nothing, choosing to focus his attention warily upon the warriors before them instead.

Chia dropped to her knees at Sheba's feet. "Truly, you *are* the daughter of the Blood Goddess!" she whispered. Her companions, upon seeing their leader prostrate herself before Sheba, were quick to follow her example.

"I have not yet ascended the throne," Sheba told them. "Rise to your feet like the warriors that you are." Joktan couldn't help thinking that she almost seemed embarrassed by their actions.

"We are your servants," Chia said, standing slowly while keeping her eyes trained upon the ground.

"No, you are not," Sheba replied. "You are King Xalton's servants. There is no need to bow before me."

"As you wish, My Lady," replied the other, "but may I speak openly?"

"By all means."

"When we left Zebulon to search for you, it was at the request of King Xalton. I had my doubts, as to who you really were, but now I have seen with my own eyes. Please forgive my disbelief."

Joktan's eyes narrowed at the mention of King Xalton's name, and he stared at her with growing unease. The name elicited memories of dark, reeking dungeons filled with death and decay, of being hung by his wrists from manacles anchored high on a stone wall, sentenced to die by the hands of the priests of Dhampir. Zebulon was the last place in the world he wanted to see.

"It's quite all right," Sheba replied, "but now is not the time or place for discussion. We need to get out of this area before more of these accursed priests of Dhampir come looking for their friends."

Chia looked surprised. "I don't mean to pry, but why were they attacking you? It is a very unusual thing to be hunted down by a group of priests."

Sheba looked at Joktan with a mischievous smile. "Perhaps you should ask my partner that question," she replied.

Joktan grinned, barring his teeth at her, then changed the subject. "We need to gather up our weapons and leave at once." He turned to Chia. "You and your company may keep the spoil from the men you have slain, but the rest is rightfully ours."

"We have no need for spoils of combat," Chia replied, somewhat disdainfully. "However, my women would be honored to assist you."

Joktan shrugged. "Suit yourself."

Chia smiled. "Meet my companions."

She proceeded to call out their names, and each woman stepped forward in turn when introduced, bowing their heads respectfully to

Sheba. There was Shyla, from Carianthe; Brashi, from Redon; Nephtia, from Dendera; Liona, from Sidon; Fjora, from Isaheim; Sonya, from Erech; and Thallianna, from Kish.

Joktan wondered silently as Chia made the introductions. Never had he met such a diverse group of women, and he was immediately struck by the beauty of each one. It took little discernment to realize that they were not merely warriors chosen at random. They were obviously of noble decent.

"It is an honor to meet all of you," Sheba replied. "Perhaps someone could bring up our horses."

Soon the area had been thoroughly searched, as well as the bodies of the slain priests, and they started out once more across the plains, now joined by the eight warriors.

Joktan took the lead, steering them in a southeasterly direction and spurring his mount to a brisk trot. Few words were spoken. They traveled in relative silence for most of the day. The gentle, rolling hills became increasingly larger, occasionally accented by barren outcroppings of reddish-brown shale and sandstone. Scattered thickets of dense brush dotted the land, interspersed by small stands of evergreens that grew tall and close together. As dusk began to fall, Joktan reined his mount to a halt beside one such stand of trees that crowned the top of a large hill. A narrow stream of clear water ran nearby in the gully, and he decided that it would be a good place for them to spend the night.

Within the grove they soon discovered a circular patch of open ground, and he noted with interest numerous granite stones that stood along the perimeter of the place, as if erected there purposefully. Twenty-four massive rocks had been hewn into tall, rectangular blocks, then stood on end to surround the clearing like silent sentinels. At the center of the circle Sheba found a small pit where once a fire had burned.

"This was once a sacred place," she noted.

"Aye," Joktan replied anxiously. The grove seemed peaceful enough, but for some strange reason he felt uneasy, as if something lurked within the trees, watching, waiting. "Perhaps we should keep moving."

Sheba laughed lightheartedly and shook her head. "Our mounts are spent, and a good night's sleep would do wonders for all of us. Besides, I sense our coming here was no accident. It is truly a beautiful spot."

"Very well," he grumbled.

Some of the women tended to their horses, while others laid bedrolls around the fire pit and gathered wood for the night. Sheba set out provisions of meat, cheese, bread and mead, and soon all were gathered close around the warmth of the fire.

Joktan ate in silence, listening to the women as they spoke in subdued tones. Each had a distinctly different accent or dialect, unique to their respective lands of birth, but all seemed to share a common bond, almost as though they were all of the same family.

Darkness had fallen swiftly, and as they sat around the fire he gazed up at the sky. It was a cloudless night, lit by the pale light of the moons, but the place in which they now sat brought strange feelings to his mind. It seemed somehow familiar, as if he had been here before, though he knew he hadn't. He closed his eyes to listen more intently to the sounds of the night. The air was still, and somewhere off to his left a purple martin gurgled it's song in the shadows of the trees. He could hear the distinct sound of insects buzzing about out in the grass; of the stream splashing down at the bottom of the hill as it meandered it's way across the plains to the south. All was as it should be, but still the feeling of apprehension persisted.

After they had finished eating, Chia poured herself another cup of mead, then moved to sit cross-legged directly across the fire from Sheba and Joktan. The other women with her seemed to sense that she was about to speak, and their voices quickly fell silent.

"My Lady,"she addressed Sheba respectfully, "I must tell you of the dreadful things which have befallen our King, and of why he has sent us to ask for your assistance."

"I will make no promises," Sheba informed her, "but say on. I must admit that I am more than a little curious why a king would go through so much trouble to find me."

The woman then related the story of King Xalton's sudden and mysterious illness, of how Skeltar had offered to cure him, and of how the king now suspected that he had been wickedly deceived. She told them of how the wizard was even now searching for her with a detachment of the king's Imperial Guard, that he had went straight away to Luxantia, and of how the mage claimed that Sheba could cure his ailment if brought before him. She said that it had become clear to them that Skeltar had some other plan for her as well, a scheme to which no one else was privy.

Joktan began to grow increasingly uneasy as Chia told them of these things, and now he voiced his misgivings openly.

"We are bound for the southern lands. Zebulon is a great deal out of our way. It would almost be backtracking from this point, and I have no intention of doing such a thing."

Sheba laid her hand upon his gently. "Surely this is not the only misgiving you have regarding the proposition these women have put forth."

"Of course not," he replied, then looked at Chia. "A year ago this king you value so much had me thrown into a dungeon and sentenced to die, and by the hands of the priests of Dhampir, no less! I have no desire to aid him, not when he nearly had me killed. And have I yet mentioned that he has set a price on my head as well? You truly must take me for a fool."

"Perhaps I have not made myself sufficiently clear," Chia replied. "We have been ordered to bring both of you to Zebulon at any cost and by any means necessary. The King will surely pardon you, if you but lend him your aid. Of that you have my word. He has also made it explicitly clear that no harm befall either of you. There will also be a generous reward for your service, and I by no means think of you as a fool."

"Joktan has good reason to object," Sheba said. "I know that the aid your King requires of me would involve the exchange of blood. That is the only way I could cure his sickness. But tell me more of this wizard, the one you call Skeltar."

Chia sighed heavily. "He is a vile lout, that one," she spat resentfully. "In truth, he has been secretive about his designs for you. I don't trust him one bit, and the King feels likewise, of that I can assure you. We presume that since you are the daughter of the Blood Goddess, he plans to use you in some type of arcane rite, but this is merely conjecture on our part." She looked up at Sheba gravely. "Make no mistake. His intentions can be only evil."

"You have not told me yet why Skeltar seeks me out as well," Joktan said.

Chia noticed the light of the fire reflecting on his large, fanged teeth, and a sudden shiver went down her spine. "He believes that you have some sort of talisman which can be used to cure the King, or at least so he claims. He fears you greatly, however. This we have deduced by the fact that he requested the use of one hundred of the King's soldiers. Your people are known to be fearsome warriors."

Joktan nodded at her, a wry smile twisting his lips. "I'm flattered."

Sheba glared at him. "Is that the object you sold to Paltro in Luxantia?"

"I suspect that it must be," he grunted. "That thing was cursed, if you ask me. It brought me nothing but ill fortune, and I can only hope that it does likewise for the mage. If he went there in search of it, we can assume that he must have the thing by now, and that some terrible fate has befallen our friend."

"I told you that you should not have sold it to him!" Sheba exclaimed.

Joktan snorted. "By that time it was too late. We were already well on our way to the Black Mountains....." he frowned thoughtfully.

"Do you remember when we were nearing the foothills? There was a large caravan heading toward Luxantia."

"Aye," she affirmed.

"I wonder now if that was not a caravan at all, but Skeltar, with the soldiers given to him by the King."

"I doubt it," Sheba replied. "From the sounds of things, Skeltar could not have arrived in Luxantia until we were nearly over the mountains. It is a two week journey between Zebulon and there."

Chia sat staring into the fire. "I am torn at the moment. You must realize how I feel, for I am not to harm either of you, and in truth, I never would. That I swear to both of you upon my own life. But if I return to Zebulon without you, I will be put to death, and not just me, but those who accompany me as well."

Sheba looked at her. "The final decision will be made by Joktan. I will not force him to go to Zebulon, and his feelings of resentment toward your King are appropriate, notwithstanding the fact that if he had not tried to rob a temple, he would never have had to stand before the King for sentencing. King Xalton was only doing his duty, and he cannot be faulted for that."

She smiled at Joktan teasingly, then grew serious once more. "I believe that I should go to see this King, but if you do not come with me, then I will head for my homeland. You have a price on your head, and I don't, so in the end it is only right that it be left up to you to decide." She leaned close and kissed him. "I will not be angry with you....no matter what your choice may be."

Joktan growled discontentedly. "I need to be alone for a while. You will have my decision tonight." With that he rose to his feet and strode into the darkness of the grove.

Sheba watched him as he disappeared into the night, then turned to Chia. "So tell me of your journey then," she said. "How long has it been since you left Zebulon?"

Chia began relating everything that had happened to them since they had first set out to find her, and as Joktan moved further away into the shadows her voice slowly faded behind him. He moved stealthily, gliding through the trees like a ghost to the outer edge of the grove.

The night air was deathly still, uncommonly so, he thought. The sounds of birds and insects could still be heard from time to time, but even they seemed to be much quieter than they should have been, and the unease he'd felt throughout the evening now grew even more profound within him.

Joktan skirted the perimeter of the grove, going in a circle that eventually brought him back to the point from which he'd started, all the while his senses alert, searching for any sign of danger. He discovered nothing, but this only served to heighten the tension he felt inside. There was a large rounded stone that rested beneath a massive, ancient tree, and he sat down upon it and drew his feet up, considering what he should do next.

He knew that Chia and her company would resist any decision he made if it did not entail them heading for Zebulon, but his reservations about going to see the King of Straltonia were no less than immense. The mention of Skeltar had caused his mother's last words to echo in his ears. She had said that the wizard would seek him out, and by the looks of things she spoken the truth. Ever since leaving his homeland he'd been wondering just how long it would be before Skeltar finally found him. He had sworn an oath to his mother, to slay the mage, and that was not something to be taken lightly.

He also knew that, while she had said otherwise, Sheba's curiosity had been piqued, and although he felt certain that she would accompany him no matter where he decided to go, there was little doubt in his mind that she was considering the King's request.

It seemed to him that destiny had brought the two of them together--for what purpose he wasn't sure. Could it be that this turn of events had been guided by fate as well?

He stared grimly out across the grass-covered hills, wrestling with the urge to turn south, to leave in the dead of night and be far away by dawn. He could kill Chia's guardians easily enough in the darkness, but the thought of slaying women was deeply disturbing. On the other hand, if going to Zebulon meant that he would have a chance to fulfill the oath he'd made to his mother, then perhaps that was not such a bad idea after all. It would be a risky decision, but also an opportunity to honor his word. It would enable him to avenge his father too. All the years he'd spent as a slave, yearning desperately for freedom, could be repaid......

Suddenly his thoughts were interrupted by the cool touch of sharpened steel, the point of a blade being pressed firmly to the back of his neck. He froze instantly, wondering how someone could have stolen upon him unawares. Surely he should have heard their approach! His body tensed, ready to move at the first chance.

One of Chia's lot! he thought instantly. He felt his own blood trickle warm and wet down his back as a woman's voice addressed him from the shadows. He was not in the least surprised by the fact that it was feminine, but he was truly startled by it's unfamiliarity.

"Long has it been since a fire burned in the sacred circle of the Standing Stone."

Joktan forced himself not to shudder as a chill rushed down his spine. The tone of the voice was unearthly, without the slightest hint of any recognizable accent. *Definitely not one of Chia's women,* he thought, *but whom.......?*

"Who is it that sneaks up behind me like a thieving coward!" he growled lowly. His demand was answered only by quiet laughter, and he sat silently, his anger growing by the second.

"Who is it that intrudes upon this hallowed ground?" came her reply. "You have no business here."

"My business," Joktan retorted hotly, "is none of your concern."

"Oh, but I beg to differ!" the woman's voice countered. "I am the Guardian of the Standing Stone. You and your company of warriors are trespassers in this place."

"I saw no one when we entered," Joktan said flatly. "There are only nine women here this night, and I know that you are not Sheba, nor Chia, so which of the remaining seven are you? Who is it that Chia has sent to do her dirty work?"

"So am I to assume that you do not trust this one you call Chia, nor those that accompany her?"

"You may assume whatever you wish," he replied dryly.

More humorous laughter ensued. "And this Sheba...." The voice said softly. "Do you trust her?"

"Why should I tell you?" he said. "I don't even know who you are."

More pressure was suddenly applied to the blade at his neck, and he felt his blood begin to flow freely. "You shall tell me because I have asked you to."

Joktan's nostrils flared in anger. He was not one to take orders from anyone, but there was nothing he could do about it at the moment, a fact which only served to fuel his silent fury.

"Yes," he admitted, his teeth clenched. "I trust her, though I cannot say the same for you."

"Ah!" the voice laughed, "but as you said, you do not know me. How then can you decide whether to trust me or not?"

Joktan made no reply, but his fingers slowly worked their way toward the hilt of his dagger. Another urgent prod from the blade at his neck made them retreat.

"We have much in common, Joktan of the Sabertooth Tribes."

"How is it that you know my name?" he demanded. "You have been listening in on our conversations this night around the fire."

The mysterious female let out a quiet chuckle. "I hear everything. Even now as we speak, I can hear the words which are being spoken in the circle, just as clearly as the sound of the beating of your heart."

He thought for a moment. "What is it that we have in common, wench?"

In a flash the blade moved from the back of his neck to the front of his throat. His head was yanked back viciously by the hair, but still he was unable to see who it was that held him captive. The woman pressed her lips to his ear and spoke in an angry tone.

"Beware! Your life hangs but by a thread, and a thin one at that!"

"Go ahead. Cut it, wench," he snarled through gritted teeth, adding even more emphasis to the last word.

She slowly released her grip on his hair, but the blade at his throat remained. "For a start, we share in our mistrust."

"If you put away your blade and let me see your face I would not have reason to mistrust you. I give you my word that I will not harm you."

The voice laughed merrily. "Nor could you if you tried!"

He felt a warm tongue suddenly caress the back of his neck, and instantly his flesh broke out in goose bumps. Soft lips kissed the spot where the blade had drawn his blood only moments before, and the bleeding ceased abruptly.

"Interesting," the voice commented.

"What?" he demanded.

"Your blood," came the reply, whispered softly in his ear.

"It is red, like any other mortal," he growled, feeling the sword begin to cut into his throat. "If you do not let up upon that blade there will be a great deal more of it for you to lap up."

"That *would* be a pity now, wouldn't it?" the woman commented, and he could tell by the sound of her voice that she was smirking.

"I certainly believe so," Joktan remarked dryly.

"Yes, it definitely would be! To spill the blood of one as..... unique.... as you. *The blood of Elves.....*" she paused briefly, touching her tongue to the wound once more. *"The blood of the Watchers.....*and of men. Quite unique indeed."

"Are you Sheba's mother?" he wondered aloud.

"The Blood Goddess?" she laughed. "No, I am not. She is merely *called* a goddess by those who do not understand her powers."

"I grow weary of your games, woman!" he grumbled. "If it is my life you seek then slay me, but if that is not your intention, state your purpose and be done with it."

"As you wish!" the voice exclaimed. "Behold me!"

Suddenly a brilliant light exploded before his eyes. The blade at his throat was gone, and in the same instant a woman appeared as if from thin air in front of him. She was completely naked, save for her long, blonde hair, which cascaded down over her lithe form to conceal her large breasts and femininity in shiny, golden spirals. Her eyes were as blue as sapphires, her features exquisite, and beautiful beyond compare.

Joktan stared at her in disbelief, his jaw agape, eyes nearly popping out of their sockets. One moment she had been merely a voice somewhere behind him in the darkness. Now in the blink of an eye she stood before him, real as any mortal, glowing with a radiance that seemed to emanate inexplicably from her very flesh.

The blade that had been held to his throat now gleamed brightly in her hand. It was a broadsword, made of the finest steel he had ever seen. The hilt was intricately engraved and adorned with sparkling jewels, and the sides of the blade were etched with mystical designs. Strange words were inscribed upon it in an ancient hieroglyphic script. An amethyst crystal, fashioned into the shape of a human skull, glittered in it's setting upon the pommel.

Before she spoke he knew that this was no mere mortal woman which he beheld. So great was the radiance about her that he fell upon his face at her feet. She looked down at him and laid her hand gently on his head.

"My name is Lamashtu!" she declared. "I am of Old, She who was worshipped by the ancients! I am the First Queen of the Earth, the first to be called into this world when men crawled out of the primordial waters! It was I who sustained them and gave them sustenance! I called them my children, but now they do not know me. There are few now living who remember my name, and those that come to seek me in the midst of the Standing Stone are fewer still. Even so, I yet remain."

Joktan was speechless. He had no doubt in his mind that the woman standing before him was a Goddess in the truest sense of the word. There was a power about her that had compelled him to fall at her feet. It was overwhelming and dreadful, yet loving and protective at the same time, and for a moment it felt as though he couldn't catch his breath. He could feel his heart pounding wildly in his chest. It seemed as if time stood still.

"We have a common enemy, Joktan," Lamashtu said, raising him slowly to his feet.

He stared at her, still unable to speak a word. Her gaze was piercing, and it seemed as though she looked in upon his very soul. He tried to avert his gaze, but found himself mesmerized, and for the first time in his life he felt truly afraid. She was reading his mind, listening to his thoughts, and it terrified him.

Lamashtu smiled. "I once had a consort. His name was Shamash, and I loved him as I loved my children and life itself. You probably do not recognize that name though, do you?"

Joktan shook his head, and the sound of his own voice startled him. "No," he said weakly.

"He was beautiful to look upon in those days, before his heart was corrupted by greed and power," she continued. "I knew his glory was fading, but there was nothing I could do to stop it. As men began to increase upon the face of the Earth, Shamash sought to make them his servants, to bend them to his will. He demanded the sacrifice of animals, and in their eagerness to please him, mankind slaughtered thousands of creatures upon altars of stone in the sacred groves."

She looked at him again, and he could feel the bitterness in her eyes. "That was how he first tasted the blood of the living. It was like wine to him. His lust for it became unquenchable, and the blood of animals ceased to satisfy his thirst. He commanded his servants to offer him the blood of humans, and in their ignorance, they were only too happy to oblige him. First they gave him their newborn babies, still wet and bloody from the womb. But Shamash wanted more."

"Soon the groves were stained with the blood of innocent, murdered virgins. He glutted himself upon the lives of his helpless victims, raping, then killing the poor women brought to him as sacred offerings. His appearance began to change. In the beginning it was hardly noticeable, but with the passing of years he became a monster, horrible to look upon, and a disgrace to all our kind."

She shuddered in revulsion at the memory. "Yet I still loved him, for he was my consort, without which I was incomplete. I tried everything I could to make him stop, but he wouldn't listen to me. He wanted me to join him in the abomination, but I refused, and he became very angry. I knew then that it would not be long before the blood of men no longer satisfied him, and shortly thereafter my worst fears came true."

Her voice lowered and her eyes narrowed. There was no mistaking the hurt in her voice. It was edged by anger. A quiet anger, that had settled but grown harder with the passage of time. "He tied to kill me."

She paused for a moment to wipe the tears from her eyes, then continued. "By this time even men were terrified of Shamash. I fled to the Elder Gods, pleading for them to intervene, and they came swiftly to my aid. Together we banished Shamash, imprisoning him in the Underworld. We stripped him of his power, and called him Dhampir, meaning *'Drinker of Blood'.* Ever since that day he has dwelt in the black realms of the eternal Abyss."

Joktan stiffened. He had listened with interest as the Goddess told her tale. Now he thought he understood. "Are you telling me this because I killed some of his priests today?" he inquired.

She looked at him sternly. "I am telling you this because Dhampir grows strong once more. Temples dedicated in his name have sprung up all over the lands of the Westermarch, and his power has increased greatly. He now has an ally, a wizard who foolishly intends to release Dhampir from his prison in the Underworld and bring him back into the world of men. He thinks that he can control him, but he is utterly deceived. Dhampir will bide his time, waiting to be brought forth into this world, but he will never be the slave of a wizard. He will bring legions of demons with him, and together they will destroy every living thing upon the face of the Earth."

Her voice fell to a whisper. "*Your world will end!*"

Joktan frowned. "Why does this concern you? You are a Goddess!"

Lamashtu shook her head in dismay. "Everything owes its existence to another," she replied, "just as the grass and trees need the warmth of the sun to flourish and grow. Without purpose, all living things perish. If there is no one left to believe in the Gods, if our names fade from memory and we are forgotten....*even we can die!*"

Joktan stared at her in silence. He had never considered the idea that the Gods might be dependent upon men, but it did make sense in a strange sort of way.

"The wizard that will bring Dhampir into the world again is known to you," Lamashtu said lowly. "His name is Skeltar."

"I should have guessed!" Joktan exclaimed bitterly. "It seems his name haunts me at every turn of late."

"He is preparing to go up against the King of Straltonia, and Dhampir will lead the assault."

"I have the Face of Death," Joktan confessed. "I stole it from the priests in Luxantia, along with a strange blade."

"I know," Lamashtu smiled. "And it must not fall to them again, nor Skeltar, and most certainly not Dhampir. It would not be wise to take it to Zebulon."

"Then what should I do with it?" he asked.

"Give them to me. I will hide them where no one can find them," she replied.

"How can I be sure that all of this is not some elaborate trick?"

"Look into your heart," she said softly. "Tell me what it says."

He closed his eyes and stood quietly for a few moments. "It tells me to trust you," he whispered.

"You must go to Zebulon," the Goddess urged. "You must challenge both Skeltar and Dhampir. And you must also protect Sheba."

"That is a pretty tall order!" he snorted.

Lamashtu smiled. "I have faith in you. I always have. When you were still far off across the plains, I called out to you, and though you knew it not, you answered. I told you what to look for as you drew closer, riding straight to the sacred grove and the Standing Stone. That is why this place seemed so familiar to you earlier."

"You know much," he mussed with a frown, "but killing a wizard.....that is a very dangerous affair."

"Yet you have sworn an oath to do just such a thing," she reminded him.

"Aye," he agreed reluctantly, "that I have, and I shall perform it, or die trying. But *slaying a God?"* He sighed doubtfully. "I am mortal. My sword did little against the sorcery of a few priests today. Dhampir may be beyond my abilities."

"I admit, no sword crafted by men can kill a God," Lamashtu replied. "However, long ago an ancient star fell to the Earth. It was composed of a very precious metal, unlike any that can be found in this world. It was a gift to me from the Elder Gods, and I carried it away to the land of Svartalfheim, the home of the northern Dwarves. There it was expertly crafted, into this very sword which you see in my hand. It was a process that took many years to perform."

"The blade was tempered with my tears. The handle is wrapped and bound with my own hair." She moved closer and held it out to him. "And now I offer this sword to you. No other is it's equal, the blade called *Avatare."*

Joktan studied it briefly, then grasped it firmly in his hand. The balance was superb. It looked as though it should be very heavy, and he was amazed to discover that it was remarkably light. The silver blade had been polished to a mirror finish. It gleamed brightly beneath the pale moonlight, it's keen edge razor sharp. Never had a sword fit his hands so perfectly.

"This is a fine blade," he said reverently, "but should it not be you who wields such a weapon?"

"Aye," she replied, "you are right, of course. But my love prevents me from killing Dhampir. What is more, I cannot kill *any* living thing, lest I am tainted by the act, and become what I most despise. The Elder Gods knew as much, and in their mercy ordained that this sword be forged and placed in the hands of a mortal of my choosing....one who had within him the power to accomplish this great task. One who would not fall before the evil of Dhampir."

Joktan handed the sword back to her and sat down on the rock to considered what she had just said. "Can Dhampir not turn this blade against me by the use of magick? If sorcerers can do such things, I fear to imagine what a God can do."

"Never," she assured him. "This sword was created for a specific purpose, and it will always serve its master. When it was crafted, a spell was placed upon it, that it should serve only the one who claimed it with his blood. Never has this blade known blood until tonight, when I held it to your throat. That makes it rightfully yours. You are its master. It will never forsake you in times of danger."

"How very clever of you," Joktan muttered. "And what if I were to decline?"

Lamashtu laughed softly. "You forget that I am a Goddess. I know you won't. Besides, you already have it in your heart to kill the wizard. That is a path you willing set foot upon with the oath you swore to your mother. What you did not know at that time, however, was that in order to honor your word, you must also kill Dhampir! He will surely stand against you, and you will have no choice but to slay him if you continue after Skeltar. Avoid him if you like, but it will be only a matter of time before he discovers you. Destiny guides both of you, as well as Dhampir himself, but only one will be victorious."

She held up the sword once more. "I believe that one will be you!"

Joktan sighed wearily. "Never have I dealt with a wizard before, but of late this Skeltar seems to haunt my every step. My mother said he would seek me out." He shook his head. "Although I did not place much faith in her words at the time, with each passing day they ring ever more true."

He looked up at the Goddess grimly. "Perhaps you are right. Too long have I wandered aimlessly now, waiting for Skeltar to find me. Too long have I put off what must be done, but no more. In the morning I leave for Zebulon to meet this shadow that darkens my dreams. You will find the Face of Death in the circle of the Standing Stone."

Lamashtu smiled. "Long has my heart awaited the coming of this night!" she exuded. "Now rise up and stand before me!" she cried. "You were naked when you first came into this world, so strip away your loincloth, and remove those boots from your feet, for you now stand before the Queen of all the Earth!"

Joktan obeyed instinctively, his body responding to her voice before his mind even had a chance to consider the import of her command. She stood silently for a moment, scrutinizing him closely with her piercing, sapphire gaze. His eyes met hers briefly, but the power emanating from within her was overwhelming. He quickly averted his gaze to stare at her feet.

Lamashtu reached out and touched his cheek tenderly with her hand, compelling him to stare once more into her eyes. She moved closer, so near that the fullness of her soft lips almost touched his when she spoke.

"It is the custom of men to tower above those that serve them," she said. "In that way they feel powerful, and believe themselves to be exalted above all others. But I am a Goddess, and I say that only in humility of heart can true strength and power be found. So I kneel before you this night, and place my blessing upon you with the Fivefold Kiss."

Joktan was startled as she knelt before him, the features of his face vividly portraying his bewilderment and awe. Her hair was a golden cloak that covered her nakedness and spilled onto the ground like a robe of fine spun silk.

"Blessed be thy feet, that have brought you to me," Lamashtu intoned, kissing first his right foot, then his left. She raised her head .

"Blessed be thy knees, that shall kneel at the Sacred Altar." She kissed his knees in the same order as his feet, then her head moved up slightly higher.

"Blessed be thy phallus, which shall bring the seed of life into this world." She pressed her lips firmly against the engorged head of his fully erect manhood and kissed him there.

A throaty groan escaped him, and she looked up, a wry smile playing upon her lips. She paused as their eyes met, then continued.

"Blessed be thy breast." He could feel her breath, moist and warm upon his nipples as she kissed first the right, then the left.

"Blessed be thy lips,*"* she whispered, kissing him suddenly, her eyes closed*. "May they utter the Sacred Names."*

Joktan's body began to tremble uncontrollably. He felt dizzy and lightheaded, and it took every last bit of his willpower to keep his feet rooted firmly to the ground. He mentally commanded strength into his wobbling legs and forced his knees not to give way beneath him. His vision blurred to the point of blindness.

"Will you accept this sword that I offer you this night?" Her voice resounding like thunder inside his head. "Will you claim Avatare?"

"Yes," he answered as she held it out once more.

"Then it is yours," she declared, placing it in his hand. She touched his face again, and instantly his vision returned, his head cleared, and the trembling ceased.

"You are it's master. With this blade you will defeat Skeltar and Dhampir. It will enable you to dominate, subdue and punish the rebellious spirits and demons they may summon against you. With this sword you may persuade even the Watchers and good spirits to aid you in times of peril! Now fasten it about you, and bear it in the knowledge that my love and trust are perfect, and both I extend to you, without reluctance nor restraint."

Joktan quickly replaced his clothes and strapped the mighty sword about his hips. The weight of it felt reassuring and strangely natural. Lamashtu watched him approvingly, then her face grew stern once more.

"Swear to me that you will fulfill this," she commanded. "Swear that you will honor your word to both myself and your mother."

"I swear it," Joktan replied solemnly. "May this sword turn against me if I break my oath."

Lamashtu smiled proudly. "When you face Dhampir, I will distract him with the face of Death. Remember this! Call my name and I will answer."

"Aye," he assured her. "I will remember."

"There is one last thing you should know," she informed him. "I sense your distrust of Chia and her company. We spoke of it earlier."

Joktan nodded.

"I have looked into their hearts, and they will not harm you. Chia bears no ill-will towards you, nor do those who accompany her upon this mission. Of that you have my word. Their friendship will remain true so long as you allow them to demonstrate it to you."

"Very well," he replied. "I will take that into consideration."

Lamashtu laughed. "Then I bid you good night," she smiled. "May you rest well this evening, and be refreshed both in body and spirit, for tomorrow will dawn soon enough, and you must be strong. You will be tested soon."

Suddenly she was gone, and with her the radiance which had shone so brightly. The darkness of the night came rushing in, leaving him momentarily blinded, and as his eyes slowly adjusted Joktan considered the Goddess's final words.

Will I be tested tomorrow? he wondered, but at that instant he felt weariness sweep over him. He turned into the grove and carefully made his way through the trees back to the camp.

The women still sat comfortably about the fire, and Sheba rose to meet him as he approached, a look of concern upon her face.

"I was beginning to think you had gotten lost," she said, obviously worried.

He smiled and pulled her to him, looking deeply into her emerald eyes. "You should know better by now," he replied. "I had much to consider."

She kissed him, then noticed the sword at his side.

"Where did you get that?" she asked curiously.

"That is a long, strange story. I will explain it to you later, when we are alone."

Together they joined the others around the fire. Liona, the Sidonian, offered him a tankard of mead, which he accepted gratefully. He sat down cross-legged next to Sheba as they looked at him expectantly, waiting in silence while he downed his drink and refilled the empty tankard.

"Do you wish to go to Straltonia?" he asked Sheba at last.

"I do," she replied sincerely, "but only if you choose to come with me."

Joktan took a long draught. "I will go," he said. "On one condition; I would like to meet this wizard of whom I have heard so much about of late. He must die by my hand. No one else must interfere, or they too will have to deal with my sword." He looked at each one of the in turn. "Skeltar is mine. I claim the right to slay him here and now. My reasons are my own."

Chia looked at him and nodded gravely. "As you wish. The wizard is yours. "You have my word. Our priority is to protect the King."

"An oath must be sworn this night," he told them evenly. "You must swear that you will protect Sheba from harm, even if your life be forfeit. That no harm shall come to either of us, whether it be by your hand or that of your King. This oath I require in blood, for if we are to go to Zebulon, I must be sure that we can trust you. I know that you must feel likewise as well."

"You shall have it," Chia agreed. "We have sworn to protect King Xalton, and that we will do. Which is why we sought you out. If Sheba can cure his ailment, he shall owe her a great debt, and you will be generously rewarded for your efforts."

Joktan stared at her across the fire. "It is not my concern for your King that compels me to go," he told the woman flatly. "I mean you no offense, but he is not my King. I have met him only once, and it was not a pleasant experience, so you can understand when I say that I care not if he lives or dies."

He drained his drink, refilled it, then continued. "If Sheba chooses to aid him, then I will give her whatever assistance I can. It is for the wizard that I choose to go."

Chia turned to her company. "If you swear an oath this night, you shall be bound by it forever. If any one of you breaks it, the rest of us shall require their life. Is this understood?"

The other women nodded, voicing their consent.

Joktan smiled a toothsome grin. "Draw your blades and let's be on with it!"

My father was a tyrant,
His heart was like a stone,
I took his crown and kingdom,
When I slew him on his throne.
His blood yet stains my dais,
His face still haunts my sleep,
His faithful servants linger,
In the shadows of my keep.
Poison taints my wine-cup,
Assassins stalk my dreams,
Whom can it be that seeks the crown,
I've shed blood to receive?

----Ancient Fragment from the Steedman Scrolls

Joktan awoke long before the crimson hues of dawn crept over the horizon. The evening fire had reduced itself to a heap of smoldering ashes, and he crept from his bedroll, stealing silently away from the circle toward the trees. Two of Chia's women stood watch within the cover of the grove; he regarded them mutely, heading down to the stream to bathe. His body was caked with dust from travel and battle, and the cool water felt soothing as he immersed himself completely.

By the time he returned to the camp, every one was up and about. Sheba had stowed away her belongings, as had the others, and he quickly rolled up his blankets, lashing them down securely behind his saddle before joining the women for breakfast. The meal consisted of thick strips of salted back bacon, some cheese and a chunk of bread, washed down with liberal portions of mead and wine. As they were preparing to leave, Joktan drew Sheba aside.

"There is something I must do before I go to Zebulon," he said in a low tone. "Ride out with the others. I will catch up with you in a while."

Sheba looked at him quizzically. "You're not having second thoughts, are you?" she asked, her voice filling with concern. "I told you last night that we do not have to go if you don't want to, and I meant it. If you feel….."

"I want to go to Zebulon," he cut in abruptly, "but first I must be rid of the Face of Death. In Zebulon there will be many priests of Dhampir, and you yourself said that it must not fall back into their hands. I fear we will have enough to deal with once we are there."

She studied his face for a moment. "Are you sure you know what you are doing?"

"Yes," he assured her quickly. "You must trust me. Tell the others that I am merely scouting out the area."

Sheba slipped a pale arm around him and pressed her soft lips against his firmly. "Very well," she sighed reluctantly. "Just hurry back when you are done."

"I won't be long," he replied.

He started to pull away, but Sheba drew him back, her eyes fixed upon his, searching. "You still have not told me where you got that sword," she whispered.

"You will know soon enough," he promised. His gaze roamed the circle of Standing Stone briefly. "This is a very ancient place. Once it was a sacred grove, and we entered last night unaware, but ever since we stepped foot within the trees we have been watched. Surely you have felt it…… as though unseen eyes stare at you from the shadows….."

Sheba nodded affirmatively. "Yes," she admitted. "I too have sensed that we are not alone here, but I said nothing. I didn't want to give rise to any superstitious fears the others may have."

"And that is why I have said nothing about this sword," he confided. "Once we are away from this place, I will tell you all."

She looked at him thoughtfully. "That is probably best then."

He kissed her again, then mounted his steed and headed off into the grove alone, and Sheba turned to Chia, who stood there watching curiously as he rode away.

"Joktan is going to do some scouting. He will catch up with us shortly."

"If it pleases you, I can send one of my company with him," the woman replied. "This land can be a very hostile place."

Sheba laughed and shook her head. "No, that won't be necessary. He would not approve. Besides, at times he can be quite hostile too!"

Chia nodded, but Sheba could tell that the warrior had misgivings about seeing him ride off alone. She sensed the woman's suspicion, too, but made no further comment, and presently they doused the fire and rode off in a easterly direction.

The morning was warm, and a light breeze drifted across the plains, rustling through the tall grasses. Birds flew overhead in the crimson gold of sunrise, and a herd of antelope that had come down to the stream to drink bounded quickly away as the women rode past in silence.

Once they were gone, Joktan rode back through the grove to the center of the Standing Stone. He dismounted quickly, rummaging through his saddlebag, then knelt beside the ring of stones where their fire had been.

"Good morning," came a familiar voice. He turned sharply to see Lamashtu standing before him. Her long hair flowed in golden locks down her back, and she stepped forward lightly to meet him. The corners of her full, red lips twitched gently, smiling, and Joktan knelt respectfully before her.

"You don't have to bow before me!" she laughed, amused.

He stood slowly, not sure if she would blind him once more with her radiant glow, and the Goddess read his thoughts instantly.

"Don't be afraid," she said softly. "Last night I had to make sure that you believed me."

She drew close and touched his cheek gently, lovingly, and he felt a rush of energy course through his body. "Even for a Goddess, it is not wise to flaunt power vainly."

"I give you the Face of Death," he said, thrusting two cloth-wrapped bundles toward her. "And the dagger that I stole from the priests of Dhampir as well."

Lamashtu accepted the bundles graciously, but she held them as if they smelled of some vile substance. "Thank-you for keeping your word to me," she replied.

She bent down and placed the objects upon the remains of the morning fire, then moved her hand above them slowly, uttering a strange series of words. She spoke in some ancient, long-forgotten tongue, once known only amongst the gods themselves. He watched the bundles begin to sink into the ground, as if it were quicksand, and quickly disappear beneath the ashes in the circle of stones.

Lamashtu paused, then stood and faced him, her piercing gaze looking in upon his soul. Her mind probed his thoughts, discerning his emotions at once, and he felt the sudden urge to turn away, but something within him would not allow it.

"I wish to show you a thing which I myself have witnessed from afar," she murmured, her voice as soft as velvet. "You need to know for yourself why Skeltar must be stopped, and why Dhampir must be defeated. I have sensed your own reasons for slaying the wizard, but you are only one person among millions. Dhampir threatens not only you and I, but them as well. His coming will be the dread of the Earth."

She put her hands to his face and touched her forehead to his. "Close your eyes, Joktan," she intoned, her words vibrating like low the rumble of a mighty drum. "See what has befallen Luxantia."

He did as she said, and instantly his mind was filled with horrible scenes. He saw the small trade town in which he had lodged wreathed in rolling waves of flame. Black smoke rose high into the sky, and charred corpses littered the ash-covered streets. Huge locust-like creatures, nightmarish and foul, gnawed at the incinerated bones of men and women.

Amid the rubble could be seen the carcasses of the hellish creatures as well, innumerable, and those that had managed to survive the flames feasted just as eagerly upon the ruined remains of their own kind as that of men. The small lake on the far edge of the town was stained red with blood, and vile beasts moved hideously within the shallow depths of the festering water.

"How did this happen?" he asked. "Who would do such a thing?"

"Let me show you,"Lamashtu whispered, and suddenly he saw the soldiers outside of the town wall. A powerfully built man sat astride a stallion, obviously a captain of the Straltonian Army, and beside him stood a darkly robed and hooded figure. Somehow Joktan knew that the stark form belonged to Skeltar, and he instinctively let out a low, throaty growl at the mere sight of the mage.

He saw the citizens of the town fleeing in terror through the gates, streaming toward the soldiers for protection, and he watched in revulsion as the soldiers drew their bows and rained arrows upon them till their bodies lay like pincushions upon the blood-soaked soil of the Plains of Kabril.

"I have seen enough!" he cried out impulsively, jumping back as if struck by a mighty blow.

Lamashtu still stood motionless, her head down, tears streaming from her eyes, golden locks fluttering like strands of brilliant silk in the morning breeze.

"How long ago did this happen?" he demanded.

"Nearly four days now."

"At the very least this is treason," Joktan muttered. "I'll be damned if the troops I saw were not Straltonian. I can recognize them anywhere." He gazed at her for a moment, unsure. "Tell me that what I have seen is not real."

"It is real."

"How can it be?" he asked. "What king would allow such a thing?"

"As of yet King Xalton has no idea," she told him sorrowfully. "And yes, this is treason. Skeltar lusts for power."

"There has never been any love lost between the civilized kingdoms and the savage tribes, least of all between us and Straltonia." He looked at her grimly. "In truth, I care little for them. Let them fight their own wars, I say. Many have been the times we have stained the dusty plains with their blood, till it ran like a river to the seas. But this has nothing to do with my people and their past."

"Skeltar seeks world dominance," she said softly. "He will take the civilized lands first, but rest assured, the savage tribes will fall before him just as easily as the rest once his attention has been fixed upon them."

"Luxantia did not deserve this," he growled thoughtfully. "Word will travel fast."

"Yes, it will, but this*.....this is what awaits Zebulon!"* she lamented. "The first step on the road to bloody ruin."

"I don't need further convincing," he replied throatily. "I will slay the wizard. By the edge of this sword I will hew Dhampir to pieces. That I promise you."

He touched her face, lightly brushing away her tears. He hated to see a woman cry, even if she was a Goddess. Unexpectedly, Lamashtu threw her arms about him, the wetness of her parted lips pressed firmly against his own. She kissed him deeply, and as her tongue explored the warmth of his mouth, a sensation such as he had never known began to sweep over his body. Like a blazing fire he felt her power surge through him uncontrollably, and she pulled him tighter to her. His senses were overwhelmed as an inexorable force inundated them. She moved her curvaceous form against him sensually, and he swooned in her embrace, melting into her. Joktan's manhood stiffened erectly, the instinctual response to the closeness of a woman's naked body.

Something within him sought to break free of her, but another part of him yielded willingly to her touch as the Goddess's hands gently explored him. Her touch began to cause another feeling within him to grow as well.

Perhaps it was due to the fact that he had drank Sheba's blood only two nights before, and it had created a burning lust within him, a desperate yearning for more. Even Joktan himself did not know, but in the heat of the moment he tore his lips from hers, and with the lusty growl of a ravenous tiger he opened his mouth wide and sank his ivory fangs deep into the soft flesh of her neck.

Lamashtu gasped in surprise as his teeth ripped deep into her soft warm skin. As her blood began to flow into his mouth Joktan bit down even harder, his long canines gripping her like talons of ivory steel.

Now it was she who fought to break away, but he held her there, sucking her thick, red blood, drinking it madly like a man dying of thirst amid the waters of a cool mountain spring.

Suddenly she disappeared in a burst of blinding light, leaving him standing alone in the center of the Standing Stone. He was confused, overpowered with lust for her blood, and alone. He spun around, glancing quickly this way and that, but she was no where to be found. Slowly his senses began to return, reason began to reclaim his wits and seep back into his mind, and in the silence Lamashtu's voice boomed like thunder.

"I know you are in love with Sheba, and I would not have done that if it where not for the fact that you will need great strength to accomplish the task before you. I chose to impart some of my power to you by means of a kiss. But even I did not expect you to bite me, much less drink my blood! *How dare you!*"

Suddenly she stood before him once more, in the full radiance of her splendor, but somehow it did not seem to blind him as much now as it had before.

"You know that I am a mortal man," Joktan growled, the burning passion he had felt moments ago slowly beginning to subside. "You moved against me with purpose. You wanted more than just a kiss."

"Perhaps," Lamashtu smiled demurely. "Is that such a terrible thing to you?"

"No, it is not," he admitted. "But my love for Sheba forbids it."

"I hadn't planned on imparting my very blood to you!" Lamashtu retorted. "Such a thing is unthinkable! The audacity of it!" she exclaimed almost furiously. Then she paused a moment, her brow furrowing in contemplation.

"Dhampir will smell my blood in you. You do know that, do you not?"

"Aye," he lied, unsure himself of why he had bitten her.

"Do you seek to make him jealous then?" she demanded.

"Of course!" Joktan replied. "If I must fight him, I will need every advantage I can get. I want him to be so angry that he cannot think clearly. If he is now mortal enough to die by the blade of a sword, then he ought also be mortal enough to make rash mistakes."

"That is your reasoning for biting me?" she asked curiously. "Come now! I can peer into your soul and discover the answer for myself if I must."

"Alright!" he laughed mirthfully. "I did it because I wanted to! What mortal has tasted the blood of a goddess?"

Lamashtu shook her head, but her expression was not one of complete disapproval. *"You are a willful creature, aren't you!"*

"At times," he answered, then frowned. "I have lingered here too long already," he said suddenly. "I must rejoin the others, else it will take me all day to catch up."

"Then go with my blessing," Lamashtu replied. "We will meet again, after you have honored your oaths and vows."

"Aye," said Joktan. "I will not forget about you."

She laughed. "Nor I you! But do not worry, our time will come soon enough."

With that the Goddess disappeared once more. Joktan stood for a moment longer, his brow furrowed in thought; then he turned and strode away from the circle of stones. Within minutes he was riding at breakneck speed over the hills of the plains, and the sacred grove of the Standing Stone slowly receded into the distance behind him.

King Xalton peered down at his emaciated body and moaned miserably. His skin sagged upon his bones in loose flabby folds. Each rib, every bone in his face, even the small bones of his frail hands, stood out starkly. He looked like a skeleton in a baggy suit of flesh. He sank back into his floating bed wishing silently for death to overtake him, to end this long, pain-ridden suffering he was forced to endured day after day.

There had yet been no word from Luxantia, nor the warriors he'd subsequently sent out in search of the woman and savage of whom Skeltar had spoke.

Quan Chang Xu, the strange little wizard from Zhenya's Golden City sat by him constantly, whispering weird sounding incantations in strange tongues, burning sandalwood and sage, and administering tiny cupfuls of steaming liquid that seemed to be some sort of herbal tea.

So far the King's condition had not improved, but then the wizard had already told him from the start that he alone would not be able to rid him of the mysterious illness that sapped his life force, draining his energy and vitality a little more with each passing day. However, the constant servings of teas and potions at least helped keep the pain and agony at bay, so it seemed that--thus far at least--the curious old mage had been true to his word. This fact, combined with his obvious dedication, had earned him a degree of respect from Xalton, something very few people outside of his bevy of beauties would ever boast.

Quan Chang Xu was a curious little fellow. It seemed rarely a day went by that the King's interest was not piqued by something the wizard either said or did, or both. He had scarcely left the King's Royal chambers since his arrival, save for his morning prayers and meditation, and all the women within the inner sanctum of King

Xalton's Palace had taken quite a liking to him, something that was unusual indeed.

Each day of the week Quan Chang wore a different colored robe, adorned himself with different jewels and precious stones, burned a different type of incense and herbs.

"Sometimes I think that the only thing keeping me alive is my curiosity," King Xalton told him, laughing painfully. "Every time you leave my chambers, you return dressed more strangely than before. Is it the custom of your people to change robes so profusely?"

The aging wizard smiled merrily at him, his eyes sparkling gleefully. "Perhaps you are not accustomed to seeing people wear clothing at all, my Lord!" he jested.

The King laughed good-naturedly, but his mirth was cut off abruptly by another series of ragged coughs that left him gasping for breath. At last he recovered and peered at the mage seriously.

"In truth, I am perplexed," he managed at last. "I am no fool, old man. I know that nothing a wizard does is without purpose. So tell me, what is the meaning of it? Indulge a dying king."

"If I tell you," the mage chuckled, "you must promise not to laugh at me. It makes it very difficult for you to breath."

The King smiled back at him. "You're telling me! he exclaimed wearily. "But please, say on, for I am truly interested."

"Very well, as you wish," the wizard obliged. "Each day of the week is influenced by different planets, astrological correspondences, and spirits," Quan Chang told him. "As a wizard, all of my workings and spells are greatly improved if they are conducted in harmony with not only the heavenly bodies and spirits, but those of the Earth as well. Everything has an aura--an energy--about it, from the most common stone to the beasts of the field and men. Also, it was discovered in ancient times that every color gives of it's own, unique energy too."

"It sounds more like science than magick to me," the King replied.

"You are quite right, of course," Quan Chang told him. "I practice astronomy and astrology, mathematics and what some might refer to as simply mysticism. I study minerals and soils, birds and fish, beast and reptile, spirit and soul. All things are connected."

King Xalton frowned, and the mage enthusiastically continued. "The first day of the week belongs to the Mother Moon and the Sisters of Mercy; therefore, I wear robes of silver and white, the colors that are most beneficial and appropriate, and the candles that I burn are designed in the colors that comply with the guardians of the Moons--generally blue. As you might have noticed, I wear a lot of silver adornment on this day."

"The second day of the week is ascribed to the governance of Mars. I likewise wear colors of red, scarlet, and rose. That is also the day when sexual activities are most beneficial, a fact that you, Oh King, may well desire to make note of!"

"The third day belongs to Mercury. Colors that are harmonious with that planet are orange, violet, light blue and gray. On the fourth day the planet Jupiter holds sway over the heavens, and I accordingly dress in purple and azure blue. It is a most propitious time for matters related to prosperity, growth, and the fruition of things."

"The fifth day belongs to the planet of Venus, a most important celestial body indeed, my lord, for it is also the one by whom we calculate the days of the year and the equinoxes. Many sacred places are built in alignment with Venus. I wear shades of green and brown on such days, and find it to be most beneficial."

"The sixth day is governed by Saturn. On such days one can effect great changes in things if the art of it is known, and the intention is pure. The colors most helpful on such days are gray, black, and silver."

"On the seventh day, the glorious energy of the sun presides. I dress in robes of red, crimson, yellow and gold. As you may have noticed, your health improves quite noticeably on these days, and it is also a good time for pleasures of every sort. At such times I highly recommend your indulgences in the more carnal activities you so enjoy."

The King considered his words for a moment. "I had not realized that you put so much thought into such seemingly commonplace things," he told the wizard.

Quan Chang Xu nodded. "When various energies are found to compliment each other, we call them *sympathetic.* Thus most of the magick I perform is referred to as sympathetic magick. By combining a wide variety of things which function well together, the power is made that much greater, and ideally, more effective."

"Do all sorcerers conduct themselves in such a manner?"

"That I cannot say, my Lord," Quan Chang Xu replied humbly. "I only follow the teachings of my order. I am sure there are differences in every land, for not all religions agree with each other, and that is even more true of wizards. We are a very strange lot at times!" he smiled broadly. "I can hardly imagine how others must think of us, we whose ideas and conceptions appear strange and eccentric to the uninitiated at the best of times, dark and sinister at the worst."

"There was a time when I wanted to outlaw sorcery altogether,"

King Xalton admitted with a weak grin. "But my counselors advised against it."

"We are not all evil, my Lord," the mage responded quietly. "Men will be corrupted by whatever means they choose."

Xalton sighed heavily. "I suppose that you are right," he considered. "A knife in the hands of a skillful cook is merely a tool, used to prepare a magnificent meal that both excites the senses and nourishes the body. But in the hand of an assassin, it is an instrument of death."

"A most fitting analogy," the wizard responded thoughtfully. "I shall have to remember it for future use in discourses with my students."

The King lay back once more upon his bed, considering. At length he turned again to the wizard.

"My father was a tyrant. He brought only destitution and the sword. Straltonia fell from greatness under his rule, and in the end, I slew him with his own sword and made myself King."

"Does that weigh heavily on your mind at times?" asked the wizard.

"Aye," Xalton replied ruefully. "That it does, though more particularly of late, for it was the only treacherous act that I have ever committed."

"So now you wonder if perhaps the gods are repaying you for what in retrospect may have been a sin."

King Xalton shrugged. "Possibly. But then, perhaps the gods are merely deaf."

"In that regard, I am afraid that I cannot help you," replied the mage. "You see, I have no dealings with the gods. Such things are best left to priestesses and priests. Whether or not the gods hear the prayers of men makes little difference to me, for I am a wizard. I specialize in manipulating energies in the performance of my will." He smiled ever so slightly. "I have no need of gods."

"You are a strange one indeed!" the King sighed, then asked. "Could you perhaps discern what has become of the women I sent out in search of the savage and his companion?"

Quan Chang Xu smiled, his eyes sparkling like polished jet. "I have already made the necessary preparations, my Lord."

Elliasha suddenly emerged from the edge of the chamber, wearing only a string of pearls about her neck and another of abalone shells around her waist. She hurried toward the King, bowing respectfully before seating herself near the edge of the pool. Although he loved all his women, Elliasha was the one for whom he felt the most affection, the deepest passion. At the mere sight of the woman the King's expression brightened, but seeing the look on her face today made him frown. It seemed as though there was something on the woman's mind that troubled her greatly. He could see she was on the brink of tears, and it was highly unusual for her to appear so distressed. He pushed himself up onto his elbow and gazed intently at his favorite mistress.

"What is it?" he asked tenderly, momentarily forgetting about the throbbing pain that stabbed at his withering body. "I know that look well, and there is something amiss," he intoned.

She hesitated momentarily, her lower lip starting to tremble uncontrollably, and the King became impatient. "Out with it girl!" he commanded. "You have naught to fear from me. Speak your mind this instant!"

"It is your son, Gerinth….."

King Xalton's features instantly became taut with fear at the mention of his only son's name, the heir to the throne of Straltonia. *"What about my son!"* he whispered, his voice shaking with alarm.

"I have just been informed that he has fallen ill, my Lord."

"Ill?" Xalton echoed hollowly. "How is that possible? I saw him just last night, and he was fit as a lion, healthy as a wild ox!"

Elliasha nodded, her dark eyes brimming with tears. "Aye, my Lord," she wailed bitterly. "Never has he been sick a day of his life! And yet only moments ago the court physicians delivered the news to me personally."

"I must see him at once!" the King demanded abruptly. He motioned to the wizard. "You must accompany me to Gerinth's chamber and heal him immediately!"

Quan Chang Xu rose quickly, nodding his consent, and the King pulled Elliasha into his shivering arms. He stroked her head lovingly, and she buried her face in his chest and wept.

"It's going to be all right," he mumbled perfunctorily. "Send for the others to bear me to him."

Elliasha began to sob hysterically. "It is too late, my King!" she replied. "No magick can save him now."

King Xalton refused to accept what he was hearing. "Calm down, my dear," he told her gently. "I'm sure it is only some sort of minor malady…."

Elliasha looked at him, tears streaming down her cheeks. She held a dark hand to her mouth and shook her head, her eyes wide and full of sorrow; then she fell back into his arms, her slender body trembling with grief and despair.

"It is too late, my Lord," she whispered, staring blankly across the room. *"Our child is already dead!"*

Skeltar sat back upon a cushion in the dark interior of his carriage. The initial journey to Luxantia had seemed to take forever. The return to Zebulon felt like it was taking even longer, and Skeltar was not a man of patience at the best of times. They had left seven days ago, and Zebulon was still another nine days away.

He thrust a withered hand into the folds of his robe and felt the talisman. *How fortunate that the Eye had already been mounted upon it!* he thought again. It was another piece in the puzzle of the Black Scroll, but there were still eleven other pierces out there somewhere, waiting to be found and brought together. There was a specific scroll containing arcane incantations for each piece. He possessed four of these scrolls, but only the one talisman, or more correctly, seal. He sighed anxiously, leaning his head back to rest against the padded interior of the carriage, wondering how long it would take him to locate the other pieces, to decipher the other scrolls and unite them. No one had ever done it--at least not as far as he had ever heard tell of. *He would be the first in the history of men!*

He parted the curtains slightly, gazing out over the endless expanse of dessert plains. His eyes shifted from the horizon to study the troop within the scope of his vision. They were certainly not the elite soldiers that King Xalton had promised him, but that was probably better in the long run. Most were becoming quite content to be in the service of a wizard. Before leaving Luxantia, Skeltar had allowed the men to loot through the ruins of the town, and each of them now bore a small fortune in their packs, a fact which made their progress all the more cumbersome and slow. It would take a day longer to reach Zebulon, but it was a small price to pay for their loyalty.

He let the curtain fall shut and closed his wrinkled eyelids. In spite of obtaining the seal, he was no closer to capturing Sheba and her companion than he had been before leaving Zebulon. Capturing her would make his youth return, his bones strong, his flesh supple and smooth.

King Xalton would have sent out a search party for her by now, of that he was certain. He would be motivated by the need to be rid of his terrible illness, by his distrust of wizards--particularly Skeltar--and his insatiable lust for beautiful and exotic women.

Finding the Seal had been of utmost importance, but now he needed to capture Sheba before the King could get to her. Skeltar leaned forward and opened a hidden compartment under his seat. From it he withdrew the sacred parchment he'd been given by the priests of Dhampir. Taking out a quill that had been fashioned from the feather of a vulture, he opened a vial of black ink and began writing an incantation.

The bumping of the carriage made it difficult to draw the magickal characters and sigils, but soon the spell was drawn and ready. He laid aside his writing implements and held his palms above the surface of the parchment, then closed his eyes and breathed deeply to calm and center his thoughts. His face twisted malevolently as he focused his will, then he opened his eyes and began to speak the arcane words of an ancient rune that was once often used in ages past by none other than the fabled wizard Therion himself. As he intoned the spell, he carefully folded the parchment in such a way that, when he was done, it resembled a flying bird. Skeltar cupped it in his hands and held it out before him reverently.

"Servants of shadow, legions of dread!
Hear the voice of your master,
from the land of the dead.
Rise swift at my bidding,
Fly over the plains,
Bring me the ones who are known by these names!"

He tossed the parchment into the air, and instantly it burst into flame. It hovered there before him like a spirit, taking on a life of it's own and transforming into an ethereal bird of ghostly fire. The specter beat it's flaming wings, staring at the wizard with bright yellow eyes, the pupils of which glowed like burning embers, then it shrieked and turned away. It flew off through the wooden carriage wall as though it wasn't even there, and Skeltar settled back upon the cushioned seat, his thin lips upturned in a horrible smile that was frightening to see.

He sat there for a long while, gloating silently to himself. *Sheba will be mine!* he hissed. *Soon I will be young once more!*

Suddenly the carriage wheels ground to an abrupt halt. Commands were being shouted hurriedly outside, and someone rapped on the door.

"Who's there?" Skeltar grumbled belligerently. This journey was already taking too long. The last thing he needed was another delay.

"It is I," came the familiar sound of Brutus' voice.

"Come in!" said Skeltar, and immediately the door swung open. Glaring sunlight flooded the dim interior of the carriage, nearly blinding him completely. His eyes watered and he shielded them with his hand, blinking furiously.

"My scouts just relayed word. There is a merchant caravan coming this way, sir," Brutus told him quickly. "It's headed for Luxantia."

The wizard's black eyes narrowed. "That does present a problem," he agreed. "If news gets out that Luxantia has been razed…. it will not bode well for us."

Brutus nodded affirmatively. "What would you have me do?"

"We will continue on our way," Skeltar advised. "The sight of a detachment from the Imperial Army shouldn't frighten them. They see the King's troops quite frequently, to be sure."

"They are well armed," Brutus informed him factually. "I suspect, however, that upon seeing the King's banner they will be friendly enough, thinking us to be merely on patrol."

"Then signal them to halt when we meet," Skeltar conferred. "Have a few of the men barter with them for wine or what not. While they are distracted the others will surround them, but be casual about it. Don't raise any suspicions."

Brutus smiled grimly. "Very well."

"How long will it be before we meet up with this caravan?"

"I estimate about three hours."

"It will be getting dark in five," Skeltar noted.

"Aye," Brutus confirmed. "They are heavily burdened and moving slow."

"Good!" Skeltar exclaimed. "They will be easy prey. Once they have been subdued, we will move off a ways and set up camp for the night. That will leave time to distribute some of the spoils to the men and reorganize things." He fixed his eyes upon Brutus darkly. "Kill them all. See that none survive."

The officer turned to leave, then paused. "There are many women in this caravan," his said uneasily.

"And that troubles you?" Skeltar asked coldly. "It wasn't a problem at Luxantia."

"Aye," Brutus replied. "But what I mean to say is, when it comes to plunder and spoils, my men value women just as highly as gold and silver."

"And men consider *me* to be vile!" the wizard ejected.

"If they are to die anyway…." Brutus started, but he was cut off.

"Let your men do as they wish with them," Skeltar ejected. "But they must be slain before we break camp in the morning. There must be no witnesses."

50

In waves as black as midnight,
I slaughtered the hounds of hell,
The butchered hordes of Dhampir,
In heaps about me fell.
Upon the bank of the Tsargul,
Like sands along the sea,
I left their rotting ruin,
Yet still their eyes I see.

----Excerpt from the Padden Stone

The Tsargul River was unusually low for this time of year, yet from his vantage point on the hills of the western shore, Joktan estimated it to be at least two hundred cubits wide. Often he had heard men speak of it, for the Tsargul was one of the mightiest rivers in this part of the Westermarch. At the head-waters it started out high up in the Black Mountains as a tiny stream, fed by glaciers, natural springs, and melting snow. By the time it reached the foothills at the southeastern region of the mountains, the Tsargul was a raging torrent of treacherous white-water rapids.

From there the Tsargul wound it's way south and east, widening out into the vast Keddishyan Plains. Here it served as a natural boundary between western Straltonia and the land of Gershom. Farther south, it divided western Lagash and Kahsdim from their eastern borders with Korava before emptying out into the Tethys Sea.

It had taken the better part of three days to reach the Tsargul from the Standing Stone, riding hard and sleeping for only a few hours each night. Chia kept her women warriors tightly in line, and it seemed to Joktan that she would have driven them even harder had it not been for the presence of him and Sheba.

The fear that King Xalton would die before their return weighed heavily upon her mind, and although the others shared the same worry, he sensed that they much preferred the freedom of the open plains and the possibility of battle to the daily routines of life as a palace concubine. The relentless pace that Chia set for her companions was wearing on them more and more each day. It was readily apparent that they had maintained it for quite some time now. As for the women's prowess as fighters, Joktan had no doubts.

They moved with the ease and agility of prowling leopards. The blades of their weapons--all finely crafted in every respect--bore notches and chips that had clearly been sustained in combat. Each woman carried herself with the confidence and self-assurance of a soldier who has seen countless battles and knows what their abilities truly are.

However, the fact of the matter was, the larger portion of their time was usually spent in more peaceful pursuits. The endless riding, the meager hours of sleep and rest, all were slowly taking their toll.

Joktan and Sheba were practically unaffected by such hardships. They had been traveling now for weeks, through land that was far more inhospitable and forbidding than the wide-open hills of the western Keddishyan Plains. With the exception of a few scratches and bruises he'd received during their last battle, he was in excellent shape.

Looking at Sheba, one would be hard pressed to tell if she'd ever seen the slightest hint of combat. She bore no bruises, no scratches or cuts, not even a single tiny scar. She showed no signs of weariness or fatigue, no burning from the wind and sun. Her skin was still as pale as ivory, a fact which Joktan had at first deemed odd but now took for granted. His skin by comparison had been burnt severely at the start, but now it was tanned a deep bronze.

Sheba seemed to greatly enjoy the company of the other women. Since the day they had met, Joktan had been her only companion. While they had become very close to each other and now shared an undeniable bond, having the pleasure of conversation with new friends was a welcome change. At times, however, the constant presence of the others became more of an interference.

Today Chia had been forced to slow their pace. It was more for the sake of the horses than her women, who nonetheless accepted the break from hard riding like a breath of fresh air. Joktan, however, had chosen to ride out ahead, enjoying the chance to be alone for a while without his thoughts being interrupted by the others.

Since leaving the Standing Stone, he still hadn't had a chance to pull Sheba aside and tell her of his meeting with Lamashtu, of how he had obtained his new sword, and of giving her the Face of Death. Several times he'd begun to speak of it, only to be interrupted by Chia or one of her women.

Now, as he sat upon his horse searching for a spot to cross the Tsargul River, he reflected on the events that had transpired only a few days before.

He felt somehow different. It was difficult to explain, but he knew that Lamashtu had inexplicably changed him on some level. He could feel it in his body, in the strength of his muscles, in how quickly his wounds had healed--wounds he'd received fighting the priests of Dhampir. But it was also inside of himself that he noticed a change taking place, as though a power now resided within him which had never been there before. It was like an energy that seemed to have no end, and it affected him profoundly.

He knew she was a goddess in the truest sense of the word--just as surely as he knew that he'd been born a savage. It was a knowing beyond question, belief unfettered by doubt, the understanding that comes when mortal flesh has touched the purity of the Divine.

Try as he might, he could not fathom what it was that had possessed him to bite her, to drink her very blood. Only two women had ever made him feel the uncontrollable urge to drink their blood; one was Sheba, and the first time he had bitten her the experience had overpowered him. It had very definitely changed him forever.

With Lamashtu, however, it was altogether different. Sheba's blood was intoxicating, enthralling, even rapturous.

Lamashtu's was pure power.

It went far beyond description, surpassing definition. It surged through his body like a living entity, as though it had a consciousness all it's own. Just how much of this mysterious force had been imparted by her kiss or her blood, Joktan could not know.

His physical senses, which because of his bloodline were naturally keener than most men's, had become even more acute. He wondered just how long these sensations would last, or if they would ever go away at all. And he also wondered how on earth he was going to try explaining it to Sheba, when he himself could scarcely understand.

Perhaps the presence of Sheba's blood, still burning fresh within his veins from the night before, had caused him to bite Lamashtu.

He jumped down from his mount and seated himself in the grass along the crest of the hill. From here he had a commanding view of the surrounding land, and it was an excellent spot from which to study the flow of the Tsargul River. Crossing it would prove a challenge, he surmised, but they did have the unexpected advantage of the river being shallower than usual, a fact which would certainly be in their favor. Chia and her companions had crossed here recently, and if they had managed it without incident, Joktan figured he could do it just as easily. Besides, horses were strong swimmers, and his mount was in excellent shape.

For some inexplicable reason, a tiny black speck on the distant horizon caught his eye. He sat watching it for several minutes, chewing on a stalk of wild oats, which grew in abundance throughout this region of the Keddishyan Plains.

As he studied the tiny dot it quickly grew, and he realized suddenly that it was moving in his direction with astonishing speed. Soon it was a the size of a small cloud, and he jumped to his feet, shielding his eyes from the brightness of the sun for a clearer view. He turned and glanced back to the west, noting that Sheba and the others were not far off, then peered once more at the eastern skyline.

What had been an insignificant speck only moments before was now a dark mass of flapping wings, and as it moved steadily closer, a feeling of apprehension began to grow deep within him.

He could hear the others coming nearer, and with a mounting sense of dread he leapt onto his horse and motioned for them to join him. As they reined up their steeds beside his, Joktan anxiously drew their attention to the cloud in the sky, which had moved even nearer in the matter of just a few minutes. Together they studied the strange black shape with uncertain looks.

"I saw it only minutes ago," Joktan informed them seriously. "Then it was only a speck, but look at it now! It is nearly ten times larger and growing quickly." He shook his head and spat angrily into the dirt. "Whatever they are coming, those things are headed our way at a furious pace."

He glanced over at Sheba. She had her eyes closed, and her expression was one of intense concentration. She suddenly looked at Joktan.

"I don't know what it is," she confessed, "but I feel that it will not bode well for us to linger on this ridge. We must get to lower ground, and quickly."

"Aye," he agreed, then turned to Chia. "Do you have any idea of what it might be?"

She merely shook her head. "In my homeland, I once saw a bird that some villagers had killed. It was very big, nearly forty feet from each wing tip, with skin that resembled a Leviathan, and wings quite similar to those of a bat. I have never seen such a creature since, nor do I care to for that matter, but at this distance......" She gazed at Joktan uneasily. "Sheba's right. We had better get off of this hill….and fast."

"Look!" exclaimed Liona, the auburn-trussed Sidonian, her voice betraying her fear. "There must be three score of them!"

"Aye," agreed Brashi, "maybe more, and I'll be damned if those are any sort of bird I've ever heard tell of."

Joktan grunted. "Some evil is at work here, and I like it not. What are we waiting for? While we sit here discussing what it may or may not be, it gains upon us."

He turned his steed and spurred it down the hillside, and the others hastily followed his example. When they reached the river's edge, Joktan turned and called to Chia. "Is this the general area where you crossed before?"

The woman looked about hurriedly and shook her head. "I think we crossed just upstream from here, a few miles up beyond that bend," she indicated a place where the river rounded a wide, sloping point of land.

Joktan gazed back at the sky. The dark cloud was within a league from them now.

"How fast is the current?" he asked.

Chia shrugged. "I don't know. The water was a littler higher when we came through last, and it washed us down river a bit, almost to where we are now I'd say."

Sheba drew up beside them. "Forget about crossing the river," she said gravely. "By the time we are half-way across those things will be here, and us sitting ducks."

"I agree," Joktan replied. "Perhaps they will pass over us and be gone, but I highly doubt it. I prefer to fight on solid ground. I wish there was some cover to be had, but such is our luck, I reckon. There is nothing we can do but stand our ground and wait."

No sooner had he spoken then a shadow passed over the sun and the sky became dark as dusk. Sheba's eyesight was far keener than that that of all of the rest, and she gazed up to the heavens and let out a startled gasp.

Joktan looked to see what it was had made her to cry out, and what he saw turned his blood instantly to ice. Several of the creatures flew ahead of the rest, and now they swooped down toward the small band of warriors with astounding speed.

Their wings looked like those of a bat, dark and leathery, but the span was nearly twenty feet across. They had bear-like heads, and at each corner of their fanged mouths protruded wicked, curving tusks, very reminiscent of the wild boars in Joktan's homeland. Their bodies were similar to that of a boar as well, but the legs were powerfully built and bulged with corded muscles like those of lion. Long, terrible-looking claws extended from massive paws, and a rat-like tail trailed some fifteen feet behind them. Like the rest of the creature's bodies, it was covered in scales and sparse, coarse hair that was black as coal.

"Saurgs!" Sheba cried, leaping to the ground. "Get off of your horses!"

Already Chia's companions had dismounted. Their crossbows swung skyward, and the descending creatures were greeted with a hail of steel-tipped bolts. The air was rent by the awful sound of their hideous shrieks and roars, as the demonic beasts fell upon them in such great numbers that the light of the sun was all but blotted out completely.

Joktan ripped his sword from it's scabbard with a barbaric battle cry. His bared blade flashed in a deadly arc, cleaving the head of the nearest saurg in two. Brains and filth spilled onto the ground, and the beast went down as another sprang toward him to become impaled on the blade of Avatare. It bellowed painfully and fell away as he rushed to meet the next beast with a throaty growl.

Sheba tore her axes from her belt, and the space about her became a swirling circle of death and broken bones. She screamed vengefully at the creatures, swinging her weapons with binding speed and fury. Black, oily, blood spouted into the air, and around her the bodies of slaughtered saurgs began to mount as she fought them back with reckless abandon.

Chia and her companions quickly discovered that their crossbows would do them no further good. They joined the fray wholeheartedly, their blades rising and falling in unison as they formed a line and slashed a path through the frenzied swarm of beating wings. The creatures fell in mangled droves like grain before the reaper's scythe, but it seemed as though their numbers yet continued to increased.

For each one that fell writhing and bleeding, three more descended from the blackened sky to take it's place. All was chaos and madness, a hideous storm of leathery wings and rending claws, yet the warriors fought on tenaciously, refusing to yield their ground.

Joktan spun as a snarling pair of gaping jowls rose up before him. He struck savagely at the horror, hacking off the lower part of the creature's fanged jaw with a vicious sideways cut. It shrieked insanely, swinging at him with talon-tipped wings, and he struck back with all his might. The saurg's head was severed from its body in a single stroke, and instantly he was covered in a spray of reeking ooze. He saw one of the horses go down beneath a cloud of flapping wings, saw the steed kick desperately, and the saurgs close in upon it.

The horse bellowed in terror as the creatures tore it apart, and the sight of its blood drove the rest of the spawn into a hellish fervor for flesh.

A brief moment the creatures fell back from before him, and Joktan took up his bow, loosing a score of arrows before the beasts flocked in upon him once more. The ground became slippery with the tar-like sludge that bled profusely from the butchered fiends. The air filled with the thunderous dim of their horrible shrieks and visceral roars, the stench of the carnage noxious as a poisonous, deadly fume.

In the midst of the tumult Sheba saw Brashi fall under the weight of a massive saurg, but alas! There was nothing she could do to save her. Brashi's screams were short-lived as the creatures ripped her body asunder, fighting each other like rabid dogs for strips of the woman's freshly slain corpse.

Liona howled furiously at the swarming beasts, shield in one hand, ax in the other. Her lithe form was covered in grime from head to toe as she chopped her way through the carnage toward the creatures that hovered over her fallen comrade. By this time their line had fallen apart, and she cried out for the others to rally about her.

Her shout was answered by Fjora, the blonde warrior from Isaheim. Her blue eyes burned an unearthly hue of violet, and the woman's long golden locks were drenched with gore. Fjora's pale skin was dark with the vile blood of mangled saurgs. She swung her steel-spiked mace and battle-ax with all the fury of the legendary Berserkir warriors from her homeland.

Joktan wheeled as a saurg lunged at him, it's great mouth open wide, teeth dripping putrid, festering slime. He thrust his blade into the creature's gaping maw, then wrenched it free as it fell back shrieking in agony and two more swept in to take it's place. He met them like one possessed, azure eyes blazing, his hair clinging to his face, and Avatare singing a song of death and slaughter all around.

"Come on, you spawn of Hell!" he challenged the creatures as they scrambled toward him. "Come meet my sword! Meet Avatare, and die upon my blade!"

Suddenly his sword began to glow with a silvery-white light, and he struck out at the closest saurg, aiming at its nightmarish head. He swung so hard that he nearly lost his balance. The tribesman stumbled forward, and his sword almost missed the creature's head completely, but it sprang back instantly, howling as if it had been dealt a mortal blow. Joktan leapt at the beast and thrust his blade at its broad chest, but the saurg pulled back desperately, it's eyes bulging in terror.

He thrust again, and this time his blade sank into the monster's scaled flesh. To his startled surprise, the saurg's skin began to burn as though it had been doused with acid, and the creature staggered back into the swirling chaos, then fell dead upon the ground.

Joktan wondered what was causing his sword to glow so brilliantly, and he marveled at the effect it had upon its victims, but another saurg clawed at him from behind. He spun and thrust instinctively, and the beast fell thrashing upon a heap of butchered carcasses.

Sheba's voice rose above the tumult, and he glanced around hastily, searching for her amidst the flurry of bloodthirsty saurgs. He spied her some thirty or more paces to his left, her axes whirling like a windmill, her face contorted in violent rage. At her feet and behind her lay dozens of mutilated beasts, yet the creatures swarmed in upon her, their talons and claws reaching out fanatically.

Joktan suddenly realized that they were not trying to kill his mate. It seemed as though the creatures merely sought to capture her, attempting to catch her off guard from the sides and behind. Against all of the other warriors the beasts fought like the enraged souls of the damned, but with Sheba they were holding back, circling but not striking, reaching but not lunging, as if she were the prize they had been sent to retrieve.

Joktan remembered Chia's warning, that the wizard was searching for her, to use her for some mysterious, arcane purpose, and he surged forward with renewed vigor and wrath.

He called out to Chia and the other women to join him, but even as he shouted for their aid he knew it was no use. They were bitterly fighting off hordes of saurgs, each of them embroiled in a deadly struggle from which they could not extricate themselves.

Avatare still glowed brightly in his fists, and the beasts fell back in terror every time he struck, but still they managed to cut him off from Sheba. He cursed them insanely, striking out even harder. In growing numbers the hell-horde fell before the gleaming bloodlust of his sword, yet it seemed that no matter how many creatures he slew, their numbers only swelled. They pressed even thicker about him, wave after endless wave of horrible wings and racking claws.

He couldn't tell if the sun had sank below the horizon or if the thousands of leathery wings were simply blotting it from the heavens, but Joktan refused to surrender. His body dripped with vile, oily sludge, and the carcasses of massacred saurgs rose high in sickening heaps about him.

He heard Nephtia, the Denderian beauty, screaming desperately as nightmares clustered innumerably over her frantically struggling figure. Their talons ripped her bronze flesh to pieces, and the monsters feasted upon her with hellish delight.

He saw Shyla, the ravishing warrior from Carianthe, dragged down to the ground. Her body was quickly mangled and torn to bloody shreds by saurgs as they piled upon her corpse in demonic droves.

And then Thallianna, from the far away kingdom of Kish, her ebony skin glistening with the blood of a multitude of grotesque lives which her sword had reaped, also fell before the onslaught of slavering teeth and hideous claws.

Still he fought mercilessly, his blade wove death and dealt slaughter like a hurricane of razor steel, fighting relentlessly to reach Sheba's side, but hemmed in by endless tides of horrible snarling demons. They swept upon him like an angry tide of seething wings and menacing fangs, desperate to sink their teeth into his flesh.

His heart sank in his chest like a lead weight tossed into the sea as he saw Sheba, utterly surrounded, her axes notched and riling with gore, forced down upon the ground. And he screamed the most blasphemous profanities as a gargantuan saurg rose high into the air on pitch black monstrous wings, and clutching her securely in it's dreadful claws, soared off into the east.

If ever he had been close to losing all love for living--if ever he had been nigh to tearing out his own heart from within his chest and hurling it to the ground like a bloody stone--it was at that awful, terrible moment.

One by one the saurgs rose on dreadful wings, following the wretched beast that pinned Sheba helpless in it's talons. He heard her desperate cries fade slowly into the distance, and as the creatures that had darkened the heavens retreated beyond his grasp, Joktan took up his bow and shot down as many as his arrows could reach.

The ones that yet remained behind, too wounded to fly away, he bitterly slew and hewed to pieces upon the western bank of the mighty Tsargul River, till they all lay dead before him, and there were no more left to slay.

Then he fell to his knees upon their butchered carcasses and at last threw down his sword as bitter tears streamed down his blood-stained face.

TO BE CONTINUED……..

www.ingramcontent.com/pod-product-compliance
Lightning Source LLC
LaVergne TN
LVHW020657110826
845149LV00012B/2023

* 9 7 8 0 9 8 7 6 9 2 1 2 2 *